THREADBARE

THREADBARE

A NOVEL

JANE LOEB RUBIN

Author Photo Credit: Jai Catalono

First edition

ISBN: 978-1-68512-581-3

Cover art by Level Best Designs

This book was professionally typeset on Reedsy.
Find out more at reedsy.com

To my husband, David, my cherished family, and Mathilda.

"If history were taught in the form of stories,
it would never be forgotten."

— RUDYARD KIPLING

Praise for Threadbare

"Rubin's novel, *Threadbare,* is a classic, delicious immigrant story with a twist. Set in 19th century New York City— not the 20th— it's loaded with history, and its protagonist, Tillie, is a headstrong, visionary teenage girl. Although Tillie becomes a woman far too fast, her indomitable spirit prevails. Her compelling story is one of resilience in the face of discrimination, economic hard times, and epidemics— and it resonates for the 21st century."— Susan Jane Gilman, bestselling author of *The Ice Cream Queen of Orchard Street*

"In *Threadbare,* Rubin weaves a vivid tapestry of hope, heartbreak, and resilience amid breath-stopping challenges, opening a window to a transformative time in women's history."—Audrey Blake, *USA Today* bestselling author, *The Girl in His Shadow, The Surgeon's Daughter*

"Jane Rubin's *Threadbare* harkens back 150 years stylistically and thematically to Louisa May Alcott's Little Women, echoing exquisitely. Universal matters such as the power of family ties, the conflict women face between marital and childrearing responsibilities versus vocational ambition, sisterhood, and emotional resonance, are richly enhanced by compelling narrative layers involving the fin de siècle German Jewish immigrant experience, NYC farming and tenement life, the development of the garment industry, access to healthcare and the agony of loss from epidemic and cancer, and women's reproductive rights. Rubin's loom weaves a plush pile, in fact—not threadbare—and is as rich and inviting to the touch as a tapestry of classical antiquity from which one loathes to part." —Peter Bolo, MD; Chair Psychiatry, Overlook Medical Center, Summit, NJ

"Jane Loeb Rubin wins us over again in *Threadbare,* the captivating prequel to her earlier novel, *In the Hands of Women.* Readers follow resilient Tillie Isaacson Levine from her adolescence on a farm in 1879, through her marriage and move to a Manhattan tenement, and finally to her work in the city's garment business in the 1890s. Against all odds, given biases against women and Jews, she starts a business while raising a family. Readers will race through *Threadbare,* rooting for Tillie in every chapter." —Marlie Parker Wasserman, author of *Inferno on Fifth*

I

Part One

"Life is not a matter of holding good cards, but of playing a poor hand well."
—Robert Lewis Stevenson

Chapter One

October 1879

W*here was she?* Mama commanded the morning, waking first, placing fresh logs on the shriveling coals in the fireplace, brewing coffee, its deep woody aroma waking us from sleep. Fire, coffee for Papa, the family's breakfast, then get the children off to school. The melody in her voice as she lifted Hannah from her crib and sang her morning song always cheered me.

Summer had passed, and autumn's chill crept into the evening air, lingering until morning. Papa set a large fire at dusk from the mountain of logs he had chopped, split, and stacked over the long summer. Each year, the dry wood, neatly stacked on the porch under the roof's eaves, shrank through the winter months, always lasting until the yellow and white daffodils opened their petals in early spring. Stoking the coals at bedtime and adding a couple more logs, he would leave our bedroom doors open so we would stay warm through the night.

I longed to linger beneath my heavy quilt tucked in my dreamy haze, but my daily chore before breakfast was feeding the chickens. I dragged myself from bed, wrapped my new purple shawl around my shoulders, lifted my school clothes off the wall peg, and tip-toed from the bedroom, careful not to disturb the baby. My younger brothers, Nate and Joe, were still sound asleep in their narrow beds beneath the bedroom window.

Mama, why haven't you added more wood? Creeping through the parlor,

3

I peered into the kitchen. Mama's usual place by the stove was empty. Perplexed, I threw a fresh log on the embers, watching it ignite. The wood spit and smoked as it caught, spurting hot air into the room. *Get on with your chores.* I tugged my new brown muslin school dress over my head, inches longer in the sleeves and hem than the year before, braided my heavy brown hair, fastened a ribbon around the end, then crept through the front door onto the wood porch where my stiff leather boots stood waiting. Two sizes larger than last year's boots, they felt smooth inside but cold from the night's chill. Papa accused me of having feet almost as big as his. How could he say such a cruel thing? I wished I would stop growing. It was hard enough being a full year older than my classmates. Mama held me out of school when I was six because of a diphtheria epidemic that swept through New York City. Now, in seventh grade, I was also taller than all my classmates, even the boys.

The temperature was bracing, my breath shooting puffs of smoke into the crisp air. Mama's vegetable patch beside the chicken coop was brown and dry. Weeks earlier, her summer harvest had been picked, canned, pickled, and stored in the root cellar for the winter. To my left, south of our farm, tall buildings, some nearly ten stories high, cut into the distant skyline. To my right, beyond our outhouse, livestock farms stretched as far as the eye could see.

Where was she? In the privy out back? My eyes paused at the outhouse. No lantern.

The crystallized grass sparkled in the dawn light, crunching beneath my feet as I approached the barn where we stored the feed barrel. Chickens twitched and rushed to the fence, knowing breakfast was near. Handfuls of feed sprinkled down on them, setting them abuzz, clucking, bumping, their hungry beaks pecking their seed. After returning the bucket to the barn, I walked inside, more perplexed than ever. Did Mama run to a neighbor's home for a missing provision?

Our chicken farm was the only home I knew. My father named it "Sam's Kosher Chickens" and sold poultry to Jewish butchers on the Lower East Side. Avi Schulman, whose land we leased, was a wealthy friend of Rabbi

Friedman. He owned most Jewish farms in northern Manhattan, and we rented our small patch from him. When my parents arrived from Germany in 1866, I was barely a baby.

I heard Mama's sniffles as soon as I opened the door. She stood in the kitchen facing the small northern window, still dressed in her tattered flannel nightshirt, her waist-length hair hanging like a damp brown mop. Steam rose from the tea kettle in her hand. Her saucer-shaped eyes were misty when she twisted her body to face me.

My stomach clenched with concern. I took the kettle from her hand. "Mama, where were you? Are you hurt?"

She wiped her face on her sleeve, speaking dispassionately in her native German, "*Nein.* Papa wants to take me downtown to that Bellevue Hospital. To see a doctor. They may not speak German. So, you must come and help us speak to them. Get Nate and Joe ready for school and pack their lunches. Papa will take Hannah next door to the Cohens until we return."

My bare feet stuck in place as I tried to digest her instructions. "Why?" We'd never gone downtown to the doctor before.

She patted her chest, shifting her eyes to the wooden floor planks.

Was it her heart?

I set the kettle down and stepped closer. Fearing the worst, I wrapped my long arms around Mama's short, slender body. At first, she pulled back and shuddered, a sob escaping her lips. Then she fell onto me, leaning her head on my shoulder. "I'm scared. It's my bosom."

Heavy footsteps pounded into the small kitchen. "Sarah, everything will be fine." Papa's words rushed from his lips, firm and hurried. "Tillie, get the boys up. You know what to do. We'll be leaving soon."

Dread filled my chest as I roused my brothers, set out their school clothes, and packed their lunches with an extra apple and slice of cheese. While they ate eggs and toast, I wrote a note to their teachers explaining Papa would collect them late in the day, then tucked it securely in Nate's book bag. Maybe if I did everything right, things would be fine.

In the meantime, Papa packed our open wagon with blankets and a few provisions for lunch. He pulled our horses, Zero and Infinity, from their stalls in the barn and hitched them to the wagon. Whenever someone asked about their odd names, Papa would explain, "I named them for the two parts of our lives. We arrived in America with empty pockets—that's Zero. And Infinity, he's for much later when we're old, and our cup overflows with happiness and wealth."

Papa took baby Hannah to the Cohens' and returned moments later to the kitchen. "Poor child didn't have a clue what was happening. She kept calling for her book."

Mama dropped her head, seeming as confused as Hannah by the morning's disruption. "We read stories every day after the others leave for school. She must feel upside down, like me." She pulled two books from the counter. "Nate, please drop these at the Cohens' on your way out."

Nate turned to her, his face pinched with anger. "It's not fair! Tillie gets to miss school. Why can't we come, too?"

Part of me wished Nate could go in my place. He was two years behind me at school and always dawdled at recess, the last to head back to class. I was the opposite, excited every day of seventh grade, learning new facts about the world. But my ability to translate between English and German was seamless, far better than Nate's.

Joe, the youngest and beginning his second year of school, stood at Nate's heel, his brow knitted together in concern, lips quivering. "Where are you going?"

Mama pulled Joe into a hug. "Only a quick trip downtown to see the doctor, my darling. It will be fine."

Papa scowled at Nate. "Can't you listen? Do what you're told and count your blessings. Half the boys your age in New York don't go to school. They go to work." He paused. "And they don't eat three meals a day."

Nate knew better than to argue with Papa. He pouted, gathered his tattered schoolbooks, and moved to Mama. After a quick hug, Nate took Hannah's picture books and left the house, the screen door slamming behind him. Like a shadow, Joe copied Nate's every move, twisting his concerned face back to me as they rushed together down the dirt road.

I returned the best smile I could muster, hoping I made Joe feel more reassured than me.

Moments later, Papa, Mama, and I were sitting on the wagon's perch, watching the sun rise over the horizon, jetting its razor-sharp red and orange streaks into the sky. As the wagon bumped over divots in the dusty road, we could see the city buildings huddled together in the distant south, belching smoke to the clouds above. Our life in the farms of Harlem already felt a world away.

Chapter Two

My wagon trips downtown typically took place on Sundays with Papa, the day after the Sabbath. Those were his delivery days to the butcher, and if my chores were done, Mama allowed me to join him. The ride took most of the morning, and the caged chickens never stopped squawking. But once we left the quiet of the farms and entered the city, we scarcely heard their racket or, for that matter, the horses' clip-clops. The clamor of Manhattan's East Side swept over the wagon, drowning out all sound and conversation. We watched a sea of carts and wagons move through the crowded streets, stray animals baying in hunger and fear as they wandered aimlessly, and persons in all manner of dress, calling out greetings, walking in family clusters to grey stone churches dotting the avenue.

When the wind blew from the southeast, we could smell the city a mile away. The streets were a foul mixture of rotting garbage and decaying manure that permeated the air. Despite the stench, we were ravenous when we reached Orchard Street and the butcher on the Lower East Side. Papa slowed the cart, guiding the horses to the shoulder for a rest, and we ate the egg sandwiches and apples Mama had packed. Papa always laughed and said the exact same thing, "Time to build strength for battling the hondler."

The butcher's storefront was outdoors, just a simple table, stained pad, and knife-sharpened pencil, with an overhead sign in Hebrew letters signifying his kosher enterprise. As our cart approached the shop, my excitement grew, my arms tingling with anticipation to hear their negotiation ritual. First was the tipping of their heads, showing each other their worn yarmulkes, a signal that they intended to conduct business within the boundaries of our many religious trade laws. From that moment on, I held my breath for the heated, at times thunderous, negotiation. The butcher didn't speak plain German like Papa, only Yiddish—the language European Jews shared, a hodge-podge of Hebrew, German, and other tongues. They haggled over the price of the chickens as if their head nods moments earlier were a hollow courtesy. From these trips, I learned a few words, even though Mama insisted I speak only English and pure German.

"Learn English and help us speak it too," Mama told me in her fractured tongue. "Become part of this new, exciting world. Forget about Yiddish. It's an old-country language we left behind."

But the adults spoke Yiddish when they argued or told secrets. No matter Mama's opinion, Yiddish was all around me up north on the farms, too. Even my friends in school shared odd-sounding and naughty words, so I learned them as well. That old language wasn't disappearing as quickly as Mama would like.

It wasn't until we were heading back to the farm that Papa let on. "Tillie, it was a good day. The butcher was low on birds, and I got an excellent price." He snuck open his trouser pocket and showed the bills to me a moment later, buttoning his pocket before anyone on the chaotic street noticed. "Ve will eat good this month, da?" he struggled in his fledgling English.

* * *

Unlike my jovial Sunday trips with Papa, today's trip was thick with apprehension. We rode silently, each wrapped in our thoughts. Papa and Mama were probably thinking of the day ahead while I tried to pretend all was normal and push my worries aside, drinking in the cool air and autumn colors. Finally, we reached the packed dirt road beside the newly fashioned Central Park. Mama sat stiff as an oak tree in the middle of the perch. From time to time, I saw Papa squeeze her hand.

Moving closer to Mama, I savored her warmth. I held her free hand, curling my other fingers around the seat's edge to steady myself from the pitching and bumping. Mama's eyes were closed, her lips forming silent words. Was she praying? Mustering every bit of strength to remain calm? I forced myself to pray, too. *Please make Mama well. Please, God.*

Prayer was a personal matter for my parents, each having their own version. Neither came from religious families in Germany. Although we belonged to our local synagogue and celebrated the Jewish holidays, our family made most of our own rules for food and clothing. Many of our German Jewish neighbors did the same. But one thing was certain: whenever Mama or Papa worried, they took time for a few private words with God.

Mama broke the silence, attempting to use her English. "I vant to go home, not hospital. Dis is not good." She closed her eyes, and her lips moved again, reentering her thoughts.

Papa said firmly in German, "Sarah, we have no choice. All will be fine."

A cobblestone surface replaced the packed dirt road. We passed Mount Sinai Hospital on 66th Street.

I pointed to the sign. "Are we here?"

"No, we are heading further downtown to Bellevue," answered Papa.

I persisted. "Why? Isn't this the hospital for Jews?"

He glowered, fixing his eyes straight ahead, jaw clenched. "Mostly the rich ones. We can't afford to bring Mama here."

I squeezed her hand again.

Papa said flatly, "Not too much further. We're almost there. Did you know Bellevue's the oldest hospital in New York? They'll take good care of you."

Mama shook her head, agitated. "It's a lie. That hospital's dirty. Rats from the East River roam the halls at night spreading terrible diseases."

Papa persisted, his voice calming. "Oh, those are just rumors. Besides, Tillie and I will stay with you the whole time." Finally, he stopped talking.

I was thankful to sink back into our quiet worrying. When Mama had her hot winds, my brothers and I knew it best to hold our tongue. I didn't know who was right, but I hoped it was Papa. Besides, I was used to mice in the barn, but giant filthy rats were another story.

* * *

We were covered in a thin blanket of grime when we reached Bellevue Hospital. Papa dropped us out front and took the horses to a nearby stable for water and hay. While we waited for him to return, Mama and I took turns brushing off each other's clothing.

I pointed upward. "Mama, look how high the hospital is." I counted, "One, two... It's practically eight stories and fills the whole block." A new wave of apprehension swept through my chest. How would we find our way?

Papa hurried up the steps to join us beneath the arched doorway. Entering the lobby, our eyes searched the immense space, taking in the ceilings and windows. But my admiration was short-lived. They expected me to figure out where to go next.

As if reading my thoughts, Papa said, "Tillie, go ask where to take Mama."

Mama hung tightly to Papa's arm, trying to look brave.

I left them in a frightened huddle in the middle of the lobby as I approached an official-looking woman standing near a hallway. She wore a floor-length, starched white apron over a plain, long-sleeved black dress. A large white hat with curled wings was perched crosswise on her head as if she were wearing a miniature Viking boat. I would have laughed if not for her sour, puckered expression.

The woman's hawkish eyes followed me as I approached, pointing at Mama. "Do you speak English? What's the matter with her?"

Her strident voice frightened me. I couldn't find words.

"And?" she insisted, her face pinched and red.

I took a breath for courage. "My Mama has something wrong with her chest. You know, her woman parts."

She peered back at me with disdain, disinterested in our plight. "Can you read English?"

I straightened my back, insulted by her rudeness. "Of course I can."

She settled a little, her color returning, and pointed across the lobby to a hallway. "Take the elevator to the 6th floor and follow the signs for the Women's Clinic. Her eyes ran up and down our bodies. "Make sure she washes in the lavatory first. The doctors won't examine her if she's this dirty."

I stepped backward, absorbing the force of her insult, my ire replacing fear. I spun around, returning to my parents, and said, "Follow me." I didn't want to embarrass or upset Mama further, knowing how hard she worked on the farm to keep everything clean. Just that morning, I saw her wash her body with a soapy cloth before we left. Her simple dress and shawl had been pristine a few hours earlier. She'd never been dirty a day in her life!

We walked to the end of the corridor and stood spellbound as a man in a grey uniform opened the solid, heavy door and folded the open grate. The word "Otis" was engraved on a brass plaque over the entryway. Papa and I stepped into the tiny room, but Mama held back.

"Oh, Papa, this must be the moving box you told me about! The one you read of in the newspaper." I searched my memory, recalling the word. "An elevator!"

Papa's eyes grew wide with excitement. "Indeed. Come, come, Sarah. This is a marvelous invention."

Mama shook her head. "I'll take the stairs. This scares me."

"It's perfectly safe." Papa reached out, pulling Mama inside the room as she gripped her satchel.

We rose to the sixth floor, watching each floor pass before our eyes. The elevator man opened the grate, dropping us in a large white room with clusters of people sitting on chairs. I saw the sign above the entryway, "Women's Clinic." Another woman wearing a crisp white apron sat at a desk on the far side of the room.

Papa squeezed Mama's arm, leaning into her ear. "See, the elevator was not so bad, eh?"

I turned to Papa. "Could you find seats? I'll give them Mama's name."

My empty stomach began to churn for lunch as I wove around groups of people unwrapping sandwiches, offering their children scraps of bread and cheese, I reached the desk, introduced myself and gestured to my parents.

She wrote our names at the bottom of the list. "Take a seat. It will be a while before a doctor is available."

Returning to my parents, I glanced about the waiting room. It teemed with couples, pregnant women, and large families sitting in clusters. Like us, most wore some version of homemade muslin garments. Their hats and scarves reflected their poor backgrounds, flat felt working caps for men, scarves, and straw bonnets for the women. And their voices filled the air with a cacophony of accents and foreign tongues that bespoke their origins.

"There're many before us in line. We might be waiting a while, so let's have lunch," I said.

Papa stroked Mama's back. "Perhaps a sandwich will help you feel better."

I pulled our lunches from Mama's satchel and passed the chicken sandwiches and apples around. Mama barely touched her food.

As I drifted into the stillness of waiting, other families faded into a back hallway or through the elevator, some with relief and others crying into their handkerchiefs. Occasionally, I glanced at Papa holding Mama's trembling hand, leaning his face to her ear, softly recounting a memory. He tapped his toe with urgency, making my apprehension grow, repeating in German, "We've traveled through danger before. *Meyn bashert*, we'll get through this, too."

I loved watching them share their love. It was the only good thing about the day.

Mama bent her head into Papa's neck. But her worried face could not conceal her fear. Finally, she pulled her knitting from her satchel, concentrating on the deep green shawl she'd recently begun.

The familiar clicking of Mama's needles and Papa's calming words settled me further. Everyday thoughts of friends and school crept into my mind.

I reached into Mama's satchel, looking for my book, *Little Women*. Flipping through the pages, I found where I'd left off. Jo, the second eldest sister, had sold her hair to raise money for Marmee's train fare to the army hospital. Papa, a war chaplain, was injured, and Marmee, like many other wives and mothers, was determined to help nurse him back to health. I couldn't imagine her bravery, witnessing the brutality of war, or cutting off all my hair. In no time, immersed in the story, I lost notice of the minutes ticking by.

"Mrs. Isaacson," a loud voice cut through the room. Startled, I dropped my book.

We stood abruptly, Mama setting her knitting on the chair. I took her hand and approached the receptionist. Papa, who knew he'd wait with the men, sat back in his chair, fidgeting.

A third young woman with a silly Viking boat hat entered the waiting room and walked toward Mama and me, smiling. Her soft grey eyes were friendly.

She spoke calmly in German. "My name is Nurse Sophie. Please come with me."

Nurse Sophie led us into a hallway lined with small rooms. She opened a door and gestured for us to follow. The room was furnished with a narrow table and sturdy wooden chairs. A tall window covered with a white gauzy drape faced the city street below. So much white!

Nurse Sophie handed Mama a thin white robe. "Please remove your outer garments and corset, put on this robe, and sit on the table. The doctor will be in shortly." Unlike the other nurses, she wore four brooches on her smock, each depicting angels playing harps. I'd never seen such jewelry. What did they mean?

Lowering myself into the chair, I braced for another long wait. At the same time, Mama disrobed, handing each item of clothing to me. We were accustomed to bathing and dressing together, but undressing here, in an examination room at a hospital, felt unnatural. I folded her things on my lap so they wouldn't wrinkle, averting my eyes, affording her extra privacy.

A loud knock startled us. The doctor, a middle-aged man with sparse grey hair parted on the side, a thick white beard, and spectacles walked into the room without waiting for us to answer. A younger doctor followed close behind. Both wore knee-length white coats. Nurse Sophie remained at the doorway and nodded at Mama reassuringly.

The older doctor asked, "German or English?"

I answered, "I can help my mother with your English. I speak and read it well."

The doctor cleared his throat, seemingly indifferent, glancing at his papers, and then spoke in English. "I'm Dr. Montgomery, and Dr. Arnold is my surgeon-in-training. Your name is Sarah Isaacson?" He waited for Mama to respond. "I understand you have a problem with your breast?"

He turned to face me. "You are the daughter? How old is your mother?"

"Ja, tirty-two," Mama interrupted in her thick accent.

I nodded. "My name is Tillie."

Dr. Montgomery studied Mama. "Lie back, and I'll examine." He listened to her chest with an instrument, then opened her gown.

Mama squirmed uncomfortably, crying out as he touched her.

He asked, "Does it hurt, madam?"

Mama nodded, her breathing ragged.

Speaking to Dr. Arnold, he rattled off, "This young woman has a large tumor in the underside of her left breast. It's the size of a walnut and may be advanced. It must be removed. We'll keep her at the hospital tonight and operate tomorrow. She's very young, so there's no time to waste. Find space on the operating schedule for a radical mastectomy."

While Dr. Arnold stepped from the room, Dr. Montgomery shifted his attention back to me. "Can you stay with her tonight? We'd like to schedule the surgery early tomorrow. Your mother has a dangerous growth in her breast that must be removed immediately."

I stared back at him, mouth ajar. I could barely understand what they were talking about.

Nurse Sophie added, "So, she can get better, dear."

I helped Mama sit up and held her hand while translating his brief message. She took a deep breath, quivering. She then turned to Dr. Montgomery, locking eyes, and cried in Yiddish, "Take the damn thing out."

"Mama!" I'd never heard her speak Yiddish or swear at anyone before.

Dr. Montgomery, unfazed, turned to Nurse Sophie. "Make sure she bathes tonight. I want her scrubbed clean." Then he turned back to me. "Tillie, did you say?"

"Yes," I whispered, terrified to hear more.

He looked into my eyes and instructed me. "It's your job to keep her calm. After we're done tomorrow with surgery, she'll remain at the hospital for a few weeks to heal. You should stay with her and help translate. We'll see you again in the morning." Dr. Montgomery bowed at Mama and left the room.

Mama searched Nurse Sophie's face. "He'll take care of a Jew?"

Nurse Sophie set her hand on Mama's shoulder. "Of course, he will. This is not Germany. It's America." She continued in a gentle voice. "I'll help translate too. My family is also German." She turned to me and winked. "Tillie is my younger sister's name. She can read English, just like you."

She was reassuring, and I volunteered, "My real name is Mathilda, after my Oma, Miriam. But everyone calls me Tillie. I like it much better." Mathilda sounded too heavy, as if laden with the weight of a challenging foreign life, whereas Tillie felt light and breezy, a name I could fill with my dreams.

I helped Mama dress. She was still trembling. "It'll be fine." But her fear made my skin crawl as this foreign experience had also begun to frighten me. Still distracted by Nurse Sophie's brooches, I asked, "What are the angels for?"

Nurse Sophie smiled. "It never hurts to have a little extra help from the Almighty." She held Mama's shoulder, firmly supporting her. "Now, let's go tell your husband the plan."

We reentered the waiting area and Papa hurried to Mama taking her in his arms. As he held her, Nurse Sophie explained the plan in German.

When she finished, Papa turned to me speaking in his bravest voice, "You stay with Mama. I'll leave soon to arrange for someone to watch the other children and return first thing tomorrow. Is there anything either of you need me to bring back?"

Mama shook her head.

Worried about my schoolwork, I asked, "Could you collect my books? I don't want to fall behind. I can work on my assignments here while Mama mends." I didn't want to surrender my coveted place, first in my grade.

He knit his brows. "I'll try if I have time. It may have to wait for another day."

His impatient tone made me feel ashamed to have asked in the first place.

16

This horrible place made us all unsettled.

We walked stiffly to the elevator, Papa holding Mama's hand. He stopped, took her arms, and gazed into her eyes. "Be brave, Sarah. You'll return home in a few weeks and be back with our beautiful family." He swept a wisp of hair off her face. "I'll be here when you wake tomorrow."

Mama threw her arms around his neck, holding him tightly for a long time, rocking side to side. Finally, Papa pulled away, boarding the elevator, never taking his eyes from hers.

Chapter Three

The patient ward, up one floor from the Clinic, was lined with twenty narrow beds, ten along each wall, each bed separated by a starched white curtain. Grown women occupied each bed but Mama's. It sat, sheets firmly pulled across the top, cleanly tucked corners, waiting for her. Towering, evenly spaced windows covered the side walls, sent fractured early evening light through layers of grit on the outer panes crisscrossing the center of the room.

Nurse Sophie had recounted the hospital's history during our walk to the ward. I figured she was trying to distract Mama. "Before my time, this part of the hospital was filled with wounded soldiers during the Civil War. Many of our doctors traveled to the front for months, helping care for them, bringing badly injured men back in covered wagons."

I imagined wounded Union and Confederate soldiers lying in the beds in place of the women. Chills shot up my spine, conjuring the old newspaper pictures I'd seen of men with amputated limbs and piles of discarded arms and legs outside hospital tents. I was grateful the war ended before we came to America. It was less frightful to see women in the beds.

I looked about, curious what ailment brought these women here. Some slept, while others held new babies. The infants' mewing set the air alive with new life and hope. Visitors sat with other patients, sipping tea, reading, and knitting colorful scarves, gloves, and hats for the winter ahead. Women of all ages filled the room, emitting an odd sense of peace.

Nurse Sophie spoke to Mama in German while she pulled out a basin, washcloths, and a fresh gown. Handing the washcloth to Mama, she explained. "Recently, scientists discovered 'germs,' particles that spread disease. They're so small we can't see them without a microscope. They're the reason we wash everything and everyone. As they say, cleanliness is next to Godliness." She smiled gently at Mama. "Andrew Carnegie even donated a laboratory to Bellevue so we could continue to learn about these microscopic creatures."

I smiled at Mama. "That helps explain things." Then my eyes darted to the filthy windows, wondering how the staff could possibly fend off all the dirt.

"You should feel reassured, Sarah, that between the spotless operating theater and a modern surgical approach, you will be safe." Nurse Sophie said.

"See, Mama, it will be okay."

Nurse Sophie poured water from the bedside pitcher into the basin. "Most women heal well after surgery. We'll administer medicine during surgery to make you sleep deeply, and I'll be beside you in the operating room. Afterwards, I'll give you a strong drug to relieve your pain when you wake."

Little by little, Mama's body relaxed as she sank into the bed. Nurse Sophie seemed to know exactly what to say, and in German, no less.

What would her body look like after surgery? On the farm, Mama, Hannah, and I bathed together. I shuddered, thinking of her chest without the soft curve of her breast. But even though thoughts of Mama were uppermost, I didn't know what I should expect. Where would I sleep? What would I eat? What about school?

As if Nurse Sophie could read my mind, she said, "I know this must seem alien to you as well, Tillie. Try not to worry. Leave it to the doctors and nurses to fix your mama's problem. I'll fetch a cot and dinner for both of you tonight, so you can stay close. Mama may have a small bowl of clear soup for dinner but shouldn't drink anything after bedtime. We'll see how she feels after surgery tomorrow and then decide what's best. In the meantime, you can help her wash and get to sleep."

After Mama finished a thin chicken broth, I drew the curtains and helped Mama sponge bathe and change into a fresh gown. Her shoulders softened as I brushed and plaited her hair. "Feel fresher now?"

Her eyes filled with tears. "Oh, my sweet girl. Someday, you'll be a wonderful, caring Mama." She wiped her eyes with her lace handkerchief. "Did I ever tell you Oma's story when she got sick?"

"No, Mama." I folded her clothing and laid each garment neatly on the bedside table.

"It was back in Baden, before we came here. She had something awful growing in her bosom, like me."

"Mama, do we need to talk about that now?" I wanted to shut my ears to anything bad.

Mama ignored me. "Since we were Jewish, the Germans at the hospital wouldn't examine her. I had no choice but to bring her home. A doctor we knew from the shul came and said he couldn't fix her. He only gave me medicine to give Oma for the pain. I was just seventeen and had never taken care of a dying person. I was terrified, heartbroken." Mama paused; her cheeks streaked with tears. "It took months for my dear Mama to die. She couldn't sleep at night, nor could I, with all her moaning. The medicine barely kept her comfortable. She pleaded with me to end her pain."

My skin prickled with fear. "Oh, Mama, that won't happen to you. I squeezed her hand. *Oh, God, please protect Mama.* "Remember what Papa said about getting home to the farm again."

She looked deep into my eyes. "There I was, with you, my precious infant daughter and a dying mother. The circle of family is what binds us together. Forever."

An uneasy sensation grew in my belly. After all, I was supposed to keep her calm. "I know, Mama. Please rest."

She sighed loudly as if compelled to continue. "Your papa and I treasure each of you, and there are things I need to tell you while we're alone." She cleared her throat. "In case something terrible happens."

I interrupted, my eyes filling with tears. "Please don't talk like that. You're scaring me. You're supposed to rest."

Mama reached for my hand. "You must listen. It's important." She drew a slow breath. "If you care for the important people in your life, they care for you. Like now. Who's here helping me?"

I nodded and wiped my eyes.

"My girl, you're smart and beautiful. You may only be fourteen, but you have a grand life ahead of you. Make your dreams come true. If you work hard, many will. But not always as fast as you want, so don't give up." Mama gently kissed my temple. "Will you promise?"

"Yes, Mama, I promise." I was confused. What was Mama asking of me? Perplexed, I kissed her temple in return. Since I'd been little, this spot on our faces was Mama's and mine, our love spot, reserved for special kisses. I'd have her explain after she was well again.

We lay on her narrow bed. Mama roped her slender arms around me the way she had when I was small. I felt reassured, cuddling against her body. Her breath in my hair felt like a summer breeze.

"Would you like me to tell you *The Beginning*? It's been a while."

I nodded as the day's weight pulled me deep into the mattress.

She began recounting my favorite story, our grand adventure to America. Mama called it *The Beginning*.

"I remember the crystal-clear sky when Papa and I set sail from the port in Hamburg to New York City. It was 1866, the year after you were born. We were married two years by then, and life in Germany was terrible. The Germans hated the Jews, and the only safe place was south, in our village in Baden, close to our own kind. When we wanted to marry, Papa was forced to seek permission from the Town Council. Can you imagine? They'd only allow the oldest son in each family to wed, and he also needed a profession. Papa was the firstborn, but he was a farmer, raising chickens like he does here, and farming wasn't considered a profession. So, he lied. Afterward, we were afraid we'd be discovered and the officials would arrest Papa. We had to escape."

"Mama, that's so unfair. It's not like that here in New York, is it?"

She shook her head against mine. "Your Oma lived in our home back then."

Hearing those words made me jumpy. This couldn't happen to Mama, too, could it?

"After she passed, little else kept us in Baden. We had to take you somewhere safer."

The sheer thought of leaving my home sent shivers down my spine. "Were you scared?"

"Yes, but excited too. Everyone at the synagogue talked about America and how they went to war to free the African people from slavery, just like the ancient Jews in Egypt." Mama ran her fingers through my hair. "We thought if American soldiers would stand up for the Africans, they'd protect us too."

I hung on every word, soothed by her silky voice, even though I'd heard her recount the journey numerous times. Something about this time felt different, as if she was handing the story to me for safekeeping.

"Others in our shul were going to America for a fresh start. We knew we'd make friends who spoke German. After the snow thawed, we packed our belongings in our wagon and traveled north by foot—all three hundred and fifty miles, sometimes walking ten miles a day, until we reached Hamburg. Along the way, we found synagogues where the rabbis helped us find food and a safe place to sleep."

I pictured the three of us trudging mile after mile, my heart pounding with all the hardship they endured. "Did you carry me the whole way?"

Mama smiled, recalling, "Oh no, dear. We made a soft bed on the wagon for you. The wagon's rocking lulled you to sleep most of the time."

The image of me napping in the back of the bumping wagon kindled thoughts of little Hannah only a year ago.

"Papa had just enough money to buy passage for us. When we arrived north in Hamburg, he sold our two horses and wagon and bought tickets on the *Eugenie*. We set sail on May 14, 1866."

Suddenly, the hospital curtain was pulled open. A nurse's head appeared around the edge of the drape. "Time to check on you." Scanning between my empty bed and me cuddling with Mama, she said, "Dear, I'd like you to get into your cot. Let your mama get her rest."

I nodded, wiggling off Mama's bed, giving the nurse space to listen to Mama's heart.

As the nurse left our little white enclosure, she turned back and said, "Please quiet down. It'll be dawn before you know it."

"Oh, Mama, please finish," I whispered as I settled into my cold cot.

Mama knew precisely where she'd left off. She lowered her voice. "We sailed for three weeks. The sea was rough, and the crew separated the men and women at night. I carried you to the top deck during the day and spent hours with Papa looking out at sea, imagining our lives once we reached land. On clear nights, we'd watch the stars. There were more than I'd ever seen."

I yawned.

"Finally, we docked at the southern tip of Manhattan, at a place called Castle Garden. It was a funny name because there was no castle and no garden."

I smiled and nestled my head deeper into the pillow.

"We walked through a gate into the city and headed north, just like when we left Germany, but this time to our new home. So many people crowded the streets," Mama murmured. "They spoke languages we'd never heard and dressed in odd clothing, some fancy, others in rags. It felt like we landed on the moon, but we kept walking north like our friends from Baden told us to."

"North, just as in Germany." I found the similarity amusing.

Mama yawned, turning onto her side. "By early evening, we left the city buildings behind and entered the countryside. The land was hilly and rocky, scattered with farms and German settlers, mostly Christian. But they were good people and pointed us to the synagogue, our first stop."

I reached across my cot onto her bed, holding her hand in mine, drawing in the faint smell of her lavender soap from her sponge bath that morning, knowing she was comforting both of us.

"Rabbi helped a lot of families. He called us 'fresh off the boat.' First, he gave us a hot meal and a safe place to sleep. They had worked out every step at the shul like an instruction book."

"Hmm," I said as her voice lulled me to sleep. "You were brave, Mama."

"Our neighbors were kind. Some journeyed from Baden like us, some from other cities. They helped us start Papa's chicken farm, find a midwife for me when Nathan was born, invited you to the synagogue school, and became our new family over the years."

I shifted toward Mama and kissed her cheek goodnight. "I love you. Everything will be fine." It must. I resettled into my cot and prayed with all my might Papa was right.

Chapter Four

The bright sun cut through the dirty windows, sending streaks of light over my face. I woke from a thick, dreamless sleep, disoriented at first. Wiping the crust from my eyes, I sensed something was wrong and bolted upright. Mama was gone.

A nurse stood at the back end of the ward. I stumbled around the beds and ran to her. "Where's my mama, Sarah Isaacson?" How could I sleep so long? My job was to reassure her.

The nurse approached me, her hands sending a settling message. "Your mama's fine. The doctors took her hours ago, but she didn't want to disturb you. She said to tell you not to worry and," the nurse paused, a gentle smile crossing her face, "that she loves you very much."

Still unsettled, I implored, "How much longer will it take? Will she come back here?"

The nurse glanced at the wall clock. "They should be about halfway through. Go wash up in the lavatory and I'll get tea for you." The calm smile never left her face.

I didn't trust her. She probably said that to everyone. I doused my face with cold water. Looking in the mirror above the sink, I thought about my promise to Papa. *Do something!* I crept from the washroom, checking the hallway, ensuring no one would stop me, then ran up the stairwell until I reached the top floor. Wandering down the dim hallway, I saw the door to the operating theater. A rectangular windowpane covered the upper section above the sign. Stretching on my toes, I could see through the glass.

The room was shaped like a theater. Dr. Montgomery and Dr. Arnold stood in the center, wearing red stained aprons over their street clothes. Was that Mama who lay on a table between them, her untethered hair dangling off the edge of the table? Bleachers of seats lined two walls. In them sat doctors wearing white coats and nurses in their aprons and hats. Many had notebooks open on their laps, writing and drawing while puffing on pipes, smoking cigarettes, and eating. Windows flanked the other two walls, the ceiling practically all glass. I'd never seen an indoor space so brilliantly engulfed in light.

White sheets draped Mama's body except for her chest and head. The bright sunlight bathed her upper body. Her breast and nipple were gone—in its place, a red triangular valley extending from her chest to her neck and shoulder. In the center of the room, Dr. Montgomery reached over the table with bloodied tools.

Am I still dreaming? This is a nightmare! I swallowed my scream, my stomach churning. *Think, think.* Yesterday, Nurse Sophie had explained what the surgeons would do to Mama, but I'd never imagined it could possibly be so gruesome.

Nurse Sophie had explained that she and two other nurses would assist. One sat by Mama's head, pouring droplets through a small strainer over her face. Nurse Sophie stood calmly at the bedside, bending her ear over Mama's mouth, holding her wrist. A third nurse held a pan with bloodied cloths, periodically walking to a table at the side of the room, replacing the dirty pan with a clean replacement. *It's like the chicken slaughterhouse.*

The knot in my stomach grew tighter as I watched. Am I allowed to be here? I wanted to run down the stairs and bury my head under the pillow—to go back to last night when we were cuddling. But I couldn't leave Mama behind, helpless. I repeated Papa's words to myself, "She'll be better soon and back home at the farm." This awful day would be behind us.

Dr. Montgomery's voice interrupted my thoughts. "I've finished my part." He began to lecture the students. I placed my ear to the door.

I could only make out tidbits, barely understanding their meaning, "The tumor was larger than expected...all the muscles in the left chest...hold off on a blood transfusion...cut close to the nerve...better crippled and disease-free."

My head spun. She wasn't supposed to be crippled. Would Papa be angry that I let this happen?

Dr. Montgomery asked if there were questions, then continued without waiting. "Nurse, attend her with utmost caution...post-surgical infection is our greatest risk...use carbolic acid on every dressing change...Dr. Arnold, please close."

My toes were throbbing, but I was determined to see more. I shifted my weight, reaching higher.

Dr. Montgomery looked at the clock. "This was my fastest time yet, five hours, twenty minutes. Clear her out soon. I've another big surgery and must begin before the midday light is gone." He glanced at the ceiling windows then walked to the sink. His eyes darted to the door—and caught mine.

"You!" he pointed, shouting, turning to the nurse. "Get that girl away from here."

At that warning, I darted back to the ward to wait.

* * *

Over the next three days, Papa and I sat vigil, never leaving her side. Papa had arranged for the boys and Hannah to stay with neighbors, not knowing how long it would take for Mama to heal.

Nurse Sophie vigorously followed Dr. Montgomery's instructions, applying clean bandages to the wound and cold compresses to her head. But despite her fastidious care, Mama spiked a fever which soon grew worse, never releasing its tortuous grip. Although she briefly surfaced from a medicated fog, long enough to recognize Papa and me, hour after hour, she idled in a fitful, unconscious state.

The fourth morning, with no respite, Dr. Montgomery came by with Dr. Arnold and Nurse Sophie to check on Mama and her wound. I gasped as Nurse Sophie removed the bandages. Her soft breast had been transformed into a gaping raw wound with oozing red rings over her chest and shoulder.

Was that bone I saw? White pus dripped from the area's edges, and her body emitted the foul odor of rotting meat. I covered my mouth and nose, trying to hold my breath.

Papa's anguished voice rose in concern. "What the hell happened?"

Dr. Montgomery cleared his throat. "Her wound is deep and infected, causing the fever. This sometimes happens, no matter how hard we work to maintain healing." Turning to Dr. Arnold, he continued, "The carbolic acid dressings should've been more effective. Please review every detail of her post-operative care."

Dr. Montgomery placed his hand on Papa's shoulder and spoke, "Regrettably, your wife is very sick. I doubt we can pull her through."

It seemed Papa already knew. He locked eyes with the doctor and nodded. "She's in God's hands now."

I tried to restrain my tears, pleading. "But she can get better, can't she?"

Dr. Montgomery averted his eyes, shaking his head from side to side.

Nurse Sophie pulled me against her. "Your papa's right. It's in God's hands now. We need to wait and see. I'll stay close and help her."

* * *

The day dragged by as I lost grip of time, my ears fixed to the sounds of Mama's shallow breathing, sometimes rapid, other times slow. The room grew heavier, as if the heavens were thickening, descending with a suffocating force, crushing all hope. Nurse Sophie stood beside us. Papa held Mama's hand to his cheek, praying.

My head pounded with apprehension. I could sit still no longer. *Do something.* Crawling from my chair onto Mama's narrow hospital bed, I placed my head against her good shoulder. "Live Mama! Please, live." I pleaded in her ear. "Don't leave us."

She coughed, a strange wheezing sound, air swimming through her chest with no direction, then a rattle. Her hazel eyes peered at the ceiling.

I shouted, "Mama, look at me!"

Mama stared upward, intoxicated by an otherworldly grip. The rattling continued.

A hollowness in my chest grew as if Mama was taking my heart, my love, on her next journey. I'd never considered she might die. That was the fate of old people, not young mothers. Sometimes a child died from fever, but I'd never felt the relentless, terrifying power of death, stronger than anything I'd ever known. How could this happen? Our family needed her. I needed her. *Please, God, shield her!*

Nurse Sophie set her hand on Papa's arm and whispered in German, "Sarah's leaving us."

A pained howl erupted from my mouth. Was that me screaming? Nurse Sophie moved closer, softly stroking my back. "Don't be afraid. Your mama will be at peace soon."

My eyes darted to Papa's, our protector. "Papa, make it stop!"

But his helpless tears dripped onto Mama's body as he rocked, praying. He lifted her fingers to his lips, kissing each one, bearing the weight of truth that his most beloved was departing. His shoulders quivered. *"Meyn bashert!"*

The rattling stopped. The air froze. I sat, mouth agape, as Mama exhaled her final breath.

Chapter Five

For weeks, my family drifted in a fog, muddling through the days, dependent on the goodwill of neighbors to get through. Although we children trudged to school each morning, our minds and our hearts remained harnessed to Mama and the gaping hole she left behind.

Papa haunted the farm like a ghost, caring for the chickens and fixing fences, but barely speaking or eating. At night, he slept fitfully, crying out in his sleep. I suspect, like me, he was plagued by images of Mama's terrifying wound and the way her soft, lovely face lost its life.

In a short time, like all good gestures, the generosity of our community ended. The dinners and offers to help watch Hannah dwindled, our lifeline slipping though our fingers. Even in our compromised state, we knew we must carry on alone. Mama's death, like a flash storm, had swept away the family I loved, unearthing our happiness, the everyday joy we had taken for granted.

Papa assigned Mama's indoor chores and Hannah's care to me when I wasn't in school, arranging a barter with the neighbors in exchange for watching Hannah during my classes. Nate and Joe worked the farm with Papa after school, helping with the chickens, fences, and other repairs. Dirty clothing piled up during the week, and I spent all weekend boiling water in the fireplace for the washing and scrubbing—clothes, bedding, floors, and chamber pots. Little by little, the once pristine clothing I hung on the line outside turned discolored and torn.

My library books, stacked beside my bed, gathered dust. I stopped reading, no longer having time for pleasant pastimes or escape. The housework and cooking Mama handled with ease were awkward in my clumsy hands. Frustration and resentment simmered under my scowl. I wanted to hide in a cave and sleep, to pretend this new way of living was a dreadful dream.

* * *

Mrs. Schwartz, the Headmistress of my school, beckoned me after class to sit with her. "My mama died when I was your age. It was a terrible time, but eventually, the sadness lifted, and so will yours."

I searched her eyes, not believing a word.

"It gets better slowly. You'll keep your mama alive in your heart, making her proud and treasuring her memory."

My eyes welled. "Mama wouldn't be proud of me now. I'm doing a terrible job."

She reached for my hand. "Look at me, dear."

I lifted my tear-filled eyes to hers.

"What I'm saying is true. It takes time, a lot of it. For now, do your best at home and try to leave time for studying. You are one of my finest students. She was always proud of your performance in school."

Although her words and the distraction of school helped stoke my spirit, it wasn't enough. I needed more time in the day. During the winter, I continued to fall behind, my homework partially finished or untouched. I wasn't equipped to step into Mama's shoes—cooking meals, cleaning, watching the boys, and caring for Hannah. And, as I fell behind in school, my resentment grew.

"Nate, why can't you leave Joe alone? You're so mean to him." I yelled when he poked fun at his brother, making him cry. Mama always had a tight grip on the boys, but I had no clue how to handle them.

Nate would then run outside into the cold, leaving the door open behind him. "You're not my mother. Quit bossing me!"

Did they think it was my fault Mama died? Didn't they know I missed her just as much as they did? Day after day, I sensed the doors to my future closing. *Mama, how can I possibly follow my dreams?*

Papa occasionally slipped out of his silence to reassure me. "Tillie, do the best you can. We're all sad."

"But Papa…"

He no longer had his ordinary patience. "You heard me!"

So, I tried harder to engage the boys, distracting them with a game of dominoes or tiddlywinks. Who would care for me? How could I help anyone when my heart was so heavy and abandoned?

Walking home from school, anticipating the ruckus of the household, I imagined Mama strolling right beside me. "Mama, how'd you make stew? I forget how long it cooks. Mine is tough, and everyone hates it. What am I forgetting?"

I was desperate for a sign from her. She was constantly on my mind. In private, I invented conversations with her, imagining her loving words and gentle advice.

That winter, Hannah stopped sleeping when her molars erupted, whining in pain all night. I stayed home from school, caring for her, once again struggling to remember Mama's many remedies, finally recalling one—a concoction of tea, cloves, and honey. I washed her little face with a cool rag, helped her sip the tepid tea, and sang Mama's German songs until she settled. That night, I dreamt Mama returned to us.

"Someday, you'll be a wonderful Mama." She hummed in my ear. "Look out for each other, especially Hannah." I relaxed, stroking Hannah's hair as she slept beside me, then dissolved into the first restful sleep since Mama passed.

* * *

In the meanwhile, life as we'd known it on the northern farms was changing fast. In Current Events at school, we learned that Europeans from many countries were pouring into the southern city, many packing into apartment houses in the Lower East Side. Housing was scarce, and some neighborhoods had fallen into terrible times. Poverty and crime were growing at an alarming rate throughout the city.

New apartment buildings with elevators were shooting up all over. The construction forced people outward in every direction, including north towards our farmland. Our teachers warned us that our Harlem livestock farms would be pushed out of the city to the north, east, and west to make room for apartment buildings and businesses. No matter where we looked, we saw change. It was only a matter of time before our little enclave left, too.

Joe was fascinated with buildings, always curious about their construction. He glued himself to Papa when there was any project needing repair. Now that Nate and I were busy with weekend chores, Papa took Joe downtown on his deliveries to the butcher. At dinner, they talked non-stop about the new bridge connecting Manhattan and Brooklyn, the mansions, and buildings under construction in between. The bridge, in particular, captivated Joe.

"Did you know architects built stone towers in the river to hold up the bridge? Workmen died when they went up and down inside those buildings too fast." Joe caught his breath. "Someday, I want to be an architect and build bridges."

I ached to see for myself. But instead, I was trapped with housework and watching Hannah. I listened attentively to their conversation, recalling Mama's message about dreams. Joe already had his.

Mama's words came straight out of my mouth. "You will be an architect someday, Joe. Keep up your schoolwork, and your dream will come true."

Papa cocked his head, wearing an odd expression. "Your sister's right."

Nate interrupted, "Not me. I hate school. I'm going to work with Papa on the farm."

Papa patted Nate's head. "Good thing. I can't manage the farm without you." He turned to Joe, adding other observations from their trip downtown. "So many new inventions! Steel and elevators. This will be a great city rising high above the ground, reaching into the clouds. I wish your mama were alive to see it."

Papa spoke more words that Sunday than we'd heard from him in a long while. Later, as I washed the dishes, thoughts filled my head. Was Mrs. Schwartz telling the truth? Would our life as a family become happy again?

He must have read my thoughts. Right after I put Hannah to bed and opened my book in the parlor, he said, "Next week, there's no delivery. How about we make a picnic lunch and see that new Central Park? The cold weather's beginning to break and the cherry blossoms are starting to bloom."

I could scarcely believe my ears. "I'll pack lunch, and we can go after our chores." Even though life would never feel complete without Mama, a shot of hope raced through me. "Can we talk alone? Outside?"

We stood outside on the front porch. I wrapped my purple shawl tightly around my shoulders. Papa leaned against the house; a rare, contented smile crossed his face.

"Papa, what happened today?"

He shook his head, looking off in the distance. "Something snapped inside me when we were bouncing about in the wagon. It was as if your mama reached down from heaven and slapped me."

I smiled at the image. "Why would she do that?"

His voice caught. "Before we left for the hospital, she made me promise to take care of you children. She said, 'You are our future, our legacy.' Then she reminded me that after she and I were deep in the ground, you four would be left behind to carry on. She insisted that it wasn't only her job to prepare you for adulthood. It was mine, too."

I reached for his hand.

Papa's eyes filled with tears. "I've been so mad at her for leaving me, I forgot my promise." He filled his chest with air, releasing it slowly. "I'm sorry."

I leaned into his powerful chest, thinking about how she came to me, too. But instead of sharing my dream, I savored his deep hug, a reassurance I had missed for months. "It's so hard, Papa. I can't stop missing her."

"We'll miss your mama till the end of our days. But we'll be fine. I'll keep my promise and be the best Papa I can be."

* * *

34

Papa was chattering away the following Sunday as we arranged our blanket on the grassy meadow in Central Park, but I barely heard a word. My eyes were fixed on the fancy New Yorkers wearing expensive, stylish clothing, strolling by us on the well-groomed paths. The women took dainty steps in their colorful dresses, tight at the waist with full bustles in the rear, holding open parasols, shielding their faces from the sun. The men were drab in contrast, donned in dark suits with tall hats. Unlike the men on the farms with their long hair and beards, these gentlemen shaved their faces, leaving only a mustache behind, cutting their hair close to the head.

I imagined them living in the palaces hugging the side of the park. Some mansions had footmen standing guard out front. How on earth did they make so much money? I could barely imagine living in such luxury. They probably don't ruin their hands washing clothing and sheets every weekend.

Papa was still talking, indifferent to the parade of wealth, as he made up for those months of silence. "We're lucky. We can pile into our wagon, hitch the horses, and settle in for a picnic by the hour's end. You know this park is for everyone, not just the rich. We're lucky we live close by. The streetcar costs too much for most poor folks to bring their big families up here for the day."

I looked around and saw very few families like ours. "It's hard to believe that it's for the poor, too. Most everyone is dressed fancy."

Nate laughed. "Those ladies look like sausages in their dresses. It's no wonder they hobble slowly."

I swatted him on the arm. "Don't make fun. They're beautiful, wearing the finest fashions." I wondered how a dress so grand would look on me.

Papa was undeterred. "The man who designed the park, Olmstead, had to build north, the only open land left in the city. Simple people like us will eventually find their way here.

He lay back on the blanket, cradling Hannah, seemingly indifferent to the stares of passersby, until she fell into her nap. From time to time, a smile crossed his face. Was he thinking how he'd kept his promise to Mama?

We spent the end of that April afternoon riding along the labyrinth of paths, admiring early white and pink dogwood blossoms, sparkling ponds with families of ducks, and meadows sprinkled with early wildflowers. The hilly paths curled around clusters of daffodils and flowering trees, all breathtaking in their early spring bloom. It was an unseasonably warm day, so we threw our coats in the back of the wagon, laughed, and sang, celebrating the start of a new season in our lives. I was the only one silently bothered by our simple muslin clothing.

Chapter Six

May 1880

Like a slow drain, our neighbors sold their livestock and moved away, leaving abandoned parcels of grazing land in their wake. Papa watched his friends herd their remaining livestock to vacant land—west to New Jersey, east to Long Island, and as far north as Sullivan County, New York. But he wasn't sure where we should go.

In May, a few weeks after our picnic, we were outside, turning the soil for the vegetable garden. Papa hammered stakes for the fence into the muddy ground, eventually passing the sledgehammer to Nate. While Papa rested, he pointed in the direction of our school. "Did you see the men with their instruments? They're measuring the streets and blocks."

Joe was quick to answer. "They're called surveyors. I talked to one at recess. He said they're dynamiting the granite hills to level the land. It's too bumpy for building."

"When are they planning to do that?" I handed Hannah small rocks to set atop her growing rock mountain.

"In the next year." Joe picked up the dead plant stems from the summer before and dropped them in the mulch pile, calling back to us over his shoulder.

Concern washed over me. Just as we were adjusting to our new life, everything would change again.

"Our farming world's shrinking fast." Papa pulled at his beard. "Soon, I will need to decide where to move. I don't want to live far from the butchers, but we'll be forced to leave. I understand Rabbi is working on a plan. Oy, imagine schlepping those noisy birds across a river, from up north of here to the Lower East Side."

Joe piped in. "Last week, when Papa and I rode downtown, the trains spooked Zero. The horses fear the clatter."

Papa paused, reflecting. "It's getting busier and busier by the month. Streetcars are crossing the city every which way, taking so many to work. The apartments and factories are spreading north, too. The future is here."

* * *

The following week was time to plant. We were well into spring. The air warmed and smelled of new life, buds were opening around us, helping lift the heavy weight in our hearts. Fewer days were overshadowed by the aching wound of our loss, replaced with recounting happy memories of Mama. With that, Papa worked hard to keep his word, reading to Hannah at night and helping the boys with their numbers, freeing my time to stay abreast of my schoolwork.

I led Hannah to the freshly sowed soil and inhaled the heady smell of spring soil. I opened my fist to reveal a handful of green bean seeds. "Hannah, see these seeds in my hand? Help me plant them in Mama's vegetable garden. Now that it's sunny, they'll grow, and later this summer, we'll pick the green beans for dinner." Keeping Hannah beside me, I planted the beans, onions, and corn from seeds Mama had stored in the barn last summer. I prayed that each new seedling would bring a happier future.

Hannah sat on the cool ground, running her fingers through the burlap seed bag as I once did. She knelt beside me, digging shallow trenches in the soil, spreading the seeds. *Yes, Mama, I'm watching out for my little sister.*

Although the boys continued their rambunctious play, when not at school, they were happiest helping Papa around the farm. During the weekdays, the nearby mothers watched two-year-old Hannah. To repay their kindness, we supplied baskets of fresh eggs and occasionally a butchered chicken. Our neighbors were more than satisfied. After all, who wouldn't be delighted to spend a day with our enchanting Hannah, whose sparkling green eyes, engaging giggle, and precocious babble charmed everyone?

With the delicate days of our mourning behind us, another new development came our way. Papa had become a target for marriageable women who studied him from the pews in the synagogue. Out of nowhere, dinners and sweets showed up at our home, just like right after Mama died. The older women were especially eager to introduce Papa to other widows. Death took many lives in our community—men and women alike, and there was never a shortage of single adults.

We teased Papa about the parade of mediocre dinners and women. Who was this Greta Goldman offering us dry chicken and stale cookies? Why were they lathering us with treats? It made me miss Mama all over again.

* * *

A few weeks later, Papa gathered us in the parlor. "I'd like to speak to you about something important." He cleared his throat, his dark brows furrowing, plunging right in. "It's time for me to meet a new woman."

I gasped. "Why?" My eyes darted to the boys. Nate's mouth had dropped open, and Joe looked confused.

As if reading our minds, he said, "Don't worry, no one could ever measure up to your mama, but Hannah needs care, and Tillie is doing far too much."

Had he been planning this all along? "Papa, it's not yet one year? Don't you think I'm doing a good job?" I pressed.

Papa sighed. "My sweet child, all this work is too much for you. You need to finish your studies, and when you're ready, you'll want to marry and set out on your own. It's wrong for me to keep you from your future."

My dreams, my future, all over again. I nodded cautiously. I'd never thought seriously about marriage and all it entailed—either his or mine. "I'm in no hurry, Papa. I like things this way just fine."

He turned to the boys who had begun tittering. "I expect all of you to be respectful and polite." His eyes snared Nate's. "No nonsense." Papa, a man of few words, had said his piece. He directed Nate and Joe outside to help close the farm for the night.

I tried to consider Papa's reasons. I'd been too busy with the endless chores to contemplate my future or his feelings. I looked around our little home and saw families of dust balls clustered under the furniture and in the corners, spider webs along the ceiling. Mama would never have let things deteriorate to this extent.

Mama always took pride in how we dressed. Every day before school, she checked that our clothes were clean and mended, hair and teeth brushed, and homework finished. When the weather turned cold, she knit colorful sweaters, hats, and mittens. Looking critically at us now, I realized we'd outgrown most of our clothing, and what fit was stained and threadbare. As much as I marveled at the new fashions, I had no interest in constructing ordinary clothing, dreading the notion of spending the upcoming summer sewing new school clothes. But what we wore now would never stretch another year. Exhaling a deep sigh, I thought perhaps Papa might be right. It was time for more help.

* * *

For the past year, I stopped thinking about boys. But as my grief lifted, my curiosity about those mysterious, exciting feelings returned. I'd started my monthly the year before. Thank goodness Mama had shown me how to fold and wash my rags, keeping them on hand for the following month. She told me everything about my body in such a kind way that I was neither frightened nor ashamed. Other girls in my grade had gotten their monthly, too, but they were fearful of the blood. No one explained things to them ahead of time.

Marriage, what a strange idea. What would it be like? No more school? Making babies of my own? Would I have time to read? Would I work? Would I see Papa, Hannah, and my brothers again? The more pieces of my life I sorted through, the more anxious I felt. It was certainly not my dream, at least not now. Curious or not, all I cared about was already right here in my home. Now that I was back on top of my grade, I knew that reading and learning were my main interests. Maybe, I told myself, I didn't want to marry after all.

Besides, all that touching scared me. People told me I resembled my mother with my long, wavy hair and big hazel eyes. But, unlike her, I was tall, up to Papa's nose! He called me his little beauty. Since I was small, he'd pinch my cheeks and say, "What a *shayna punim!*" He knew his sweet words made me happy.

Mama told me, "You grew tall so young because you're impatient, like your papa. Always wanting to taste things before they're fully cooked. Don't rush. All will come in time." Then she warned, "Keep the boys away until you are much older, and remember, it's wrong to become impure before your marriage. Don't let the boys touch you."

I had no intention of letting any boys touch me!

Chapter Seven

The word was out. Women at the shul kept up their attention, circling Papa, visiting our home with platters of brisket and roasted chicken. Eventually, one woman , determined to give Papa a second chance at love, introduced him to Rebecca after Sabbath services. Rebecca was a very young widow, not even Mama's age. I learned later that she'd been married briefly to a man who became stricken with consumption, fought the disease for over a year before finally succumbing from pneumonia. Afterwards, lonely, childless Rebecca assisted at the synagogue.

Papa and Rebecca lingered outdoors, talking until the sun set. Her energetic, upbeat personality impressed him. A few weeks later, after they walked out together several times, he invited her home to meet us.

"Children, I'd like to invite a very nice woman here for tea on Sunday. Please make sure you wash, and Tillie, I'll need your help cleaning the house."

"What's her name?" I asked.

He proceeded to share how they'd met.

The boys charged out of the house into the yard, whooping and teasing. "Papa and Rebecca, sitting in a tree. K-i-s-s-i-n-g. First comes love, then comes marriage…."

I watched Papa's apprehensive face. "Don't worry, Papa, we won't embarrass you."

That weekend, I poured my energy into cleaning the house, gave Hannah a morning bath, and made sure the boys had clean faces. She arrived punctually at two.

Rebecca stood at the door holding a honey cake still warm from the oven, the delicious aroma filling the air, wordlessly winning over Nate and Joe. Both dumbstruck, they stared at her or perhaps at the cake, as if she dropped out of the heavens.

Rebecca wore a lovely green calico frock with a modest bustle in the back. She was small and talkative with dark brown curly hair and matching brown eyes, vastly different from Mama in both looks and personality. We quickly introduced ourselves and settled in the parlor for tea and cake.

"I'm Tillie. I love your dress. Did you make it?"

She smiled at me. "I did. I love sewing and designing copies of the latest fashions."

I shook my head. "I don't know the first thing about sewing and need to make larger clothes for everyone this summer. Nothing fits."

Hannah, who was settled on my lap, wiggled off and headed for the cake.

"Hannah, just one more piece," I warned.

Rebecca watched Hannah stuff the cake in her mouth. "Oh my, let's clean you up, little one."

Hannah scooted to her, climbing on Rebecca's lap, crumbs and all.

I reached out, uncomfortable at Hannah's ease, running into the arms of a virtual stranger. "Hannah, come here. You'll soil her dress."

Hannah paid no mind to me, perfectly happy sitting on the lap of the cake lady.

Rebecca reached for the tea napkin, wiping off Hannah's face and hands. "It's fine, I'm happy to help."

My shoulders melted, the tension easing, watching Rebecca handle Hannah with care.

Rebecca's eyes met mine. "Would you like my help with the fall clothing? I'd be happy to give you some pointers."

Perhaps this woman would be alright.

* * *

Rebecca's visits to the house became more frequent—tea, a walk with Papa, sometimes playtime with Hannah. No matter her purpose, she always spent time helping around the house, never leaving before she tidied up, washed the dishes, or helped me with my mending. She occasionally offered to take Hannah for the day, who began to tag behind Rebecca instead of me, calling her Mama. I wasn't sure I liked that, but I knew Hannah didn't remember Mama the same way we did.

One afternoon, I walked home after school, and the delicious smell of chicken roasting in the coal stove practically knocked me over. I heard singing coming from the kitchen, and when I entered the room, I was surprised to see Rebecca cooking and holding Hannah on her hip. "Rebecca, what are you doing here, today?"

"I had a free afternoon, so I thought I'd get Hannah early from the Cohens and bring her home for her lunch and a nap," she answered with a laugh. "She's adorable! How was school? Do you have a lot of homework? Want to try to get it done before dinner?"

I stood in shock. *Could my life return to normal?* "Of course, I'll be in my bedroom. Call if you need help," I smiled, skipping to my room.

More days like that followed. My initial reserve gradually dissolved, convinced that Papa was right, as usual.

* * *

On a lovely autumn day, several months later, Rebecca and Papa married in our apple orchard beneath the blossoms. They left me in charge of the family for the weekend and honeymooned in the countryside of Sullivan County. Their wedding was the happiest day we'd had for more than a year.

Months passed, every day feeling perfect. Papa was always smiling. Rebecca was loving and patient with Hannah, and we no longer needed to send her to the Cohens on school days. Even the boys calmed. But as time continued to pass, a subtle shift surfaced in Rebecca, a short-temperedness, at first, with the boys and their antics. Initially, I was glad for their extra discipline. They were loud, always forgetting to close outside doors and take off their dirty shoes.

One school day, they ran into the house with muddy shoes right after Rebecca had washed the floors. She grabbed Nate by the collar. "How many times do I need to tell you both to take off your shoes! Now go to your room and do your homework."

Nate stopped in his tracks, his mouth open in surprise. "Yes, ma'am." Both removed their muddy shoes on the porch and shut the screen door. Then, slowly, Nate walked to his bedroom, grabbing Joe's hand on his way.

Order was restored, and I was pleased with the calm she commanded, never expecting her to turn the anger my way. "Enough with the homework and reading. You can do your work later. Watch Hannah so I can fix dinner."

I'd assumed all along that she promised Papa to allow me time for school and reading. But now I sensed something more than irritability with the boys. I tried to pitch in a little more, knowing the dreariness of endless housework. But I thought she enjoyed it, like Mama. She tsked every time I closed my door to study. What was her problem? A flame of distrust had been ignited.

At least Rebecca was always kind to Papa, making big meals for breakfast and dinner, kissing him on the head when she served him, and listening attentively when he spoke. Sometimes, I could hear hushed laughter seeping through the bedroom walls at night, like I did when Mama was still alive. *What on earth was so funny?*

As things turned out, cooking and cleaning weren't Rebecca's favorite chores either, but she managed them far better than I did. What she enjoyed most was sewing. Since her arrival, we'd worn garments made with care, the closest, straightest stitching I'd ever seen. She asked for very little from Papa, only one monthly item, the Delineator magazine, which featured the latest clothing fashions. For Hannah and my dresses, Rebecca skillfully replicated garments without ever purchasing the Butterfield patterns. For her own, she asked Papa to purchase detailed patterns at the dry goods store.

* * *

One March day after school, Mrs. Schwartz pulled me aside at the doorway as I was leaving. She waited for the building to empty. "I am delighted to see your spirits up. You look lovely in your new frock, and your schoolwork is excellent, as before. I commend you for making up all your missed work, especially considering your responsibilities at home. But I'm happiest to tell you that you will graduate first in your class."

I could barely wait to tell Papa, knowing he would be proud. *Oh Mama, can you see?*

Mrs. Schwartz continued, "I'd like you to consider continuing your studies in high school. Have you discussed the topic with your father?"

In the commotion of our family adjustment, I hadn't thought beyond the tip of my nose. Many of my friends were beginning to share their plans after finishing 8th grade, the final grade in this school. Most were helping on their farms, making plans to move with their families. My girlfriends, Fanny and Elise, were already courting. "No, we haven't discussed high school."

"I don't recommend high school for all our girls, but you have so much promise. Would you like me to speak to your father?"

My chest expanded with pride.

Mrs. Schwartz's eyes gleamed. "There's a Jewish high school in midtown connected to our shul that you could attend. If your father agrees, I will write an introductory letter and take you for a visit."

I was ecstatic, imagining how exciting it would be to continue through upper school. "I'd love that." I'd have all new books and subjects to learn.

Mrs. Schwartz clapped her hands together. "Well then, I'll come by on Sunday around noon and have a chat with your father."

I thought of Mama's words at the hospital. She was right to remind me to work hard for my dreams. My heart soared as I skipped back to the farm, something I hadn't done since I was a tot. High school would be a dream come true!

* * *

The days dragged, waiting for Sunday, my secret gnawing at me. Finally, Mrs. Schwartz appeared at the farm door standing erect as a soldier at arms, a woman with a mission. Unlike her drab school week dress, she wore a deep violet frock with white bric-a-brac trim and a straw hat with spring flowers decorating the brim. Earlier that week, I told Papa she would call but let him assume it concerned the boys. Besides, Nate and Joe were pranksters, and I figured he'd be relieved when he discovered her true purpose.

I greeted Mrs. Schwartz with a full smile and was immediately struck by the delicious, familiar fragrance of baked butter, sugar, and cinnamon.

"Yum, that smells delicious. What did you bring?" My mouth watered as I lifted the corner of the muslin cover hiding the delicacies beneath. It was rugelach, my favorite pastry. Memories of Mama flooded my mind while my nose tingled.

When Mama was alive, Friday mornings were a special time. Preparation for our Sabbath meal began before we left for school. After we returned, I watched her braid challah, our Sabbath bread, and then roll sweet dough on the heavily floured kitchen table for dessert. Once flattened, she spread nuts, cinnamon, and her homemade apricot preserves over the surface, cut the dough into long triangles, and rolled each into an individual pastry. It'd been a long time since we'd baked sweets. The memory of that heavenly aroma permeating the house hours before we gathered for candle lighting, prayer, and a family dinner reminded me how fragile happiness was.

Rebecca, not quite the ambitious cook, kept our Sabbath meals simpler. Roast chicken, vegetables, and challah. Dinners were always plentiful, but she never ignited the meal with Mama's magic touch.

"Please come in." I led Mrs. Schwartz into the sitting room where Papa and Rebecca stood, set the pastry on the table, and hustled into the kitchen to boil water for tea. I pulled cups from the cupboard silently so I could hear their conversation, praying for the meeting to go as planned. As good fortune had its way, Hannah was napping, and the house was uncommonly quiet. Once the boys heard her name, they hid in their bedroom, likely expecting the worst.

Papa got straight to the point. "I hope Nathan and Joseph are behaving," he used their full birth names, the ones reserved for occasions requiring discipline.

She smiled, warm embers in her dark brown eyes. "They've been good boys and have shown much improvement since your marriage. Both are making steady progress with their reading and numbers and will be well-educated young men when they finish school. Joseph is particularly talented at mathematics. I believe he has an academic gift, like Tillie."

My eyes were fixed on Rebecca. I saw her self-satisfied smile. She clearly thought she was responsible for their improvement. It irked me that she didn't mention the truth, that it was me who checked their schoolwork and practiced multiplication and fractions with them every night. My face flushed with annoyance.

Papa knit his brows. "That's good to hear, but then I'm confused. What brought you here today?"

"I would like to discuss Tillie."

On cue, I brought the tray into the room and smiled. Setting the tray on the table, I looked at Papa and asked, "May I stay?"

Papa gestured to an empty chair.

All eyes turned to Mrs. Schwartz.

She cleared her throat and paused, the same exact pause she used at school when she had an important announcement. "Tillie is one of the brightest students our school has seen in years. Other than the Jacob boy, who went on for medical training, and your son, Joe, we haven't taught a child with her academic gifts for quite some time. She'll complete eighth grade at the top of her class in reading and is performing mathematics at the high school level."

Papa nodded, a proud smile on his face.

"As you know, we don't have a high school in this part of town, and it will be some time before there's one where you're headed. I came today to encourage you to send her to the Jewish high school in midtown next fall."

Papa's eyes widened with surprise. Rebecca squirmed in her chair. I held my breath, waiting for Papa to speak.

He drew a deep breath. "I'm pleased to hear your praise, and I know school has always been important to Tillie, but we haven't discussed high school. Frankly speaking, we've been preoccupied with decisions about the farm." He looked at the floor, shaking his head, then lifted it to Mrs. Schwartz's eyes. "The time escaped me since Sarah passed. But don't most girls finish school after eighth grade?"

Mrs. Schwartz spoke slowly, giving her words weight and emphasis due to her status as Head Mistress. "That's true. Many do from these parts, but Tillie is different. She absorbs knowledge like a sponge. It's my considered opinion that she's a gifted child who should be given the opportunity to continue her schooling."

Papa's forehead wrinkled deeply, then he asked, "I don't know any of the details, for instance, the cost? Where would she live? Even with streetcars, it is too great a distance and dangerous to travel back and forth alone at her age." Papa looked at my hopeful face and then at Rebecca's, whose lips were pursed in a tight frown.

Mrs. Schwartz studied Rebecca while she spoke. "Those are all good questions, Mr. Isaacson." She shifted her gaze back to Papa. "I know of scholarships and there is a well-supervised dormitory beside the high school where many students board, some only for weekdays. At this point, I wanted to present the idea to you." She handed Papa a brochure on the school. "This covers the specifics."

Papa glanced at the brochure. "Who pays for the scholarships?"

"Some of the wealthy German patrons of the synagogue who settled in Midtown years back, like the Seligman family."

I released my breath. Would he agree?

Papa glanced at Rebecca. Her lips had all but disappeared, her eyes glowing pits of fire.

Why couldn't she be happier for me?

Mrs. Schwartz's eyes swept from Papa to Rebecca, resting on Rebecca's face. "I'd like to take her downtown to see the school in the next few weeks. In the meantime, perhaps you and Mrs. Isaacson can discuss the idea further." She shifted in her chair, again facing Papa. "I haven't formally announced my plans yet, but I will be teaching there in the fall, if it has any bearing on your decision." She paused, "I'd like to know your thoughts by the end of the school year, as it will take the summer to work out details."

"I'll get my decision to you soon." Papa then called the boys. "Nate, Joe, come out from wherever you are hiding and have some rugelach your Head Mistress baked."

The boys charged into the room, yelping with relief, their hands darting to the tray.

Papa stormed, "What are you forgetting?"

The boys pulled back their hands and sang in unison, "Thank you, Mrs. Schwartz."

* * *

Later that evening, after putting Hannah to bed, I heard Papa and Rebecca arguing in their bedroom. I tiptoed by the closed door to listen.

Rebecca's voice was strained. "Sam, I know you wanted Tillie to have time to study after Sarah passed. I gave her that time and will admit, it's to her credit that with all the ups and downs around here, she completed eighth grade at the top of her class. But you must know something important."

"What is it?" Papa asked, concern in his voice.

"I've missed two of my monthlies."

Papa whooped with excitement, clapping his hands. I heard the rustling of a hug as he sang, "Such joy! Such wonderful news! Another child, our child!" He quieted for a long time, then added with concern, "But why so serious? Are you feeling alright? Do you need the doctor?"

"No, dear, just the usual symptoms. But I'll need Tillie's help with Hannah and the boys more than ever. You know what a handful they are. And then there's the endless housework."

My fury grew. She's making my life, my future, all about her needs.

He answered softly, "Rebecca, high school is months away. Tillie can help you all summer."

Rebecca forged on. "She's completed eighth grade like all the rest of her friends. Why should she move to a dormitory downtown and live like a princess while the rest of us work ourselves to the bone? And the expense? The money must come from somewhere. Should we stop paying for the boys' school, or clothing, or food?"

"You're not being fair. She helps you every day."

I heard the edge in his voice, that strained warning when he enunciated every word more carefully. It always came straight before he lost his temper. The boys and I knew it well.

Rebecca interrupted. "She knew why that Head Mistress wanted to visit and yet didn't tell us in advance. Surely, she could have spared us the humiliation of being unprepared for the discussion."

I wanted to blast through the door and defend myself. But my better judgment held me back.

Papa let out a loud sigh, "Rebecca, there's no humiliation. Why are you spoiling our wonderful news?"

"Right now, it doesn't feel wonderful. I'm sick every morning after breakfast and am tired all day. What am I supposed to do?"

"Shouldn't all that pass soon?" Papa asked, but his voice sounded more like a statement. After all, he was an experienced father.

"Hopefully. Sam, I love you. But your big family is more work than I ever imagined. I need help, and she's the only one who can do it." She huffed. "High school, of all things! She has quite grand ideas for herself."

Papa's anger threatened every word. I wondered how much longer he would hold his temper. "Sarah always encouraged Tillie in school—which is likely where she got her ambition. Besides, I want more information before I decide. In the meantime, don't discuss any of this with her. She's still young, and I trust Mrs. Schwartz on the matter."

Another interruption. "But Sam..."

"Enough!" he said tersely.

Finally, she'd pushed him too far. A perverse surge of victory shot through me.

"Let's enjoy our happy news. I've heard you, and now I need time to think."

Despite his rebuke, my belly soured as I knew high school was far from certain. Rebecca's resentment was no longer a secret. I crept from their door to the kitchen and dropped heavily into a chair, picking up my library book.

Chapter Eight

Early the following Sunday, when the last of the overnight coolness still hung in the air, Rabbi Friedman knocked on our door. The boys were in the yard playing ball, and Papa, Rebecca, and I were finishing breakfast with Hannah. I wasn't sure why Rabbi had come, but I hoped it was Mrs. Schwartz's influence. If he told Papa I should go to high school, I'd be allowed to go.

"Good morning, Rabbi. Please join us for breakfast." Papa gestured to an empty chair. "We have challah toast and fresh eggs."

"Danka, but not today, Sam. Let's walk. There're things we need to discuss." Even though Rabbi Friedman was close to Papa's age, he always looked worried. His back was bent forward as if in mid-prayer, his hair and beard long, streaked with premature grey.

"Can I come?" I jumped from my chair, my curiosity nibbling at my better judgment.

"Me, me," Hannah echoed.

Rabbi didn't hesitate. "Not today. This conversation is for the adults."

Annoyed, I wiped off Hannah's messy face and hands with a damp rag and waited for Rebecca to get busy tidying her bedroom.

Peeking out the front window, I saw the men walk behind the barn under the shade of the apple trees. Without a second thought, I left Hannah and crept out the front door, scurrying into the barn, hiding against the rear wall so I could overhear their conversation. I crouched among the chickens, hoping my careful entrance wouldn't create a ruckus.

The Rabbi's voice was grave. "I'm afraid I've pressing news. I got word from Avi Shulman. You remember the farmland owner?"

Papa was silent.

I peered through a crack in the wall boards.

"Last week, the bank withdrew his land loan. He'll need to return all this to the bank." Rabbi stretched out his arm, sweeping it across the horizon.

Papa's eyes opened wide. "But why?"

"I hear from friends downtown the city is behind it. What the city wants, the city gets."

"But...I don't understand," said Papa.

Again, with his upturned palm, Rabbi raised his arm to the horizon. A strained impatience crept into his voice. "They want our land for development and have pressured the banks. Take a good look around, Sam, because this part of New York will be nothing more than a memory in five years. It'll look like southern Manhattan, full of stone streets, apartment buildings, and businesses."

Papa sighed loudly. "I hoped there would be more time. When must we go?"

"We're talking months."

"I know you've been looking for a resettlement location. Did you find anything?"

Rabbi placed his hands on his hips. "That's what I wanted to discuss. There's a parcel Avi and I found that you must see. I convinced him to reinvest in a new area north of here. The land's more fertile than what we have now. It's in Sullivan County, but we need to lock in our tenants so he can close the deal with the bank." Rabbi looked at the horizons around us. "It's large enough to relocate the community plus some. You realize, of course, some of it will be used for the new synagogue and school."

"I understand, Rabbi." Papa nodded, wiping his brow with his shirt sleeve.

"Part of our congregation has already moved their livestock to that county and are eager for us to join them. But we need to vacate after fall harvest at the latest."

"That's awfully fast. You know Rebecca is expecting."

"Yes, of course. But the men look up to you and will take your lead. I want to keep the community together. There will be plenty of women to help Rebecca when her time comes." Rabbi continued, "Can we take a group there this week to see the area and decide?"

I couldn't believe my ears. A voice inside shouted, No! This wasn't the plan. I straightened my legs, stepping backward to catch my balance, accidentally stomping on a hen's claw behind me.

"Craw! Craw!" The wounded hen skirted angrily around the barn, flopping her wings, disturbing her pen-mates. The racket grew as the other chickens caught her distress, flailing their wings, squawking in empathy.

"What's going on in there?" shouted Papa. "Who's in the barn?"

I peeked my head through the doorway. "I stepped on a hen."

"Have you been listening to us?" the Rabbi scolded. Without waiting for an answer, "Shame on you, girl!"

Papa looked at my worried face and knew my thoughts right away. "Rabbi, are you aware of the discussions we've had with the school Head Mistress about Tillie's future?"

Butterflies fluttered in my belly. I held my breath. *Please, oh please, take my side.*

"Mrs. Schwartz can be quite convincing, and I know she supports the girl's education. But high school simply isn't a priority. Your whole family comes first. You'll need at least a year or more to settle into a new home and farm."

Rabbi saw me blinking back tears, shrugged, directing his next words to me with a softer edge to his voice, "Dear, this isn't your time. It's a big change for your Papa and Mama, and they'll need your help more than ever."

He didn't even know my name! It wasn't fair. Remembering what I'd overheard Rebecca say when she and Papa had discussed high school and her strained behavior toward me since then, my restraint unfurled. "She's not my Mama! She doesn't care what's good for me. She only wants me to watch my real Mama's children and doesn't think school's important!" I stormed. "My Mama would have found a way."

"Don't put yourself first," Rabbi scolded, his patience short lived. "An entire community is being uprooted, and we need everyone's help. And don't forget, your most Godly role as a young woman is to help with your home and family."

Rabbi dismissively turned back to Papa and added, "I hope you have savings put away. You'll need it."

Papa nodded, squirming uncomfortably, avoiding my eyes. "Now, how about that coffee?" They headed back to the farmhouse.

I trailed behind, holding back furious tears, kicking the cursed dusty soil on the ground.

Chapter Nine

June 1880

N o one besides Mama cared a fig about my dreams, and she was no longer here to fight for me. After working so hard to regain the spot of first in my class, there was no way I'd reduce myself to a life filled with the drudgery of housework. Deep in my bones, I was certain I was meant for more importance. Feeding chickens and washing clothes on our chicken farm would never make me happy. I would not give up so easily.

Papa's reasons for delaying my high school during the move were fair enough, but I didn't want him to dismiss the idea entirely. I stewed all week, struggling to find another way. By week's end, I approached him with a bargain. "Papa, can we hold off on high school for a year while I help Rebecca unpack and with her new baby? After that, you'll be settled, and then I could travel home on weekends to pitch in."

Papa held his hat, circling the brim in his hands, considering my request. "I'm sorry, Tillie, but I can't promise anything right now. I don't know how long it'll take to get the new farm on its legs. I won't agree to a thing until I have a roof over our heads and food on the table."

That was the last straw. "It's so unfair! What about the scholarship? If they offer to help, would you change your mind?"

He shook his head. "I said no! There's simply too much change in our lives. And Rebecca—"

I snapped, parroting back in a singsong. "And Rebecca wants me as her slave. She never wanted to care for any of us and thinks it's my job now that she's having a child of her own. Can't you see that?" I paused, my head exploding with frustration, grappling for a way through his resistance.

Papa's face reddened, his voice cross. "Enough, Tillie. Accept what it is."

I persisted, channeling Mama's message to me. "If she were here, I'd be going to high school, move or no move!"

Papa's face fell.

I knew my words cut deeply, but I couldn't give in. "I miss her so much and before she died, she made me promise to work hard for my dreams."

Papa pulled me into his outstretched arms. "Come here." He held me tightly. "Sometimes, we must let go of old dreams and make new ones. Good things will come your way in time. You'll see."

* * *

My eighth-grade graduation was around the corner. Papa offered to host a celebratory party, but I refused. On the afternoon of the graduation ceremony, I bid my friends and teachers farewell at the school and walked home before the rest of my family, who lingered for refreshments and conversation, acting as if they were the proud parents. Rebecca especially wore my valedictorian recognition as if it were her own badge of honor. I saw no point in playing a part in their charade.

Immediately afterwards, my summer fell into a pattern, an eternal repetition of the worst toil imaginable: sorting, packing, cleaning, and minding Hannah. Rebecca, the evil stepmother, unleashed her every frustration in my direction. "Get this, Tillie. Do that, Tillie."

I cringed at the sound of her shrill voice. My wrath festered like an open wound. Even little Hannah, who typically clung to me, sensed my foul mood and sought out Nate and Joe when she needed help. Rebecca was the only member of the house undeterred by my fury. She worked diligently beside me, avoiding all eye contact and conversation. New orders were issued at the heels of the last task completed.

The men, on the other hand, simmered with excitement as they hatched plans for a Jewish resettlement community in Sullivan County. Were they not aware of the burden they'd placed on everyone else? My resentment deepened. What on God's green earth was exciting about moving to a desolate farm community far from the city's excitement and opportunities?

Any shred of past appreciation for the sewing Rebecca had done for me was gone. As she struggled with morning sickness, fatigue, and, later, swollen ankles, she expected more and more from me. How could our relationship change so dramatically in under one year? Was I evil to feel satisfaction when she ran to the basin holding her mouth?

Her strident voice shot fire through my veins, "Tillie, are you done with the laundry? I need help in the kitchen."

In my rebellion, I worked slowly, leaving clothing stains, intentionally forgetting to pack items, and feigning deafness. It was my only retaliation, the single way to rebel until I worked out a better plan.

On rare occasions, I had a moment to relax and read a library book, inhaling the pungent smell of the leather cover. But sensing my contentment, Rebecca would call for more help, spoiling the mood. "No time for idleness. I need your help now."

Infuriated to no end, I returned all my books to the library and abandoned reading altogether. Rebecca of course didn't care, viewing books as frivolous play. Papa was so preoccupied with the move; he barely took notice. He offhandedly said, "Chin up. Things will get better."

Thinking back, I'd never seen Rebecca read a book or newspaper during the months I'd known her, only fashion magazines for her endless sewing projects, continually reminding me that she needed to make maternity dresses. As much as I admired her ability, it was increasingly obvious we shared no other interests. I toiled in the farmhouse as she sat by the window, stitching by the hour.

One morning, after cleaning up breakfast, I took Hannah and snuck away from the farm while Rebecca was in the outhouse. We walked to the synagogue to play on the matchbook-sized playground, the only one for miles. It had a teeter-totter and two swings. From time to time, my classmates brought their younger sisters and brothers during summer mornings before lunch and afternoon naps. When I arrived, I felt a rush of happiness for the first time when I saw Elise and Fanny. A smile cracked through my frozen frown. All of us were taking a break from the tedium at home. We clucked like hens at feeding time while pushing the children on the swings.

Elise was excited to fill me in on the news. "Our families are going north with the rest of the community, but Fanny and I decided to get married! We won't be joining them." She pushed the swing harder as her younger sister called out, *higher, higher!*

I was dumbfounded, anxious to hear more.

Fanny giggled with glee. "Our fiancées live in the Lower East Side with their parents. We'll live there, too, until we can afford places of our own. We'll be near each other."

I was incredulous. "This all happened in one month?" Fiancées sounded so fancy.

"You know Talia, the matchmaker? She knows lots of good men," Elise explained, "Courting was fun! We're going to work in stitching factories until we start a family."

Fanny looked at my confused face. "Maybe you should think about it too. There are lots of men looking for brides."

Elise added, "Rabbi said that those terrible old laws in Germany denying Jewish marriages haven't changed. Men are coming to New York, looking for wives and a new start. The first person they speak to is the local Rabbi. That's where Talia comes in."

I was shocked. This was all news to me. "The rabbis are all in cahoots, and they marry us off like cattle. They could care less what we want!" I thought angrily about how much control Rabbi Friedman wielded over our lives. And I didn't like Talia, either. She had a reputation for pushing her hand in everyone's face for payment, even before marriage decisions were made. I'd heard some girls complain they felt like a sack of flour sold at market. Had the worth of smart young women fallen so far?

Fanny interrupted my thoughts. "Don't be angry. It's good to go through the rabbis. They make sure the men are reputable. They protect us from bad people who've broken laws in Europe, like stealing or hurting others."

I calmed down slightly. "I suppose. But are you ready to have a husband? A child?" As I asked, the seeds of a plot began germinating. Perhaps I finally had a way to use Rabbi to my advantage.

Elise waved her open hand at our cluster of younger brothers and sisters. "I think so. I've had plenty of practice watching them."

While the girls chattered, I pushed Hannah in her swing, half-listening, thinking. Admittedly, anything was better than the isolation of farming and living under Rebecca's thumb. But marriage as a way out?

My mind raced. Could I marry and attend high school? Would my husband support such a thing? Could I insist on that condition? Once married, my decisions would no longer be up to Papa and Rebecca. My husband would be in charge. It was risky. I was only turning sixteen in August, and Rebecca had fought hard to ensure I'd be around to help her. The hard part would be convincing Papa to let Rabbi find a husband for me now, amid a move. All told, it was worth a try. "Maybe you're right. I'll talk to my Papa."

Moving to the Lower East Side, with its reputation for overcrowding, was worrisome. Would it be safe? Growing up on a farm, I knew little about life downtown. I'd seen tenements from the outside when I joined Papa on his chicken deliveries, but I'd never gone inside any buildings to see for myself. And the smell of the streets in the heat of summer was atrocious.

I was conflicted, weighing the unknown life downtown against life ahead. *How bad could it be?* Excluded from the men's discussions during their evening planning meetings and relegated to the boring jobs they gave to the women had become intolerable. Despite everything I didn't know, I decided to take things into my own hands.

* * *

Returning to the farm, I heard Rebecca's screech a half-acre away. I cringed.

"Where were you? I needed your help!"

Holding Hannah's hand, I slowed down on purpose, approaching the door. "I took Hannah to the school to play with other children and met my school friends. We all needed a break."

"Next time, ask permission. You can't just take off without a word," Rebecca snapped.

"You would've said *no*." I fumed. "Hannah needs to have fun. She's barely a baby, and I'm not your servant!"

She stood shaking with anger on the dusty patch of earth. "What a mouth! Who do you think you are, Queen of the Nile?"

I snapped back, "I wish Papa never married you!" and stormed past the house, leaving Hannah crying in the dirt. I kept going until I reached the pond, standing there, stewing.

Later, hours after things calmed, after I washed the dinner dishes and tucked Hannah in bed, I whispered in Papa's ear. "Can we take a walk, alone?"

We strolled down the dusty road, watching the sun sink in the western sky. Surveyors had hammered hundreds of stakes into the ground, marking the future streets. The granite hills were roped off for demolition. During the day, the exploding dynamite vibrated through the floorboards. Sometimes, the rattling knocked a dish from the cupboard onto the floor, sending shards of pottery everywhere. Some of the hens even stopped laying eggs. Time was ticking fast.

Papa reached down and scooped a handful of dry dirt. "Our world is disappearing. Soon all this land will be leveled, built into roads, apartments, and businesses. It's good we'll be gone."

Gone with Mama and all my beautiful memories of her on the farm. A shower of sadness threatened to rain down, but I resisted, drawing in a fortifying breath, attempting to forge forward.

Papa, sensing the sad turn in conversation, asked me, "What's on your mind? I'm not happy you were fighting with Rebecca. You know I can't allow that."

I sighed. "I'm sorry, but I can't stand it anymore." I reminded myself to act like an adult.

"Change can be hard, but sometimes it brings better things for everyone."

I was afraid Papa wouldn't listen to anything that didn't fit into his plans. "Why can't you understand? You and Mama came all this way from Germany for new opportunities, and now I want mine."

He took my hand. "You're acting selfish. We have a big family to worry about, and this move must go smoothly. When we came to America, it was only the three of us. Soon, there will be seven, too many to put your needs first."

Except Rebecca puts hers first. "Papa, I was talking to my friends today, and Elise and Fanny are getting married." I waited a moment before going on. "Would you consider letting me marry too? I'd miss you, but now that I can't go to high school, I need to think about my future, and I can't see a future for me north of the city, on a farm in the country."

I held my breath. Papa stopped in his tracks, facing me, his face puzzled. "What's going on behind that *shayna punim* of yours? I know you're disappointed about high school, but this is new. Marriage shouldn't be a way out of moving. You should be in love with someone first."

"It's true. I don't want to move north, and I'm tired of being under Rebecca's thumb. My future is over if I move to the farm." I was meant to be more than a servant in my own home. Pushing forward, I added, "The girls said many good men are looking for wives, and Rabbi is helping them. I thought he could find someone for me."

Papa's face shrunk with concern. "Let me think about it. We'll talk again in a few days. More than anything, I want you to be happy." He sighed. "Sometimes you remind me of your mama, with her big ideas. We'd still be in Germany if it weren't for her." He reached for my hand and kissed the palm.

I was relieved he hadn't said no. Of course, he hadn't said yes, either.

And then he added, "But while I think it over, please apologize to Rebecca. She's working very hard and not feeling well. I can't have the two of you battling."

Chapter Ten

After the house quieted and the younger children were tucked in bed, I heard Papa and Rebecca arguing in hushed tones. Aching with curiosity, I again tiptoed to their closed bedroom door.

"Now she wants to marry?" Rebecca's whispers were as shrill as her voice. "Why is she so unhappy? Most girls her age help their families, especially during difficult times. She's so full of herself."

Papa explained patiently. "She wanted to go to high school, but since she can't, she needs to set her own course." He paused, "Sarah would've found a way to make high school work."

Rebecca bit back. "Neither of us wanted our spouses to die young, but God had different plans."

Papa didn't miss a beat. "Yes, he did, and I thank God every day he had you waiting for me, and the two of us moved forward together. But Tillie was never meant for farming. She has bigger dreams."

"She's going to be in for a big surprise when she learns how much work it takes to run a household alone. Not to mention babies," Rebecca scoffed. "In the meantime, she'll have to work in one of those awful factories. It'll be misery for her. She can't sit still long enough to sew on a button."

"She'll learn." Papa sighed. "She's been through a lot of heartache. Perhaps a loving husband will help her heal, like you helped me."

It was quiet for a moment, and then Papa laughed and said, "And besides, it's not a sure thing. Maybe after she meets a few *schlemiels*, she'll change her mind and see that staying home a while longer isn't a bad thing. Then, at least joining us will be her decision, not ours."

"But that doesn't help me one bit. Three young children and a new baby, plus a move?" Rebecca's voice rose. "It's simply too much!"

"Let's cross that road when we get there. I can always trade eggs and chickens for help with the children, like I did before we met. That's how I made sure Tillie stayed in school after Sarah." His voice trailed off.

Rebecca huffed. "I suppose, but I still think she's too young to marry."

How would she know? She barely knows me.

Papa's voice sounded tired. "And let's face it, having Tillie around with that gloomy attitude isn't helping anyone. It's a shame we don't have more money set aside. She's smarter than most of the boys heading to that high school. It's a damn shame."

"It's the way of the world, Sam. She's a girl, and her duty is at home. Sarah filled her head with big ideas, and now look at her, miserable about doing the right thing. Even Rabbi said so."

Papa spoke in a strained, angry voice. "We took away her dream of high school and I won't take this away, too. I'll talk to Rabbi this week and he can get Talia involved. We'll see what comes of it."

Rebecca snapped back. "I hope you don't regret it."

I slid across the floor to my bedroom replaying their words, *smarter than the boys, how's she going to take care of a family*, while I sadly thought about the aching hole Mama had left in my heart. If only Papa had fought this hard for high school.

* * *

At lightning speed, one week after Papa spoke to Rabbi, Talia arrived at the farm, raring to make a match. I led her into the parlor, where Papa and Rebecca waited. She was exactly as I imagined: pushy, indifferent, and preoccupied with her payment. Although quite small, with a face full of random dark hairs sprouting from places where hair did not belong, her domineering personality made up for her lack of size.

While they introduced themselves, I prepared a tray of tea and cookies, setting it on the table.

Talia got right down to business, making no pretense that her priority was payment, not my happiness. "What's the dowry?"

Rebecca interrupted, eyeing the woman distrustfully. "Not much."

"I'm afraid that's true," Papa agreed. "But I have chickens."

Talia brushed a few wiry whisps of hair under her black scarf; her face pinched in thought. "Well, I suppose a woman has to eat."

Papa cleared his throat, turning to face me. "My daughter, as you can see, is lovely and just as smart as she is beautiful. We'd like to find a worthy man."

"With chickens?" Talia harrumphed, eyeing eyeballing me from the top of my hair to my shoes.

How dare she talk to Papa that way!

"I may have two men for her to meet, if they're not already taken." She rattled off their ages, employment, native language, if either had children, and so forth. She had no photos, nor could she describe their appearance. Standing at five feet seven inches, I preferred a man taller than me.

I blurted out in frustration, "It sounds like you're describing livestock. Have you met any of these people? What kind of men are they? They all seem like strangers on the street!"

Talia was unfazed. "I got their names from my contacts. They don't go to our shul. This is how things work. You meet, you and your papa decide, then you pay."

* * *

I heard the knock and shooed my brothers outside as I greeted him. "Hello, I'm Tillie." I smiled.

His head was bent to the porch floor. Seconds passed before his eyes darted briefly to mine. "Dov."

"Would you like to come in? I made fresh lemonade, not too sweet." How could a young man this shy be ready to wed? Besides, he still looked like a young boy, skinny as a rake and a face sprinkled with pimples—a stray dog.

He glanced up again. "Thank you."

66

I gestured to a chair. Papa and Rebecca were already waiting for him in the parlor. Papa stood and firmly shook Dov's hand.

"Where do you live?" Papa asked.

"About a mile north," Dov answered softly in German, staring at the floor.

Papa and I exchanged glances. I mouthed, *don't go.*

"I'll get the lemonade." I excused myself and went into the kitchen, straining to hear Papa's conversation.

"What do you do for work?" Papa asked.

"I raise sheep with my Pa."

"Do you butcher as well? We don't here." Papa pointed to the barn.

"We do both." Then, silence until Dov turned my way. "You do know how to butcher livestock, don't you?"

I practically dropped my tray of glasses. I shot a glance at Rebecca, who had buried her face in her handkerchief, suppressing a laugh. Recovering, I commented. "I do not butcher, and I don't remember you from school. Do you go to the shul?"

"Nah, I stopped school after fourth. Didn't like it. We don't go to shul anymore."

Rebecca asked, "How old are you, Dov?"

"Eighteen." He squirmed in his chair. "We're moving north as soon as Pa's ready."

Rebecca leaned in his direction. "Have you brothers and sisters? How does your mama feel about you marrying?"

He raised his eyes to hers. "I have four youngers. My ma's been dead a while.

A trap! That Talia was wicked.

The next hour was interminable as Papa and I politely attempted small talk with the most introverted, dull boy imaginable. It didn't take a high school graduate to figure out that they needed a woman to run their home and help clean up after the butchering. Papa was right. There were worse fates than moving north.

Once Dov left, Papa, Rebecca, and I all shook our heads in unison and began to laugh.

"Tillie, you won't be happy with that one." Rebecca reached for Papa's arm. "You'll run circles around the poor boy." Mirth filled her face. "Something we finally agree on?"

"Yes." I laughed, surprised to be of the same mind.

* * *

The second boy, Elijah, who visited the following Sunday, irritated me from the start, boasting about himself and vainly styling his hair with his fingers. His visit was as unsatisfying as Dov's.

After a quick introduction to Papa and Rebecca, I suggested we take a walk. The moment we were out the door, he asked, "How many men have you met?"

"You're the second."

He brushed back his dark hair and shook his head to the sun. "I've met more girls than that. Most of them weren't pretty like you. My mother didn't think they were good enough for me."

I was stunned. His mother? I tried to turn the conversation, "Do you like to read?"

Elijah laughed. "Are you kidding?"

The conversation went downhill from there. I learned more than I cared to know about him—his penchant for lamb and love of horses and hunting. He never thought to inquire about my likes or dislikes. And then, out of view from our house, he tried to kiss me.

I jerked away. "Stop it."

He frowned. "What's the harm in a little kiss? It's a warm-up for later."

I wiped his saliva from my lips. "Didn't your perfect mother teach you any manners? I don't even like you," I marched in the direction of our farmhouse.

Elijah called after me, "I'm going home. You were a waste of time."

"You're a disgusting pig!" I shouted over my shoulder.

Fuming, I stormed past Papa and Rebecca into my room, throwing myself on the bed. Maybe I didn't want to get married after all. If Dov or Elijah were my choices, then I was stuck. I had no intention of marrying a self-involved, rude imbecile or a dull, boring dolt and being trapped for life. Was this the best Talia could do? Did she send dregs because we were poor?

Papa walked in quietly and sat beside me. "You don't have to go through with this. There's no rush to marry."

I sat up and leaned my head on his shoulder. "I don't know what to do. Isn't there someone out there like you?" For that moment, I felt like his little girl again, savoring a moment of rare attention.

He started to laugh. "Oh, you'll see. There's a special person just for you. Do you want me to talk to Rabbi again? He said he may have one more, but he's older. What do you want to do?"

"I'm not ready to give up. But I need to learn more about him first."

* * *

The following Sunday, Rabbi stopped by the house. This time, Rebecca set up the parlor with breakfast. Rabbi filled his plate with eggs, challah, and applesauce and relaxed in his chair. "I heard you didn't care for the two men."

I shook my head, afraid to say a word and insult him with my vile description of Talia, the matchmaker from the underworld.

Papa cleared his throat. "Rabbi, the men Talia brought to the house were barely men, in no position to support a family. Could you tell us something about the older man?"

"I'm sorry to hear that. Talia assured me they were ready for marriage." Rabbi stroked his beard. "I wonder why she sent them."

You know why! She saves the best for her wealthy clients. My chest caught, thinking about the permanence of marriage and how far I'd be from my family. Could I trust the rabbi to do better than Talia?

Rabbi straightened his yarmulke, pushing it back on his balding head. "I heard Abraham Levine, who's originally from these parts, is looking. I believe he's twenty-eight." He glanced at Papa. "Talia doesn't know of him."

Papa shot back, "Let's leave it that way. If you could, we'd like to know more about him."

Rabbi set his half-eaten plate on the side table, the runny applesauce leaching into the scrambled eggs. No one made applesauce as well as Mama had, with its soft, firm texture and hint of cinnamon. "Years back, before you arrived, the Levines had a farm up here. The father was not cut out for farming and started an imported button business downtown. He sold fancy buttons to dressmakers in Manhattan."

I listened attentively, realizing how little I knew of the city and its commerce. But my memory hadn't dulled. I thought of those fancy dresses worn by the ladies in Central Park. *It would be lovely to dress like them.*

The Rabbi gazed through the front window at the orchard. "Mr. Levine was married before, but tragically, his wife died from consumption. The baby perished, too…such sadness. A common story."

My heart fell. How does anyone recover after such loss? Would he have room in his heart for me? "That's terrible."

"He's a lonely man and deserves happiness. Frankly, I'm concerned the age difference could be a problem."

I interrupted. "I'm not some silly girl, Rabbi. Why does everyone underestimate me?" Was this why he let Talia send two dunces my way? He must view me as a dim-witted, selfish child.

Rabbi ignored my comment. "I must caution you it's different marrying a man his age who has been through so much loss. You need to think about that."

I was clueless. What did he mean?

Curious to hear more about Mr. Levine, I pursued. "Where does he live? Does he have other family? Is he a good person? Do they still sell buttons? Is he taller than me?" I rushed from question to question, not stopping to let Rabbi answer.

Papa cut in. His bushy eyebrows furrowed. "Is he a man of reasonable means? Can he take care of my Tillie and a family?"

Rabbi held up his hands, defending himself from our barrage. "Enough questions! I can't answer everything, but this is what I know."

I dropped back against the ladder back chair, ready to listen.

Rabbi drew a deep breath. "He's rebuilding the family's button business. The parents passed a few years back, and I don't know if there's any more family. The last time I saw Mr. Levine, he was still a boy. As I recall, he wasn't short then."

Papa and I moved to the edge of our chairs.

Rabbi rubbed his hands together. "To answer you, Sam, he's living in the Jewish tenements. When the market sank, his family gave up their apartment, a rather nice one, from what I heard. They practically lost everything. But he's ambitious and has worked hard to restore their business."

Papa's face flushed. "I thought you said he was a worthy match. Those buildings are a disgrace, not even fit for my chickens. I can't have Tillie living there. Her mother, God bless, would strike me down."

The rabbi kept his voice calm, patting his hands down. "Many people suffered hardship in the last bank collapse. As I said, Mr. Levine is enterprising. I don't think he plans to stay there long."

Papa cast his head down and sighed.

The rabbi continued, "And business has picked up. There's a steady demand for imported buttons by dressmakers, especially the fancy ones." Rabbi paused to consider further. "But marriage takes two, and Tillie must support his efforts and help him get back on his feet."

Both of their eyes turned to search mine.

I firmly nodded, determined to take this last chance. "Papa, may we meet?"

* * *

Rabbi scheduled a meeting with Mr. Levine two weeks later. He was my last option, and I was a wreck. I worried he'd think I was too young, and my fate would be sealed. I'd be banished to the farms up north.

Sitting in front of my small wall mirror, I changed my hairstyle three times. First, I brushed it down to my waist and tied a yellow ribbon in the back, but I looked like an overgrown child. Then, I pulled the front half upward, fastening it with a comb. Studying my face in the mirror, I decided I still looked too young. Finally, I turned my head to the floor and brushed my thick mop to the top of my head to form a bun, but it fell apart in my hands. In a flash of anger, I threw the brush across the room, where it crashed noisily against the wall.

"Is everything alright in there?" Rebecca called out. Her concerned tone irritated me even more.

"I can't do anything with my hair!" I cried, frustrated and nervous about the meeting.

Rebecca's voice remained calm. "May I come in? Perhaps I can help."

I didn't want her help, but my hair was impossible. At this rate, I'd make a poor first impression. I acquiesced. "Thank you."

Rebecca studied my hair as I watched her in the reflection. Her face was full of concentration. "Let me try something I saw in a magazine." Within minutes, she had tied my tresses atop my head and fastened a braided bun, much like Queen Victoria's hairstyle, pulling short tendrils of curls free around my ears. "How's that?"

I was stunned, amazed at her deftness.

"You have beautiful hair. I can teach you how to fashion it properly if you'd like."

I smiled at my reflection. "I look so sophisticated! I can't believe it." I twisted about to face her. "I owe you an apology. I'm sorry for being rude."

Rebecca hesitated, her shoulders softening. "I understand, Tillie. We've both been overburdened. Let's try to be friends now that you're taking this big step. We'll be much happier, and it will cheer your papa. We both love him in our different ways."

I placed my arms around her small frame. "You're right."

Rebecca had sewn a pale peach summer dress for my courting. I slipped it over my lightweight corset and fastened the small buttons up the bodice. It fit perfectly, and the color complemented my hair. Papa walked into my bedroom as I finished dressing, handing me Mama's pearl combs. "Tillie, I think your mama would've wanted you to wear these today, for good luck. Shall I help?"

I bent my head forward as Papa slid the combs into the sides of the braided bun Rebecca had fashioned. He kissed me on my temple. *Did he know that was Mama's spot?*

I whispered. "I hope this one isn't another disaster. Maybe Mama's been warning me not to bother with marriage quite yet."

Papa smiled softly. "Be patient. If he's not the one, the perfect man will come along when the time is right."

He left the room, and my eyes drifted back to my reflection. *Mama, can you send a sign? Am I doing the right thing?*

No reply came.

I sighed. I would have to rely on Papa's judgment. Although excited to meet someone older and worldly, I felt so unprepared, a little girl wearing dress-up clothes and a fancy hairstyle, pretending to be a grown woman. Down deep, I knew I wasn't ready to meet this man, or marry.

A knock at the front door jarred me from my reverie. I heard Papa greet Mr. Levine. I took a deep breath and stood straight as a tree, just as Mama had always instructed me. My fingers shot to my hair, touching the combs for good luck. Then, I closed my eyes and prepared to make an entrance.

Papa called, "Tillie, would you join us in the sitting room?"

I entered the room, my eyes immediately locking with Mr. Levine's. Surprised by his youthful appearance, I stumbled on a loose floorboard then caught my balance. *He must think I'm a jester!*

He jumped toward me, extending his hand. "Are you alright?"

I straightened my dress, flushing with embarrassment. My plans for a fine entrance had backfired. "Yes, of course, how clumsy of me."

He defied my expectations. Prepared to meet someone older and balding like Papa, this man was youthful and handsome, with thick, wavy brown hair and blue eyes reflecting a glint of humor. He was taller than Papa, his hair and beard neatly groomed. Even though the day was steaming hot, he wore a black, lightweight suit and carried a small package in his hand. *Was it for me?*

Mr. Levine studied me with a curious smile. He had the straightest white teeth I'd ever seen on a grown man. "You must be Tillie. I've been looking forward to meeting you." His voice was deep and smooth like base notes on a piano, again setting me off balance, this time while I thankfully was seated.

I wondered what the Rabbi told him about me. He couldn't have been more opposite from my low expectations. My fear dissolved, only to be replaced by a tingling new excitement, even more disarming than my first impression. My body was floating. Barely able to maintain my composure, I gestured to the kitchen. "May I offer you some cold lemonade? You must be thirsty after traveling so far. I'll be right back." I didn't wait for an answer, skirting to the kitchen to prepare refreshments and collect myself. Arranging the tray with glasses, a pitcher, and cookies, I was eager to get back into the parlor and learn more, already feeling optimistic. *Please, let this time be different.*

As I reentered the parlor, I looked about for any missed motes of dust from my morning sweeping. Suddenly, I cared what Mr. Levine thought about the condition of our home. Pleased Rebecca and I had caught them all, I poured everyone a glass and sat back in my chair. Papa and Mr. Levine were engaged in an animated discussion about the streetcar and his ride north to our farm. None of my family had ever ridden one.

As Mr. Levine recounted the interesting people he'd seen on his trip, he stole glances at me. "Maybe you'd enjoy a streetcar ride? If it's agreeable with your father, I can take you downtown to a museum. I read in the newspaper that the Metropolitan Museum of Art reopened. Would you like to take a tour together?"

I nodded, equally listening to the deep tone of his voice as to his words. This was a far cry better than listening to a pimply boy talk about farm animals and horses. "I'd enjoy that, Mr. Levine. That is, if Papa agrees."

Papa's head nodded slowly, never taking his eyes off Mr. Levine.

Rebecca shook her head. "Sam, she needs a chaperone, and we're all up to our ears."

Was she trying to spoil this for me?

Mr. Levine interjected. "Would you be more comfortable if we took one of the boys with us?"

Papa looked at Rebecca, who nodded back to him. "Yes, that would be fine, Mr. Levine. Take Joseph. Nate is needed here."

Mr. Levine shot Papa and Rebecca a full smile, then turned to me. "How does that sound to you?"

"Of course, I'd love to go." I relished being treated like one of the grownups, with an opinion of my own, finally.

"Please, call me Abe."

Papa reached for a cookie. "You can call me Sam and my wife, Rebecca. And, of course, Tillie."

Abe's eyes searched mine, dissolving my defenses. "Your Rabbi told me you have many interests and love to read. As a matter of fact, so do I."

I felt a rush of excitement at the prospect of an adventure downtown with this handsome man whose voice was a growing symphony in my ears. "I've never been to an art museum. And yes, I love books. But with the move and caring for Hannah, I haven't had much time to read this summer."

I tried to catch my breath and settle. *Ask him about his life.* I was talking too fast, my words tumbling out of me before I had time to think. "Rabbi Friedman told us you sell buttons to dressmakers?"

"Indeed, I do." Abe set his package on the tea table, carefully removing the string and unfolding the brown paper. Inside were the most unusual buttons I'd ever seen.

Rebecca drew a sharp breath. He had her under his spell, too.

Abe turned to her and explained, "I brought these for you as a wedding gift. Rabbi told me you and Sam were recently married and that you're an accomplished seamstress."

Rebecca spoke in barely more than a whisper, "How thoughtful of you. They're exquisite."

Abe said, "I agree. These were made in Germany. The brass is very strong, perfect for life in your new country home."

I leaned closer to look. The buttons were brass, stamped with images of farm life, different rural scenes on each one, a field of hay, livestock, flowers. My eyes shifted to Rebecca, whose face was brimming with excitement. I turned to Papa, puzzled, as if to ask, *Why did he bring Rebecca a gift and not me?*

Papa nodded with a little smile. "Thank you. As a matter of fact, Rebecca's expecting and will need to sew some new frocks. She'll enjoy using these."

Rebecca held the buttons in front of her eyes. "I've always felt buttons were as important as fabric, like jewelry. The designs reveal a story about the woman wearing the dress." She laughed lightly, "while closing the frock properly."

Abe nodded. "I couldn't agree more. Small, sturdy pieces of art." Turning back to me, "Tillie, I thought you might be curious to see more of my collection and then select buttons for yourself."

I met his eyes with a smile, realizing this man was no simpleton. He knew exactly how to handle Rebecca. I should be so smart. Will he know how to handle me, too?

Just then, Hannah called from our bedroom. "Can I get up?"

A quick smile shot across Abe's face.

He likes children, I delighted.

Papa rose. "Please excuse me. I have a few jobs to attend to. Tillie, maybe Abe would like to see the farm and pond? It'll all be history in a few months."

Abe nodded. "You probably know I lived up here when I was a child, but I have no memories of the place. Before you arrived, my parents moved us downtown to start their own business. I'd love to see where they started out."

Knowing Papa and Rebecca were eager to talk things over, I said, "I'll get Hannah so she can walk with us. But Abe, leave your jacket here, it's awfully warm today."

Chapter Eleven

Autumn 1880

The large painted murals in the Metropolitan Museum were spectacular. Portraits, battle scenes, and biblical stories filled its vast halls. Sitting on a bench, encircled by the magnificent art, I let my emotions wash over me, losing myself in each painting. My brother, Joseph, carried his small sketch pad, drawing likenesses of the buildings in the paintings.

Enjoying this new experience, I remarked, "Everyone in the city should have a chance to come here." Over the last two months, Abe had shown me other treasures like this museum, in the city proper.

Abe, sitting beside me, agreed. "I'll bet the museum will grow larger still. Many new artists in Europe and some of the rich families in New York are donating paintings to build the collection."

My eyes glittered with excitement. "Can we come back and see the new ones after they're hung?"

He glanced at Joseph, who had his head bent, absorbed drawing perspective lines in his sketch, then drew me to him for a quick hug. "Of course."

A week after the museum trip, on an unseasonably warm afternoon, we spent the afternoon strolling through Central Park. I stopped in my path and looked up into Abe's eyes. "You've shown me a whole new world. It's wonderful! You're wonderful."

Abe's eyes darted around, checking to see if we were alone, then leaned down and kissed me gently on the lips. Joseph was indifferent, having taken his place on the park bench, sketch pad open, pencils busy at work, filling the page with the buildings lining the park.

Like Papa in my directness, I probed, "Abe, how do you see our future? Together?"

He stood straighter, lifting his dark eyebrows in amusement. "What exactly do you mean?"

I flushed, afraid I'd gone too far. "I know it must sound forward, but this summer's been dreamy. Would it stay like this if we became a couple?" I longed to hear his intentions.

Abe laughed lightly. "Why don't you tell me how you'd like our future to look?"

I drew in a deep breath and began to share my hopes. "I would like to finish my schooling. I'd hoped to attend high school, but Papa couldn't afford it because of the move. And I'd like to marry someone special, like you, and have children." I lost myself in his deep blue eyes. "And I'd like to learn more about the world."

Abe held my eyes. "There's a high school downtown. It's a city school for everyone." He looked down sadly. "It's no secret that I lost my wife and newborn a few years ago. I hope to have a second chance. With you, if you feel the same. I'll be thirty in two years and don't want to wait much longer for a family. But I hope no matter what God has in store, we will always explore and learn together."

I was speechless. He was perfect.

"I love your curiosity and the spark of excitement you show when you see something new." He added with a warm smile, "And you are very attractive."

He gently kissed me. I reached up to his lips, savoring the affection. My face and neck flushed while an exciting new sensation raced through me. Then the realization struck—I was falling in love. Life on the farm seemed like a universe away, already fading into the past.

From that moment on, my future was sealed. The following Sunday, Abe visited for dinner. Afterwards, he asked Papa to walk with him. Rebecca hid a smile as she cleared the dishes, for once, not demanding my help.

My stomach was dancing, filled with a fluttery feeling. Was this was the moment Abe would ask Papa for my hand?

When they returned, Abe led me outside to the edge of the apple orchard, knelt, and held my hands in his. "You are my dream come true. I promise to love you forever and take good care of you and our family. Please make me the happiest man on earth and marry me."

"Yes, yes, Abe, I will marry you." I laughed as he rose from his knees, brushing the dirt from his trousers. We kissed until we heard Nate and Joe imitate our kissing sounds in the background. Ordinarily, I'd be angry with them for spying, but today, I just threw my head back and laughed along with them.

* * *

Elise and Fanny returned to the farm to help me prepare for the wedding, nattering about their newly married lives. They were particularly proud of having pried coveted recipes from the women at the shul for the three of us to take downtown to our new homes: Mrs. Cohen's brisket, Mrs. Schwartz's rugelach, and Mrs. Korn's apple cake. Quite a feat!

Elise tied the cards together with a yellow ribbon and placed the packet in my valise. As she secured the recipes, she broached the topic that had been troubling me. "Did Rebecca talk to you about, you know, the wedding night?"

I looked at my lap, full of apprehension. "No, not yet. What do I need to know?"

Elise smiled mischievously. "She really should have by now. For me, it was a bit awkward. We both felt self-conscious taking off our clothes. I'd never seen a man naked before. You know, with only sisters, I didn't know what to expect. Men are so different."

"And then?" I asked, confident with two younger brothers, I knew plenty about boys.

Elise squirmed in her chair. "Even though I knew he'd put his thing in me, I never expected him to move around so much. It hurt, and I bled all over the sheets. I cried when he finished." She sighed. "I made him wait a few days before we did it again. The second time, it didn't hurt much, but I still don't understand all the fuss." She scrunched her face.

I scrutinized Fanny to see if she agreed.

"I didn't mind," she said with an eager smile. "I loved the way he kissed and touched me all over before doing it. Especially down there." She pointed to her bottom and giggled. "That part was divine. When the time came, it hurt a bit, a strange, full feeling, and then it was alright." A second giggle escaped. "I'm fine with it, especially now that I know what to do."

My fear grew. "What do you mean, know what to do?" More than ever, I wanted Mama's guidance. She and Papa always seemed happy together.

Fanny turned to Elise. "It would be more fun if you touch each other first. It's like my mama told me before the wedding, 'It's your special time. There's no rush.'"

Confusion registered across my face. I hadn't a clue what either girl was talking about. *Enter me? From where I bled monthly?*

Fanny turned toward me, her brows knit in disbelief. "I wonder why Rebecca didn't talk to you about any of this."

I shook my head. After I met Abe, Rebecca had returned to her frenzied state of packing, cleaning, and mending. We didn't speak much.

Fanny said, "I don't want to get pregnant yet, and Mama said the only way is to make him come out before he finishes, then wash well afterward. But Marc wants to do it all the time!" She giggled. "He's hard to control."

Undressing in front of Abe would be strange. Where was Mama when I needed her? She had told me about making babies when I started my monthlies but hadn't given me the actual details. Clearly, there was much more to know.

* * *

Rebecca had found time to sew a simple white gauze dress for my wedding day. Abe gave her mother-of-pearl buttons for the back closure, around the neckline, and hem. Mama hadn't brought her wedding dress to America, so

I wore her combs again. Perhaps Hannah would someday use them. Elise and Fanny stacked my hair atop my head and held the waves in place with the combs. *Are you watching, Mama? I miss you so much.*

Papa, misty eyed, stood at the door. He took two long strides and drew me into his arms. "You're a beautiful bride." Then he examined the combs in my hair. "I'll never forgot those combs in her lovely hair. You bring back the happiest memories of my life. I hope today is the start of a joyous life for you and Abe."

The heavens treated us to a clear, mild October day for our vows. We arranged the chuppah outdoors, facing the northern hills where orange and red foliage saturated the horizon. My friends tied branches of colored leaves, some holding large acorns, to the fabric covering the canopy, weaving fall flowers through the white muslin they stretched over four poles.

A week earlier, Abe and I met with the rabbi and had the most unexpected discussion. We sat in his tiny office, the rabbi behind his desk, Abe, and me in stiff wooden chairs. "Are you both ready for this big step in your lives?" he asked.

"Yes, Rabbi," said Abe.

I nodded.

"I see your friends have been decorating the chuppah. They've made a simple muslin cloth quite beautiful with the fall leaves."

I studied the rabbi, not quite trusting what he'd tell us next, especially after my high school ordeal.

Rabbi studied our faces. "Do you understand the significance of the chuppah?"

I answered, "Doesn't it go back to Abraham and his hospitality to others?"

"Good Tillie, you remembered well." He cleared his throat. "But there's more to it than that."

Abe and I listened intently, curious what he'd say next.

"Do you believe in demons?" The rabbi asked, completely straight-faced.

I squirmed in my seat, shaking my head. Abe sat motionless.

"I do." The rabbi let his words sit before continuing. "Like Abraham, it's good to be hospitable and a welcoming member of your community, but there will always be demons wanting to get under the canopy, set to wreak havoc."

I drew my brows together, not understanding. Abe sat back, his eyebrows raised, waiting for more.

"Here are a few examples of demons." He began counting them on his fingers. "Money, children, parents, in-laws, work." Rabbi took a deep breath and continued. "That holy space under the chuppah is reserved for the two of you. It represents your bond under God. You must commit to keeping the demons outside that holy space."

Abe nodded, a smile spreading across his face. "That's the best marriage advice I've ever received."

I was left wondering what Rabbi was getting at.

A week later, I thought about Rabbi's words as I stood under the canopy with Abe and Papa, my two favorite men. It was doubtful Papa and Mama's rabbi in Germany shared the same advice about demons before their wedding, but nonetheless, I believe my parents understood. Their separate bedroom, private conversations, and secret laughter signaled to my brothers and me that they shared a private space, one that did not include us. Their bond made us feel secure in the family. I committed to doing the same, creating a secure, happy home too.

Our family and members of the congregation stood on all three sides, surrounding us as we exchanged vows. The warm day was glorious, so we continued our celebration outdoors. With a wedding following Rosh Hashanah, the Jewish New Year, we had prepared traditional foods for the feast. Tables of succulent beef brisket, chicken, roasted honey-glazed carrots, string beans, and sliced apples were arranged on tables with cheesecloth towels shielding the food from bees and flies. While Abe and I greeted our guests, women from the shul helped uncover the platters and hand out plates after the service,

The musicians assembled their instruments during our meal, and the dancing began, continuing into the early evening as the sun began its descent toward the horizon. One by one, families broke away from the dance floor, slipping over to wish us well. Before leaving, they presented their simple gifts—a set of dish towels from the Levys, kitchen utensils from the Kaplans, a pot and lid from the Blooms. All practical, all intended to help set up our new home.

Mrs. Schwartz, my Head Mistress, handed me two books tied together with twine. "These are two of my favorites: Charles Darwin's *On the Origin of Species* and Charles Dickens's *Hard Times: For These Times.* You're a bright, intelligent girl. No matter what lies ahead, always make time to read and think about what you're learning."

Was she as disappointed as me that high school didn't work out?

After all the guests and musicians departed, the platters emptied of food, and the wine consumed, we returned to the farmhouse to change into our everyday clothes. Everything I owned was packed except for those items I couldn't hold in my hands—my love for my family and my rich memories of childhood with Mama. A tear escaped, and I quickly brushed it away, latching the valise. Papa would bring our gifts when he visited next.

Crossing the yard to the wagon, I gazed at the house, imprinting every detail: the chicken coop, gentle hills, apple orchard, and open sky.

"Goodbye, everyone. Goodbye, farm!" I cried out as I handed my suitcase to Papa and scooped up Hannah for a tight hug. "Please visit soon. I'll miss you.

Abe put his arm around my shoulder. "You know we'll see your Papa when he makes his trip to the butcher next week. That's only a few days from now." He turned to Papa, adding, "Sam, I hope you'll have room for the gifts in the wagon next week. Maybe if the weather is good, Hannah can come, too, and we'll show her our home."

Papa was sitting on his perch behind Zero and Infinity, ready to drop us off at the streetcar stop. He nodded, eyes glistening, "Hop up. Time to go."

Chapter Twelve

And so, just weeks after my sixteenth birthday and a whirlwind courtship, I was a married woman. My entire family was bracing for major changes, clinging onto each other and the community for courage. Papa, on the cusp of moving, showed constant fortitude, acting as the Rabbi's right-hand man, and I was becoming a woman with a future. Every day began with a renewed sense of excitement, something I hadn't felt in a long while.

I'll admit five months was a short period to court and could have been quite risky, but the fact was, my life snapped together surprisingly well. Abe kept his promise, and together, we visited resplendent sites in the city. My aspiration to see more of the world was coming true.

But despite my loving feelings toward Abe, a strange reality set in that evening after the celebration, riding downtown on the streetcar after the wedding. Was it wedding night jitters or the vast unknown of my future ahead with Abe? I did my best to quell my fear, rocking and singing to music that had long since dissolved into the air, pretending I didn't have a worry in the world. Finally, we arrived at our stop and the Brunswick Hotel in Midtown.

The past months had been my first time for many things. The hotel, the doorway into my next adventure, was yet another first. But I wasn't fully prepared for my new name. When Abe checked us in as Mr. and Mrs. Levine, I found it hysterical, triggering a fit of giggling. Had I become an actress in my own theater?

The skinny clerk winked at Abe, "A plucky one! Your wedding night?

Hmmm, I'll give you a special room."

Suddenly embarrassed at my childishness, I turned away from the counter, distracting myself, studying the hotel's interior and its heavily decorated lobby. Gleaming, mahogany panels wrapped around the room. Dark green upholstered chairs were arranged in conversational clusters, each one hugging a shiny wooden coffee table holding a vase of freshly cut autumn flowers. I closed my eyes for a moment, gathering my nerves, determined to act properly.

Abe reached for my hand as we walked to the elevators. The porter took our luggage, and we rose to the seventh floor. At our hotel door, Abe handed the porter a coin.

In one swoop, Abe leaned down, picked me up in his arms, and carried me over the threshold into our room, gently setting me on my feet in the parlor.

My eyes popped with delight when I saw our room. Part parlor, part bedroom, it was the most gorgeous place I'd ever slept. Pale green brocade wallpaper covered every wall, and two chairs in a darker shade of green sat around a low table, much like the hotel lobby. Another colorful fall bouquet, a bucket containing a champagne bottle, and two crystal goblets were tastefully displayed on a lace doily. A folded note sat between them.

"Oh, look, Abe." I picked up the card. "'Congratulations on your marriage.' How thoughtful!"

Abe laughed and took my hand. Beyond the chairs sat a massive wooden poster bed covered with a blue and green bedspread and deep blue velvet decorative pillows. Matching window drapes cascaded down the far sides of the wall. To the left was a door leading into a private bathroom with a sink and privy.

"It's like a palace." I couldn't have been more delighted.

Abe turned to me. "Let me put our valises in the closet; then I'll pour that champagne."

"I've never tasted champagne." I swept my hand across the room. "And this opulence, like a castle, makes me nervous."

Abe filled the crystal goblets halfway and handed one to me. "Maybe this will help you relax," he said.

The bubbles in the champagne tickled my nose, making me sneeze. I'd never tasted anything quite like it before. Bright, fizzy, a bit sour. Another giggle slipped out. It took all my self-control to settle down and behave like an adult.

I burrowed into the plush chair, studying the light from the lantern as it cut through my glass goblet, splintering its rays into the colors of a rainbow on the wall beyond. "It's so beautiful. I want to remember every detail."

Abe studied me with a pleased smile. "I wanted to make everything perfect."

I savored the moment we were in, reflecting on the details of our wedding. "The Rabbi was thoughtful to talk about your parents. He remembered them so well and Mama too. It made me feel as if our whole family was standing with us under the chuppah."

I wondered if Abe had thought about his first wife and child. I couldn't imagine how strange this second wedding must have felt for him. I said a silent prayer for a long, happy marriage.

As we recounted the day, my head began to spin. "I'm feeling a bit dizzy."

Abe took my goblet and set it on the table. "Come with me."

He took my hand, and we crossed the room to the bed. Lighting the oil lantern on the nightstand, he pulled down the covers and faced me. Gazing into my eyes, he leaned in and kissed me, unthreading Mama's combs from my hair and setting them on the nightstand. My hair dropped freely to my waist. He whispered. "Are you ready?"

I nodded, slightly unsure what I should do as he began unbuttoning my dress. Frozen in place, I watched my dress pool on the floor. I stepped over the fabric circle, and then he lifted it, draping the garment over the bedside chair. He drew me into his arms, kissing me lightly, guiding me backward onto the bed. Once I was sitting, he stood beside me, removing his clothing, placing each piece atop my dress. I was mesmerized, never having witnessed such an undressing ritual nor having seen a grown man completely naked. I was stunned at the amount of hair and the size below, considering how much larger he was than my younger brothers. Before I could react, he lay down beside me, brushed his fingers through my hair, and started kissing me again. I helped him slide off my undergarments, one piece at a time, then pulled up the blanket, covering our exposed bodies, reminding myself, *This is permitted. He's my husband.*

Abe traced my breasts with gentle hands until I moaned. As he explored my most intimate places with his fingers, I felt a deep ecstasy, a divine sensation that grew quickly. Suddenly, the most delightful wave of pleasure swallowed me. Before I could react, he tenderly leaned his body on top of me. I opened to him.

He whispered, "I'll try to be gentle."

After a few uncomfortable moments, just as Fanny described, I began to relax and enjoy his movements, dissolving into a new physical dance, reaching for sensations with a sense of urgency. Lost in our closeness, I was surprised when he moved with more determination, as if an otherworldly force had seized control. Then, he abruptly stopped.

Seconds later, we separated. He lay next to me, catching his breath. I knew there was something beyond the soreness and wanted to explore it more. These were powerful feelings. I finally understood why Mama told me to wait until marriage to share my body and share it only with my husband.

Resting on his forearm, he tapped the tip of my nose. "I'll love you forever, Tillie Levine."

Smiling, I kissed his lips, "I never believed marriage would be like this." Pausing for a moment, I asked, "Can we do that again?"

Abe lay back, a content smile crossed his face. "Of course. But would you like a glass of water first? I know I could use one."

Our honeymoon was the best two days of my young life. We spent most of it in bed, exploring one another's bodies, talking about our lives, and resting. In between, we ventured downstairs or across the street to the steakhouse for meals, my eyes avoiding the desk clerk's knowing eyes, thinking that he'd always remember me as the giggling young girl. But I was no longer that girl. I was now a married woman.

Chapter Thirteen

Tuesday morning, Abe hailed a coach to drive us to my new home on Orchard Street. As the carriage clip-clopped through the busy streets, he warned me, "You already know the story about my parents' business and our losses during the 1870s depression. It meant returning to the tenements. But I promise we won't live there long, a year or two at most, while I put aside money for a more spacious apartment."

"I've only seen the apartments from Papa's wagon. What's it like inside?"

"Small and crowded, cooking smells from other peoples' apartments." He took my hand. "I saved money for our wedding weekend so we'd start our marriage with a wonderful memory."

"It was wonderful," I said, still dreamy after our morning intimacy. *Why is he telling me this again?*

Abe persisted, forcing me out of my distracted state. "I want you to remember how beautiful the hotel was. Soon, we'll live in an apartment even larger than the hotel room, and it will have a private bathroom." He cupped my hand. "Promise me you will be patient."

I wished I'd seen his home. Without knowing what to expect, Papa's concern about the tenements festered in my stomach. "I'll find ways to help. You'll be surprised at how much I can do," I offered, attempting to reassure myself as well as him, tamping down a growing apprehension.

Abe's tenement apartment was in the Lower East Side, not far from Papa's kosher butchers. From my trips downtown, I recalled the crowds and carts, but this morning, it was far more congested. The streets were so crammed with people and pushcart peddlers that our coach could barely squeak through, jostling about as the driver attempted to control the horses. "Whoa, Bessie, take it easy, girl."

As he turned onto Orchard Street, a band of young boys darted wildly across the cobblestone street, spooking the animals further. Bessie began to rear. The driver shouted into the din. "Damn, those boys. Doesn't anyone bother to watch them?"

Abe sat beside the driver, pointing to breaks in the crowd, trying to help him wind his way to his building. But the beehive of activity frightened the animals. Finally, Abe patted the driver's arm and climbed down from the wagon, grasping the horses' halters, guiding them through the mass.

My ears were fixed on the cacophony around me. These were my new neighbors, shouting in words I could barely understand, wearing little more than rags, hats and scarves in all shapes and sizes. A cart peddler yelled, "apples, apples" while another bellowed to the crowd, "*Schmattas, schmattas,* good price!"

I stared at a woman standing off by herself, selling pots and pans, clanking on either side of her cart, shouting to the crowd. Her open mouth was a black cavern where teeth once dwelled, her pendulous breasts swayed in a lightweight tea dress, too flimsy for the crisp fall weather. These people are my new neighbors? Fear squirmed through my stomach. What had I done?

Flocks of women clustered on front stoops, hands punctuating the air in their frenzied conversation, watching out of the corner of their eyes, their small children playing in the street while their older ones ran amok through the crowds.

The knot in my belly clamped tighter. I held back my fearful tears. Only hours before, I was snuggled in Abe's arms, full of contentment. I looked at my husband guiding the horses, calming them, and took a deep breath of courage. Mistake or not, my fate had been sealed.

Finally, Abe and the driver managed to wedge the carriage through the peddlers' carts to Abe's front stoop. It was a miracle no one was injured.

Once the women on his stoop recognized Abe, a chorus of whooping rang through the air. They rose gleefully, scrutinizing me with backward looks while they crowded around him. "Mazel Tov!" they half-sang, turning their heads from me to him, boxing me out. They might as well be chanting, "*outsider, outsider.*"

I forced a smile, determined to hide my hurt, wondering why they were so flirtatious. Determined to win over these new neighbors, I let Abe help me from the cart, pulling me to his side, showing them we were a couple. Slowly their offhandedness melted, and one by one, they greeted me with half smiles, sharing their names and apartment numbers.

Abe, pleased with their eventual reception, said, "Enough introductions for now! I'd like my beautiful bride to see her new home. I spent days scrubbing it clean. There will be plenty of time to meet and talk later." He picked up my bags and entered the tenement house.

Following behind, leaving the bright sunlight, I was hit with a wall of darkness. As my eyes adjusted, I made out a narrow, tall central hallway that encased a set of steps, snaking back and forth up five stories, passing four apartments on each floor. But its sparse design and lack of natural light paled in comparison to the revolting stench of spoiled food, unattended chamber pots, and unwashed bodies. Gripped with an immediate queasiness, I held my breath. Up three flights, I climbed to his apartment, praying to reach our landing without retching.

Our apartment door opened directly into the smallest kitchen I'd ever seen, with barely room to cook. But aside from a teakettle on the bulky iron stove, it didn't appear Abe did much cooking. There was no trace of food in sight, not a crumb.

From where I stood, I could see the entire apartment. To our immediate right was a tiny parlor with two tall end windows overlooking the street. Half-full open barrels of buttons of all sizes, shapes, and colors claimed half of the parlor floor, leaving a few feet of space for a small dropleaf table and two wood chairs. To the left of the kitchen was a small bedroom, barely fitting the bed he'd squeezed in. Thin wall partitions with adjustable transom windows on top allowed air and light to pass through the three adjacent rooms. Noticing the chill when we entered, I asked, "Where's the fireplace?"

Abe answered. "There isn't one. The coal stove in the kitchen doubles for heat and cooking. We get our water from the spout in the back of the building. That's also where the privies are. I'll show you in a moment."

My sense of adventure vanished at the base of the staircase, replaced by disgust and fear. I'd be shoehorned into this dreadful place for a year or more. How would I manage through the winter? "There're so many people, all on top of each other. Is it safe to use the privy at night?" Did Papa truly know how terrible it was here? Had Abe lied to Papa's face to close the marriage deal?

Abe took my arms in his hands, summoning his most reassuring voice. "Don't worry. I'll take you at night and bring the oil lamp, so you feel safe. Remember, I promised to find a better place for us in the next year or two. I just need more time."

I couldn't hold my disappointment any longer. "I feel sick." I sat in a chair, sniffling. "Can you at least open a window and let air in? The smell is disgusting."

Abe pounded on the window jam, wedging it open. "I'm sorry. I knew this would be a big change for you. I normally open the windows every morning to freshen the apartment, even in winter. Then, I pile coal in the oven and heat the rooms. You'll see, it's not usually so bad."

"I'm sorry to act like a baby. It's just so different, but I'll be fine so long as I'm with you." I lied, ashamed to spoil our first day at home.

The cool air rushed in through the two front windows, helping cleanse the room of its stale odor. I breathed in deeply while my stomach settled, studying the apartment. I could see Abe had spent time cleaning and organizing. Even though the curtains were tattered, and the wallpaper was bare spots, he had given every room a thorough scrubbing before the wedding. A picture of his parents hung on a parlor wall. Beside it was a dark rectangular shadow. Had he removed a photo of his first wife? Desperate for a silver lining, I figured a tiny apartment would be easy to keep clean.

Abe pulled up the other chair. "Feeling better now?"

"Much," I answered, filling my chest with the fresh air. "I can see why people stay outdoors. I wondered about that when we pulled up."

"I'll run downstairs for coal and fresh water while you unpack." Abe lowered the window to a crack and grabbed the coal scuttle and empty bucket by the door. "Then I'll show you the neighborhood, and we'll pick up ingredients for dinner. Tonight, we'll cook together, and I'll teach you how to work the stove."

I forced a smile, determined to do my part. *This will be my new adventure, exploring the city and studying.*

Later, unpacked and ready to explore the neighborhood, he faced me. "Tomorrow, I need to leave for the day. I made a few dress shop appointments scattered about town. While I'm out, why don't you meet some of our neighbors?" He pointed to the apartment across the hall. "Most of them are very nice, especially Sadie. But be careful how much you share. There're a lot of *yentas* who'd love to get into our business."

* * *

Wrapped in Abe's arms, I stayed warm through the night, but a frosty chill seeped under the covers the instant he rose from the bed. I followed him, wrapping my body in the dressing gown Rebecca had sewn for my trousseau. Abe lit the stove before we made our way downstairs, through the back door, and outside to the privy. He brought a rag and soap to wash the seats. Once again, the smell of the hallway hit me like a sledgehammer. Could the *privy be any worse?* I held my breath in the filthy wooden room. "It's disgusting in there!" I choked, walking back to the outer building door.

"I know. Especially if the night soil men don't visit." He filled one pail with fresh water from the spigot for coffee and washing and another with coal, carrying one in each hand.

One more nasty thing to do in this vile place. Chances were, I'd also be the one schlepping those buckets up three flights of stairs.

The room was toasty when we reached the apartment, helping me relax into the new day. I made coffee, and we sliced the hard cheese and challah we'd bought the evening before. Abe described his customer deliveries for the day, displaying the buttons they had purchased. He mainly sold to dressmakers who designed and sewed garments for women uptown. They were quite particular, insisting on keeping abreast of the European fashion trends. Fascinated, I hoped one day I might wear such lovely garments.

Abe picked buttons from the boxes on the table. "Evening dresses require pearl, glass, or ivory buttons. The metal and wood buttons are for daytime garments."

His dressmakers selected their buttons from sample boxes they could also show their customers. I'd never realized how important buttons were. They gave each outfit a unique touch. My interest was piqued.

He pointed to a pile of empty boxes. "Could you assemble more sample boxes today? I'll pull out stock from the barrels before I leave and give you boxes to fill."

I nodded, eager to assist.

"A new shipment of winter-weight metal buttons arrived last week, and I didn't have time to prepare the samples. I'll show you how to line them up. Check them over carefully to confirm they aren't chipped or scratched."

I approached the boxes curiously, reaching in, holding various button to the window's light. "Don't forget, I need to find the high school and sign up for classes. Mrs. Schwartz gave me my paperwork to share. Can I do the samples tonight?" I thought for a moment. "I'll need directions to the school."

Abe scuffed his shoe on the floor. "Ahem, there's something I should tell you." He looked down as if afraid to meet my gaze. "I may have exaggerated. The school is a long walk across town and then north. It's not anywhere near this neighborhood."

"What!" A flash of anger shot through me. "You lied? You knew how important high school is for me."

Abe's eyes flickered back and forth, avoiding me. "I didn't exactly lie. I just didn't check the details." He quickly added, "But I'll give you directions if you'd still like to check it out. The shul has a library, and it's much closer, on Henry Street. They have a night school too, but mostly to help immigrants learn English." He turned back to me sheepishly.

I was furious, both at him and myself. How could I be so naive?

Had he lied about anything else? My head spun. Now, what would I do?

"What about the high school in midtown? Where Mrs. Schwartz wanted me to go? Maybe I could still get in?"

A grunt. "Oh, sweetheart. That school is even farther and far too costly."

I couldn't restrain my angry words. "But you knew that was my main reason to marry. Not only to stay in the city!" I shouted. *How could I have been such a fool?*

Abe placed his arm around my stiff shoulder, pulling me into his chest. "I thought you'd fallen in love with me. Is that not true?" He lowered his face to mine. "We'll find a way. Trust me."

I slowly melted as the tears came. I was trapped and confused, not feeling a shred of trust, wondering what other bad surprises lay ahead. But he was right about one thing. I was in love and didn't want to begin our first day of marriage with tears and anger. I answered evenly, "I'll check out the school and find a way to make it work."

I unlatched myself from his arms and walked into the kitchen, unwrapping last night's chicken and making a sandwich for Abe's lunch. I plucked an apple from the bowl we'd filled with fruit from Papa's orchard. Apple in hand, its sweet smell delicious and innocent, made my heart lurch with longing for the safety of Papa's farm. But in a few short weeks, it would be no more. *Nothing stays the same.*

Abe bent over the parlor table and scribbled on a piece of paper. "I marked the main streets, but for the small ones, I jotted landmarks so you won't get lost." He stopped for a moment, a quizzical expression on his face. "Why don't I take you there tomorrow? That way, I can keep you company."

"No, I'll be fine," I said tightly.

He filled a large satchel with completed button orders and another with sample button boxes, strapping them tightly together. "Let's work on the sample boxes together tonight. That way, I can show you a few tricks and you can explore today."

I forced a smile, trying to appreciate his effort.

Abe held my shoulder. "Be careful. Some people steal down here. It's best if you keep only a coin or two in your coat pocket for emergencies." Abe gathered me in his arms with a kiss goodbye, and in one long stride was out the door. "I'll be home for dinner. I love you, sweetheart," he called back over his shoulder.

The door clicked behind him.

* * *

I dropped into my chair, staring at my cold coffee, the cream congealed, small clumps swirling on the surface. *What did I get myself into?* I spread out the city map Papa had given me, determined more than ever to find the high school. I traced Abe's directions with my finger.

Barely ten minutes later I heard a tapping at the door. I opened it a crack. A comely young woman stood in the hallway wearing a bright smile and simple muslin dress. Her untied dark brown hair extended to her waist. I'd never seen such a mop of long, corkscrew curls. At her side stood a darling little girl about Hannah's age.

"I hope I'm not bothering you, Mrs. Levine," said the woman. "My name's Sadie Stern. I was working when you moved in yesterday and didn't get a chance to greet you. I live across the hall. You can call me Sadie."

"Oh yes, Abe mentioned you." I opened the door wider, worried about letting in the putrid air. But, instead, my nose lit up when I was greeted with a waft of freshly baked cake.

She continued in her heavy German accent. "I baked this morning, hoping you'd have time to stop by. My older boys just left for school, but little Eva and I have a free hour before we get busy sewing."

Such a familiar, happy sensation swept through me, evoking memories of home and Mama. "I'd love to. And please call me Tillie. I only need a minute to finish tidying, then I'll be right over." I gently closed the door, glancing into the parlor with its stacks of button containers. Maybe living here won't be so horrible.

Moments later, I sat in Sadie's tiny parlor at her oak drop leaf table, sharing coffee and warm cinnamon nut cake. While I sipped my coffee, she assembled books and a doll for Eva on the braided rug beside us. The child was a miniature of her mother. Her cherub face, ringed with tight brown curls, danced with mischief. As I watched her play, I felt a new pang of loss, wondering what Hannah was doing at that moment, perhaps also playing with her dolls. I'd never had a sister or an aunt, and as we sat eating sugary crumbs, talking, and laughing, I began to see that even in this squalor, people found joy in friendships.

Sadie handed Eva a thin book and a small kit of paint. "Eva, come sit by the window, and I'll fetch a tin of water."

I stretched my neck to look. "What did you give her?"

"A painting book, she loves them, keeps her busy while I get my *mansion* picked up." Sadie mocked, looking about. "But the paint gets messy. I'm not sure it's so smart."

"I'd like to buy one for my little sister, Hannah, when she visits later this week. Where did you find it?'

"I'll show you later."

We sat together for close to an hour, exchanging our stories, chatting as if we'd known each other our whole lives. Sadie's apartment was the same size as mine, but even with a family of five, it felt roomier. Everything was well organized and neat as a pin. The three children slept in small cots lined against the parlor wall, and Sadie and her husband, Max, slept in the back bedroom like Abe and me. The small bed was surrounded by bolts of cloth he sold to dressmakers. My eyes drank in this new concoction of sights—buttons, fabric, a world so different from the farm.

Keeping Abe's caution in mind, I limited our discussion to the obvious facts of our courtship. However, I did share my plan to finish high school.

She looked at me, brows drawn in a doubtful knot. "Tillie, that's a grand plan, but only a few of us in the neighborhood even squeak through eighth grade. The high school is far across town, and the Jewish high school uptown costs a fortune. Most families need everyone to pitch in. Then, of course, we marry, and babies come." She watched my face fall. "I wish you luck, though."

I had married and moved a world away, only to be trapped in the same dilemma I had at the farm. Everywhere, families needed all hands to help contribute. I admonished myself. When will I ever learn?

She patted my hand. "I can see you're disappointed, but don't fret if high school doesn't work out immediately. You should check out the Settlement House. It's next door to the shul on Henry Street, only a few blocks from here. Everyone goes there when they arrive to learn residents English. They have classes and a lending library. There're plenty of books if you like to read. Best of all, their Clinic comes in handy." She gestured to Eva. "Especially the midwife."

* * *

Undeterred, I left the building moments later, entering the tumultuous din of Orchard Street. Following Abe's directions, I arrived at the high school forty minutes later after walking my toes off on the bumpy, ungroomed roads. The large brick building was indeed far across Manhattan and sat beside Washington Square Park, a treacherous walk on rainy or snowy days. Yet, despite my concerns, I climbed the front steps, remembering to brush the dirt from my clothes, and headed to the main office. Recalling the hospital years ago, I knew it was important to make the correct impression.

A well-dressed, bespectacled woman in a grey suit and starched white blouse looked up from her desk at me. "May I help you?"

"Good morning. My name is Tillie Levine. I moved here two days ago and would like to enroll in high school."

Her critical eyes scanned my body while she pointed to a chair. "Please have a seat. The Headmaster's in a meeting. He'll be tied up for a while."

Did I pass the first test?

I waited close to an hour for Mr. Tompkins, the headmaster, to beckon me into his office. His secretary introduced me as I walked in.

He looked up from his desk, not standing. "Please have a seat Mrs. Levine. How I can be of assistance?"

"Good morning, Mr. Tompkins. Last spring, I completed eighth grade at the top of my class up north on the farms." I handed him my papers. "I'd like to enroll in high school. The letter from my Head Mistress shows my grades."

He pointed to the letter in his hands. "You say your name is Levine, but it says Isaacson here."

His sharp-edged question felt like an accusation. "Yes, sir, I'm recently married and moved to Orchard Street last week." My hands clenched on my lap. Perspiration dotted my forehead.

He reviewed the letter again and narrowed his eyes. "And you think you can handle high school as a married woman? You need to know we don't allow small children here, nor do we allow women in the family way to attend classes."

A streak of defiance coursed through my chest. Was everyone against me? I answered him tightly. "Yes, I understand, but I can manage. As you can see, I'm an excellent student, the top of my class."

Mr. Tompkins scarcely waited for me to finish my sentence. "You've earned the marks, but the school year has begun. You'll have to wait until next fall. Why don't we meet again this summer? Who knows, by that point, you may be a mother, and this desire of yours will be moot." He lifted his cold eyes to mine. "Good day, Mrs. Levine."

"Wait, please. Can't you consider an exception?" I stammered. "This is my dream."

"I'm afraid not. Good day, Mrs. Levine." Mr. Tompkins rose abruptly to see me out the door.

* * *

Back outside on the high school steps, my tears flowed. If I'd only checked things out beforehand. How could I be so stupid to trust everyone around me? Papa had led me into this trap, and then Abe snared me, counting on my innocence. Rebecca could care less, and Mrs. Schwartz, the only one with nothing to gain, warned me with her wedding gift of books. The fact that I'd been a star pupil didn't impress Mr. Tompkins. Now, my dream would be delayed at least an entire year, that is, if I didn't get pregnant. I kicked the stone steps in disgust.

Consumed with disappointment and repulsed by the filthy tenements where I now lived, I stormed down the steps onto the street, forgetting to mind the directions. Fuming and wandering, I soon found myself twisted around on unfamiliar roads. I reached for my map. It wasn't in my pocket. *Damn!* I'd placed it in my purse and then proceeded to leave my purse at home. *What else will go wrong today?* I searched my memory for Abe's description of the main roads on the east side.

Papa, with his endless nature lessons, had taught me one helpful lesson I needed now. He repeated time after time, "Reading the sky is an ancient skill. Knowing the sun and stars will always lead you home."

I turned in the sun's direction, now tilted by a hair in the eastern sky, and followed it, trudging through narrow, garbage-strewn streets, past run-down shanty houses and ragtag people living in the open. The pungent stench of excrement was everywhere. Children ran about barefoot on this cool autumn day. Why weren't they in school? Who cared for them? Finally, a shaggy-haired boy approached me, reaching out his hand, "Lady, spare a coin?"

"I don't have money to give you." I looked at his thin face, forgetting about the coin in my pocket, and pulled out my apple. "But I have an apple. Would you like it?"

Before I finished speaking, the child grabbed the fruit and bit into it. Juices dripped down his dirt-stained chin onto his clothing, leaving streaks of stickiness behind. I wished I had more to give. How awful to be desperate and hungry. No matter how brisk or slow Papa's chicken business was, he always managed to keep food on our table and ensured we were safe.

When our teachers discussed the poor conditions in lower Manhattan, I had imagined something better than Dickens's *Oliver Twist*. I didn't have a clue how well I'd had it. "Do you go to school?" I asked the boy as he wiped his mouth with his forearm.

"Nah, lady, no school here," he answered before scampering away.

I took a deep breath and carried on, finally reaching Bowery Street, making a right and then a left on Houston Street with its sweeping boulevard. A few minutes later, I was back on Orchard and at our building. I rested on the stoop, not wanting to reenter the filthy building, considering my options. Despite my annoyance at the school, I was far more shaken by the terrible deprivation surrounding me. The word "poverty" now had the pitiful face of a hungry child, a face I'd never forget. Papa and Abe had failed to warn me about that, too.

A short, round woman dropped next to me on the landing with a loud "oomph". She cleared her throat and yammered in Yiddish, "So, are you the Levine bride? I heard you were a pretty one."

Without waiting for an answer, she continued, "I'm Pessy Cohen from the 2nd floor; just call me Pessy. I was married for twenty-two years, then my poor Milton died, God rest his soul. But he didn't leave behind a penny. It's been no picnic. We had five children, and two died when they were infants. I still cry for them at night." She bent her body forward, holding her scarfed head tightly between her hands, rocking to and fro.

"I'm so sorry…." I struggled to understand her Yiddish. Before I could console her further, she launched back into the diatribe of her life.

"I work in the factory on the fifth floor, ironing before the pieces go out. My arthritis and eyes are so bad I can no longer sew." She flung her gnarled fingers in front of my face as proof. "My other children have grown and moved to Brooklyn. I barely see them. They rarely take the ferry here to visit. Ungrateful, not even a penny for their mother. What did you say your first name was?"

I looked at Mrs. Cohen, scarcely believing how much personal information she shared in one breath. "My name is Tillie. It's nice to meet you. Can you point me in the direction of the shul?"

"That way." Pessy pointed. "Next time, we'll talk more."

I forced a smile. I must get out of this place before I become like her, planted on this crumbling stoop, growing roots from my behind into the steps, complaining to any stranger who stumbles by.

As I hurried away, my hunger pangs signaled it was past lunchtime. I reached into my coat pocket for my apple and realized it was no longer there. A wave of guilt hit me. Thinking of our bowl of freshly picked apples, I decided to keep several in my pockets so the next time, I'd have more to share.

My thoughts grew dark. Except for Sadie, people living in these parts felt faceless, empty of hope, full of desperation. I missed my friendly, intimate farming community. *Stop dwelling on it. That place no longer exists.*

The rabbi should have warned me about the terrible living conditions and poverty where I'd be moving. Did he know that I could live or die in this part of New York, and no one would care? Was a young girl's worth so little?

Expecting another rebuff, I entered the shul, looking for the rabbi's office. Young women dressed in tattered clothing, holding babies wrapped in rags, and small children's hands filled the hall, inspecting me with their harried eyes. *Here we go again.*

A squat woman with piercing dark eyes and disheveled hair barely held together in a loose brown bun wove her way through the families and approached me. Her melodic voice defied her looks, disarming me. "And who are you? You're not a familiar face around here."

My mouth opened like a stopped-up drain, then an unstoppable stream of words poured out of my mouth. I no longer cared what Abe thought about me speaking to strangers. "I'm Tillie Levine, and I just moved here. I was married last week, and my neighbor, Sadie Stern, told me you had a lending library. I love reading and want to continue my education, but the high school won't let me start this year. Besides, it is so far away. I barely know a soul."

Her face softened. "Well then, dear. Welcome to the neighborhood. My name is Mrs. Simon. Where did you live before your marriage? And where are your parents?" She took my hand, leading me deeper into the building, away from the crowd.

I drew a deep breath and recounted my mother's story and my father's need to relocate the farm to Sullivan County. Despite Abe's warning, I needed to share, to connect with an adult close to Mama's age. Abe wasn't enough.

She listened intently, her eyes drifting to mine while we walked. "I've been reading in the paper about the farms moving north. The city's growing fast, and there's not enough housing for everyone." She paused. "I don't think Abe Levine wanted to stay a member of our shul after he lost his first wife, but we heard about you through our rabbi. Would you like me to arrange an appointment with Rabbi Meyer? Perhaps you'll join. We have a lovely lending library. How does that sound?"

I had few other choices, and Mrs. Simon, with her all-knowing eyes, had me convinced.

Chapter Fourteen

Before long, I'd met most of the women in my building and was surprised to learn that during the daylight, many of their apartments functioned like industrial beehives. They called them factories. When I woke, sipping coffee with Abe, I could see a parade of men and women from other buildings arriving at ours in the morning. Sadie said they sat all day by the tall parlor windows, working hard, sewing together pieces of garments until dusk. Before leaving at twilight, the foreman marked the number of garments completed. He delivered the pieces to the next stop, where the process continued until the shirts and dresses were fully assembled. They were paid a pittance based on the number of completed units. Most workers were barely scraping by.

I would help Abe instead, but with no high school in the immediate future, I knew I'd need something else to fill my time.

After Sadie's sons and Abe left for school and before the parade of workers showed up, Sadie and I began to share what we soon called "morning lessons." She told me everything I needed to know about the city, where to get the freshest meat and the best prices, who I could trust in the building, and who to avoid. Having lived in the tenements for four years, her family of five had wholly outgrown their space and was also eager to find a larger home.

Best of all, Sadie had mastered the simple coal stove, and she taught me to cook the delicacies I missed. "With the stories of your mama's great cooking, I'm amazed how little you can make!" Sadie teased me after we prepared dinner together one afternoon. "You need to know how to roast a flavorful brisket and chicken in your oven, or else Abe will starve. The important ingredients are onions, carrots, garlic, and many hours of roasting. In the cold months, a hot stove keeps your home warm. You know, we're lucky our husbands earn enough to keep our stomachs full." Her gaze shifted from me to her apartment door. "Many of our neighbors can barely afford soup."

Once again, I was reminded that the life my parents had eked out wasn't so bad. "Mama let me read and tend my homework after school. When I finished, I played with Hannah while Mama cooked." I winked at Eva, who was busy undressing her doll. "But I know she would have eventually taught me her recipes if only…she had lived." I caught my breath, shaking off the sadness. "I can't tell you how much I appreciate your help. Abe was disappointed the first few nights with my bland, tough dinners. He probably thought I was only good for one thing!"

"He is a man, after all." Sadie chuckled with a knowing edge. "Did you know," she paused, deliberating whether to share, "Mrs. Simon had asked if I knew any eligible men for a young woman from up north. Rabbi Meyers was helping your rabbi on the farm find a match for you. I knew Abe was widowed, but he couldn't bring himself to join the synagogue, always squirreled away in his apartment when he wasn't working. I was the one who gave Abe's name to the rabbi."

Stunned, my words stuck in my mouth. The city, full of so many thousands, suddenly felt as small as a thimble.

After leaving Sadie, I spent the rest of the morning tidying, rinsing clothes, and making sample boxes for Abe. All the while, I was lost in my thoughts, replaying events from the two years since Mama died. Where did I go wrong? Could I be happy in this life?

I resolved to never become a victim, like Pessy upstairs, promising myself to stay alert to new opportunities. There must be many. I only needed to find the right one. My future did not have to be tied to high school. Were my eyes set on the wrong plan all along? Money was the indisputable path out of the squalor. I vowed never to grow roots from my tuchus into the front stoop.

CHAPTER FOURTEEN

***

One late October evening after dinner, sitting at the table beside the lantern, Abe began teaching me more about his button business. He set several shallow wooden trays on the table. Each had a lid and was partitioned with rows of vertical and horizontal dividers holding hundreds of buttons. "I arrange the sample boxes by their use. That works best for my dressmaker and tailor customers." He selected a few buttons from the tray, then handed them to me.

I inspected the buttons in my hand, first holding a brass button with openwork up to the lantern's light. "This is far more detailed than I realized."

Abe set the first tray to the side, selecting certain buttons from the second, setting them before me, and pointing to each in turn. "Buttons are made from more delicate-looking materials for women's day and evening wear. Compare these three: bone, pearl, and glass. They're hand-painted with domestic and floral designs. This one is religious." He picked another ceramic button from the tray and handed it to me. "See the fine artistry, the delicate flower petals?"

I examined the button. "It's beautiful, like a piece of jewelry. The artist must have used a miniature brush. But won't it get damaged on a dress?"

"No. Even though it's a lovely piece of glass, it's quite strong." Abe dropped the button back into its compartment with a cling. "Like you, a delicate but sturdy flower."

I was confused by the comparison. Was I a mere sturdy button to him? Did he think I'd sit pretty while he went out and mingled with the world? Just as I was still learning about him, Abe had much to learn about me.

***

The temperatures dropped as autumn shifted into winter. In the morning, webs of frost appeared in intricate lacy designs on our front windows, sending fractured rays of light into the room, a beauty that mocked us while we aired out the parlor and scurried to stoke the coal stove. After Abe left for work and I shared coffee with Sadie, I returned to our apartment, settling into the warm parlor and assembling the sample trays Abe needed for customers. Once finished, I filled his orders for the next day's delivery. But the final job, one I'd taken on without being asked, was sorting through his disheveled stack of paperwork that included factory bills, invoices, and payments due and organizing each category into a separate file. That was how I learned about the operation of his little button business.

Just as Mama helped with Papa's books, I wanted to be Abe's trusted partner. One evening, I showed him the files I'd created. "I've organized your paperwork for you," I said.

He leafed through the files, examining their contents. "My God, you're a wizard. I've never been this organized."

Eager, I turned to meet his eyes. "I can do more. At the farm, Mama and I helped Papa prepare orders, write checks, and keep the ledgers. That will take a burden off you, so you're free to make more sales."

Abe kissed me on the cheek. "How about we stick with the sample boxes and filling orders for now?"

My excitement deflated. How quick he was to dismiss me. I knew I must find a way to gain his confidence. In the meantime, I continued my afternoons at the Settlement House, vanishing into its haven of books and people. Sitting in the window seat of the little dusty library felt like home. I'd found a copy of *Little Women*, the book I was reading but never finished when Mama died. Vividly recalling where I last left off, Marmee leaving her daughters to help tend Papa's war wounds, I found the exact page in minutes, transported back to their world.

I was drawn to the complex of buildings and the hubbub within, surprised by my level of comfort. The synagogue, which we referred to as the "shul" and its attached Settlement House, was the epicenter of Jewish life on the Lower East Side, a safe haven for new residents. The buildings were only a few blocks south of our apartment, and the Settlement House library contained an excellent selection of books in residents engllish and German. Like my old shul in the lost Harlem farmland, there was a school for children. Additionally, Mrs. Simon had arranged English classes for adults and hosted evening speakers who discussed adjustment to the city and happenings beyond our crowded streets.

Next door, the Settlement House sponsored a Clinic staffed by a doctor, nurse, and midwife. The Clinic was a remnant of the Jew's Hospital, which had closed and moved uptown, renaming itself Mount Sinai Hospital. Patients with serious problems were generally transferred to the charity hospital, Bellevue Hospital, by ambulance coach. Some with money went uptown to Mount Sinai Hospital or cross-town to Beth Israel Hospital.

From time to time, Mrs. Simon shared tea with me. We'd discuss books, my adjustment to the Lower East Side, and the ever-growing needs of the neighborhood. Occasionally, she introduced me to other young women my age.

One day, sitting alone with Mrs. Simon, I glanced up from my cup and saw her studying my face.

"Tillie, I have a proposition for you."

"What kind of proposition?" I asked eagerly.

"We're overwhelmed with requests for language classes. How would you feel about teaching some of the new residents English?"

My excitement bubbled to the surface. "You know I only finished eighth grade. Do you think I'm qualified?"

"Of course. You're smart and outgoing. Watching you maneuver between Yiddish, German, and English at teatime is a marvel. It would put your skills to good use while helping others begin their lives here."

Anticipating my next question, she continued, "You'll be paid. Not a great deal, but it's something."

Me, a paid teacher? Imagine that! I can add my wages to our savings for the new apartment.

"I'd love to, but I need to check with Abe."

* * *

That afternoon, instead of my usual hour in the library, I hurried home to cook dinner, stopping at my favorite butcher and vegetable cart on the way.

Hours later, the roasted chicken, potatoes, onions, and carrots shot curls of succulent steam into the parlor. I leaned over the plates, inhaling the heavenly aroma, hoping this fine meal was the potion needed to make my new dream come true.

Abe sauntered into our apartment and hugged me tightly. "It smells like heaven on earth."

"You might want to thank Sadie. This meal was her first cooking lesson," I said. "Let's eat while it's hot."

Very shortly, only scraps of dinner remained. Abe gnawed on the chicken bone, making faint slurping sounds. He was full and sated, the perfect time to discuss teaching. Mama always waited until after dinner to raise new ideas with Papa. I remember how she said, "Never propose anything to a hungry man. He'll be far more willing to listen with a full belly."

"Mrs. Simon had an exciting offer this afternoon," I said, my eyes twinkling with suspense.

"What do you mean, offer?" He set down the bone, his voice serious.

"She'd like me to teach an English class, for money!" I sat straight in my chair and clapped. "I'm thrilled."

Abe sat, digesting the news. "I don't think it's a good idea."

My body sunk into the chair. "What do you mean?" How could he possibly deny me?

He pulled at his beard. "Aren't those classes at night? What about our dinners at home together?"

Memories of my dashed high school plans resurfaced. I pleaded, "It would only be a couple of evenings, and I can leave your meal on the counter." *How could he do this to me?*

"I want you home at night," he said firmly.

My jaw tightened. My voice raised in anger. I no longer cared who could hear us through the walls. "That's unfair. I've already sacrificed too much."

Abe said tightly, "Your papa made it clear it was my job to protect you. Walking about this part of the city at night is too damn dangerous." He reached out for my hand.

I recoiled. "Let me see what I can work out."

A thread of annoyance laced through his words. "What is that supposed to mean?"

I didn't answer. Instead, I picked up our plates and returned to the kitchen to clean and wrap the leftovers. Next time, I wouldn't ask first.

* * *

Mrs. Simon, concerned about spoiling the harmony in our marriage, offered two afternoon classes in place of the evening. I immediately committed without checking again with Abe. Although I knew ignoring him would bring strife into our home, I was determined one way or another that he treat me as an equal. Somehow, Mama had figured out the intricacies of marriage, and so would I. Her words echoed in my head. *Don't be afraid to have dreams for yourself.*

This time I informed Abe instead of asking for permission. He nodded in consent, but there was no joy in his expression.

As winter's frost descended on the city, I felt happier and busier, balancing my language classes at the Settlement House, assisting Abe with the business, and selecting food and supplies from my favorite shops. On an occasional Sunday, Papa and Hannah visited after delivering the chickens, injecting my family's familiar warmth into our lives. Eva, across the hall, was the main attraction. To the annoyance of other neighbors, the girls ran between Sadie and my apartments, feet pounding on the wood floors, concocting games with their dolls, squealing with delight.

But I should have known their joyful visits wouldn't last because tucked into the back of my mind, I hadn't forgotten about Papa's now lengthy trip from up north. I simply hadn't wanted to think about it.

But for Papa, the extra distance from Sullivan County down to the Lower East Side butcher was formidable, more than doubling his old trip. As New York City buildings sprang from the ground like weeds in midsummer, dragging chickens in his rickety wagon every week had become impossible. Papa had to leave home well before dawn, and it required staying overnight with us, which was exhausting for both Papa and the horses. I must hand it to him, though; he may have lost a few chickens who managed to jump ship, but he never lost a wagon wheel. He cared for his few possessions with abundant care.

"A new butcher is setting up in Sullivan County," Papa announced one Sunday. "When he does, I'll use him to slaughter, and he'll distribute to the kosher meat shops around the city." He quickly added, "Business has doubled since we moved, so many new Jews. The time is right to expand the hen production and let others do the schlepping."

A lump grew in my throat. "When will we see each other?"

"Don't fret, sweetheart. We'll find a way." He changed the subject. "And, what's this I hear about you teaching? Your mama would be proud."

Did he know I was also working with Yiddish, the language Mama forbade us to learn?

He smiled as if reading my mind. "You didn't fool me. I knew you were learning more Yiddish than you let on. Just watch out for all the bad words. There're are many."

I laughed, relishing this new, more mature relationship growing between us.

* * *

I knew Abe, in his particular way, was relieved I was happier. Although I didn't want to keep rubbing it in his face, he felt guilty, misleading me about high school. He certainly didn't want to come home to a miserable wife.

Watching other families in the building and listening to the heated arguments and shrieking that made the thin walls vibrate, I knew in my gut Abe was special, more giving, more loving. Moreover, my help with the business, especially keeping his paperwork orderly, made Abe's life more efficient. Hesitant to argue further, he no longer discussed my teaching, accepting it as if it was his idea in the first place. "The Settlement House is a good place to spend your afternoons. But please be home in time for dinner and to help me in the evening. You know, my business has never run so well."

I was thankful for a truce.

As we changed for bed, Abe said, "I think you're ready to take on more with the books. What do you think?"

Patience had paid off. With my careful attention to collections, we should be able to move in months. "I'd be happy to help more. Since I already set up the orders, how about I write invoices, enter payments into the ledger, and prepare the deposit slips for the bank? Then I'll give you the names of our late payers."

"Very well. We'll start tomorrow evening. The list is a good thought. I'll gently remind those dressmakers when I make deliveries, and hopefully, they'll stay caught up." He embraced me tightly.

I rubbed my head on his shoulder. "I'm happy, and I love you. But I'd be lying to myself if I said I didn't miss school. It's a shame we grow up so fast." I sighed.

As we lay in bed later that evening, he turned to look at me, searching my face. "I know I should have done more about high school, but honestly, I was so smitten I would have said anything to have you." He stroked my hair, twirling the loose curls around his fingers.

"I wish you'd told me more about life here, the poverty and filth. It's incredible people cross the sea for this. It's so close to the edge. Makes my high school dream seem small."

Abe thought a moment. "I suppose I was used to it. When my family passed, the hole in my heart was so big I stopped noticing much around me."

I placed my hand on his cheek and studied his eyes. There was a deep sadness buried beneath the blue surface. He had lost more than I could possibly imagine.

"I intend to keep my promises."

I exhaled deeply; my concern melted away. "It'll be better once we get a decent place. For now, that's all I want."

He kissed the tip of my nose. "I promise. At this rate, we should be out of here in a year or so." The corners of his mouth turned up. "Besides, maybe by that time, we'll have another Levine on the way."

My stomach caught. Abe could be right. We were so active in bed at night a baby was inevitable. But there was no way I'd give up relations. It was the best part of marriage.

Abe held me closer and breathed in the scent of my hair. "You smell lovely." He played with the top button of my dressing gown, kissed me on the lips, and I melted into his caresses once more.

Chapter Fifteen

I groaned as I tried to sip tea with Sadie. "I feel miserable. I can't hold anything down." Every day that week, I'd woken in a nauseated fog, barely able to lift my head from the pillow.

Sadie dragged her chair by mine and rubbed my back, her tenderness reassuring. "It's normal. Most women feel queasy for a few weeks in the beginning. Try nibbling on toast."

Since early November, I suspected I might be pregnant, but I wanted to be certain before telling Abe. Now, in early December, I was lethargic from the moment I dragged myself from bed. I scheduled an appointment with Marta, the midwife at the Settlement House Clinic. She confirmed my suspicion. Although a small part of me was happy for Abe, my queasy stomach and lack of energy were making me short-tempered and gloomy. No one warned me pregnancy was so dreadful. I needed Mama's reassurance.

Later that evening, I sat staring at my dinner plate while Abe talked nonstop about his day. Suddenly, my mouth filled with a metallic taste. I ran to the kitchen and bent over the bucket.

Abe followed me, concerned. "What's wrong? Did you catch something at the Settlement House?"

I grabbed a rag from the counter and wiped my mouth. "I'm pregnant."

His face broke into a delighted smile. "How wonderful!" He clapped his hands, singing, "We're going to have a baby." Suddenly, he stopped, looking at my glum expression. "I'm sorry you're not feeling well. Can I do anything to help?"

I gripped my belly. "I don't think so. Marta said it should pass in a few weeks."

"Let's buy a warm coat for you. Do you need boots, too?"

I dropped back in my chair. "No, my coat and boots are fine. Besides, we need to save everything so we can leave here." I scanned the crowded room. "This is no place for a baby."

Abe's eyes sparkled with excitement. "Yes, of course. God sent me a second chance with you, my darling." He gently placed his hand on mine as he realized once again that he alone was celebrating. His words spilled out. "You must get plenty of rest. Perhaps a nap in the afternoon instead of working at the Settlement House."

His words unnerved me, making my world close in. "That's not necessary. Marta said that it will pass. Remember, I'm a farm girl and don't need pampering. Where I come from, women do their normal jobs, and everyone gets on fine."

He didn't look convinced, so I added, "I promise to see the midwife regularly, and she'll let me know if I need more rest."

Abe shook his head. "I want you to stop teaching and stay home. Stay away from the Settlement House. Who knows what kind of diseases those people brought here with their rags."

A rush of annoyance swept through me. *Again, Abe with his control.* "I finally let go of my grand high school plan and found something purposeful to do every week. My class depends on me." I huffed, settling my pounding heart. "And my students are poor, not sick. Can we talk about this later when I start to show? Right now, only you and Sadie know."

Abe reared back, surprised. "If Rabbi learns you're working while expecting, you know he'll make you stop, and I'll have hell to pay. He'll say it's indecent."

I snapped back. "All the more reason to stay quiet. Don't suffocate me." I was unwilling to have the rabbi, any rabbi, meddling in my personal matters. Not again. Not this time. "We'll talk when I'm further along."

He studied me carefully. The seconds ticked by. Finally, he reached for my hand. "I'll agree for now," he said. "But when you start showing, we'll have a different conversation."

His voice held a cautionary edge, unwilling to relinquish his authority. I'd bought myself some time, but I had no intention of giving up teaching until I was good and ready.

* * *

The Settlement House was buzzing every day with new faces and needs, drawing me closer to memories of my parents. I now understood their disorientation years back, arriving in New York with so few possessions, not speaking the language. I saw my mother in the young women who brought their babies to class, eager to learn English and assimilate into the crowded neighborhood they now called home. The men reminded me of my father, proud to be called an American, grateful for his new freedom, eager to find his way.

I memorized their Eastern European names as they entered my class—Moishe, Mendel, Rivka, and Freyde. Most of my students were Orthodox Jews, who, unlike me, stood apart from the established crowd in their traditional garb, yarmulkes, and tallits with their twined and knotted fringes for the men, and modest dark dresses with head scarves for the women. But once we were comfortable with each other, our surface differences melted away. Beneath our clothing, we were more alike than different. They shared stories of their hardships, the lives they'd left behind. The more I learned of their struggles, the harder I worked to ensure their success.

My English classroom was filled with twenty students and their families, even during inclement weather. Sometimes, forty people jammed into the small space. Once settled, we took turns naming what we ate for last night's dinner. Sometimes, I gave them choices: "Soup? Cheese? Chicken? Bread?" Often, my questions were met with downcast eyes or embarrassed stares. Through this exercise, I realized the depth of their poverty.

I thought about Papa's pride, providing for his family. "Be thankful you eat three meals a day," he'd scold us when we refused the food on our plates.

Thin, unwashed faces and glassy eyes studiously peered at me. I began bringing a couple of loaves of bread and a block of cheese to class, sharing it with my students. "I hadn't time for lunch today. Please join me." I typically took a portion first. Not a crumb was left behind; mothers always pushing their children ahead first.

* * *

By the end of the second week of class, I knocked on Mrs. Simon's office door. "Do you have time for tea?"

"Of course, always!" We walked to the kitchen to boil water.

"Dear, how are your classes going?" Mrs. Simon fussed with the tea canister, scooping out leaves. "I'd love to hear what you think about this new group from Eastern Europe."

A perfect opening. "I was hoping to share an idea."

She poured the boiling water over the tea to steep. "I'm all ears."

"I'd no idea how poor the people were. They must have come to America with nothing but a change of clothes and their names."

Mrs. Simon strained the tea water into two cups, humming in agreement.

We sat at a small table by the snow-encrusted window. "After class settles in, they take turns naming what they ate for dinner the night before. You know, vocabulary building. I found that many aren't eating properly, or much at all. And they're ashamed to admit it."

Mrs. Simon drew her lips together, snorting in disgust.

My voice hitched. "Some of the children have only an apple or broth for dinner. They're all thin as garden rakes. So, I started bringing bread and cheese to share, but it's not enough. As we get further into winter, I'm afraid they'll get sick."

Mrs. Simon set down her cup. "What's your idea?"

I'd rehearsed my plan in my head all morning. I took a full breath, quieting my emotions. "Back on the farms, when something bad happened in a family, the community cooked and helped with the children until the parents got back on their feet. I'm sure that happens here, too. But these newcomers don't have friends yet, and they need help now." I drew a deep breath, hoping she'd like my idea. "I thought if we created a larder here at

116

the Settlement House, we could distribute food to the neediest."

She watched me carefully while I laid out my plan. "Interesting. Go on."

"The teachers can give you a list of families who need help, and then you meet with them in private to see what they need."

Mrs. Simon knit her brows, studying my face. "I like this idea. But what if there isn't enough food donated? And where will we store it so it doesn't spoil?"

I contemplated her questions, wishing I'd thought of these issues beforehand. "We can start slowly, testing it with just a few families." As I spoke, the answers rolled out of my mouth. "Perhaps you or Rabbi could announce the idea after Friday and Saturday Shabbos services? You could ask members to bring an extra loaf of bread, a block of cheese, potatoes, or vegetables each week to put in the larder. If they drop the food off on Sunday, we could distribute it during the week."

She nodded and smiled. "Yes, I can see this working."

"In the meantime, we can store the food in the root cellar down in the basement so it doesn't spoil. It should last a week or more in the cold weather."

She bobbed her head as she spoke. "I like the way you think, dear. We can use more people like you. Our shul is growing fast. So many of our newcomers need more than we're providing. I'll speak to Rabbi later today and if he agrees, we'll start this weekend."

I clapped my hands, pleased. "Wonderful!"

"I imagine you'll need a partner to help you." Mrs. Simon stopped moving and gazed out the window as if her options were standing in line on the snow-covered sidewalk. "Perhaps someone with experience in the community. I can't take on another thing, but hunger can't wait."

"A helper would be great." I knew I hadn't the faintest idea how to take this project on alone.

She tapped the table with her nail, the clicking quickening as a broad smile filled her face. "I know just the person. She mentioned last week that she's itching for a project." Mrs. Simon's eyes gleamed. "Mrs. Katz, one of our long-time supporters, and a wonderful cook, would be perfect. This is right up her alley. She's always baking treats to welcome new synagogue members."

* * *

Within two weeks, we were filling the food larder on Sunday, and it shrank daily over the course of the week. The teachers shared names with Mrs. Simon using the utmost privacy. In no time, our helper, Mrs. Katz, had more donations of food and money than we had families to receive them, as she also contacted the old-timers who had left the tenements and moved to fancier neighborhoods, but never forgetting their humble beginnings. Her gift of gab got her through every door, and she always returned to the Settlement House with names of those needing other assistance as well, such as a nurse visit or work. Mrs. Simon then connected the family to Dr. Boro at the Clinic or an apartment-based factory. We kept our new neighbors fed over the winter as they blended into our synagogue family.

One morning, I saw Mrs. Katz preparing soup in the Settlement kitchen, boiling chicken and chopping celery and onions. She was short, only reaching my shoulders, her apron tied tightly around her thick waist. I approached her. "We did it! Our pantry is running as if it's been around for years. It's all due to you."

"It's exciting, isn't it?" She smiled. The skin creased around her animated brown eyes. "Now that my children are grown, I feel useless if I'm not involved in a project. If it weren't for Mrs. Simon keeping me busy, I don't know what I'd do."

I waved off her words. "I'm learning from you. You're a wonderful teacher."

Indeed, the food pantry had become an important accomplishment that winter. And, as I envisioned, the faces kept changing. As one family found work and no longer needed assistance, they began donating food to the larder for the newer arrivals.

Mrs. Katz explained one afternoon. "Tillie, always remember, it takes more than one person to make big things happen. You discovered the need.

Mrs. Simon helped connect me to families, and I used my years of goodwill to encourage friends to reach into their pantries and contribute. Together, the three of us started something important. We should all be proud." She placed her palm on her heart.

I felt the satisfaction, too. The memory of the ravenous child last fall, as I made my way home from high school, had been seared into my memory. This project was far bigger than a single apple; it kept our entire community full while they all found work.

The success of the pantry project fueled my imagination. I began a mental list of ideas to discuss with Mrs. Simon. I thought my energy would go on forever. But, as luck and nature had their way, my body forced me to slow down before I could explore more ideas with Mrs. Simon.

Chapter Sixteen

With the coming of spring, my belly grew at lightning speed. Despite Marta's prediction of a June baby, March had just arrived, and I looked ready to deliver. Infant movement pounded me from within as I pushed feet, elbows, and a rump back into my pelvis. Panicking, I made an appointment with Marta at the Clinic. "Are you sure there's only one in there? How could I possibly be so big? I'm up and down all night using the chamber pot, and barely anything comes out. Look at my ankles and fingers—they're so swollen."

Marta helped me onto the Clinic table.

I unbuttoned my oversized day dress. "I can't get over how clumsy and uncomfortable I've become. I feel like an old woman, and I'm not yet twenty!"

She set her short, metal stethoscope on my mountainous stomach, pressing the earpiece against her right ear and sliding the smooth end over the surface of my belly. "I hear one very strong heartbeat. Even so, I don't like the look of your ankles and hands. It's time to get off your feet."

My eyes bulged in disbelief. *Off my feet? I'll go mad!* "Marta, I'm not ready to stop working." My head spun with concern.

Marta pointed to my stomach. "No matter. The baby must be your first concern. Now climb on the scale." Her brow knit in consternation.

I gathered my skirt and stepped on the scale, overwhelmed in every way.

Marta grunted. "Far too much weight. No more sweets and no more salt. Only fresh food for you and that baby from now till birth. Stick with milk, chicken, and vegetables."

Unnerved, worried about going crazy at home, I bargained, "I'll lose my mind lying around for months. Is it alright if I sit in the morning while I work on Abe's books, teach my English class in the afternoon and then go home and rest? The Settlement House is desperate for teachers and my students depend on me. I promise I won't eat any more sweets."

Marta's eyes met mine. She understood. The Clinic was equally overwhelmed by the influx of immigrants. "I suppose we can try it for a few days and see if the ankle swelling goes down. But I want you back here to see me in one week. If things don't improve, you'll be confined to your apartment and off your feet until you labor. And I won't listen to another word." She paused, her eyes hooded in thought. "Besides, if Rabbi sees you working, he'll send you right home, and we'll all be in trouble. Honestly, I don't know how you've gotten away with it this long."

Could I trust her with the truth? I decided to take a risk. "I've been hiding, careful to stay far from his office, and my shawl covers a lot."

Marta sighed loudly, shaking her head at me. "As I said, your baby must come first."

I decided not to tell Abe at dinner that night. He'd agreed to my schedule so far, and I didn't want him interfering. But as luck turned out, he ran into Marta on the street that very afternoon, and she cautioned him to keep an eye on me.

After dinner, as we changed for bed, I found him watching me. "I hear you saw Marta today. She's worried about you. Just look at your ankles."

I averted my eyes.

Abe demanded, "What did she tell you?"

"She wants me to cut out all sweets and salt." I sighed. "She said we'll see how the next week goes, and I promised to take it easy. Please don't worry."

His voice rose with frustration. "What do you mean, don't worry? You're my wife and carrying our child. This has gone on long enough. As of now, I want you home."

"But Abe, I feel fine," I disagreed weakly. *Of course, I didn't, but if I told him that, he'd never allow me to keep teaching.*

"You always say you're fine. But I don't believe it. You can't begin to imagine how you'd crush my heart if you or the baby…" His voice broke as he led me the three steps to the edge of our bed, helping me stretch out on the blanket. "Tillie, your happiness means everything to me. But now, you must listen. I want you home and off your feet."

I pleaded. "But Marta was willing to give it a week. Can't you, too?"

He sat beside me on the bed and took my hand, speaking gently. "No. I'll not risk losing my family again."

The weight of his authority pressed down on me. "Can I at least meet with Mrs. Simon and my class tomorrow to say goodbye?"

He sat silently, his hand playing with a loose curl of my hair, exhaling a deep sigh. "Yes, you should say your goodbyes, and I'll talk to Sadie about picking up groceries. Maybe you can watch Eva in the apartment to return the favor." He lifted my chin so he could look directly into my eyes. "But, after tomorrow, I want you to stay in. Do you understand?"

This time, the sigh was mine, knowing I had lost the argument and that he was probably right. A knot of regret tightened within me. All I'd ever wanted was to attend high school. Teaching was a poor substitute, but I loved it anyway. *This infant better be worth it!*

Abe slid into bed beside me. "Look at it this way, darling. You have a few extra months to read to your heart's delight. I'll come with you tomorrow, and we'll stop at the Settlement Library and stock up. Then I'll exchange the books as you finish them."

"How do you always do that?" I cried. "Just as I start to get good and mad, you find a way to make me love you more." I rolled, facing him, knowing he would always protect me, no matter what.

Abe threw his arms around me. "I don't think there's a way I could love you more. But it's my job to keep you safe, even when it makes you mad."

* * *

Gradually, the swelling in my hands and feet subsided, but my belly continued growing at a staggering speed. I no longer could see past the mound to my ankles or feet. But controlling my sugar cravings was near impossible. Every few days, Sadie returned from the market with an expensive orange and brought up a few apples left over from the winter root storage room at the Settlement House. My friends from the building and Settlement House didn't help matters. Wanting to cheer me, they occasionally appeared at my door with a delicious honey cake to eat with afternoon tea. The aroma was irresistible, but I was too grateful for their company to complain. After taking a nibble with my visitors, I offered the remainder to Sadie for her family, forging a life-long friendship with her sons.

The stream of visitors, evenings with Abe, and my stack of unread books created a tranquility I had missed since Mama died. Reading beside the gas lamp while I roasted a chicken in the oven kept the apartment warm and cozy. In time, I accepted my confinement while silently counting the days until my due date.

Mrs. Simon, always my favorite visitor, stopped by regularly. On one occasion, I handed her a cup of tea and shared my plan. "I'd like to keep teaching. I'll bring it to class like the students bring their children. I miss everyone and don't want to sit at home." My hand swept across the room. "I've had enough of these four walls."

She winced. "Your baby is not an 'it.' 'She' or 'he' will be your beloved child, not a basket of potatoes to lug around with you. Besides, trust me, you have no idea how you'll feel after your child's born." Her face relaxed, transforming into a wistful expression. "Becoming a mother is special. You'll see. I wish I'd had the chance."

Her words troubled me. Somehow, I thought I could pick up right where I'd left off.

She saw my face fall. "Don't worry, dear. There'll always be a place for you when you're ready."

Tears pooled in my eyes. "I didn't want a baby this soon. I was just getting comfortable with my life. Teaching saved me. You can't imagine my disappointment when I was turned away from high school."

She cupped my cheek in her hand. "You've done a remarkable job, and your mama would be proud of you. Don't try to plan the future today. Take it slow." She placed her arm around my shoulder and squeezed.

* * *

In the predawn hours, six weeks later, I jolted awake. My body quaked with severe cramping. "Abe, fetch the midwife. Hurry!" My baby was coming too early.

As he shot out of the apartment, I tried rolling on my side, desperate to find a more comfortable position. Then, I was struck with an uncontrollable urge to pee.

Struggling to rise from bed, I inched my way to the chamber pot and crouched. I felt an explosion in my lower body as water poured out. I grabbed a towel to hold against myself and dropped onto the floor beside the mattress.

A loud knock at the door. "Tillie, it's me, Sadie. Can I come in? I heard you scream."

"Come in." I had never been more grateful for thin walls.

Sadie set her lantern on the floor, eyeing the puddle around the chamber pot, then helped me onto the bed. "You're in labor. I'll stay and help until Marta gets here, or longer if you want. I'm an old hand with babies." She sat beside me, pushing her open hand into my lower back, rubbing.

"Yes, yes, stay," I moaned, feeling slightly better with her hand's pressure.

By the time Abe returned, the early dawn had begun casting its light through the parlor windows, shooting jagged beams through the kitchen transom onto the bedroom walls. He charged into the apartment with Marta at his heels, both carrying bundles of clean sheets, towels, and soap. She held a satchel with her birthing instruments tucked inside.

"Oh Marta, thank God you're here! My water broke." I panted. "Do you know Sadie? Can she stay?"

Marta leaned over the bed. "Sadie and I are old friends. Of course, she can stay. Lie down and try to relax." She spoke in a soft voice. "Let's get you straightened up, and I'll see how far along you are. In the meantime, Sadie, wash your hands with the soap I brought."

"Can Abe stay, too? I'm scared." I asked breathlessly.

Just then, a forceful contraction hit, making me groan. Marta pulled up my gown and slipped her fingers inside me while I cried out.

She waited for the cramps to release, then said, "Tillie, this baby's coming soon. You must have started labor during the night. You're far along." Marta examined my belly with her stethoscope and shook her head.

Abe watched her expression. "What is it?"

Marta cocked her head at Abe. "Not certain yet. Let's get Tillie ready."

"What should I do?" Abe cried out, hovering over me.

Sadie grabbed his arm and led him to the kitchen, pressing her lips together with authority.

"Abe, go join Max for coffee and breakfast in my place. He might need help getting the boys off to school. I'll get you in a while."

"Don't go!" I pleaded, my emotions raw with desperation.

Sadie looked down at me. "He'll just be across the hall in our apartment."

"No, please don't leave me," I begged.

Marta took command. "The fathers always wait outside until the baby's born." Her eyes softened, eager to calm me. "But perhaps we can call Abe in when it's time to push."

I nodded as I caught my breath. The truth was, the labor pains had intensified, consuming me in a manner so complete I could think of nothing beyond the pain. I would have agreed to throw my loved ones into a blazing fire pit at that moment if the pain would only stop.

Once Abe left, Marta and Sadie set up for the birth. Attempting to catch my breath between contractions, my eyes caught a brilliant halo on the wall from where the parlor light reached. I stared into the ring of light, catching my breath, imagining Mama tethering me to the bed with her gentle words. *You can do this, Tillie. All babies come into the world this way.*

Marta and Sadie laid padding beneath me on the bed, cleaned the bedroom, boiled water, and prepared a special area for the infant. Sadie warmed towels on the stove.

I howled with every contraction. Pain and fear had joined forces within me, lacing into an excruciating, all-encompassing force, transforming me into a wild animal. At times, I gripped Sadie's arm so hard she had to pry my fingers off, leaving red marks on her pale skin.

Finally, Marta leaned into my face and commanded, "Stop screaming. It won't help and will only exhaust you. You must breathe. Try to concentrate on breathing. In…and…out."

My contraction eased. She was right. At this rate, I'd die from exhaustion before I gave birth.

Marta leaned into my head and, with a firm tone, spoke to me. "With the next big cramp, I want you to breathe along with me, in and out. I promise it will help."

I lost track of time as my labor ravaged me, the contractions excruciating. Eventually, the pain became so violent I could barely breathe. Finally, I hollered, "Mama, help me! I'm dying."

I heard Marta call to me from the foot of the bed. "The baby's ready. Time to push. The pain will lessen only if you push down hard when I tell you to. Sadie, get Abe."

Dimly, I saw Sadie slip out of the apartment.

Marta set her hand on my lower belly. "I feel another one coming. Take in a big breath and get ready to bear down. Help me get this baby out. Push!"

Abe ran into the room and grabbed my hand as I bore down. His eyes were wild with fear. Sadie reached out to steady him.

Marta looked at his frightened face. "Abe, this is normal. Help Tillie sit up and support her while she pushes."

He stood frozen in place.

She barked. "Do what I say or leave." Then, turning to Sadie, she continued calmly, "Sadie, get the warm baby blanket ready and help me at this end."

"Help me!" I yelled out as an overwhelming force shook my body. I pushed with more strength than I knew I had. *I'm going to die.* Finally, the contraction passed.

Marta's voice came from a distant place. "Almost there. I can see the head. One or two more pushes and your child will be born."

My panic didn't upset Marta. She was so comfortable in charge that I clung to the reassuring sound of her voice. She was my anchor. I'd barely caught my breath before another tidal wave of squeezing drove through me. Without volition, my body clenched down, pushing our little boy into the world. "Oh my God, oh my God," I gasped as he began to squeal. I looked at Abe. He was still holding my back upward, sobbing.

Sadie swaddled the infant in the towel she'd been warming on the stove and set him in my arms. "You have a son."

I looked from the infant to Abe, feeling a rush of love.

"We have a boy! Thank you, God," cried Abe, wiping his face on his sleeve. "Let me see."

I lay beside my emotional husband, peeking under the infant's blanket to count his tiny fingers and toes. Suddenly, nothing but my helpless baby mattered to me. "Yes, thank you, God, for giving us this miracle. I will protect him with my life," I murmured from the deepest part of my heart.

But my reaction didn't last long. Another cramp seared through me. "Good God, more?" I shouted. "What's going on?" My face crumbled in pain.

Marta, who had finished delivering the afterbirth, looked up. "Let me check." Seconds ticked by as she examined. "We're not done. There's another baby."

Another contraction squeezed down as she slid her hand out.

"No!" I cried.

Marta ordered. "Abe, take the boy. Sadie, I need your help here."

Abe reared back, shouting, "What? Two? Why didn't you tell me?"

Marta's angry face stopped him cold. "Mr. Isaacson, we didn't know. I couldn't hear the second heartbeat."

"Hell on earth!" Another contraction gripped me at the heels of the last. *Good Lord, here we go again.* Waves of involuntary pushing began another time. So lost in the sensation, I had no time to think. Minutes later, a tiny baby girl slid onto the sheet. She was silent, so different from the first baby. "What's wrong?"

"Come on, little one," Marta urged the infant, vigorously rubbing her back.

The seconds ticked by. Panic set in as I strained to sit upright. Then, finally, I heard a slight cough followed by the slightest whimper. Together, the adults released a synchronized sigh. I dropped backward on the bed, too exhausted to speak or cry with relief.

Sadie hurried to wrap the infant in a warm towel, placing her under the blanket against my bare skin.

Abe whispered to Marta. "She's so small. Can she survive?"

Marta's worried look told me something wasn't right, but she forged on through her birthing ritual. "Sadie, let's clean the babies. Afterward, we'll have them nurse." She met Abe's eyes. "Both babies came early and are small. The boy is stronger. For now, let's be thankful they're both breathing."

Sadie squeezed my hand gently. "One step at a time. Lie back and relax. You earned it. That was hard work today." She waved Abe toward me. "Get ready to help Tillie hold the babies close to her body to keep them warm. They'll like that."

Sadie took each infant from me, one by one, and wiped them off with care. She then rewrapped each in a warm blanket, placing one on my right side and the other on the left. Abe stuffed pillows behind my back until I was partially sitting. Then Sadie helped me cradle the boy to my breast, positioning his tiny mouth on my engorged nipple. He started sucking immediately.

"Ouch!" I startled. "No one told me it would hurt."

Marta smiled. "It's a good sign he's suckling. You'll get used to it, but with two, try to feed them close together so you have time to heal and rest." She lifted the baby girl to me in the same manner so I was cradling both, one on each side.

Abe supported the boy while I guided the infant girl to my other nipple, but she closed her eyes, showing no interest in latching on. "What should I do?" I bounced her gently.

Sadie uncovered the baby, rubbing her skin. She opened her little eyes, upset by the chilly air, her lower lip quivering. Again, we positioned her tiny lips on my breast. She suckled, but before long, stopped and fell asleep, more comforted by my warmth. She didn't seem eager to be part of the cold world outside my body.

Marta cleaned the birthing area and washed her instruments, instructing Abe, "Make sure Tillie nurses each baby every three hours, day and night. If you must, unwrap the girl and expose her skin. It will encourage her to latch, even if for a short while. Infants don't typically work up a big appetite right away." She snapped her bag closed. "There are three things to remember at all times: keep them clean, warmly swaddled, and regularly fed."

Abe nodded. "Is there anything special we can do to help the girl?"

Marta placed the dirty towels in a sack. "I'm glad you reminded me. Only let healthy, close relatives hold the babies. We don't want them sick before their bodies grow big and strong." She warned us, "Remember, they were born almost a month and a half early."

Before leaving, Marta carried the bassinet into our bedroom. "I suggest putting them together in the bassinet, keeping them near you at bed and mealtime. They'll stay warmer together on chilly spring nights and after all." She gazed at me while I cuddled them, "They're already used to sharing a bedroom."

* * *

Over the next few days, I lost my grip on external time. Instead, I tuned into the clock of motherhood, sleeping, feeding, and changing the babies. Sadie came every morning with our morning coffee, food for the day, and fresh diapers. Then she left with the soiled. I had no idea where she found time to add my chores to her already hectic day. Marta stopped by twice that week to check on the infants and me.

Abe stayed home with me for a full week. I'd never seen him happier and, unlike me, with boundless energy, helping in any way he could. When I opened my eyes, I'd find him rocking one baby or the other in the parlor, singing nursery rhymes in his deep, soothing voice.

My understanding of his terrible losses sharpened as I watched him cuddle the babies. Childbirth was precarious, the instantaneous bewildering attachment overwhelming. Thank God he had a new family now.

By the second week, I could move about the apartment without difficulty, and Abe returned to his customers. He made his rounds, handing out cigars right and left, dutifully returning mid-afternoon to check on us sometimes with infant outfits from his customers.

If it weren't for my lingering concern for our baby girl, whom we named Sarah after Mama, all would have been idyllic. She nibbled at her meals, not a voracious eater like her brother, Julian, who grew more robust by the day. Where he was the vision of vitality, Sarah was delicate. I feared she was too frail.

Marta's smile faded at her second visit when she examined Sarah. "I'll ask Dr. Boro to stop by later today and check the babies, especially Sarah. Perhaps there's more we can do to help her. Let's see what he says."

Contrary to my earlier expectations. I had fallen deeply in love with both infants, willing to do anything to protect them. Mrs. Simon was right. Two months ago, I'd been clueless. Parenthood had already changed me.

Marta returned to the apartment with the doctor after dinner that evening. I noticed the dark circles of fatigue beneath their eyes as they removed their coats and hats. She introduced Dr. Boro, a gentle-looking man of average height and build.

I studied the doctor, a man about Papa's age. "It's nice to meet you. Can I get dinner for both of you? We have enough food to feed an army."

Although Dr. Boro's brown eyes were hidden behind his rimmed spectacles, he radiated warmth and ease. "Danke. Perhaps a quick bite after I check your babies. I've three more stops this evening and can't stay for a proper meal."

Dr. Boro studied the twins in their bassinet while, like a mother hen, I fidgeted behind him. He lifted Sarah in his arms. "Ah, little Sarah, so nice to finally meet you. I'm Dr. Boro," he cooed as if she could hold a conversation. "Mama will undress you, and I'll examine."

I gently set Sarah on the bed and unwrapped her swaddle. Her lower lip trembled as the cold air struck her bare skin.

"It's alright, darling," I reassured her softly. "The kind doctor wants to check you."

Dr. Boro took a miniature instrument from his bag. "Your eyes look fine, and so do your ears—and you don't like the cold, that's good." His soft words soothed Sarah. "Now, let's use my stethoscope to listen to your heart and lungs. Hmm, perfect." He unpinned her diapers, examining her lower body. "Your tum feels soft, and your body is fully formed." He turned to me. "Tillie, you can dress her now, but leave her on the bed. I'll check your son."

I wrapped her quickly and kissed her forehead as Abe helped maneuver Julian through his exam.

"Let's try to fatten you up." Dr. Boro regarded Sarah on the bed, continuing to speak directly to the infant. "More milk will make you strong like your big brother." He glanced into the bassinet at Julian. He took Sarah's little hands in his and tried to pull her upward from the bed. She lay limp.

Dr. Boro's tenderness did not ease my concern. "How do I get her to eat more?" I asked. "I give her plenty of time at my breast."

His soft eyes studied mine. "My dear, little Sarah is fighting hard to grow and build strength, but it's a difficult battle for her. Both infants were born weeks early, often the case with twins, and certainly no fault of yours. Mother Nature designed a woman's body for one baby at a time."

I trembled. What was he trying to tell me? Would she live? Was Julian in peril, too?

He interrupted my thoughts. "Feed Sarah first when your breasts are full, so she doesn't need to work hard. Don't worry about Julian. He's a fighter. He's tightly tied to instinct and will work harder to fill his belly. In no time, you'll see your milk supply increase to fill both babies." He studied my face, waiting for a nod before continuing.

"Last things. You must drink plenty of water and eat healthy meals like eggs, meats, dairy, and vegetables. Remember, what you eat becomes the food for your babies."

Abe interjected. "I'll see to that."

Dr. Boro looked deeply into my eyes. "I know you're worried. I wish I could predict the future, but I can see you are both doing a fine job. Keep up the good work."

I exhaled. He'd given me the spark of hope I needed.

He then set his hand on Abe's forearm. "You must keep the babies away from visitors. Sarah doesn't have much reserve to fight infection. If your family comes to welcome them, put the infants in your bedroom and let the family peek in. Absolutely no passing them around with the neighbors."

Abe squeezed his determined lips together. I knew he took every word to heart. "I understand."

Dr. Boro closed his medical bag while finishing his instructions. "The plan is to put weight on them before the cold and flu season starts six months from now." He paused thoughtfully. "It's better to be born in the spring. We'll have a nice stretch of good weather to work with." With those simple instructions dispensed, he wolfed down a brisket sandwich on my home-baked challah, gulped a cup of tea, and headed to the apartment door, Marta at his heels.

Marta slid her sandwich into her satchel and winked back at me. "My next stop is home, and I'm going to savor every bite before tucking myself in!"

* * *

Word in the tenement building traveled until all our friends knew we were concerned about our little Sarah, and Dr. Boro wanted her isolated. His word was gospel in this neighborhood, sometimes more than the rabbi's directives. But nothing could stop the tide of good wishes. Abe intercepted our guests in the hallway, their arms full of hand-knitted booties, blankets, and baked goods. He regaled them with stories of the tiny babies, but no one came inside. Instead, their infectious laughter echoed up and down the stairwell.

During the short stretches alone with the infants, I thought about Mama and Papa and our days on the farm. In less than one year, I had undergone a staggering number of changes. Nursing gave me time to settle, reflect, and think about Mama and her gentle lessons. I'd sit back, close my eyes, and conjure her sweet face. *Are you watching, Mama?*

* * *

"There's a letter for you," Abe announced as he entered the apartment after work. "Looks like it's from your father."

Excited, I snatched it from his hand and hurried to our new rocking chair beside the parlor window. Abe had bought the chair days ago from a street vendor. Although a much-needed addition to our sparse furniture, it creaked with every rock, often in tempo to the lullabies Abe sang to the infants. I ripped the letter open, unfolded the paper, and read it aloud.

> *May 31, 1881*
>
> *My precious Tillie,*
>
> *Mazel Tov on the birth of Sarah and Julian, my first grandchildren! We are filled with joy for you and Abe. I'm now an Opa!*
>
> *We are coming to visit in two weeks, Sunday the 12th. This time we'll travel on the train and then streetcar. The boys and Hannah understand they must stay away from the babies, so don't fret.*
>
> *I'm bringing a sack of early vegetables from the garden: peas, beans, and asparagus.*
>
> *With love,*
>
> *Papa*

I could barely wait. Hannah had just turned five and would start school in the fall. She was a precocious child with wispy blond curls, vibrant green eyes, and a bouncy personality. Although I missed my brothers too, all those hours watching over Hannah made me extra protective. Besides, Mama's words were never far in my mind: *if something happens, I want you to look after the children, especially Hannah. She's still a baby and won't remember me.*

These days, with Papa further north and doling the chicken transport to others, we rarely saw each other in person. Instead, we wrote letters. He came every month, recounting stories about Rebecca's baby girl, Abby, born months earlier in the fall. I imagined she must be crawling by now. Papa's chicken business was booming, too, and my brother Nate planned to work with him after eighth grade. It had been months since we'd all been together. I missed them terribly.

The babies began crying. Could it be time to feed them already? My exhaustion kept me rooted to the chair.

Abe gazed at my exhausted body through his own bloodshot eyes. "Looks like it's time. Let's get them taken care of and then we can eat and rest too."

I nodded. "Could you take Julian while I nurse Sarah? Then we'll switch."

Moments later, we repositioned in the parlor. Abe held Julian against his chest, rocking in the chair. "Tomorrow, Rabbi Meyers is coming to the apartment with the mohel. It will be eight days, and Julian needs his circumcision." Abe twirled the short brown ringlets on Julian's head. "Poor thing doesn't know what's coming."

For me, circumcision was a barbaric ritual. Cutting off a baby's foreskin seemed downright cruel, but I had no choice in the matter. Who was I to challenge an ancient tradition? No wonder the mamas were kept in the kitchen crying, away from the infants.

Abe knew I was unhappy, and my growing fatigue didn't help matters. "I saw Mrs. Simon while I was meeting with Rabbi, and if you agree, she'd like to come as a witness and bring sweets to enjoy afterwards. She misses you."

These days the drop of a pin could make me dissolve into tears. "Mrs. Simon can cry with me in the kitchen." Sarah pulled away from my breast. I positioned her on my other breast feeling much like Papa's milk cow in the barn.

* * *

The next day, I paced the floor, nervously picking up a stray button here and there, looking for dust. The circumcision ceremony was not as bad as I feared. The rabbi and mohel came and went within an hour. Mrs. Simon distracted me while the mohel's scalpel cut off Julian's foreskin. A touch of wine on Julian's infant lips quieted him and my aching heart. I mopped my tears and headed into the parlor to take him from the men. We then officially toasted our first-born son.

The next two weeks passed in a tired fog. If it weren't for my family's upcoming visit, I would have lost complete awareness of the days. My life was defined by the infants' needs: feeding, changing, washing diapers, and hanging them on the window clothesline with a bite of food for me in between. The endless repetition was driving me mad. Sadie's daily visits with coffee in the morning and my anticipation of Papa's visit were the two distractions keeping me moving forward.

I thanked God every day for Sarah's growing appetite. Just like Dr. Boro predicted, once Julian smelled my milk, he became ravenous and emptied every drop from my breasts. But as much as she grew, Julian remained twice her size.

Chapter Seventeen

June 1881

A rap at our apartment door woke me from a catnap. I'd finished feeding the babies, and they were fast asleep in our bedroom. Sitting in the rocker on my own, I'd also drifted into a dreamless sleep.

Abe shook my shoulder. "Time to wake up. Your family's here."

I startled, jumping from the rocker and shaking my head awake while Abe opened the door. Papa stood smiling with my two excited brothers beside a troubled-looking Hannah. Rebecca and Abby were not with them.

I hadn't seen my brothers for close to a year, and they'd shed their childish looks. "You boys have doubled in size! Nate, look at that mustache. You're so handsome and manly. And Joe, you are the spitting image of Papa, tall and lean. Are you two staying out of trouble?" I knelt to face Hannah. "Hi, sweetheart."

Nate and Joe nodded knowingly to each other and hugged me. But Hannah's face held an odd expression, clown-like and stoic, as if she were holding back tears, unusual for her. Did she recognize me?

"Come in! Come into our little home." I settled my family in the parlor while Abe opened the drop leaf table, lifting and securing the extensions. Then, I set down a plate of marzipan cookies, a pitcher of lemonade, and glasses.

While the boys dove into the food, I studied Hannah, puzzled. Something was amiss. Her face lacked emotion. Then it hit me. Her eyebrows and lashes were gone! Left behind were little clusters of light brown hair in clumps of two and three strands. I inhaled a shocked breath. "Papa, please come with me for a moment." I took his hand and led him the short distance into the bedroom, shutting the door. "What happened to Hannah? What's going on? And where's Rebecca?"

Papa cleared his throat, shifting his weight from foot to foot. He turned his gaze to the sleeping babies. "Mazel Tov! They're beautiful." Twisting back at me, he added, "Rebecca was feeling under the weather and stayed home with the baby."

I repeated, "What's going on with Hannah? When did she start picking at her face?"

The babies stirred, and I shushed them back to sleep.

Papa whispered haltingly. "I don't think it's serious. She developed those habits after her sister was born. You know how busy it is with a baby and getting settled in a new place. I think Rebecca is having a tough time handling all the children and isn't as patient with Hannah as she once was before...."

My face flushed red as my anger grew. "This is serious. She's pulling out her eyebrows. That's no small matter." I whispered emphatically into his ear.

Papa patted my arm. "Hannah hasn't started school yet and may be lonely for attention." He continued, "I'm sure she'll be better once she makes friends. Try not to worry so much."

"But what are you doing now to help her? Is Rebecca reading to her at bedtime? Are you?" I persisted.

He dropped his head.

"But Papa, she needs love and attention right now." I paused. "I feel terrible I'm too far away to help."

"Dear, you can't be everywhere fixing everyone's problems. Hannah will be fine, and you have your own family to care for." Papa answered, turning his head toward the infants.

I wasn't satisfied with his answer but decided not to spoil the visit. I'd discuss the matter with Abe later.

Fortunately, the infants slept another hour, so we had time to catch up on family news. When the babies woke to feed, I took Hannah into the bedroom with me. "Feeding time is for girls only." I winked at her. 'If you'd like, you can hold Julian while I feed Sarah."

Hannah crinkled her face, eyes glistening. "Rebecca won't let me touch Baby Abby. I hate babies!" she cried out.

I was surprised she'd stop calling Rebecca "Mama." "Oh, sweetheart. When you were a baby, I played with you all the time. You were so cute. I loved you to pieces, still do." I pulled her into my arms for a long hug. "Let's make funny faces and sounds and get Julian to laugh while he waits for his turn."

We settled on the bed with the babies. I changed them both and held Sarah to my breast. Hannah hesitantly reached out to touch Julian's toes. A throaty coo escaped his lips as he caught Hannah's eyes. She giggled back. "He's funny."

Before long, Hannah was laughing and tickling Julian.

"Are you sure you don't like babies? You seem like a little mama to me."

Her eyes filled. "I miss you. Can I help you make lunch when they're done feeding?"

My breath caught at the sight of her sadness. "You certainly may." *Why wasn't anyone spending time with her?*

After setting the babies back in their crib, Hannah helped prepare the afternoon meal, arranging a platter of sliced brisket, tomatoes, and sautéed sweet onions. I sliced a freshly baked loaf of challah and set it in a basket. "We did it. You're an excellent helper."

Abe bent his head around the door frame. "The family is getting hungry. Those boys have bottomless pits for stomachs." He knelt, looking gently into Hannah's face. "Did you make all this lovely food?"

Hannah smiled, digging her toe into the floor.

I handed Abe plates and silverware while Hannah carried the bread. Together, we made several quick trips with the meat platter, a tub of mustard and fresh pickles, completely covering our little dinner table, finally announcing, "Lunch is ready! Sorry, we're tight for seating so the big people get chairs, and everyone else should find a cozy spot on the floor."

"It's like a picnic!" shouted Hannah, seated by a barrel of buttons.

"That's right." I hugged her little frame. "My neighbor Sadie made all the food. But next time, I'll bake the challah, and we'll have my cinnamon babka for dessert.

"This food is great!" exclaimed Nate.

I agreed. "A big improvement from what I served after Mama passed."

Papa teased me. "We weren't sure whether it was safe to eat here!"

I laughed. "I promise I won't poison you! Sadie, next door, has been a masterful teacher."

* * *

Papa patted his belly. "How about a stroll to walk off lunch? I'll bet the boys would like to see the bridge construction."

Joe and Nate jumped up from the floor and gathered the plates and silverware. Abe carried the large black pram we borrowed from Sadie down the three narrow flights, clanking against the staircase spindles the entire way. Papa and I each took an infant.

A hint of spring warmth infused the air, making us feel lighter. The sky was dotted with puffy, low white clouds, keeping the sun's glare in check. We passed other families like us, enjoying the gorgeous weather. Blossoming dogwood and cherry trees sweetly perfumed the air around us.

I reminisced, "This weather reminds me of the day you took all of us to Central Park for a picnic." Less than three years ago, it felt like a lifetime.

Papa smiled, holding Hannah's hand. "Hannah was just a small tot then."

We strolled along the water's edge until the skeleton of the unfinished bridge connecting Manhattan and Brooklyn came into its spellbinding view, jutting sharply into the deep blue sky. Abe broke from the group and walked to a concession on the sidewalk that sold pamphlets describing the construction.

"Can we buy one?" asked Joe. "I want to learn more about how they're building it."

"Of course, read it over, and next time, you can explain to me how they keep a structure this heavy from falling into the river," answered Abe as he paid the vendor.

Joe flipped through the pages. "There have been stories about the bridge construction in the newspaper. Did you know those tall gate-like structures are called caissons? They're buried deep in the ground, far below the riverbed. The architect's son got sick after coming up too fast in the elevator shaft. Some others died."

Joe had piqued Abe's interest. "I read that, too. Something happened to his blood. He's lucky he didn't die. Now, the lifts go up and down slowly. It takes hours."

Joe settled on a bench, pulled out his sketchpad, and began drawing a picture of the unfinished bridge. "I'm going to show this to my teacher when we get back to school."

Joe's fascination was no surprise. From the time he played with blocks, he was constantly building, following Papa around the farm with his hammer.

Abe, in awe of the child, offered, "How about you visit us again later this summer? The bridge should be further along. Maybe you'll be able to walk across."

I had my eye on Hannah the entire day. Not terribly interested in the bridge, her frown disappeared as the day wore on. She and I pushed the baby carriage and sang old songs she remembered from the months before my wedding. *"Sailing, sailing, over the bounding main, for many a stormy wind shall blow 'ere Jack comes home again...."* I was convinced all she needed was love and attention to bloom again.

* * *

After Papa and the children left, I was impatient to discuss Hannah with Abe. "It broke my heart to see Hannah so withdrawn. You remember what a happy imp she was a year ago? How could a little girl change so much?"

"I saw it too. She misses the loving touch of a mother. I can't imagine how Rebecca can be so indifferent to the attention she needs."

His words struck me. Most men I knew, like Papa, were honest and hard-working, viewing domestic situations pragmatically or not at all. I was reminded of my good fortune to find a husband with Abe's tenderness and depth. I hesitantly asked, "Would you consider letting her live with us? At least for the school year?"

He looked at me, perplexed. "Sweetheart, I don't think you can handle another child. Would you have the time to give her what she needs? And we have so little space."

I couldn't let go of the idea so easily. "You're right, but she's my baby sister, and I promised Mama I'd look after her." I sighed. "She needs me."

Abe paused, running his fingers through his beard. "I'm not crazy about the idea, but you can write to your Papa and see if he'll let her stay this summer. We can test the water and see how we do together. But remember, we must stay on top of the business, too."

I knew he was right. We were both cramped for space and the only way out was by saving a bigger nest egg. But hearing the reminder in the same breath with my sister bothered me, as if they remotely compared in importance. Without delay, I composed a letter to Papa for Abe to drop at the post office the next morning.

June 13, 1881

> *Dear Papa,*

> *It was wonderful seeing you last Sunday. Twins are a big under-taking, but I had so much practice learning from Mama, tending to Hannah. Every day, I love the babies more and more. Is that how you and Mama felt about us? Julian took an instant liking to Hannah. He's an affectionate child, cuddling with Sarah in their bassinet. The other day, I saw him holding her hand while they slept.*

> *On another topic, I'm concerned Rebecca might be overwhelmed, caring for everyone: Hannah, the boys, and an infant. That's quite a handful! Abe and I thought we could help by inviting Hannah to stay with us this summer? If it goes well, maybe she could stay on for school,*

too.

I was lucky to have Mama until I was fourteen. While the boys needed attention, they always looked to you while I trailed around behind Mama. I think that's why I enjoy motherhood. I promise I'll give Hannah the same love and attention Mama gave to me. As for now, the babies sleep so much that I'll have plenty of time to read to her.

Mama instilled in me a love for learning, and now I teach. I hope someday I'll finish high school and earn a proper teaching certificate.

Please let me know your thoughts. I have my fingers crossed that you'll decide to give it a try.

With buckets of love,

Tillie

Once the letter was on its way, I returned to my non-stop cycle around our home, hoping Papa would agree. If he did, we'd put the babies and Hannah in the front room and use the dinner table for Hannah's schoolwork until we moved to a bigger home. I was sure we could find a nook for the carriage downstairs so I could walk Hannah to school in the fall together with the babies.

Upon learning of my plan, Abe cautioned me. "As always, you're three steps ahead. You and the babies are already walking Hannah to school, and your Papa hasn't said 'yes' to the summer."

I snapped back, "Why are you such a wet blanket? I only want everyone in our family to be happy and healthy."

He took my arms, dropping his face to mine. "I don't want you exhausted. You just had twins, and they should be your main concern. Besides, button sales have picked up, and my customers are accustomed to a speedy delivery—all because of you."

I wiggled free, my voice sharp, "I'll help when the babies nap and when you're back home at night. The button work is easy for me. My sister is far more important than a barrel of buttons! Is that what you're really worried about?"

He dropped into the chair, a strained impatience lacing his voice. "You don't realize how much I've come to depend on your sharp eye with the books. And we've gotten weeks behind since the twins were born. I could lose my customers to competition if we don't clean up our end. Then we'll have bigger problems."

Once again, Abe was right. The babies had turned our lives upside down. Both of us were sleepwalkers. The night feedings and coaxing two infants to nap at the same time was daunting. Julian was easier, but Sarah wouldn't sleep unless I tied her to my chest with a shawl. And that was the only stretch of time I could concentrate on bookkeeping and assembling orders. I thought of Sadie, working every day with a full house. I would turn to her again for guidance. But still, I continued to worry about my little sister.

Two weeks later, I heard from Papa.

June 27, 1881

My Dearest Tillie,

Thank you for the wonderful day. And what an exciting time to live in Lower Manhattan, so many changes since I traveled downtown with my noisy chickens. The boys were thrilled to see the bridge and read the pamphlet Abe bought for them. Maybe one of them will study engineering. And our blessed Hannah seemed uncommonly happy spending time with you.

I left with concern for little Sarah and pray for her every night. If anyone can help her thrive, it's you. You have a remarkable ability to care for others.

It's in that spirit I must decline your generous offer to welcome Hannah in your home, even if only for the summer. Although I know your offer comes from a giving place, I don't think it's right to burden you with additional responsibility while you have newborns at home. They grow so fast, and you should enjoy every moment. Losing your mama taught me to smell the flowers while they bloom. So many of us, rich and poor, don't know how to appreciate our bounty. Try to enjoy yours.

But you have made me think hard about Hannah and I want to give her a happy childhood as you had. Hopefully by the time we visit next, things will sort themselves out.

With love,

Papa

I showed the letter to Abe. "I don't know what to do next. I'm afraid if I push Papa too hard, he'll feel like I'm criticizing him. What do you think?"

Abe sat back, studying Sarah's face as he rocked her to sleep.

I knew Papa made good points. Perhaps he was also afraid of insulting Rebecca. She was his wife, and he was committed to her happiness. I waited quietly while Abe considered.

"The best thing now is to do nothing. That's what I do with tough customers, so they can change their minds later and keep face," he said.

I considered his advice. After all, there was no harm. It left Papa open to reconsider.

I took out a fresh sheet of stationery and composed a new, short letter.

June 29, 1881

Dear Papa,

Thank you for writing back so quickly and for all the compliments. So much of who I am comes from you and Mama, so you can give yourself credit.

Abe and I are available to help Hannah in any way she needs. Please trust me when I say it's no sacrifice. She's my adorable, bright little sister, and I want to give her every advantage. One thing I have learned this past year is that the childhood years are far too brief.

We look forward to your next visit, and if we're lucky, the boys can walk across the bridge to Brooklyn before school starts.

I hope this time Rebecca and baby Abby come, too.

Love,

Tillie

* * *

Although thoughts of Hannah were never far from my mind, I spent the rest of the summer immersed in our lives, putting Abe's accounts in order and, of course, tending the infants, day, and night.

They were as opposite as babies could be. Julian slept long stretches and on occasion made it through the entire night. He was a voracious eater, outgoing, smiling at everyone he met. Resembling Abe, he'd begun to spout wavy dark hair and his deep blue eyes held an engaging sparkle.

But our little Sarah continued to struggle, only nibbling at mealtime. Although she gained weight, she remained markedly smaller than her brother. She had awakened to the world and was alert, but fussed around strangers, as if she sensed danger outside her little nest, always preferring the comfort and safety of her Mama and Papa's arms. Unlike Julian, her fine blond whips of hair were practically transparent, creating the appearance of a tiny bald bird. Her large eyes were a beautiful shade of green, like the ivy that clung to the farmhouse siding, and her nose a mere little button next to Julian's. Mrs. Simon's warning was correct. My priorities had changed since Julian and Sarah were born. Teaching at the Settlement House could wait for now.

When people on the street peeked into the carriage, they were surprised to learn the babies were twins. For once, something made my gossipy neighbors swallow their words in wonderment.

As we approached the end of summer, I received another letter from Papa. His news took me by surprise.

August 27, 1881

My dear Tillie,

We look forward to our visit on September 4th and the celebration of your seventeenth birthday. The boys can't wait to see the bridge. Do you think the span will be completed?

With summer ending, Rebecca and I had an opportunity to discuss our concern for Hannah. Rebecca feels Hannah has become even more withdrawn and thinks it may help her to spend time with you. Although I'll miss my little girl, I must do what is best for her. She continues to pull at her brows, a sign that she's unhappy.

I'm packing her favorite blanket, doll and will give you money for her keep and school. Hopefully, we'll see all of you for Rosh Hashanah this fall and celebrate the New Year together.

Rebecca is doubtful that she and the baby will be up for the long trip. But we can't wait to taste what our young cook has in store.
With love,
Papa

* * *

Papa's letter filled me with excitement. I couldn't wait to have my Hannah'la in our home. In the weeks leading up to Papa's visit, Abe and I purchased a small bed for Hannah, and I enrolled her in day school at the shul, the same class as Eva, next door. I knew her transition might be bumpy and wanted everything set in place.

The last year had been the fullest of my life, turning sixteen right before my wedding, moving, delivering premature twins just seven months later, and teaching at the Settlement House. But I knew I must make space for my little sister. Would Abe and I ever have time alone? Since the babies, our marriage had grown stronger, despite my mistrust in the beginning. I began to see a new side to Abe, fiercely devoted and loving to his little family.

With that trust came a willingness on his end to discuss his past. Lying together in bed one night after settling the babies in their bassinet, he recounted stories of his first wife, Ruth. "We couldn't have been more different. Unlike you, she was dark and petite and enjoyed the quiet of home, always sewing and cooking." He reflected, "Looking back, I'm not sure she was so keen to marry. She kept her feelings locked inside."

I was quick to react. "Not like me. I wear mine on my sleeve."

Abe appraised me. "It's far better that way. I never knew if she was happy or had accepted life with me as her fate." He stroked my hair. "Pregnancy finally ignited her. She was happiest becoming a mother. But God had other plans."

I couldn't imagine the loss of a child and a spouse. Now that I was a mother, it was unthinkable.

Abe rolled on his side and looked in my eyes, "I don't dare attempt to understand His larger plan, but I will say, no matter what cross words you and I have had, you were an unexpected, astounding gift to follow such a sorrowful time in my life."

* * *

Mid-morning, September 4th, I heard knocking at the door and my brothers frolicking.

Papa scolded, "Boys, keep your voices down."

Pulling the door open, I laughed with pleasure as they shouted, "Happy Birthday!"

Papa's mention of my birthday had set me spinning, and I had asked Sadie to teach me how to make a fancy cake with frosting, inviting her family to join us for dessert. It was beautiful when completed, a white cake with matching frosting and eighteen pink candles, one for good luck

As I ushered Papa and the boys inside, I said, "I'm so happy you're here. I invited Sadie's family to join us for dessert."

We crammed into the tiny parlor. All but Hannah, who hung back, head down, gripping her doll by the wrist, its porcelain hand dragging on the wood floor. Her unkempt hair was tangled and hung down her back, no bows nor braids, nor eyebrows for that matter. Although Hannah was petite by nature, she looked thinner than usual. Finally, she lifted her eyes, latching them to mine, as they filled with tears.

I knelt to hug her. "Oh, Hannah'la, I am so happy you're here." I kissed her cheek and stroked her hair. "I promise to make you happy. And I know Julian and Sarah will think you're a big sister, even though you're really their aunt. Before long, you'll teach them to play games with you."

I cast a concerned eye in Abe's direction while he cradled Sarah in his arm.

He leaned down, picked Hannah up with his free arm, and kissed her on the cheek. Using his deep, comforting voice, he said, "Did you know Eva's coming later to have cake with us? Would you like that?"

Hannah stopped sniffling, wiped her nose on her sleeve, and nodded.

Abe whispered in her ear, "And Tillie is the best big sister you could ever have. She'll teach you lots of fun things: puzzles, reading, numbers. She knows everything." He looked at Hannah's baby doll, now locked into the crook of her arm. "What's her name?"

"Millie," Hannah murmured. "She's scared."

My heart ached for my little sister. I leaned over and kissed the doll on the cheek. "Millie can sleep with you in your new bed and take a bubble bath tonight. Sunday is bath night around here," I gazed at the doll, knowing she was an extension of Hannah. "Is she getting hungry? That was a long trip this morning."

Hannah nodded.

"How about we wash up, have lunch, and then we'll invite the Sterns for birthday cake? That'll leave us time to see your new school and walk to the bridge." I turned to face the boys, "I hope you're not too disappointed. You know, it's behind schedule."

To my relief, once Eva arrived, the girls instantly hit it off, playing together with their dolls as if they were life-long friends. Before long, a happy smile replaced Hannah's frown. Eva ran back to her apartment to retrieve all her baby dolls and the two found a little corner to play make believe with their babies.

Later in the day, after a visit at the school to show Hannah her new classroom, we walked further south until we came to the bridge. Its construction had continued to lag, one unexpected delay after another. The newspaper was predicting an opening the following May, but no one was certain. The majestic bridge rose from the river, an unfinished statue. Although the two towers and suspension cables were complete, they supported an unfinished roadway that appeared most dangerous.

"Too bad it's Sunday. No one's working," said Nate.

"It still looks beautiful standing above the East River on such a fine day," remarked Papa.

Joe pointed to the bridge. "I was hoping to watch them work on the suspension cables. What a view they must have way up there."

"I'd be too terrified to open my eyes." I mused.

Joe had a full list of facts he'd prepared to share with us, workday or not. "There will be a separate walkway from one end to the other, high over the traffic, so walkers and bicyclists can travel from Brooklyn into Manhattan without the danger of getting hit by a carriage."

We listened, fascinated by the extraordinary engineering details.

Some of our neighbors were talking about relocating to Brooklyn for less expensive, roomier apartments once the bridge was finished. Sadie had been discussing it for months and left me wondering if we should look there, too.

Chapter Eighteen

Winter struck New York City at the end of 1881 with a blistering brutality I'd never experienced, even during my years on the farm. Bone-chilling temperatures dropped below freezing, and the windows froze shut for two weeks, making it impossible to draw fresh air into our home, even for a moment or two. Our tiny coal stove barely heated the kitchen, leaving us stiff from the cold. Some nights, Abe and I huddled in our bed under layers of wool blankets, placing the two babies and Hannah between our bodies. How could we live in a modern city yet survive in such a primitive manner? Our apartment was one step above a cave.

To worsen matters, there was little to no air circulation in the building. With windows closed and coal stoves burning, the air grew thick and stale. Day after day, the growing stench of unwashed families and their dirty chamber pots permeated the air as tenants refused to brave the frigid outdoor temperatures to use the privies. The clean water spigot was always frozen shut, and we were forced to light a fire beneath it to coax out fresh water, returning to our apartment with frozen fingers. Although I insisted Hannah use the privy with me during the day, the smell was horrific. The nightsoil men had quit coming on a regular basis. I couldn't blame Hannah. I hated going out there, too. I'd sent a note to the landlord pleading for help, but he ignored me.

"I don't want to go outside!" Hannah complained.

I had to insist. "You're a big girl like me. We'll go together."

Despite the cold, Hannah attended school and Abe stayed on top of business. The demand for clothing, particularly winter garments, was growing faster than we could have ever imagined as waves of European immigrants poured into the ports. Button requests shifted from decorative pearl and ivory dress buttons to utilitarian metal and wood, all used for overcoats and work shirts. Our daily routine became frenzied.

Abe bundled up each morning to make his rounds, hefting full orders over his shoulder and returning home with a growing number of requisitions to fill. Once our husbands left for work, Sadie and I alternated watching Sarah and Julian while the other walked Hannah and Eva back and forth to school through deep snow and howling wind.

Within two weeks of the New Year, Hannah returned from school complaining of a sore throat. Her forehead was burning hot. After changing her into a nightshirt, I pushed her cot to the furthest corner of the parlor and tucked her in with her doll, Millie. I made tea with honey to soothe her throat, sitting beside her until she fell asleep like Mama once did with me. By the next day, her fever was gone, but her illness had blossomed into a thick head cold. Now, I understood Dr. Boro's concern. We moved Sarah and Julian back to our bedroom, keeping them as far away from Hannah as we could. But it was nearly impossible to isolate Hannah in such a small stuffy home.

I cried in desperation. "Abe, what'll we do if the babies catch it?"

Although he worried too, all he could do was shrug and shake his head. "Tillie, we've gotten them this far and they're over a half year. Eventually, one or the other will catch a cold."

The weather turned from cold to arctic snow, continuing for days. Hannah's coughing and sneezing was relentless, the apartment littered with nose rags. Within a week, we'd all caught her head cold. Although Abe's forehead was on fire, he bundled up and trudged to the Clinic, beckoning Dr. Boro, who arrived at our apartment later that day.

Dr. Boro removed his coat and warmed his hands by the stove. "I heard coughing coming through apartment doors on every floor. This influenza's infected the whole building. Whoever designed these apartments should be taken out and shot." He scowled. "There's absolutely no air circulation, and it stinks like an open sewer in every wretched building on the block. There's no way to protect yourself from disease in this God-forsaken place." He glanced at Hannah's concerned face, adding, "I didn't mean shot with a gun, darling, but definitely punished!"

His tone switched to a soft hmm as he bent over the crib, gently pulling the little ones out from beneath their blankets. "Ah, now, let's check the babies first." He listened to their chests and spoke directly to each child. "Julian, your lungs sound clear. How about we keep them that way by having you sleep upright? If you don't want to nurse every feeding, mama can give you a bottle of warm water and honey to keep you hydrated. I think you're fine."

Sarah was next. "You've grown so much since I saw you last. Mama and Papa are taking good care of you. Hmm, I do hear a bit of wheezing. I'm going to talk to your parents about what to do for you." He then moved to the bed's edge and looked at Hannah. "Hello, I'm Doctor Boro. It's your turn now."

Hannah walked over to him, gripping her doll to her body.

"It's alright," I said. "Let the kind doctor listen to your chest."

"First, Millie!" Hannah pushed her doll in the doctor's face.

"Certainly," answered Dr. Boro.

Hannah studied him carefully as he listened to Millie's fabric chest.

He turned to Hannah. "Millie sounds good. Are you ready?"

Hannah stood stiffly in front of him while he listened to her chest and checked her ears. "You're both healthy little girls. Hannah, your cold is getting much better, but I want you to stay home until we stop getting new cases at school, probably another week." He looked at me. "Lots of warm water, tea, and honey to help her cough. I think Hannah and her friend are on the mend."

He then gestured for Abe and me to follow him into the outer hallway. "I'm concerned about both babies, but particularly Sarah. Her lungs are congested, and we need to get her fever down. Put her in a sitting position to help her breathe and give her plenty of warm fluids with honey." He looked at the stove. "Also, boil water and hold the steaming kettle near her face. It'll help break up the congestion."

I grabbed Abe's hand, worried. "What if her fever continues?"

"Have Abe fetch me if it hasn't broken by morning, and I'll come back. In the meantime, the same goes for the two of you. Lots of fluids and try resting between caring for the children. They need healthy parents."

He glanced at the closed hallway window. "Force the window open and air your apartment out. Every day. There's no ventilation in here." He huffed in frustration. turned on his heels and was off to his next stop.

I rested my stuffy head on Abe's shoulder. Turning to look in his glassy eyes, I said with a burst of resolve, "We will beat this damn thing! But when it's past, I insist we move somewhere better. I can't put up with this filth another day."

"I agree," Abe said as he moved to dislodge the window.

By the next morning, all of us felt somewhat better. All except little Sarah. She continued to struggle as fever gripped her frail body, refusing to take my breast or drink from the bottle. We tried to force her to swallow fluids through an eye dropper, but the honey water dribbled down her quivering chin. Every hour through the night, we heated the teapot for a steam treatment, but she worsened until she stopped coughing entirely. By morning, her whimper was meek compared to Julian's angry howl.

Without a discussion, Abe bundled up and headed to the Clinic. Before long, Dr. Boro returned and listened to Sarah's chest. He sighed deeply and led us back to the hallway.

More bad news?

"I'm always frank with my patients and particularly their parents. Right now, Sarah's lungs sound full of illness and her fever hasn't broken. The poor child is weak. At this point, all we can do is continue with the steam, keep her body upright and hold her, so she feels safe and comforted. I'll return in a few hours to check again. I know you're both doing your best. This year's influenza has been an extreme battle for babies and the old."

"Could she die?" I whispered, my deepest fear.

Dr. Boro had deep circles under his eyes. I wondered how many other children were struggling.

"She could, if this is pneumonia," he said softly. "But we're not quite there. Give her a chance to fight. You've done an impressive job. Many parents wouldn't have the fortitude to bring a premature baby to six months." He gently squeezed my shoulder.

But all I heard was "pneumonia," a word portending death. I broke. Tears streamed down my cheeks.

He sighed deeply. "Be patient, keep doing exactly what you're doing. And perhaps, pray. Would you like me to send the rabbi?"

I shook my head. We would forge forward and help her recover.

With that he placed his hat back on his head, threw on his coat, and trudged down the stairs.

Sadie, whose door was slightly cracked, stepped into the hallway. "Tillie, let me keep Hannah and Julian here with Eva. That way, you can give Sarah your full attention."

I looked at my dear friend through my bloodshot, weary eyes. "I'm so scared. She was doing so well until she caught this damn thing." My tears flowed. "I wish I could help her more. I don't know what I'd do without you."

Sadie embraced me. "Let me pull some clothing and diapers together and move the other children to my place. I'll bring Julian back when he's hungry, or I can give him a bottle, whatever you prefer."

"I fed him a short time ago. Let's see where we are in a few hours." I sniffled with painful emptiness.

Abe and I settled in with Sarah. I put the teapot on the stove for steam and rocked, supporting her little body in an upright position.

Hannah ran back into our apartment to grab her doll, smiled, then darted back to play with Eva. Before long, I heard the girls giggling. The sound of children's laughter, the sound of healthy, lifted me.

Every hour, we alternated rocking Sarah with the steaming teapot near her face while the other rested, both struggling to stay optimistic. The morning dragged on with no change in her condition. By lunchtime, Sadie brought Julian back to nurse.

"What a relief to see Julian perky," I said, too tired to cry. "Sarah's still droopy and warm. I wish Julian could lend her some of his strength; she needs it."

Sadie handed Julian to me, her eyes deep with understanding. "How about you rest for a while after he eats? You're exhausted, and this could go on for a long time before she snaps out of it."

I nodded as Abe took my place with Sarah, and I moved to the bed to nurse Julian.

"I'll get you both tea and honey, so you stay hydrated, too."

We were interrupted by a knock at the door. Sadie answered. "Hello, Mrs. Simon. Come in."

Mrs. Simon handed Sadie several containers. "I saw Dr. Boro earlier, and he thought Tillie and Abe could use an extra set of hands. Here's some soup and a honey cake. Tell me, how can I help?"

"I'm glad you're here," Sadie answered. "I was just making tea and need to get back to the other children. I'll return soon for Julian."

Mrs. Simon set the food in the kitchen and walked to the rocking chair, where Abe held Sarah upright. "Has there been any change?" She felt the baby's forehead, her own creasing in concern. "What did Dr. Boro say?"

As Abe repeated the doctor's instructions, Mrs. Simon picked up Sarah and reached to the stove to get the kettle. "Let me get the tea and help with the little one while you finish with Julian, and then you both rest." Mrs. Simon gazed with disquiet at the listless child. "Poor thing, innocent as the first drops of dew."

Dizzy from worry and exhaustion I welcomed her help. I finished Julian's feeding, then took him along with the food across the hall to Sadie, who had left moments earlier to tend the other children.

Hannah greeted me at the door. "How's baby Sarah? Is she better yet? Can I see her?"

I hugged Hannah, doll, and all. "She's still having a rough time. How about you see Sarah before dinner? For now, play with Eva." I showed her the honey cake. Here's a treat Mrs. Simon made for us. You and Eva can have a slice after lunch."

Hannah eyed the cake greedily. "Mmm."

Healthy and sick—a world of difference, yet only a narrow hallway apart. Life seemed like a constant circus of ups and downs. For the past six months I'd been struggling against gale force winds, supporting Sarah and trying to stay abreast of Julian and Hannah's needs. Abe and I barely had time to say "Hello."

I walked back to my apartment and yawned. *After we get past this nightmare, we'll find a new home. Everything will be alright,* I told myself. *It must be.*

I reopened my door and saw Mrs. Simon's troubled face. My stomach dropped. She whispered, "Sit down, dear. I think we're losing Sarah. She's barely breathing. Take her, and I will wake Abe."

"No, no, please, no." I cried out, taking Sarah from Mrs. Simon's arms, holding her face close to my ear. I could scarcely hear her breath. Her beautiful green eyes were shut, and her face was white as a sheet—my porcelain angel. "Oh Sarah, no, please don't go. We love you so much." I sobbed, recalling the pain of losing Mama. *Was my life cursed?*

Abe knelt and gently placed his arms around both of us as Sarah struggled and finally took her last shallow breath. The three of us sat, frozen in place, as the Angel of Death took Sarah from us. Moments later, I set her tender body on the center of our bed. The two of us lay on either side, wrapping our arms around our daughter's body, sobbing. There were no more words, kettles of steam, or rocking. We wept until our tears ran dry. Then, without realizing it, I slipped into my own death-like sleep.

* * *

Later that evening, Rabbi and Dr. Boro appeared at our door with a group of men from the building. Dr. Boro entered the bedroom alone, sitting beside me, holding my hand while I cried. As my tears ebbed, he said, "Tillie, you are a devoted mother. This week, we've lost three babies on the block from this insipid flu. You couldn't have done more."

I buried my head in his shoulder.

He took out his handkerchief and wiped his own wet eyes. "I'm so sorry I couldn't save her." He shook his head. "Many others are grieving tonight.

My heart is broken for your families."

His composure returned, and he added, "Remember how well Julian and Hannah recovered because of your care. They are strong children and will be God's gifts to you for the rest of your life."

Abe stood at the doorway, watching us with the saddest eyes I'd ever seen on his handsome face. *This must feel like his worst nightmare had returned.*

Dr. Boro spoke to both of us. "The grief workers from Chevra Kadisha should be here soon. Mrs. Simon will direct them to prepare the body while I join Rabbi in prayer with Abe. I'll be in the parlor if you need me."

Mrs. Simon, who'd remained in the apartment all afternoon, took Dr. Boro's place at the foot of the bed and wiped my tear-stained face with a cool rag. She helped me stand, wrapping her arms tightly around me, hugging until her love found its way into my sorrowful heart. "Let the tears flow, child. We are all in pain with you."

An hour later, we stood against the side wall of the tiny bedroom, watching as the Chevra Kadisha women undressed Sarah, cleansed her skin, and wrapped her in a white shroud. I stood frozen, angry they were preparing her body, my child's body, for burial. Thoughts of the earth shoveled over her filled me with hopeless despair.

By the time they covered her face, her body had turned grey and shrunken. She was no longer my baby girl. Little Sarah had left us hours ago.

A surprising burst of anger shot through me. This was God's plan? For an innocent life to come into the world weakened from the start. To fight and lose her painful battle to live? Leave her Mama and Papa's love? The hole in my heart grew larger by the moment. I could scarcely breathe from my mounting anguish. I reached for the small cold bundle, clutching her to my chest. "My baby, my baby, no!"

The women stepped back, allowing me this final embrace. I knew she was no more and, after my anger ebbed, I returned to my senses, knowing they must take her body away. One woman fixed a black cloth over our single mirror in the bedroom as tradition dictated. It would remain there for seven days.

In the next room, Rabbi had gathered ten men, the minyan, the minimum needed to hold a prayer service, and handed each a book. They recited the evening ceremony, chanting a sad melody, rocking their bodies to the prayers as our little home pulsed with sorrow. An hour later, the service ended with the Mourner's Kaddish, an ancient prayer for the dead.

Without my knowing, Papa had slipped inside the apartment sometime during the ritual. I hadn't realized he was there until I peeked around the bedroom door. "Papa!" I ran to him, despite knowing I should stay in a separate room. But nothing could hold me back from his arms. He embraced me tightly, rocking back and forth while reciting the prayer from memory. *Yit'gadal v'yit'kadash sh'mei raba...*

I calmed, and he spoke. "I had this bad feeling. Last week your letter left me worried. I heard the fear in your words, so I came right down to check on you." His voice caught in his throat. "I'm so sorry. My poor little Sarah."

"All that matters is you've come," I steadied myself, "for Hannah too. She's in Sadie's apartment and doesn't understand. Having you here will help." I sniffled and searched his eyes. "I know Mama will care for baby Sarah in heaven."

Papa pulled me closer, patting his eyes on his sleeve.

Abe strode over, giving Papa a hug, and patting his back warmly. "Sam, I hope you can sit *shiva* with us. The rabbi will hold the funeral in the morning, and Sarah will be buried across the river in Brooklyn near the new synagogue. After that, we'll sit for the week. We can set up space for you and Hannah in the parlor."

"Of course. The boys know how to handle the farm while I'm away, and I'll stay and help with Hannah."

I was relieved to have Papa with us. One look at Hannah's shocked face told me she'd need his extra love to get through the loss.

* * *

How could emptiness feel so heavy? I wore Sarah's hollow place like a leaden weight. No matter what I did or said, I couldn't shake it. Hannah descended into a well of sadness, too. She spent hours on Papa's lap with her doll drawn to her chest while he read and concocted magical stories. Although Abe and I held and comforted each other at night, Papa's presence was what I needed most. Everything about him—the familiar tenor of his voice, the smell of hay in his clothing, his brow that creased in the most understanding way—exuded an understanding of sorrow that came from a full life of experience. Every morning, he gathered us to recite Psalm 23: *Yea, though I walk through the valley of the shadow of death, I will fear no evil: for thou art with me; thy rod and thy staff they comfort me.*

Despite my hollowness, the next week, I found shiva visits from neighbors and friends from the Settlement House comforting. They brought delicious sandwiches and pastries, and Sadie kept a kettle warm on the stove for tea. Hannah and Julian enjoyed the company, too, especially when our guests brought their children along. Little Julian's smiles were a constant source of entertainment, at times also boring their way through my sadness.

But even good-natured Julian felt the change. At night, when he reached for Sarah, his crib partner, he sensed something was amiss. The first night, not feeling her beside him, he clutched Sarah's doll and held it to his face.

Abe's eyes misted. "Sarah's doll carries her scent. He feels her presence."

* * *

I'd been unrealistic, not fully comprehending the enormity of raising three children, now two. Should I send Hannah home with Papa? At least until Abe could keep his word about a bigger, airier apartment building. How could the atmosphere of our sad home be healthy for someone so young?

"Abe, maybe we took on too much. You warned me. I don't know if I'm any good for Hannah, or Julian, either, for that matter," I lamented. "I feel such heaviness inside. The pain won't stop."

He drew me close. "Darling, we need to keep this week for mourning. Remember how long it took after your mama passed? It was the same for me when Ruth and the baby were no more. I promise it will get better."

I didn't think I could bear the agony. "How long will it take?"

"Every day, the pain will lessen a tiny bit. We must save big decisions for clear heads. Hannah deserves better than a hasty, emotional decision from either of us." Abe drew an even breath. "Let's see how we feel at the end of the week."

His words rang in my head. I knew from losing Mama that the deep sadness would eventually melt into bittersweet memories stored forever in my heart. I also knew my Papa. As a practical man, he wouldn't have the same time to indulge Hannah back on the busy farm. Setting my thoughts aside, I followed Abe's advice, limiting my mind to the six months of memories Sarah left me to cherish.

Abe and my grief bound us with the same power as our early lovemaking. For the first time in months, we embraced while sleeping and kept Julian near our bed. Would happiness ever return? Each day that passed felt like an eternity.

After the end of the week-long shiva, I was strong enough to run the household on my own. As if the heavens knew we needed relief, we were greeted with a mild snap in the weather. What a blessing to open the windows and air the apartment thoroughly, removing that horrible black mirror covering. Abe brought extra buckets of water upstairs, and I scrubbed the illness and sadness out of our home.

The day after sitting shiva ended, I took Hannah for a walk. "How are you doing, Hannah'la?"

She squinted in the bright sunlight reflecting off the snow, not fully understanding my question.

I tried again. "Is your cold all better? I don't hear coughing."

"My cold's better. Where's baby Sarah now?"

I squatted, looking directly into her eyes. "She's in our hearts with Mama."

"I don't remember Mama. Would you tell me about her so she can be in my heart, too?" Hannah asked.

Her words brought tears to my eyes. How could a six-year-old comprehend the gravity of life and death? "Of course, I will tell you many stories about Mama. She loved you so much. We'll find a place in your heart for her, too." Then I changed the subject. "Papa will head back to the farm tomorrow. Would you like to go with him?"

I waited, giving her time to think.

"Can't I stay? I like it here with you and Abe and Julian and Eva and Sadie." Hannah clutched my hand, listing our names thoughtfully as they came to her.

The noises of the street, the clopping of horse hooves, vendors shouting out wares, and children playing filled the air. I let her decision settle through the thick blanket of street life.

"I'm glad, sweetheart. We love you, too." I hugged her for a long time, close to my heart and those lost loved ones stored within.

I wasn't certain she understood, but I would respect her choice. For a while, sadness would be part of our lives. Where I had hoped to fulfill my promise to Mama by taking care of my sister, Hannah's love for me was an equally strong potion.

Chapter Nineteen

April 1882

As the harsh winter of 1882 relaxed its grip and gave way to spring, a new energy entered my fragile household. I had returned to the Settlement House, Julian in his carriage and Hannah at my side, teaching English while also working at a frenzied speed, keeping pace with Abe's bookkeeping. Button demand had soared over the frigid winter. At every dinner, we discussed the same two topics: moving our home and expanding the business. Both simple wishes buoyed me, distracting me from my sadness. It would be a long time before I could discuss baby Sarah and maintain my composure.

At the end of each week, Abe and I reviewed the ledger, highlighting payments and additional savings. With the unending growth in orders, our nest egg increased at an astonishing speed.

But there were new, practical considerations driving our urgency to move. Julian was crawling everywhere, and if we left the door to the outer hallway open by accident, he scooted, lightning-fast, out of our apartment.

"Watch out, Julian!" I shouted as he crawled perilously near the steep staircase that zigzagged down the three flights to the bottom. I knew where he was heading with no thought of the dangers that might be lurking.

"Sadie is at work. No treats now." I snatched him into my arms, planting a big kiss on his chubby cheek.

The next morning, Julian was up with the birds. Abe had pulled him out of his crib, and he was crawling about the apartment when curiosity got the better of the little boy, and he tipped over the chamber pot. The foul contents splashed all over the wood floor.

The smell hit my nose before I could open my eyes, still crusty with sleep. "I can't take this any longer. We must get indoor plumbing." I hopped over the splatters into the kitchen and returned with the pail of last night's dishwater and a dry towel. Kneeling on the floor, I looked at Abe while he held Julian. "Don't all the new buildings come with indoor toilets?"

Abe wiped off Julian. "Do you remember my promise after our wedding?"

"About an apartment nicer than the hotel?" I scoffed.

"I haven't forgotten. I plan to keep my word."

I thought back to those two days of blissful romance and the turbulent year that followed. "We paid dearly to get to that promise." *Would Sarah have gotten so ill if we lived elsewhere, somewhere healthier?*

Abe patted the edge of the bed. "Here, sit with me. Where do you want to live? Still thinking about Brooklyn?"

"I had thought so, but I'd prefer to stay nearby if we can find the right place." I gathered the dirty rags and set them in the wash bin. "I feel settled here, with true friends. Hannah's happy at school, and it's convenient for you."

"Are you sure?"

I blinked back my tears. "I like my friends here. But some days, I'm holding on by a thread."

Abe scooped me into his arms alongside Julian. "It's been rough, but you and I are strong and have faith. In time, we'll be fine."

I dug my head into his shoulder, nodding.

"I've heard about a few new buildings nearby. I'll check this week and see what's available. We've saved more than enough money."

I leaned his way, filled with relief, whispering in his ear, "I love you."

That weekend, we gathered the children and spent the day weaving through the busy streets, viewing available apartments in the new buildings. Finally, all weary by day's end, with Julian whining for his dinner, we settled on the perfect place at the corner of Clinton and Stanton near Hamilton

Fish Park. It had everything we'd hoped for.

Our new home was four times the size of our tenement apartment on Orchard Street, with three bedrooms and a luxurious private bathroom with a sink, toilet, and large bathtub, all with running hot and cold water. The building's basement had a large gas water heater that forced heat through individual apartment radiators during the winter and piped hot water to the bathroom and kitchen year-round. Each apartment had a fireplace in the parlor for additional warmth on frigid winter days. Simply gazing at the unlit fireplace brought back the crackling sounds and woody smell I missed from the farm. I could barely wait for our modern city home.

But as I reveled in the luxuries we'd soon possess, I was haunted by my recurrent thought. *Would we have lost Sarah if we'd moved sooner?* I knew torturing myself was pointless, but it was impossible to stop. I still craved the warmth of her sweet little body, holding her to my chest for feedings, gazing into her innocent eyes. If only my baby girl was moving here with us.

* * *

In a few short weeks, it was time to move. Abe arranged for a local wagon to schlep the few belongings we packed into the rented barrels.

Abe stood, hands on hips, in our new parlor. "I can't believe it only took a morning to get everything from Orchard Street to here. What a difference an elevator makes!"

The apartment was vacuous after we arranged our few belongings. We owned the sparest of furniture: a small wooden table and four mismatched chairs, two beds, a crib, and a dresser with an attached mirror. Every extra cent had gone into savings. There were no carpets to cover the parquet floors, no drapes, nor furniture for the parlor. Nonetheless, I was content. Furnishings could wait.

Hannah danced from room to room with Julian, now toddling close behind, as if this spacious area was their playground.

"Hannah, let me give you a tour of our new home." I reached for her small hand. "We have a fireplace, just like on the farm. Abe and I will get cozy chairs someday, but for now, we'll put our dinner table in front of the hearth.

We walked from the empty dining area through an arched walkway into the kitchen, a modern fantasy equipped with a sink plus hot and cold faucets, an icebox for food storage, and a long preparation counter. Cooking would be simpler and after dinner clean-up a quick matter.

"Open the icebox doors. See how cold it is? There's a big block of ice on one side that melts onto the tray." I was pleased there was enough space to store meals for several days and additional room to keep milk and eggs cold.

Best of all, we had electric lighting in every room. We no longer needed messy, dangerous candles or smelly oil lamps with their risk of fire.

Mama would be so excited if she could see us now.

Knowing Hannah would need to relieve herself soon, I led her to the bathroom. "Let me show you the bathroom and how to use the toilet." When I pulled the cord on the water closet, she ran out of the room screaming.

"What's the matter?" I called after her.

Hannah shouted back, "I'll go down the pipe!"

I led her back to the bathroom. "No, you won't. I'll come with you until you're not afraid. But let's not show Julian how to use it yet. It's not a toy."

Later that evening, after tucking in the children, I drew a hot bath, adding bath salt and lavender to the tub, the scent of a new beginning. The tub was large enough for Abe and me to sit upright, facing each other. It was a welcome warmth and a treat after the stresses of moving. We talked about the day and our dreams.

Abe took my feet in his hands and massaged them with soap. "I know it looks empty, but I'd like to fill the till before we spend money again."

"Oh, that feels good." I melted, my head against the tub. *Who cares if we wait?* "Can you believe we're finally here? If only we'd moved sooner." I fell silent.

"I know, darling. I wish we had gotten us out of that hellhole sooner." He halted. We both knew the words he would say next. There was no need to say them aloud.

In my grief, I'd lost touch with how much Abe had lost—a wife and now, two babies. "Abe, remember what Dr. Boro said. We can't blame ourselves. We had a plan and did the best we could. Remember, Julian was also premature. Many families would've lost both infants."

He nodded, looking off into the air.

Twisting my body around, I shifted to the other end of the tub and leaned my back against Abe's warm chest. We relaxed until the water cooled and the pain of loss dissolved. Drying off, we walked past our nightclothes and climbed under the covers, gently caressing each other, seamlessly shifting into the dance of ages, starting a new chapter together.

Chapter Twenty

A week later, I greeted Abe at the door, jumping up and down with excitement. "Guess what? Sadie and Max stopped by and have decided to move to our building instead of across the bridge in Brooklyn. They took an apartment like ours upstairs!"

Abe clapped his hands. "I had a feeling they might. You two are as thick as thieves." He looked into my eyes. "I'm happy to see your beautiful smile again."

Sadie's family settled in a month later, and we wasted no time resuming our morning coffee routine, thrilled with our new surroundings. We sat in the same mismatched wooden chairs while we fantasized about future furnishings, our voices echoing in empty parlors.

"The entire clothing business is taking off," Sadie sipped from her favorite teacup with the tiny blue flowers and hummingbirds. "Max found a larger space on Canal for his factory and is buying six sewing machines."

Always fascinated with the new inventions popping up around us, I asked, "How do they work?"

"The machine stitches the fabric instead of sewing by hand. The seamstress uses her legs to peddle, like a bicycle. The peddling makes the needle move up and down. It's so fast!" Sadie's excitement was contagious. "Once they're set up, you'll visit, and I'll demonstrate."

"I'd love that." I thought back to the hours Mama and Rebecca spent sewing simple garments.

"Sewing machines are changing everything for us. Now we're getting large orders directly from the designers at the big stores."

I wondered what would become of the dressmakers. Later that evening, after the children were in bed, I shared Sadie and Max's factory decision with Abe.

He set the newspaper on the table. "She's right. Now I have more store designers as customers than dressmakers and tailors." His exhale sounded troubled. "There's a lot of money in this business."

I studied his face. "Then why aren't you happier?"

He pulled at his beard. "I'm nervous what it'll cost us." His eyes caught mine. "For instance, I'll need a warehouse, too. Our button inventory is getting out of hand. With the autumn and winter supply coming, there'll be no more room in this big parlor." He twisted, pointing to the wooden crates and barrels overtaking the back half the room. "At this rate, we won't have space to eat."

"Have you started looking? Do you think the growth will last?" I asked. In under a year, sales had quadrupled, but with losing Sarah, moving, and the other children's needs, I hadn't taken the time to examine the books closely.

"Absolutely. Look around us—electricity, sewing machines, iceboxes; there's no going back. These machines have changed everything about our world. We either keep in step, or we'll fall behind, and someone else will eat our supper."

I thought more about the orders I'd filled over the summer. Where Abe once received the lion's share from dressmakers for a dozen suits or dresses at a clip, now he was handling more than one hundred dresses in a single order, most from store designers contracting directly with factories like Max's, some asking specifically for Abe's buttons.

The dinner dishes sat on the counter while Abe continued "Can you help me figure out how much inventory we'll need? Last week I stopped in at Lord and Taylor's new store on 20th Street. They already had their fall line of women and men's clothing in the display windows. And I heard that they were taking bids from factories for lots of one hundred, in different sizes no less. I'm sure Bloomingdale's will do the same."

My brain buzzed with calculations. I reached into the box where I kept invoices. "Let's go over your orders from last week." I flipped through the stack. "You're right. Their delivery deadlines are much tighter. We'll need to keep inventory close by."

Abe rubbed his forehead. "I wish I could figure this out, but numbers have always been difficult for me." He stood, drawing a deep breath, and began pacing the open floor space. "The factories need to keep their notions on hand to work quickly. That means needles, thread, buttons, and lace. They're buying in bulk, too. It makes sense for us to sell them notions, too. Good thing I can get them locally."

I laid out a few large orders on the table and took a clean sheet of paper from my journal. "Let's figure out what we'll need. An average dress with long sleeves uses twenty or thirty buttons; that's three thousand buttons for just one of these one-hundred-unit orders. Then, I'll tally up the notions. We'll keep enough for the season in storage ahead of time."

Abe shuffled through the invoices in a panic, dropping several to the floor. "I've never seen anything like this. It's a new world." His forehead was shiny from perspiration. "It's going to cost a fortune to buy inventory."

I tried to remain calm, but his panic shook me. "Where will we get that kind of money? We can't have our buttons in a steamer somewhere over the Atlantic holding up the factories."

Abe groaned. "I dread taking a bank loan. The memories...I can't go through that again. I told you about what happened in 1870 when the banks went under and called in loans. My poor parents were forced to sell everything on the cheap, and we had to give up our home and move to the tenements."

"Say no more!" I held up my hands, my voice agitated. "There's no way in hell we're going back to that disgusting place, ever! We'll homestead out west first." I sat quietly, my brain churning. "We'll simply grow slowly and buy as much inventory as we can from our earnings. Maybe take one bank loan to get us over the first hurdle."

There would be risk, but I was certain that without taking this chance, we could lose his business. Either way had peril. "Do you think the stores could pay part in advance? That way, we wouldn't need to borrow so much."

"I could try. I have a good relationship with Bloomingdale's. They might do it. I'll make a stop there tomorrow." Abe stopped pacing.

Another idea struck me. "Why don't you talk to Max? He should have extra room in his new space, especially in the beginning. That will buy us time before needing a warehouse, and it would be good for him, too. A little extra cash for Max and his buttons will be steps away when he needs them."

A broad smile washed over Abe's face, melting away the worry lines etched on his forehead. "Brilliant!" He kissed me on the forehead. "Why didn't I think of that?"

* * *

I felt alive again. The changes in Abe's company were thrilling, and I was eager to do my part. However, a practical concern continued to nag me. I did not want another pregnancy. My once carefree attitude in bed was tempered by endless responsibility and chores for Hannah and Julian, never anticipating the all-encompassing role of mother. I had helped with Hannah on the farm but was unaware of the nighttime responsibilities and the exhaustion the next day, especially when the children were sick. And, of course, I continued to ache for my little Sarah. No new baby could possibly replace her. Besides, I had concerns about another pregnancy, having lost one young friend in the neighborhood to childbed fever. So, we made love less often, and I pushed Abe to withdraw before he finished.

The morning of Abe's meeting with Bloomingdale's, I dropped Hannah at school, then pushed Julian's carriage across the street to the Clinic. Marta was standing by the reception desk when I entered.

"It's so nice to see you, Tillie! Don't tell me," she paused, smiling, "are you with child again?"

"Heavens, no! And I'd like to keep it that way," I exclaimed. "But I need your help. Any chance you can squeeze me in this week?"

"Sure, as a matter of fact, I'm free right now. My first appointment didn't show." Marta led me back to an exam space while Julian played in his carriage by the receptionist.

Sitting on the exam table, I asked, "How can I prevent another pregnancy, beyond the obvious? Abe and I agreed we would wait for another baby. It isn't a good time right now."

"There are ways, but legally, I'm not allowed to discuss them. Do you know about the Comstock Act?"

I shook my head, confused.

"It was passed about ten years ago, and it outlawed the distribution of pregnancy prevention devices. Completely ridiculous, laws concocted by hateful controlling men."

I was astonished. "Are you joking?"

Marta looked directly into my eyes. "No, I'm not. I'll help you, but only because we're friends. You must promise not to let anyone know, or I could go to jail."

Still flabbergasted, I asked, "Why would the government make such a thing illegal? There's no Jewish law forbidding it that I know of, and there shouldn't be public laws against it either."

"I agree. But it's men who make the laws." She rolled her eyes. "They prefer us homebound, making babies. And they cite the Christian Bible, no less," Marta scoffed. "It keeps families trapped in horrible poverty. Some of the women I see can scarcely take care of the children they have; forget about adding more."

Her words brought back memories of the hungry child I'd passed on the street less than a year ago. How did this make any sense?

Marta, now visibly upset, continued, "The worst is when women become desperate and try to end their pregnancy, sometimes by themselves. It's awful. Some die, and others get injured and can't have children when they're ready. Quacks take their money and don't care how much harm they cause."

I was stunned. *How could I not know any of this?*

Marta shook her head in disgust. She reached into the cabinet, pulling out an odd-looking device. "Women should have more control over what they do with their bodies. This diaphragm will help you."

My eyebrows rose. "How do I use it?"

"First, I need to measure you and then give you a size that fits your body, like shoes." Marta laughed, shedding her annoyance. "I'll show you how to insert it. But wash it well after every use and keep it somewhere safe. We get them from Germany and deliveries are sporadic. It can take months to replenish our supply." Marta paused. "Imagine, they're legal in Germany and England, but not here."

A half-hour later, I left the Clinic with the gadget. Another modern appliance to add to the growing collection in our home, I thought, amused.

Chapter Twenty-One

July 1882

Within a few weeks after settling in our new home, I'd become fully engaged in Abe's business. No longer wasting hours schlepping clean water upstairs and dirty down three flights to dump in the backyard, I had had the luxury of directing my time to the business.

My obsessions had changed from my childhood dream of high school to the precarious winter of parenthood and now to our flourishing livelihood. How naive I was, thinking high school would fulfill my dreams. Only money would ensure our safety and comfort. I'd never forgotten the high school headmaster's discouraging words last year and was humbled by their truth. He had been dismissive for a good reason. Adult life was all-consuming, full of life-and-death responsibility.

But things were looking up. New opportunities filled our conversations. Just the other day, Abe waved a ten-dollar bill in my face. "Take this to Jordan and Moriarty and buy a bigger table and chairs for the dining room." Pointing to our current drop leaf table, he said, "We can afford it, and our family has gotten too big for this one. You can use the old one as a desk."

A year earlier, I'd had an arm's length interest in fashion, viewing my clothing as a practical necessity, a homemaker's chore. Fashionable clothing was a dream. Mama had made simple, modest outfits for us, often reworking her older dresses into smaller ones for Hannah and me. The boys' trousers were purchased for pennies on the street. From time to time, Papa would return from the city with a bolt of cloth and Mama hand-sewed matching outfits for all of us, including shirts for Papa and the boys. Papa called us his carnival troupe.

With fashion trends driving our little enterprise, clothing was foremost on my mind. Colors, fabrics, styles, and buttons filled our dinner discussions. We even took ridiculous fashions, like the bustle, seriously. I knew the bustle had a purpose—less mud stuck to the hem, keeping the garment and the apartment floors cleaner. The tight waist and wide hips made practically every woman look thin, but it was a decadent fashion for the rich. No one in our part of town wore them.

I lounged on our new sofa one evening after we put the children in bed, cleaned the dishes, and reviewed the next day's orders. Flipping past the lifestyle articles in my latest issue of Harper's Bazaar, moving straight to the drawings of next season's styles, I commented to Abe, "It's about time the hems shorten to our ankles. And I prefer the soft pleating in the back rather than the bustles."

Abe half listened. "That will mean fewer buttons. You'll need to recalculate the number for inventory."

Nearing the end of the magazine, I perused an article that caught my attention. "Have you heard about the women who formed The Rational Dress Society in London?" I flipped the page, scanning the article. "It says here that they're trying to make fashion more suitable for women's comfort."

Abe, more engaged, said, "I'm heading uptown to Bloomingdale's later in the week. I'll see what Leo has to say. All these changes will affect us."

I thought more about those awful bustles and long hems. "It's about time. Did you take a good look at the undergarments used beneath the bustle? Birdcages, that's what they are." I scoffed. "Anything to slow women down and keep us three paces behind the men. I'm glad I never had one."

He smiled. "I daresay it would take a brave man to slow you down."

I rolled my eyes. "And those long hems dragging on the floor, a menace! Remember when poor Pessy fell down the stairs in the tenement building and broke her ankle? I'll never forget her shrieks." I shuddered.

Abe shook his head. "I'm glad I wasn't home for that."

"She caught her foot on the hem of her dress and fell one entire flight. They took her to Bellevue. She never walked the same after that. Her children in Brooklyn finally took her in."

Abe chuckled.

"What's so funny?"

"After all her complaining about her children leaving her behind in that cesspool apartment, she finally found a way to get them to pay attention. Do you suppose she tripped on purpose?" He snickered.

I looked at him, flabbergasted. "I can't imagine. You weren't there to see how bad it was. Pessy's crippled now and walks with a cane. A break that bad never heals straight."

I continued flipping through the magazine, thinking. "The papers call us the growing middle class, not poor or rich. The big stores are designing and selling dresses for us. But what about the poor? What will they wear?"

Abe was quick to answer. He knew his business inside and out. "They still sew at home just like they always did."

A vague notion began brewing in my mind. "Abe, how many women in this part of the city still hand sew their dresses, like Mama and Rebecca?"

"I'd say well over half. Why?"

"Where do they get their buttons?" My thoughts simmered, slowly forming into an idea.

"The peddlers on the street. They're everywhere selling notions."

"Why aren't we supplying them? We can offer something prettier, using a less costly button line, different from what you sell to dressmakers and factories. The peddlers should be ours. They're right outside our door." I looked for a reaction.

"Why would we do that? We have our hands full already."

Did I have to explain everything? Abe may have been the best button salesman in New York, but he was slow to follow my ideas. "Say we have, God forbid, another bank collapse, and women stop buying clothes from dressmakers or stores. We won't lose everything if we keep cheaper buttons in stock. People still need clothes and will sew them at home, maybe even with those snappy new sewing machines Max is buying for his factory."

Abe scratched his beard. "Ah, I see." Bit by bit, he began speaking as his thoughts gelled. "It would be simple. I know most of the peddlers."

I looked at our parlor table and the heavy accounting books from the Settlement House library I'd been studying, my brain hard at work. "But wait, what if we do even more? What if we make a parcel that includes everything a woman needs: the pattern, fabric, and notions—buttons, thread, and needles, and sell it as a complete kit?" I added slowly as the idea took form, "We can create a second business."

Abe watched me, listening closely.

I continued thinking aloud. "And Max can sell us fabrics and patterns, be our source." A flush of pride rose within me as I flaunted my newfound accounting vocabulary. "Then we sell the kits to mercantile stores. What do you think?"

He looked into my eyes. "I like it, but I couldn't take it on with the button business we already have. There just aren't enough hours in the day."

I felt overwhelmed just thinking about the challenge. *Could I do it without Abe?*

As if reading my thoughts, he said, "Neither can you. You have a full plate with the children and helping me."

My face fell. *Why was he always such a killjoy?*

I took a deep breath, tamping down my annoyance. If Abe wouldn't help me, I'd find someone who would. I said with disdain, "You may be right. Let me stew on it."

Abe gave me that look, the one I'd come to know well. He was allowing me the luxury of time to consider my fantasy but would insist on holding me back. *Just let him try!*

Chapter Twenty-Two

Clandestine morning meetings with Sadie filled the following few weeks. Once I shared my idea, she wanted to partner with me, no hesitation, no questions asked. Because both of us had an intimate knowledge of our husbands' businesses, we had the information needed to establish our own. We set pencil to paper, wasting no time designing our new enterprise. At the end of our first morning meeting, instead of a handshake, we clinked our teacups together.

"We'd best keep this plan between us for now." I cautioned.

Sadie nodded. "Knowing Max, he'll say 'No' if I don't have the details airtight."

"Same with Abe, but there's something else…" I pondered. "He worries I'll take my eyes off the children and his business."

Sadie placed her hands on her hips. "We'll show them we can do it, and once the extra money comes in, they'll quit complaining."

We met daily for the next two weeks after dropping Eva and Hannah off for school and later during Julian's nap, wrapping our plans in a tight bundle of secrecy. By the end of the second week, our simple idea had jelled into a nifty business plan. Sadie puffed out her thin chest, brushing back her tight curls. "Why should men have all the fun? For once, I'd like to bring in some money and decide how we spend it."

I laughed with delight. "Can you imagine earning more than our husbands?" I tidied our notes, drawing myself back to the open items on our list. "We have Max for fabric and patterns and a supplier for the notions, but what if Max can't share a table in his warehouse? Where will we work?"

Sadie waved my words away. "He'll come through. Knowing Max, he'll want to keep an eye on me now that the children are in school. Otherwise, he'll talk me into working at one of his tables for him." She sat thoughtfully. "But I do have one concern."

I peered at her curiously.

"We should hire a third in case you and I get tied up with family matters, you know, sick kids and whatnot. Having an extra set of hands to assemble the packets would keep our deliveries on time. You know how important deadlines are."

She was right. After Sarah's death, I couldn't fathom running off to Max's factory and leaving sick children at home, even with a sitter. I shifted my thoughts, considering the students in the Settlement House. "I know a few smart women who might fit the bill. Let me give it a bit more thought."

I recalled a Russian woman, Rivka, who attended class rain or shine. I knew she'd been living in the tenements with a relative for the past few months, having traveled to New York from Belarus, Russia. Her journey was perilous: by train to Poland, where she lived for a year working and saving for the rest of the journey through Germany to the port at Hamburg, then boarding a steamer with her much younger brother, Saul. Safe at last in New York, she was learning a new language, sewing at home for pennies, and sending Saul to school with Eva and Hannah. I was confident they could use the income.

Sadie pressed her lips together, her eyes aglow. "Then, I think we're ready to present this idea to the men."

I shook my head. "Not yet. First, we must make a sample, identical to the kits we'll sell to the mercantile stores. I don't know about Max, but I'll have an easier time convincing Abe if I can set a tea dress kit directly in front of his eyes."

The devil was in the details. Neither of us expected the packaging to be so involved. After hours of fiddling, we selected an attractive midnight blue muslin for the dress, then folded the fabric in a nine-inch square, pressing it with a hot iron to lay it flat with crisp edges. Max's standard tea dress pattern was pinned on top. The white apron fabric and pattern were measured, folded, and ironed similarly. Thread, buttons, pins, and needles were placed in a small brown paper sleeve, folded on top, and pinned to the top layer of fabric.

Every morning, while we worked, we replayed the same conversation. "What shall we name the business? It must be something special that women remember. We can't just put the kit in a brown bag and expect them to sell."

Sadie sighed. "I like using the word 'tea' in the name since they're practical tea dresses." She sat back and sipped her tea to drive the point home.

My brain was foggy from working through the maze of permutations. "How about Tea with something or another, scones, toast, crumpets...."

"Tillie!" Sadie leaped from her chair. "Tea with Tillie. It's catchy, and people will remember it."

I laughed. "But then it sounds like my company and the company belongs to both of us. What about a different first name."

Sadie rolled her eyes upward, thinking. "The most common names I can come up with are Anna, Violet, Elizabeth, Rose—"

This time, I interrupted. "Wait, I think I have it." Silently rehearsing to myself before sharing aloud, I played out the sounds and double meanings in my head. "Tea with Rose. That way, we could design the label with a tea rose in a vase beside the words. It will make the woman feel elegant, as if she's making something more than a common schmatta." I sat back, considering my words, then turned my eyes to Sadie to judge her reaction.

She smiled. Nothing more.

Did she agree or not? I didn't think the name was funny at all. "What kind of reaction was that?" Finally, weary from the endless debate, I rose, moaning, lifting my tea and saucer to set them in the sink.

"Wait. How did you come up with all that so fast? It's perfect!" Sadie beamed.

I set my cup back on the table and thrust my hand out to her, drawing a deep breath of relief. "Then let's shake on it, like businessmen. I mean, businesswomen."

"I think it's time to set up a dinner and present our business idea to the men."

II

Part Two

"A fashion is merely a form of ugliness so absolutely unbearable
that we have to alter it every six months."
—*Philosophy of Dress, Oscar Wilde*

Chapter Twenty-Three

October 1882

I lit a small fire in the parlor to remove the chill from the air while I toasted bialys. Although the autumn weather had turned colder, the building furnace wouldn't be lit for another few weeks. Sadie was due to arrive any minute for morning tea, now a less frequent event. For the past two months, we'd begun every business day together at Max's factory, wolfing down our tea and breakfast with our children beforehand and escorting them to school. My housekeeper arrived at 7:30 am sharp and stayed for the day, keeping a steady eye on Julian, no small task.

Sadie knocked and entered before I could open the door. "Oh good, you made something to eat. I'm starving." She hung her grey tweed coat on a peg by the door and followed the waft of toasted onion into the kitchen. "I miss our relaxing breakfasts."

I guided her into the parlor. "Come, let's sit by the fire where it's warm. We have a lot to discuss." I poured her tea and buttered the bialys, pulling cups and saucers from the cabinet. I set them on my new silver-plated tray. Our savings, depleted after moving, was now replenished. Little by little, we were enjoying special purchases for our homes.

Comfortably seated before the fire in my new Queen Anne chairs, I set the tray on the coffee table beside a stack of invoices and our cash box. My handwritten agenda lay on top. I poured our tea and placed the list between us.

"Let's start with the accounting, shall we?" I glanced at Sadie for her approval. "I hate that I agreed to Abe's compromise. We're already halfway through the four-month experiment he insisted on. But I think we have a strong case to make."

Sadie tilted her head. "He was right. You can't do everything. Something had to give. At least he let you hire a housekeeper to mind Julian."

I mused, "But teaching at the Settlement House…maybe I'll get back to it someday." At the time, I'd been furious with Abe. If it hadn't been for Max's willingness to try something new, I'd still be sitting around filling button orders.

Sadie lifted the lid of the money box, filled with coins and dollar bills. "In two months, we've sold all four hundred kits we assembled. Will you just look at this?"

A smile broke through my irritation at Abe. She was right. We'd hit on a great concept, something women needed and wanted. "Let's look at the ledger and get a better idea." I pointed to the box. "Remember, part of the reason it's so full is that you and I haven't taken any wages."

I began listing the outlay of costs and payments: cotton fabric bought wholesale from Max at five cents a yard (five yards per packet), patterns at four cents each, tablespace rental $10.00 a month, and Rivka's earnings at $3.75 a week, notions etc. All tallied, our expenses were $166.00 for two months. At four hundred kits, that averages to over $0.40 a kit."

Sadie watched with awe while I scribbled away, adding, dividing, and sometimes flipping my pencil to erase my calculation.

I looked away from my sheet, studying the fireplace. "On the income side, we charge the mercantile shops $0.75 a kit and they mark it up to $0.95. We agreed they'd keep each kit under a dollar. With store bought dresses five to ten times that amount, it is an undeniable bargain."

Sadie ran the numbers through her head. "So, you and I make $0.31 from each kit, and we have sold all four hundred, correct?"

"That's right, we should have $124.00 in the box. Let's count it."

We spent the next half hour stacking coins, counting bills, and totaling them. By the end, we were giggling with excitement. We'd cleared enough to buy next month's supplies and had $36.00 left in the box.

My dream of financial security was coming true. "What do you think we should do with it?" I knew that Abe, despite his initial resistance, would be pleased.

Sadie covered a mischievous grin with her hand. "Hide it from our husbands!"

I laughed out loud. "I say we take a salary and then go bigger. But in the meantime, let's finish furnishing our homes."

We were both spinning with excitement, delighted to have extra money. Both of our homes were still bare. In a few more months, there would be enough to buy drapes, wall coverings, and furniture, a dream come true.

But Sadie also heard me say "bigger." "What do you mean 'bigger?'"

I took a sip of my cold tea and winced at the temperature. "I'm not sure yet, but I have a few ideas cooking in my head."

Chapter Twenty-Four

February 1883

"I love it, darling. It's perfect." I twirled about the parlor, modeling my new wool frock. Abe had brought it home as a surprise earlier in the week, working with one of his dressmaker customers on the sly. The deep purple tones brought back memories of my old shawl from Mama, now moth-eaten, tucked away inside a memory box I kept in my bureau. The dress had soft, puffed shoulders, an inset of white ruffles around the collar and front, a nipped waist, and a bell-shaped skirt with several back pleats starting at the waist. Abe, knowing how I detested bustles and their strangulating corsets, told the dressmaker to fashion something more comfortable.

Abe sat back in his chair, a mischievous smile on his face, watching me dance. My attachment to nice clothing had changed over time. Once a measure of status, it was the foundation of our businesses, a pathway to financial security. But I was still eager to hold his attention. He hobnobbed with attractive models and fashion designers all week, and I worried temptation could cross his path. He was mine and mine alone.

His eyes shone. "Come here, beautiful."

I fluttered my eyelashes. "Oh no, you don't. We have a busy morning ahead." I lifted my hat off the rack by the front door. My velvet post-boy hat, with its high crown and narrow brim, was another current trend. "I'll wear this one. It matches my coat perfectly."

Out of the corner of my eye, I saw him reach for me.

"Abe! The housekeeper is in the bedroom tidying. She'll hear us."

He laughed, feigning a pout, his eyes filled with physical longing.

I dismissed Abe's overture, tidying my thick mane into a bun at the nape of my neck, pinning my hat securely, then calling to the children. "Hannah, would you and Julian come out and say goodbye?" I would push his desire off until the evening.

Despite the rapid growth of Tea with Rose, both Sadie and I continued to assist our husbands with their businesses. Sadie oversaw Max's workshop while working on our kits, and I helped with Abe's books, invoices and occasionally made sales calls when he needed a shrewd woman by his side. Sadie's idea to hire a helper kept us on schedule, particularly on days like today.

This morning, Abe was meeting with Leo Baum, a colorful character and Bloomingdale's premier designer. Based on Mr. Baum and Abe's prior estimates, we could leave this meeting with Abe's largest order yet. The store's decision to sell pre-made, high-end garments was revolutionizing the dressmaking industry in New York. Ever since Bloomingdale's move uptown to 59th and Lexington, Abe's sales had grown through the roof.

I checked the clock. "We'd better leave now if we plan to stop at the bakery and buy bialys."

Abe taught me to always bring a treat for the workers, something delicious to set a happy mood before talking business. My husband, walking through a customer's door with that winning smile of his, had the most affable personality in town. The bialys were a bonus. He remembered everyone's names, even the floor sweepers. Abe knew who'd lost a parent, had been ill, had a new baby at home, and who was courting whom. People loved to tell him their business. And he listened and cared.

Standing by the door, waiting, I said, "I don't know how the dressmakers are going to make it. Mrs. Polly up on 10th Street told me her business is dwindling. She's losing customers right and left to ready-to-wear."

Abe tied his wool scarf around his neck. "I'm trying to hang onto our most loyal dressmakers, but the real money is in the big stores ordering large shipments of ready-to-wear suits and dresses." He paused a moment. "I've seen familiar faces in the department store design studios. Many lost their jobs with the dress-makers and found work in the bigger factories."

"It makes sense that some dressmakers would follow the work to bigger studios." I buttoned my coat, picking my muffler off the shelf. "And I'll admit, the dresses coming off the production line look beautiful. Much less expensive than custom-made. Most need little to no alterations, perhaps only the hem."

Abe held the door for me as we exited our apartment. "Nowadays, my customers couldn't be more different. Just a few years back, the dressmakers enjoyed discussing dress details with me, but the factory owners talk all business. They've worked out the details long before I set foot in the door. I'm in and out before I finish my coffee. If all the parts—fabric, thread, fasteners, bric-a-brac—aren't there in the snap of a finger, they'll find a new dealer."

Abe attempted to stay close to the decision-makers early in the season by forging strong relationships with the head designers, like Leo Baum. It was the best way to secure business. Early involvement with the design team, seasons ahead of production, gave us time to stock our inventory from the European button factories, which also required ample lead time for the sea crossing.

Minutes later, tucked warmly against Abe in the streetcar, I felt my stomach churn, then a tightness in my throat. *Am I sick? Could it be?* I swallowed the acrid juices in my mouth and forced my mind back to our meeting ahead.

* * *

Mr. Baum's studio buzzed with creative energy. Dress patterns, fabric scraps, and finishes were strewn on every table. Designers and seamstresses jostled about the room, holding swaths of cloth to the light, seeking one another's opinions on various paddings, laces, and coquettish trimmings.

"Hold still, dammit!" an older man shouted at his model as he pinned lace on her slender curves.

She snapped back, "I will when you stop sticking me. Do you think I'm a pin cushion?"

For me, the commotion was irresistible, just like a symphony. I wanted to hear all the conversations and salty arguments filling the air.

A deep voice from the other side of the room cut through the noise. "Hell-ooo, Abe! You have a new model for me?" A little man burrowed his way through the crowded workshop while pointing at me. "Who's this exquisite creature?" He continued to shout even after reaching us, grabbing my hand, shaking it wildly, "You must be the beautiful Mrs. Levine, who Abe goes on about. I hope so, or I'll be knee-deep in trouble." His body quaked with laughter.

My eyes darted to Abe's amused expression, and then I giggled. I never expected Abe's sales call to be so much fun. "It's lovely to meet you, too."

Mr. Baum was close to Abe's age but couldn't have appeared more opposite—rotund, short in stature, with monk-like balding. His fleshy face looked as if a sculptor had dug his thumbs into clay and stretched from the center into an oversized toothy smile.

Abe shook Mr. Baum's hand while explaining.

"Tillie, I've told you, haven't I, that Mr. Baum has worked for the Bloomingdale family for close to twenty years? He started out in the custom design end of the business."

"That's right Mrs. Levine, and I couldn't get out of that workshop fast enough. Catering to rich women with no sense of fashion was a nightmare. They only wanted to imitate and outdo their friends." He waved his hands about him. "If one of those hoity-toity ladies bought a bonnet with a dead canary, the next one asked for an ostrich! Since when were we in the taxidermy business?" He roared with laughter.

I was laughing so hard I became breathless, my stomach churning, and I had to sit down. Taking a deep, restoring breath, I acted as if there were nothing wrong. "When will women tire of the bustles?"

He raised his hands to the ceiling and cried, "Exactly! The most absurd style of all. It was intended for the stage. And the models tell me those bustle undergarments are torture for you poor creatures." He rubbed his hands together. "But at the end of the day, we've made a bundle on the bustle."

Abe chimed in, "I like the ring of that, 'A bundle on the bustle!'"

We all knew that keeping ahead of style trends led to big money. Astute stores like Bloomingdale's made an absolute fortune. Abe and my challenge was to keep a step ahead of them.

Abe shifted our discussion to the business at hand. "We've brought some stunning buttons to show you today, and our new catalog as well. While we look, can I offer you a bialy? They're still warm."

I opened the bag. The smell of the warm flat rolls baked with caramelized onions and poppy seeds floated through the workshop.

"Bialys, bialys, my good friend! They know nothing of bialys in this part of the city. I don't even bother asking at the bakery anymore. Only crumb cakes, unbelievable," Mr. Baum laughed. "Bialys are one of the best things our Eastern European brethren brought to our shores." He paused, "And stop with the Mr. Baum, already. Call me Leo."

I offered, "I can put these bags in the kitchen for everyone."

Mr. Baum laughed as he patted his round stomach. "Yes, please do. Otherwise, I'll eat them all myself. Plus, those models can use a little meat on their bones. You'd think I didn't pay them enough. I'll have you know, this belly of mine cost a fortune!"

"He's so much fun," I whispered to Abe.

We arranged our buttons on the table, pairing them with the designers' pen and ink dress drawings so Mr. Baum could visualize the options.

An hour later, after reviewing his button selections, the dress factories which Bloomingdale's had contracted with, and the volumes needed, Mr. Baum studied us with sudden, serious eyes. "I'll insist the factories purchase from you, Abe. The two of you have excellent taste, and there's no one else I'd rather work with. But there is one condition."

Abe nodded. "Go on."

"You must not share our dress plans or sell the same buttons to any other designer or store in the city. Don't even show them the same buttons.

Lyman Bloomingdale insists no one imitates our look. He and Joe lose sleep over copycats. As a matter of fact, he's so suspicious that if he has an inkling, he'll cut off those factories or suppliers—for good." Mr. Baum bore his eyes into ours before continuing. "The brothers are planning an advertising splash this winter season with a 'signature' Bloomingdale's look. We're counting on big sales. This new uptown store put them in deep with the banks."

Abe extended his hand. "You can count on us."

Little by little, we were leaving our lean years behind. Neither of us ever had so much money. The Bloomingdale's sale alone would cover our family's expenses for the next year. Practically dancing on the sidewalk, we headed to the Metropolitan Museum for a rare afternoon off. We were going to view a new sculpture collection by a Frenchman, Rodin.

Chapter Twenty-Five

L ater that evening, I slipped into the bathroom and pressed a cold
hand towel over my face to quell my nausea, taking a deep breath
as my stomach settled. Flushing the toilet, I pulled my diaphragm
from the medicine cabinet and held it to the light, inspecting it for pin holes.
But there were none. *The damn thing had failed!* I wasn't ready for another
baby, but my symptoms didn't lie.

I returned to the parlor as if nothing had happened. There was simply
too much going on, and I didn't want Abe to force me to close Tea with
Rose. Fatigue hit me like a thick wall. All I wanted was sleep, but I knew I
wasn't finished for the night.

While I was in the bathroom, Abe, eager to place our orders with the
German factories, had arranged the buttons Bloomingdale's needed on the
dining room table. His plan was to confirm the quantities with me and
telegram the invoices the following morning.

I inhaled deeply, craving a burst of energy. But instead, I could only feign
interest, pointing to a series of tinted glass buttons set against a black velvet
background. "These work well. The jewel colors, especially those reds and
purples, remind me of Passover wine and our mulberry bushes years ago. I
was hoping Mr. Baum would choose them."

"That button catalog of yours was a stroke of genius. The sample boxes
have gotten too heavy and clumsy to drag about. Besides, I was delighted
when Mr. Baum asked to keep the catalogue for future ideas," Abe said.

I nodded in agreement. "You're right. But designers still like to touch and
look from every angle."

"By the way, I have a meeting with Lord and Taylor's in two weeks, and they're also selling ready-to-wear garments. So, be prepared with samples and projections. They've been pushing me off for years, but with their sales volumes climbing, they decided to give me a chance." Abe spoke over my shoulder, observing me as I filled out the Bloomingdale's orders. "I'm thankful you're good with numbers. It would take me twice as long."

Calculating costs and profits was simple math for me. To make things quicker, I created a formula for every type of order. But Tea with Rose was absorbing all my free time, and I worried I'd make a mistake somewhere. And now, another baby? I couldn't possibly manage everything.

***

Mid-morning, I met Sadie at Max's factory after Abe left for the telegraph station. Our plan was to select fabrics for our spring dress kits.

As I entered, she looked up from her cluttered worktable, strewn with cloth swatches. "This sometimes feels frightfully easy."

"Perhaps for you. I can barely mend a tear." I picked up a few sample fabrics that caught my eye. They all looked acceptable to me. "We're doing something right. People keep buying."

I had nowhere near the technical skill of sewing I should have and wanted to double-check with another woman who sewed her own clothing. My mother, then Rebecca, fashioned my dresses. Looking back, I regretted not paying more attention. "Why don't we ask Rivka to take a look?"

Tea with Rose dress kits had grown so fast in Lower Manhattan that women asked for our product by name in the stores. Our sales had doubled in only a half-year. We had outgrown Max's factory, and with his own enlarging business, Abe's button inventory, and now these kits, Max couldn't spare more space. Last week, when Sadie showed him our profits, Max told her, "I can't give up any more worktables. You need to start looking for your own factory. My business has grown, too."

After dinner and tucking the children in for the night, I walked out to the parlor. Abe had his nose deep in the newspaper. "Abe, I need your thoughts for a few minutes."

He set his newspaper down, narrowing his eyes. "What's wrong?"

Why did he assume I'd done something wrong? I swallowed my annoyance and conjured a cheerful tone. "Nothing, just the opposite. It seems Sadie and I have outgrown Max's factory. He'd like us to find our own space."

He reached out his hand. "Let me see the books." Abe took the ledger, pushing his spectacles higher on his nose, flipping the pages slowly.

I inhaled, indignant that he insisted on checking my calculations, especially knowing I was better than him with numbers. But an argument would get me nowhere. "We need to move soon. What do you think about investing some extra cash in the growth?"

He looked noncommittal. *Did he think we'd fail?*

"What do you have left after the furniture shopping?" he asked.

I walked to our old drop-leaf table where I kept my books and opened the money box. "We have over thirty dollars profit for now after paying for spring supplies."

Abe stared at the box full of cash. "This is a foolish amount of money to have sitting around the apartment. Why haven't you asked me to open an account for you at the bank?"

My face filled with rage. "Enough! First, you give us a trial period, and then you explain that we have too much cash. What do you want from me?"

"To act sensibly. This is an invitation to a burglar." His cheeks were scarlet.

Taking the conversation back to the matter at hand, I said evenly, "We need your signature to cosign a lease on a new factory."

Abe shot from his chair, startling me. "Did you find a space without discussing it with me first?"

Shocked by his reaction, I raised my voice, "Of course not! I was planning to ask for your help finding a factory close to Max's." I moved closer. "What's the matter? You should be happy. Together, we're making far more than we need."

Hannah called from her room, her voice full of concern. "What happened?

CHAPTER TWENTY-FIVE

Why are you fighting?"

We locked eyes. Neither of us wanted to upset the children.

Abe called back. "Hannah, everything is fine. Please go back to sleep." He lowered his voice, the irritation of moments earlier somewhat diluted. "I need your help filling my orders. You know I'm concerned about you having time left for the children and me. Besides, I'm making plenty."

"I can still help with your books and invoices." I took a deep breath. "Perhaps it's time to hire your own person to fill and deliver the button orders." Then, forging on, I added, "Think about it. Both of our businesses are starting to make a lot of money. We should each keep growing and hire extra help. That way, we'll still have time at home together."

Abe fell back in his chair, scratching the back of his head. "Your numbers are surprising, stronger than I predicted. And your business operates at a low price. It could protect us if the factories skip over me and go directly to the button manufacturers."

"Wasn't that the idea all along? Have two different types of businesses in case we have another bad market?" Had he forgotten it was my idea all along? But I chose not to correct him.

His temper cooled as he thought aloud. "People always need clothes, even in hard times. And your price is lower than ready-to-wear goods or dressmakers." He drew his eyes to mine. "It just might work, but I want you home at the end of the day."

"I want to be home, too. I love our family." I reached out for his hand, pulling it to my cheek. "I know I can make this work."

He squinted at me, studying my face. "There's more, isn't there?"

I smiled thinly. "You read me so well. I did have another idea."

He sighed. "Let's hear it."

"I'd like to meet with a pattern maker like Butterfield. They sell patterns all over the United States. Imagine if we could convince them to put their patterns in our kits. Then we can sell Tea with Rose nationally."

For the first time that evening, Abe smiled. "You're too crafty for your own good. I suppose it couldn't hurt to try. But you'd better be able to build volume quickly if they go for it."

It was a relief to amuse him and collaborate. "Do you have time to help us look for factory space? Then, I'll talk to Sadie about Butterfield."

"I'll poke my head around and see what's available. It might be smart to stay clear of other clothing factories. You don't want to be too obvious. And to be frank, it's surprising you haven't been copied."

Abe took Sadie and me to see several workspaces near Max's factory. The first was on the first floor of an old warehouse, sawdust covering the floor.

Sadie covered her face with her handkerchief. "What's that vile smell? Was this a slaughterhouse?"

Two steps behind her, my mouth filled with bile. "Oh God, I'm going to be sick." I ran out the door.

Abe followed me outside. "Are you alright?" He bent to examine my face.

I gulped the cool air outside, settling my shaky stomach. "I think so. We can't work there. It's disgusting. Is the next place far?"

After inspecting our other options, we settled for a partial loft space inside a building that manufactured watches and bound books on Canal Street, the same block as Max's workshop. Sadie and I wasted no time moving, scrubbing, and installing shelving to stack finished kits. Next, I bought an oak desk from a second-hand furniture dealer down the block. It had drawers with locks where we could store ledgers and handbags.

We had our attorney register our name, Tea with Rose, putting the lease under the business. An art teacher at the shul fashioned a design for our label, a blue floral teacup beside a single red rose set in a simple bud vase.

Sunday afternoon, about to begin the week in our new factory, Sadie, Rivka, and I sat at a worktable admiring what we'd accomplished. We were prepared to assemble our spring line. All that remained was fabric selection.

Pointing to the swatches on the table, I asked, "Rivka, what do you think? We'd like to add more fabric choices, and can use another opinion."

Rivka studied the swatches with a blank face, in an indifferent fog, selecting several from the table. "Women will wear these." Where was her excitement?

Chapter Twenty-Six

Despite Rivka's indifference, Sadie and I followed Rivka's advice then added five more lightweight wools for the winter tea dresses and another five calicos and linens for the spring line. Afterwards, I made an appointment at Butterfield, Manhattan's renowned dress pattern company. Their headquarters, on Broadway and Fulton Street, was only a few blocks from our workshop.

Butterfield had built a solid reputation across the United States with dressmakers and the at-home seamstress. With their widespread distribution and fashion magazine, The Delineator, we imagined selling dress kits to thousands of women across the United States. And thanks to Max and Abe, we bought fabric and buttons, the most expensive components, at cost. If things worked in our favor, we could make a fortune.

Every morning, Sadie and I rehearsed the presentation in our parlors, displaying the colorful kits with our new plaid wool fabric, button selections, and two completed dresses. Our appointment was scheduled at Butterfield headquarters with Mr. Timothy Kraft, Vice President. Taking Abe's advice to never arrive empty-handed, Sadie and I strolled to Moishe's bakery around the corner from our apartment, purchasing the freshest, most fragrant pastries we could find, then caught a coach.

Arriving early at Butterfield gave us precious time to size up the operation. The design studio was bright and sunny. Gleaming wood tables lined the room in precise schoolroom rows. Each table had a line of jars containing sharpened colored pencils. Well-dressed men and women worked calmly, occasionally whispering to each other. Everyone wore the stylish garments advertised in The Delineator. I'd never seen anything like it, a room of silent, moving mannequins.

We approached Mr. Kraft's secretary, Miss Sweeney, absorbing every detail around us, and handed the box of pastries to her. "Thank you for arranging our meeting. These treats are for you and the staff."

"Thank you," she glowed, smelling the warm sugary aroma drifting from the box. "We have a table set aside for you." She gestured toward our bundles and pointed to the right side of the workroom. "Go ahead and set up. It's the last table on the right."

Once she was out of sight, Sadie and I exchanged amused looks. "Do you think we should have brought sweets?" Sadie whispered. "Everyone here is as skinny as a beanpole. I'm not sure the staff is allowed to eat!"

Digesting the atmosphere, contrasting it to our outgoing, demonstrative personalities, I said, "They might not be so eager to accept us. We should probably discuss our credentials carefully before sharing the proposal."

Ten minutes later, Mr. Kraft, a short, serious-looking man wearing a monocle, sauntered over to our table, nodding to the designers along the way. His brown hair was slicked back, barely covered his balding head. I reached out and shook his hand firmly, just as Abe suggested. "Good morning, Mr. Kraft. Thank you for taking time out of your busy morning to meet us. This is Mrs. Sadie Stern, my partner at Tea with Rose."

He looked at his hand. Was that disdain in his eyes? "I've heard of your local outfit. What can I do for you?" he said with a touch of impatience.

With haste, I summarized our history, concept, and growing volumes. Sadie pointed to the table display and reviewed the fabric and buttons we'd chosen for the upcoming seasons. Mr. Kraft listened attentively. He had the best poker face I had ever seen.

Finally, he spoke. "An impressive display. How does Butterfield fit in?"

I drew a deep breath, preparing myself for the pitch. "We're ready to launch our next two seasons and would like to create a package with an exclusive, distinguished look. Imagine a unique Butterfield tea dress pattern for women and girls set directly atop the kit. Then, we advertise the product in The Delineator as a frugal, convenient innovation." An idea struck me.

"I must add, ready-to-wear clothing is all the rage in the stores. We can advertise with the slogan 'ready-to-sew.'"

Mr. Kraft leaned back on one leg as if he needed extra space to think. He crossed his arms and cocked his head to the side. "Why not use our current patterns? No need to design a new one when we already have tea dress patterns. It takes a long time to build a new design." He paused. "Please remind me, what pattern are you using now?"

He'd bitten. Already past discussing the idea, he was now pondering the details.

"We created a basic pattern in my husband's factory, which works well locally," answered Sadie. "But Butterfield's name is known and trusted everywhere in the country. Together, we can create a ready-to-sew product for less money than purchasing each part individually. In addition, a kit would benefit women in the territories and other remote areas who may not have ready access to the coordinated notions in their local mercantile."

Mr. Kraft knit his brows. "Where did you get the idea? You couldn't possibly have thought this up on your own."

My skin bristled. I tried to calm myself. I thought back to our pitch rehearsals when we had tried to anticipate all his questions. "It was Sadie and my invention, sir. We've worked in the garment business with our husbands for the last decade and saw the need. And, as you already know, Mrs. Stern and I have tested the kits in New York City, selling through the mercantile stores and peddlers. We rarely have inventory left. As a matter of fact, this past summer, we expanded into a larger factory to manage the growth."

His eyes burst with astonishment. "What do your husbands think about you ladies starting a business venture? It's unheard of. Don't you have children at home to tend?"

Abe's advice came to mind as my blood heated to a boil. *Keep discussing the sale. Don't let the customer bait you.* I filled my chest with air, hoping my irritation didn't show. "Mr. Kraft, our husbands are in the button and fabric businesses. Our products are interconnected, and in the end, it helps grow their businesses, too. Just as our kits will grow Butterfield's pattern sales."

Mr. Kraft nodded cautiously. "Hmm. I'll run the idea by Mr. Peters, my boss, and let you know what he decides. But he'll want to meet your husbands." He fell silent, then added, "I expect the idea may pan out in some way."

Excitement rose within me, but I kept my expression still. I was learning the art of poker, too. "Please let him know our factory is ready to fill orders immediately."

He stood. "Could you kindly leave one of your kits, as you call them, with me? Let's arrange a meeting next week. Please project costs and pricing for one thousand units, and then we can talk business." Before leaving the room, he faced us and added, "But next time, bring your husbands."

Despite my growing queasiness and irritation, I pasted a small, tight-lipped smile on my face. Mr. Kraft left without shaking our hands.

I whispered to Sadie. "I don't know how to feel. It's insulting, such a man's world."

"Galling." Sadie scoffed, then shook off her annoyance. "Let's keep our eye on the sale."

We left the building with mixed emotions and an appointment for the following week, strolling an entire block before uttering a word. It was a sunny late winter day with a hint of warmth. Perhaps, a good omen.

Sadie tugged on my sleeve with her free hand. "Why can't it ever be equal working with men? They have such an unfair advantage. Do you think Mr. Kraft has a clue how much work we've put into Tea with Rose?"

"I doubt it. I don't even think our husbands realize the hours we've spent. At least, not Abe." It felt bittersweet, but we seemed to have Butterfield on the hook. More than anything, I wanted the sale as much as Sadie.

Sadie mused, "Speaking of Abe, we should invite him to our meetings until we firm things up. He's accustomed to dealing with these types of characters. Max is too busy right now to leave his factory, and his German accent might put them off. Abe's smooth. He can sell snowballs in winter."

While I agreed, I was in no mood to share the glory with anyone other than Sadie. The two of us deserved every ounce of credit. But, I wanted the sale. At the heels of that thought, my stomach lurched. *I must do something about this pregnancy.* Just my luck, it wasn't ending on its own. But when? And by whom?

Chapter Twenty-Seven

The next morning, after dropping Hannah and Eva at school, I stopped by the Clinic, hoping to find Marta, determined to find a solution in secret. It was a simple inconvenience, a bump in my path to success, and I didn't even want Sadie to know. Certainly, if Abe found out, he'd make a mountain out of it and force me to have the child, knowing it would be the end of Tea with Rose. Any chance Sadie and I had with Butterfield would slip down the drain. Julian was a charming little boy, but a handful, and I was no fool. Another child now would spell disaster. Now, in my twenties, I wanted my future back.

The waiting area was empty. I poked my head into the back hallway. "Marta, are you in?" I called. Then I heard the scuffle of feet.

"Who's here?" Marta called back.

"It's Tillie Levine. Do you have a moment before things get busy?"

"Come on back and pick an exam room. I'll be with you in a moment."

I settled into a wood ladderback chair, leaving my coat on, impatient to hear her advice.

Moments later, Marta walked in and closed the door. "This is a nice surprise. How can I help you?"

I proceeded to fill her in on my missed period, failed diaphragm, and decision, watching her face transform from a pleased smile to tight concern.

Marta tilted her head, her eyes soft with empathy. "Tillie, I'm sorry, but we don't do that kind of thing here. Terminations are illegal and very dangerous. Isn't there some way you and Abe can see this through? Does he know?"

202

I shook my head as the tears spilled, hoping she'd feel pity and help me anyway. After all, the diaphragm she gave to me was illegal, too. "You're the only person I've told."

She pulled a chair to my side. "I'm so sorry. I know it must feel like the end of the world, but I promise, it's not."

How could I have thought this would be easy? "I know for a fact that women do this all the time. There're potions that can bring on bleeding. What can you tell me about them?"

Her face dropped. "Pennyroyal is dangerous."

* * *

I left Marta in a fury, kicking ice balls into the street, cursing myself for sharing a personal matter with her. Would she tell Dr. Boro? Would they tell Abe? That could spell disaster. I couldn't risk Abe finding out my plan. When it came to more children, he was pigheaded. But I had no idea where to find an herb like pennyroyal. I wondered if an apothecary would stock it and, if so, how much I should take. Marta told me little and made it sound as if I'd die, but I knew she was only trying to scare me. Women had been taking such potions for centuries. And before Comstock, it was legal. I just didn't know where to buy it.

I climbed the steps into our new factory, hoping Sadie left crackers in the tiny kitchen. My stomach was churning from the aggravation, another bad sign. I twisted the doorknob—unlocked. *Damn*, I'd hoped to have the place to myself for an hour until my stomach settled. As I opened the door, Rivka jumped, turning away from the bolt of blue cotton cloth she was spreading over her worktable.

"Good morning, Rivka. Are you starting the spring kits early? I asked.

She greeted me with a careful smile. "I am."

"That's wonderful...." My voice hitched as my belly unexpectedly turned, sending a thread of vomit to my mouth." I ran to the lavatory in the hallway.

Moments later, I returned, my composure restored. I lit the stove to make tea. "Rivka, would you like a cup of tea? Do you know if we have any crackers?" I called out.

Rivka walked to the doorway of the tiny kitchen. "I'll make it. Go sit, you don't look too good."

I exhaled, waiting at an empty worktable. Rivka returned moments later with two cups of tea and a small plate of crackers.

"Lovely, thank you."

She took a sip, not moving her eyes from my face. "How far along are you?"

A new panic ran through me. Was it that obvious? I had little time to waste. "What do you mean?"

"You're with baby?" she said in her thick accent, then, cocked her head.

I held my breath, not knowing if I could trust her. Then, I made a split-second decision to share my secret. After all, she might know someone who could help me. "Yes, but no one knows. I don't want it. We have big things coming our way, and another child will ruin everything we've worked so hard for."

Rivka nodded, her big eyes downcast, hooded with understanding. "Ah, many women in tenements end them too. Big families cost too much money."

My gut told me she'd know who could help. Although Rivka was one of the hardest working women I knew and smart as a tack, she had a dark, knowing side, as if she'd witnessed evils in life that I'd been guarded from, even while I lived in the tenements. She told Sadie and me that her family back in Belarus was no more. We were reluctant to press her. Had they been killed by the Cossacks? Died of sickness? Her trek across Europe and then to New York was fraught with danger. In comparison, a simple termination was nothing to lose sleep over. After all, they were once commonplace in New York City, at least until they became illegal a few years ago. Even the church agreed that life didn't begin until the mother felt quickening. That insipid Comstock must have a deep hatred of women to push through his anti-female laws.

I locked eyes with her, barely speaking in a whisper. "Who do they use? I need to get pennyroyal."

She nodded in understanding. "The potion, yes?" Rivka sat quietly, looking at her hands. Finally, she spoke in her broken English. "You don't tell anyone you heard it from me, yes?"

I reached for her hand and shook it, like men settling a business deal. "Our secret." With that, I left the building for Brooklyn with the address she'd given me.

Chapter Twenty-Eight

Lord & Taylor set its anchor in the Lower East Side long before I moved there. Starting as a dry goods store on Catherine Street, they became wildly successful. So, they opened a second store downtown and then a third on 20th Street and Broadway. By the time Abe and I settled into our business, the locals had dubbed the district "The Ladies' Mile," and except for Bloomingdale's uptown, it was our primary sales area. Lord & Taylor entered ready-to-wear early on, contracting with factories to manufacture their clothing, controlling each step of the process, and making an extraordinary amount of money. Unlike many of the clothing businesses in the area, Lord & Taylor was owned by non-Jews.

"We need to find a way in." Abe passed the saucer of cream cheese to me at breakfast the next morning. We were preparing for a sales call with their head designer, Samuel Mayfair, who'd been with the company many years and typically turned Abe away. Mr. Mayfair bought his buttons directly from a manufacturer in Paris. With their dress production, the store had been gradually eliminating middlemen.

I slathered cream cheese across my toasted bagel, then a smaller amount of fresh strawberry jam. "Their designers lack flair. They would do better if they had a wizard like Leo Baum." I bit into my bagel, luxuriating in the blend of flavors.

"Be careful, Tillie," Abe reached to my face with his napkin and dabbed an errant spot of jelly from my cheek. "Don't forget, we gave Mr. Baum our solemn word. And whatever you say, don't use the word, *signature*. People talk in this business."

"I'll remember." I brushed off his warning. "But can't we get them out of their tired rut? I could cut out pictures from the Paris fashion magazines and use them to show Mr. Mayfair alternatives, then coordinate buttons from our line rather than the ones he uses."

"That could be a good angle." Abe nodded, realizing where I was heading. "And it's a near miracle he agreed to see me at all."

"Then we could suggest he try an experiment with one or two new dress designs and see how they sell," I added.

Finally, Abe's face melted into a smile. "And here I thought you were going to get us through the door with your beauty and fancy dress. I should have known better." He rose from the table. "I have a busy day, but if you can spend time putting ideas together, that might do the trick. It would be a miracle if we could convince them to buy buttons from a simple Jewish button salesman."

"I'll take the challenge." My stomach began to churn. *Damn it, not now.* I wanted Abe out the door before I got sick.

"The real puzzle is to figure out what pastry to bring. I doubt bialys will work. They probably never heard of them." Abe pantomimed daintily eating a bonbon.

I led him to the door with a kiss goodbye.

* * *

The following day, outside the top floor office, we shot each other one final look of resolve and entered the executive office of Lord and Taylor's. Abe handed boxes of butter shortbread cookies to the secretary. "For you and the staff, fresh from the bakery!"

As expected, Abe was rewarded with an appreciative smile.

Mr. Mayfair's office, a stately wood-paneled room, was in the corner of the expansive workroom. After shaking Abe's hand, he led the way, walking with his back ramrod straight. Dressed in a drab grey suit, he was a slight, immaculate man in his fifties with thinning grey hair combed sideways across the top of his head; his bearing reflecting the gravity of his role in the company.

As we entered the room, Abe said, "Please let me introduce my wife, Mrs. Levine."

Mr. Mayfair's stern eyes scanned my outfit with an approving nod, bowing his head. "Please come in and have a seat."

We arranged our concepts on his gleaming mahogany conference table, then sat across from him.

Mr. Mayfair cleared his throat with a hint of irritation. "You already know, Mr. Levine, I have my garment assembly plan in place for the next season. I'm not sure why you've come back to see me."

"Mr. Mayfair, I'm an avid student of your business and admire your sharpness and success. Today, we would like to present a fresh idea that could lead to increased sales," Abe patiently explained.

"Go on, show me what you have." Mr. Mayfair bent his body toward the table to study our concepts. "Hmm, very nice."

After my success at Bloomingdale's, I was impatient to join the conversation. "I'm so glad to have an opportunity to meet you."

A smirk swept across Mr. Mayfair's face. Was he taking me seriously?

I pushed forward, determined to garner a better response. "By visiting designers and stores around the city, we've learned that some are taking ready-to-wear lines to new heights with an exclusive look, unique twists on European trends. No one else in the city shares their exact look. Dress designers have never been more creative combining fashion and comfort."

His eyebrow twitched with interest. "Please explain, Mrs. Levine."

A surge of excitement overrode my good sense. I was so determined to win this sale.

"We're offering to help you design a line of garments that's strictly Lord and Taylor's, something no one else in the city has, your own look, just like your signature." As the word escaped my lips, my thrill deflated. *What had I done?*

Abe shot his eyes my way, glaring at me in disbelief. He cleared his throat. "What Mrs. Levine means to say is a Lord & Taylor style of its own."

But Mr. Mayfair's eyes never left my face. I could see the wheels in his head spinning. "We have our winter line underway right now. It's close to shipment. And we must stay within our budget to ensure profitability." His voice held an uncertain edge.

Abe shot me another warning look. "We're not surprised you're ahead of schedule. You have a reputation for running a well-oiled operation. But why not plan a handful of new looks for the spring?"

So energized by Mr. Mayfair's attentive eyes, I couldn't restrain myself. "You can have a special window display with mannequins wearing sample fashions in the winter, together with an advertising campaign promising something unique for spring. If you test a limited collection, the line would carry cache and drive demand for your fall clothing the following season, all still made in volume." *Stop talking, stupid girl!*

"Abe, perhaps I underestimated you and your lovely wife." Mr. Mayfair looked up from the designs and buttons on the table. "It's a good concept, original. Perhaps we can test the idea this spring and see how sales develop." His face had lightened, the corners of his mouth carrying the hint of a smile.

I smiled at Abe, but his expression remained frozen. I realized the predicament I'd placed us in with my impulsive words and said weakly, "You'll be pleased with the success this brings. Thank you for listening and giving us a try."

Mr. Mayfair pursed his lips, nodding. "Let's plan the next steps. I want you to return and meet with my design team."

"We'll make an appointment before we leave," said Abe.

"Once we get some of these signature designs approved," Mr. Mayfair cocked his head to the side. "I like that word, 'signature,' we'll decide the quantities and advertising strategy. I'll commit to buying your buttons for this group of garments and give you a try. But please don't disappoint me."

Abe and I shook hands with Mr. Mayfair and stepped out of his office. His secretary's eyebrows shot upward. "Sounds like things went well. Do you need me to consult Mr. Mayfair's calendar?"

We set up our next appointment and left the office.

Once outside, Abe snapped, his eyes on fire. "How dare you take over the meeting? We agreed to tread carefully. You told him far too much.

Signature? The exact word Mr. Baum used at Bloomingdale's. Have you lost your mind?" He stomped to the street corner, his arms squeezed across his chest.

My ears stung. "Do you think it was that bad? I didn't mean...."

Abe's words sliced off mine. "You had to be a big mouth in there." He halted. "You threw my reputation in the gutter!"

My emotions overcame me. Tears pooled in my eyes; my delicate stomach churned with shame. "I didn't realize what I said until it came out." I groped for absolution. "I didn't share any of the designs, or fabrics. What harm is there in talking about a store having a unique look?"

Abe was unwilling to relent. "Don't give me that. You know damn well. We shook hands at Bloomingdale's. I gave Mr. Baum my solemn word."

I clutched my stomach, wishing I could reclaim my words. But it was too late. There was no way to unspool history.

"Don't be surprised if this isn't the end of it," he snarled, then straightened his hat. "I'll try to diffuse things with Mr. Baum first thing tomorrow before word spreads all over town." His harumph was so loud, a curious passerby turned to stare.

"Abe, I'm so sorry." I sniffled, dabbing my eyes with a handkerchief.

He stiffened, his eyes stormy. There was no love in those eyes, no room for an appeal. "I've been at this a lot of years. My business has more underhanded men than honest ones. Without my good name, I'm just another shyster in a cesspool of salesmen. Is that what you want to make me?"

My tears flowed faster than I could wipe them away. "My mouth got ahead of my brain. You know I would never intentionally do or say anything to hurt you or what you've built."

His voice softened to a strained whisper. "For now, I'll conduct business calls alone and you stick to the books." He turned to leave, then spun around, facing me again. "As a matter of fact, why don't you and Sadie just concentrate on your kit business and leave my business to me?"

I could barely believe my ears. Standing alone on the sidewalk, watching him disappear into the crowd, my one thought was to get home and drink the potion. For the first time in our marriage, I saw revulsion in his eyes. Any hope of another child with that man was gone for good.

Chapter Twenty-Nine

D
espite my blunder with Lord & Taylor, Abe kept his word and joined Sadie and me the following Monday for our second meeting at Butterfield. At home, I eyed the pennyroyal elixir hourly, planning to drink it once I had the Butterfield deal secured.

The three of us exited the coach in front of the Butterfield building, carrying armloads of kits. Abe chatted with Sadie the entire way in his affable manner. Not a word was spoken to me. Would he ever let it go?

Upstairs, Mr. Kraft was waiting for us in their meeting room, pacing the floor. The room, flanked by two long walls, sat in the back left hand corner of the studio. One bank of windows looked down at the street, revealing anyone who approached the building by foot or coach. The opposite partition faced the workshop and was fitted with blinds set at such a slant to allow Mr. Kraft direct observation of the studio, without his workers seeing in.

He made eye contact with Abe and walked to greet us at the reception desk.

"Mr. Kraft, I'd like you to meet my husband, Mr. Abe Levine. As you may know, he sells imported buttons to retailers and dressmakers in New York," I said as the men shook hands.

"I'm pleased to meet you, Mr. Levine. I've heard good things about you from Sam Mayfield at Lord & Taylor. Have a seat." He motioned to the chairs. "Let's get right to it. I've had an opportunity to discuss your concept with Mr. Peters, our President. He agreed to test your dress kit. But, before we dive into specifics, I'd like to review your numbers." His eyes settled on

Abe.

Abe responded with a genuine smile. "Mr. Kraft, we're happy to review our projections. Mrs. Levine handles that end of the business and can explain the numbers."

Sadie kicked my boot under the table. I knew she was irritated. She had no idea of the many reasons I was. After our Lord and Taylor's debacle, Abe had stopped sleeping in our bed.

Relieved he was softening I kept my eyes on Mr. Kraft as I worked my way through the cost of each element in the kit as well as the packaging. I referenced a paper I'd set before him. "As you can see from the comparison on the sheet, there is a thirty percent savings for the customer when she buys the complete kit rather than each part separately: fabric, pattern, thread, notions, and buttons."

Mr. Kraft held the paper to the window's light. "I see," was all he said.

I moved on. "I projected the sales at one thousand units as you asked and also multiplied that figure by two and four to show the potential profit as we grow together." I had also drawn a graph to drive my point home.

Mr. Kraft tilted his head, studied my face, then shifted to Abe. "Your analysis is adequate and shows a tidy profit. Abe, your wife is a good bookkeeper."

Stunned, I felt heat rise to my cheeks. *Breathe. Control your mouth.*

He continued. "We'd like to test the market by using our simplest tea dress pattern in a limited number of cities, say, one thousand dresses nationwide. Once we do that, we'll have a better idea where the product sells best. Advertising in *The Delineator* is free, one of the advantages of owning the advertising." He chuckled. "As for the patterns, we'll sell them at a twenty-five percent discount off retail. You'll handle all the package assembly and deliver completed kits to our factory for finishing and shipping. Butterfield's designers will create the label design that gives equal space to both company names. Finally, we'll ship the kits together with our seasonal patterns and handle distribution and sales. You'll be paid once the merchants pay us."

I started to respond, "Mr. Kraft...." but he kept his eyes on Abe, not me.

I knocked Abe's knee under the table, signaling him to take over. *Ridiculous and infuriating!* I sealed my lips, no longer trusting what angry words might spew forth.

Abe resumed. "Mr. Kraft, the proposal is excellent, but I'd like to address a couple of fine points." He paused, "We'd like you to include another one thousand girl's tea dress kits. We know from our local experience the girl's market is particularly strong. Everything we've manufactured for children has sold like hotcakes. It'd be a shame to miss out on the opportunity, particularly since your plan is to test the market. This way, we'll get double the information we need for future orders."

Mr. Kraft pushed back his chair, rocking his head from side to side like a metronome while he thought.

Make up your mind, you damn charlatan. Bookkeeper! How dare he?

Abe warned me over and over about impatience in business, and I'd certainly learned my lesson at Lord and Taylor's. My knee-jerk reflexes were dangerous. I slowed my breathing, waited, and thought about Abe's advice, "Consider every word that leaves your mouth."

Finally, Mr. Kraft said, "Yes, another thousand units of girl's kits. Two thousand total. Mr. Levine, do you think you can assemble that quantity in sixty days?"

"Yes, sir," Abe and Sadie answered in unison.

Mr. Kraft began to rise from his chair, assuming the meeting had ended.

Abe cleared his throat. He wasn't finished. "The second point is that we'd like a fifty percent discount on your retail pattern price. With two thousand additional sales for Butterfield, you'll make a tidy profit on the patterns alone."

I drew a surprised breath. We hadn't discussed negotiating the pattern price beforehand. Was this retaliation on Abe's part? Did he want me to know how it felt to have my meeting ambushed?

Again, Mr. Kraft began the insipid head rocking.

"Can you agree to a forty percent discount?" he said. "We can't cut deeper than that."

Abe turned in his chair, facing Sadie and me, casting a hard look my way.

CHAPTER TWENTY-NINE

"Ladies, is that agreeable with both of you?"

"Yes, it is," I said with a relieved smile. Abe's experience had paid off. It wasn't the same thing as what I'd done at Lord and Taylor's.

Sadie directed her response to Mr. Kraft. "We'll have prototypes to you later in the week. Once you sign off, we'll begin assembling the order."

"Excellent," said Mr. Kraft as he stood. "Next week, my shop will prepare the labels for your approval. We should have the advertising and *Delineator* campaign ready in a month. I'll have my assistant work up an order agreement and deliver it to your office for signatures tomorrow."

* * *

Once we were outside the building and out of sight of those windows, I clapped with excitement. "It worked!" I hugged Sadie and then Abe. He drew away, shaking his head as if to tell me that nothing between us had changed.

Sadie stepped away, her forehead pinched in anger, oblivious to our interaction. "He'd only look at Abe! Doesn't that make you furious?"

More relieved than angry, I said, "I'm so happy to get the deal, I almost don't care!" I took Sadie's hand. "Look at it this way, we win in the end when the business succeeds. Better to have profit than pride." I stole a glance at Abe.

"I suppose," said Sadie, cocking her head to the side, not appearing convinced. "But we're experienced businesswomen and have proven ourselves. Why is it so hard for them to accept us?"

"Be careful," Abe pulled on his beard. "I don't mind joining you and helping keep up the ruse. It's good fun, but I don't think he's ready to work directly with you both quite yet. I think it best if I stay involved."

Why did his words trigger a new caution? I wanted to believe his motivation was pure, but a deeper part of me was concerned. Didn't he just tell me that we'd watch our own businesses? Do I dare ask him to stay out of mine?

Chapter Thirty

Floating on my back in the cool pond, I felt happier than I'd been for a long time. I paddled my hands, listening to my younger brothers frolic. As I dropped my legs, my body bobbed upright, and I treaded water, checking on baby Hannah playing on the grass at the water's edge. My brothers threw a ball back and forth while I watched, proud of my strong legs, convinced they could keep me afloat, forever. I gazed at the sky as a family of birds flew overhead, lugging worms to their nests above. The chicks stretched their spindly necks, squealing in anticipation, emitting high-pitched cries of hunger.

I noticed a gentle sensation on the surface of my legs, as if someone drew a path with a finger. Was it a fish that lost its way, mistaking me for a plant? A turtle? Kicking my leg to shake it free, it gripped my leg tighter. I looked down and saw a stringy weed growing from the floor of the pond, curling its way upward like a snake. I kicked harder, but the more vigorously I kicked, the tighter it entwined me, pulling my body under the surface. I strained for air, my legs more trapped with every movement. Who would protect Hannah, sitting so close to the edge? Mama's words came back. "Look after your little sister."

I squeezed my eyes closed, reached down, and ripped at the weeds with every ounce of my strength. Hannah called for me, "Tillie, Tillie, help me." Finally, freed from the tangle, I kicked my body to the surface, gulping for air. My eyes shot open, and I woke from my dream, searching for Hannah.

She was sitting on the edge of the bed, calling my name. "Tillie, Julian's up and needs a new diaper. He smells bad."

I untangled myself from the bedsheets, never so grateful to awake from a nightmare, Stretching my arm across the bed, I felt the cold sheet beside me, the emptiness.

I could no longer bear the discord with Abe. What if he never forgave me, and sleeping on the couch was the last stop before he moved out? Was our marriage over? I couldn't delay any longer. Yesterday, we landed Butterfield. Today, I'd take the pennyroyal elixir. Abe would be home late, and I had help with the children. Marta had warned me about nausea, but what difference would it make? I'd been queasy every day for the past month. At least now, the pregnancy would be over, and my future more manageable.

I fixed a cup of tea and watched the children as they ate their breakfast, replaying my dream. *Was there another meaning?* Mama had been worried about her children, but I'd kept my word to her. I cared for Hannah with a loving heart and was equally devoted to Julian. I could not have raised happier, healthier children. But with the burdens of family and business, Abe and I had reached our breaking point, bickering far too often. Another child would end us.

The potion was buried deep in my purse. Last week, the midwife handed the vial to me in her foyer, instructing me to drink the entire contents and wash it down with a full glass of water, nothing to eat afterwards. If the bleeding didn't start by the following morning, I was to return for a procedure.

Once Sadie rounded up Hannah for school, I sat at the dinner table, listening to the children giggle as they descended the main stairway.

I gazed at the small brown vial, reflecting on my meeting with the midwife and the oddness of Rivka's familiarity with an Irish neighborhood in Brooklyn. After all, she barely spoke English. But the address she shared was in Cobblestone, a working-class neighborhood, one-half mile from the Brooklyn Bridge, only two blocks in from the wharves.

I had asked Rivka. "Do you know if the midwife is safe?"

Rivka studied my face. "My friend used her, and it worked. Take it or not. It's up to you."

I could push her only so far. She seemed to hoard many secrets. I had taken the address and left our factory, flagging an approaching carriage. Twenty minutes later, I arrived at 146 Congress Street. Exiting the carriage, I saw the steeple of Saint Paul's towering above the brownstone rooftops. Although the mud was everywhere with the early spring thaw, the neighborhood was well maintained, with wrought iron knee-high fencing separating the postage stamp-sized front yard gardens from the sidewalk. I opened the gate, walked up the steps, and banged the door knocker. Moments dragged by. I knocked again.

"Will ye wait a moment?" a woman's voice shouted. Loud footsteps, then the door opened a crack. "What's yer business?"

"I'm looking for the midwife," I said, scarcely a whisper.

Her narrow blue eyes studied mine. "Who sent ye?"

I peered into the dark foyer. "My friend, Rivka. She said you sell unblocking potions."

The woman opened the door wider and stepped onto the front landing, her head turning from side to side. "Come in quick. It's ten dollars. Let's see yer money."

A half-hour later, I was back in the factory working as if nothing had happened. The vial sat in the bottom of my purse, burning its way into my head, coloring every thought and decision. *I must get this over with soon.*

I shook away the memory, bringing my thoughts back to the present. Our housekeeper would arrive soon to care for Julian. It was now or never. I took the vial into the kitchen, poured a glass of water, said a silent prayer, and drank every drop, verging on gagging. Expelling a deep sigh, I dressed for work, determined to distract myself until the potion took hold.

Hours later, at the factory, I was laying out a plan to meet the massive Butterfield order. I called Sadie and Rivka to my worktable. "The way I see it, we need to hire additional women to make the delivery deadline." I felt my belly rumble. "Where can we find workers fast?"

Sadie offered, "Let's start with Mrs. Simon at the Settlement House. She'll know who's looking for work."

Rivka was quiet for a moment, then added, "There're a few women in my building who could help. But not until their husbands get home from work."

I knit my brows, not understanding. The gurgling grew stronger. Was I the only one who heard?

She continued, "They watch babies, cook, and clean all day. They can't leave until after dinner. They will work at night."

Sadie interrupted, "But Tillie and I can't be here. That's when we're expected home."

Rivka answered, "I can work nights and Sundays too. I could use more hours."

I glanced at Sadie to gauge her reaction. "It's not a bad thought. We could have two shifts. Then our tables would be busy day and night."

Sadie didn't look convinced. "Let me think it over. We'll post help wanted signs at the Settlement House for now."

I knew we'd speak in private later.

"I'll walk over to the Settlement House now and get signs on the public boards. We've no time to waste." As I rose, a driving pain tore down my belly. I gripped my stomach.

Sadie's face creased in concern. "What's wrong?"

I drew a deep breath. "I'm sure it's nothing. Just my monthly." The cramp released and I looked at Rivka.

Her lips were drawn tightly. "Go home. Sadie and I can handle things."

Before I could answer, another wave of pain coursed through me. I doubled over, unable to catch my breath, dropping back into my chair.

Sadie knelt beside me. "Should I get help? A glass of water?"

The pain passed, only to be replaced by severe nausea. I shook my head. "I must have eaten something bad. I should go."

But I wasn't going anywhere. The pain had only begun. The devil's dance continued, coming in waves, knocking the wind out of me. "Sadie, get a pail. I'm going to vomit."

Sadie ran across the factory, grabbing a trash pail.

I gripped my belly and whispered to Rivka, "Did she give me poison?"

Rivka sat wide-eyed, staring back at me. "I'm sorry. I was trying to help."

Within an hour, the cramping had intensified further, reminding me of labor with the twins. But there was no sign of bleeding. I crawled onto the floor and lay curled in pain. A cycle of retching, and violent cramping repeated itself until I was exhausted, I could no longer lift my head from the floor. My eyes closed. I drifted between cramping episodes into short intervals of sleep, thinking I'd die.

Rivka, frightened, spoke into my ear. "Sadie went for the doctor. Please don't tell. I don't want to go to jail."

Another wave of illness, but I was too drained to lift my head. I left it resting in a clear pool of watery bile and passed out.

I woke to a firm shaking and garbled voices. "Let's get her home." It wasn't Abe. Who was it?

"Tillie, Tillie, can you hear me? It's Dr. Boro." The voice called urgently in my ear.

I pried my eyes open into narrow slits, discerning a fuzzy image of a man. "You're terribly sick. I need to know what you ate," Dr. Boro said.

My head began to clear. *Oh God, I must tell.* "A potion."

His voice demanded, "What kind of potion? Who gave it to you?"

I floated in a cloud, longing to return to sleep. "A midwife," I mumbled before losing consciousness.

* * *

I woke from a thick haze, the lavender scent of my linens and blanket comforting me. I forced my eyes open and saw Abe standing at the doorway to our bedroom, speaking to Dr. Boro.

I mumbled, "I'm awake."

They both stepped close to the bed, Dr. Boro speaking first. "Tillie, how are you feeling?" He took my wrist, checking my pulse and feeling my forehead. "Thank God you've returned to us."

Abe cried out, "What possessed you to take poison?"

He didn't know. I shifted my eyes to Dr. Boro. Did he? But my question didn't hang in the air for long.

An almost imperceptible nod. "Tell your husband. And Tillie, it didn't work."

My head sank into my pillow. After all that suffering, how could I still be

220

with child? "I drank a potion to terminate."

"What are you talking about? Potion? Terminate? What in God's name, Tillie?" His voice trailed off. "You're saying you were with child?"

Dr. Boro stood facing Abe. "From the look of things, Tillie is about eight weeks along. For some reason, she tried to end the pregnancy. Right now, I want to make sure she begins drinking water and tea and gets back on the mend. Could you get her water?"

Abe marched out of the bedroom angry and confused, shaking his head and muttering under his breath.

Dr. Boro sat at the edge of the bed. "I would like the name and address of the midwife before she poisons anyone else. What you did was very dangerous. You could have died."

I whispered, "Why didn't it work? I'm not ready for another baby."

"I understand, but you and Abe need to work that out because, in seven months, you will have one."

Tears filled my wearied eyes.

"I want her address. Tillie, I'm serious about this."

I sunk my head back into the pillow.

* * *

Abe remained in his place on the couch for the next three nights, affording me the privacy to convalesce. By the third morning, he woke me, carrying two cups of coffee into our bedroom. Setting them down on the nightstand, he sat on a soft chair by the bed. "How are you feeling this morning?"

I pulled myself upright against the wood headboard and sipped my coffee, relishing the warm nutty flavor. "So much better." I looked up from my cup into his eyes. "I'm sorry I frightened you."

Abe sat silently while we drank. Finally, he cleared his throat and spoke each word with great care. "For the life of me, I simply can't comprehend that you'd do such a dreadful thing. Especially knowing how much I've lost, not to mention our little Sarah. I'm not sure I can live with you after this." His voice hitched. "Don't you love me anymore?"

"No, please don't go." My eyes filled. I had never intended to end our marriage. "I do love you. It's just that we've been arguing all the time, and I was afraid you'd never forgive me for my blunder with Lord & Taylor. I didn't want to add another burden to our lives."

"How could a child, our child, ever a burden?" Abe's eyes burned with resentment.

How could he possibly understand? Everything about children rested on the shoulders of the wife, the mother. Every whimper, every morsel of food, every diaper change. "Abe, it's not your burden, it's mine. I can't handle any more than I have right now." I took a deep breath. "I don't want to give up my company. Especially now when it's becoming successful."

He stared at me with indignation. "I help you. And I make enough money to take care of all of us without another company. That's the most important job a man has."

I shot back, "I know you love us, and you'd do anything for me and the children. You don't understand."

His angry eyes burned into mine. "Understand what? Tell me what I'm not smart enough to understand."

"Me, you don't understand me." I fell back on my pillow, frustrated.

* * *

The next month dragged by, Abe and I lost in our own orbits, each consumed with private thoughts. For me, every waking hour was spent pushing the humiliating incident away while working at a frantic pace to meet the looming Butterfield deadline. Despite Sadie and Rivka's probing, I refused to discuss the potion with anyone. Like it or not, this baby would happen, and I wanted my blunder buried, never discussed again. Although Abe returned to our bed at night, he was silent, falling asleep facing the wall. Reparations would take time.

The fourth week, he waited for me in bed, flipping the covers open on my side as I approached. Without a sound, I burrowed into my normal spot and pulled up the quilt.

With a tenderness I'd nearly forgotten, Abe said, "I will try to help more. I don't want to lose you."

I rolled toward him, looking into his wounded eyes, a face full of loss. It was impossible to sidestep my guilt. Lying beside him with our child growing in my belly, I wondered how I could have hurt him so deeply. My callous actions must have seemed rash, unthinkable to him. "I love you, Abe. I promise to make this child a blessing for our family."

He pulled me close, running his hands down my body, setting my skin aflame. It had been too long since our last intimacy, and neither of us could resist the pull. Later, I fell into a deep, satisfied slumber.

The sunrise cast a bright streak of light across my pillow, striking my face. As my body roused, I sensed a stickiness between my thighs. I reached under the covers and felt my bottom, checking. Blood. I cried out, "Oh no."

He threw back the covers. My lower gown and sheets were stained crimson. Panicking, Abe implored, "Did I hurt you? The baby? Should I get the doctor?"

"You did nothing wrong. But I may have miscarried." Filled with dread, I grabbed my robe and ran to the bathroom. Sitting on the toilet, my body expelled the remains of my second pregnancy, a baby that would be no more. I sobbed into a towel, muffling my shame, realizing I'd never know if this was my fault. How could I ever forgive myself? Would Abe forgive this, too?

III

Part Three

"Spring is the time of year when it is summer in the sun and
winter in the shade."
—*Charles Dickens, Great Expectations*

Chapter Thirty-One

January 1890 - Seven years later

It took time to heal. A lot of time. As if crossing an imperceptible line, our lives drifted into a new rhythm. Season after season, for seven years, our work with Butterfield expanded, making us wealthier than I ever could have imagined. Despite our financial success and newfound readiness for another child, God held back with a penance, forcing us to endure many miscarriages, tearful days, and regrets until seven years later when I had a viable pregnancy. Over those challenging years in our efforts to conceive, Abe and I drew closer, both now valuing this hard-fought addition to our family.

The winter school break was over, and Julian picked at his breakfast without a care in the world. He lined apple slices on his plate, alternating each with a torn chunk of toasted challah, pretending they were train cars on their way to Papa's farm, his favorite summer spot.

I placed his lunch in his book bag. "Enough playing. You must get to school on time. I have an early meeting at the factory."

"Can't I stay home today?" he complained, inching an apple slice across his plate.

Holding his coat and hat by the door, I scolded, "Of course not. Put this on quickly and collect your bookbag."

Moments later, we trudged through the dirty sidewalk snow. Our breaths shot puffs of white steam into the frigid air. Julian's ears were bright red.

"Pull your hat down." I adjusted his scarf higher around his neck. Turning the final corner onto Henry Street, I noticed a large white sign on the school door. "What's that?"

Julian ran ahead and read aloud, "School closed until further notice as ordered by The New York City Health Department." He looked back, confused. "What does that mean, Mama? Why would they close school?"

"Let's find out." We turned toward the Settlement House, kicking ice off the sidewalk, pulling open the heavy door.

Mrs. Simon stood at the far end of the corridor with her palm pressed against her forehead.

I called out, "Why is school closed?"

She raised her eyes, looking grim. "This weekend, there were five confirmed cases of consumption, err tuberculosis is the name the doctors have given it, among our students, and more than double that amount was confirmed in the nearby public elementary. The cases are coming from the tenements."

Despite my warm coat, a deep chill made me shudder. I thought about all the family Abe and Sadie had lost to this wicked disease. I pulled Julian to my side. "Those damn buildings! It was a matter of time before something like this happened."

Mrs. Simon wrung her hands.

I stepped closer and whispered, "Anyone in Julian's class?"

"No one yet. We're hoping to curb it before it spreads." She shook her head sadly. "School will be closed for a month. We'll make up classes this summer, outdoors if necessary."

Julian burst out, "In the summer? Aw…"

I scolded, "Julian, quiet down. This is serious."

Mrs. Simon paid the boy no heed. "Last night at an emergency meeting, Dr. Boro said we must quarantine the infected. But it's tricky. The sick confuse their coughing for a chest cold and venture out, infecting others. And the tenements have never been as packed with newcomers as they are now."

Over the last few years, with no end in sight, a rising tide of European immigrants had come to New York City. They crammed into tenements across lower Manhattan, practically sleeping on top of each other, until finally, catastrophe forced open its rusty door. The signs, all there, were misread. While we clung to optimism, convinced it was a typical round of the cold flu with its characteristic cough and malaise, tuberculosis spread its extensive tentacles through the late fall, waiting for the depth of winter to take root. By January, the final ingredient, frigid air trapped inside closed windows, unleashed the terrifying demon.

A full decade had passed since the last tuberculosis epidemic. Most people had forgotten the devasting outbreak or moved away. I was still a child living on the farm in Harlem.

The few things I knew about consumption terrified me. Although the doctors could now diagnose the disease, they had no cure.

Mrs. Simon stared hard at the floor, her eyes lost in time. "So many died the last time, before you moved here,"

My hands shot to my round belly. Could I protect my baby?

Mrs. Simon read my mind. "I've heard nothing suggesting an unborn child can catch it. But check with Dr. Boro."

More at ease, I shifted the topic to my bitterness toward the landlords. "The city should've torn down those wretched buildings years ago. They're death traps. Has anyone from the city stepped in?"

Mrs. Simon held up her hand to stop me. "Let's not get ahead of ourselves. Right now, we need to help the sick and prevent spread. This morning, we'll prepare a letter to our congregants informing them about the disease, the symptoms, and how to keep their homes safe."

"Would you like my help?" I asked. She was right. First things first.

The worry lines on her forehead relaxed. "Oh, could you?" Suddenly, her eyes misted.

"What is it?" I reached to hold her forearm.

She pulled her handkerchief from under her cuff and patted the corners of her eyes. "All this brings back such sad memories. My twin sister died from tuberculosis."

I rubbed her arm. "I didn't know. Come, let's sit." The factory could wait.

Over the next hour, we sipped tea while she shared her recollections of the last epidemic, the supine bodies carried out of the tenements, the unending funerals, the widowed. Although her nightmarish memories stoked my fear, I was her friend and tried to offer comfort. During this time, Julian sat nearby, consumed in his library book, nibbling on crackers.

Eventually, her memories ran dry. "Let's get that letter done."

Rabbi poked his head into the kitchen to share his update. "Ladies, I've sent a hand-delivered message to the City Board of Health requesting an inspection of the tenements."

Thinking back to my sweet baby, Sarah, I scoffed, "The landlords have dodged the housing office for years, full of excuses why they haven't modernized. Someone should do something about those scoundrels."

Mrs. Simon's fury was also growing. "You know how they get away with it, don't you? With payoffs. Thugs, all of them! After the last ordinance, only a couple of landlords installed running water and indoor toilets. Most won't do a damn thing unless the city issues severe fines." Mrs. Simon huffed. "Rabbi, can we bring the health department and building inspector here together? Tammany could care less if a bunch of poor Jews die, but if they come together, maybe you can shame them into action."

"Why don't we contact the newspaper, too?" I suggested. "Then, we can really make a ruckus."

Rabbi's puffy eyes were surrounded by dark rings. Had he slept at all? He extended his hands, calming us. "That's too much, and they'll resent the interference. Like it or not, we must act as if these city workers are friends, or they'll refuse to work with us on anything now or in the future."

My heart sank. I took a sharp breath to help fight back my tears. I knew my issues with the landlords were personal. They always did as little as they could get away with.

Rabbi continued, his tired voice low and even. "Dr. Boro will join us for the inspection, and I'll make sure to get commitments before they leave." He paused, "By the way, could one of you run your letter by him? I want to make sure it's accurate."

I took a second look at the post we had written. I would have it translated into Yiddish, and post both on the front doors of the buildings. "I'm happy to." Dr. Boro was just the person I wanted to speak to next. Was the high school safe? Should Hannah and Eva stay home as well?

Rabbi Meyers nodded. "Please wait for his comments and return immediately. I want it posted this morning."

"I'll keep Julian here with me." Mrs. Simon offered.

I hurried across the street to Dr. Boro's Clinic. All the windows were open. Blasts of frigid air blew across the waiting area, sending leaflets flying through the room and onto the floor. Families, clustered like bundles of kindling, huddled together for warmth. I walked through their cacophony of coughs, covering my mouth and nose with a handkerchief. The receptionist, sitting against the opposite wall, wore a handkerchief over her mouth and nose.

I unfolded the announcement, showing it to her. "Rabbi asked that Dr. Boro review this letter right away."

She pointed to the rear hallway. "Wait in his office. I'll let him know you're here."

Settling in one of Dr. Boro's worn leather guest chairs, I gazed at his bookshelves, filled with textbooks, all frayed from constant use. Elixirs in green, yellow, and brown glass vials were set in neat rows on other shelves. I wondered how this brittle army of remedies would stand up against a serious disease.

Dr. Boro entered moments later, and in one fluid motion, pulled his cloth face mask down and slurped a cup of lukewarm tea. His blue eyes were bloodshot and, like Rabbi, ringed with dark, swollen circles. Such selfless men.

Lowering himself behind his large desk, he said, "This tuberculosis epidemic is the worst I've seen in my career. If it continues to spread, we'll be in for a disastrous winter and spring." He ran his fingers through his sparse hair. "I wish we had a cure."

Fear ran through me. But despite my nerves, I needed answers. "What causes it?"

"Tiny particles, invisible to the naked eye, that enter the body while we live, breathing, talking, kissing, and eating. All innocent actions." He shook his head sadly. "It passes from one mouth into the lungs of the next, the particles burrowing deep, feasting and multiplying until that person infects the next." He stopped, drawing a measured breath. "That's why ventilation is so important. This has been stewing for months."

I sighed, replaying our final days with Sarah, wishing I could help prevent the loss of innocent lives. But I had a job to do.

"Doctor, could you review the letter we're posting this morning? Rabbi would like to ensure we have the details correct before it gets hung." I handed him the paper filled with spidery handwriting. "I hope it's legible. Then I have a quick personal question."

Dr. Boro scanned the letter and handed it back to me. "This is fine. What's on your mind? Any coughing in your home?"

"No, thank God," I answered, "But I'm worried about Hannah, Eva, and Sadie's boys. Should we keep them home, too?" Our older children attended the Jewish High School uptown and rode the streetcar together each way.

His eyes were thoughtful as he shifted back into his clinical persona. "Keep them home until Rabbi and I have a chance to talk to the Board of Health this week. We'll know more about the outbreaks after we meet with them. In the meantime, better to be safe."

I hesitated. "I'm also worried about Rivka's family. She didn't show up for work last week. Are they sick?"

Dr. Boro reached for a paper on his desk and looked through a list of names. "They're on my list of home visits this afternoon. For the moment, there're no confirmed cases from their building."

"That's a relief."

He nodded and glanced at the clock on his desk.

I was taking too much of his precious time. I stood to leave.

He warned, "Be careful and protect yourself."

As I walked out of his office, I noticed him tilting his head back in his chair and closing his eyes. *The poor, exhausted man.*

* * *

"Hi, Hannah!" I called as she returned home from school later that day. "How was school? Why are you late?"

"Eva and I missed our regular streetcar and had to wait in the cold for the next one."

"Come to the parlor. The fire will warm you up. And we need to discuss a couple of things."

Hannah hung her overcoat on the coat rack and walked into the parlor wearing her new emerald-green sweater and black wool skirt, bringing a waft of frigid air with her. She rubbed her hands close to the flames, blowing into them. "It is so cold outside!" She lowered herself into one of my Queen Anne chairs by the hearth.

I exhaled deeply. "It's been a difficult day. I heard from Dr. Boro that there's a serious tuberculosis epidemic in our neighborhood. It started in the tenements. They closed Julian's school for a month until the disease is contained." I paused. "It seems to be spreading rapidly."

Hannah turned to me, her eyes wide. "Oh no, what about my school?"

"Dr. Boro wants you, Eva and her brothers to stay home until he meets with city officials this week. Then he'll have more information to share."

"You know there are people from the tenements who go to school with us." Hannah paused, her face scrunched in thought. "Saul didn't meet us at the streetcar. He never showed up today at school." She jumped from her chair. "Oh, my God, I hope he's not sick. He never misses a day."

"Settle down, dear. Dr. Boro is stopping at his apartment later. We can check tomorrow and see if their family needs anything. In the meantime, let's stay calm."

"How bad is the disease? Is there a cure?" Hannah asked.

"I don't know a lot about it, but Dr. Boro does. The last time it struck, we were still living on the farm uptown. We were outside harm's way."

Hannah dropped back in her chair. "This is terrible. Saul's been working so hard, learning English and science. You know, he's brilliant."

"Rivka is very proud of him."

Hannah's forehead creased with worry. "Eva's been studying with him since the beginning of the year." She whispered, "She has a big crush."

Chapter Thirty-Two

The following day, Hannah and I braved the early chill, our boots crunching through shattered ice chunks on the sidewalk. Usually, I'd take this walk with Julian while Hannah rode the streetcar uptown to high school. This morning, though, we were anxious to hear about the inspector's visit and, while at the school, pick up lessons for Julian to work on at home.

As we rounded the last corner, Hannah said, "Eva hasn't heard anything from Saul. I'm worried."

I didn't want to fuel her alarm. "We're all on edge. But let's get the facts first."

We opened the wooden door to the school. A teacher stood there, barring the door, prepared to turn us away.

I said, "We've only come to collect my son's schoolwork."

She stepped aside. "Please get what you need and then go home."

We headed directly to Julian's classroom. Other parents were doing the same. No one wanted their children to fall behind.

I waved at Julian's teacher, standing at the door to her classroom. "Hannah, could you see about getting Julian's schoolwork while I go next door and talk to Mrs. Simon?"

Hannah huffed, "Don't go without me. I want to hear what's going on, too. I'm not a little child anymore."

Hannah was fourteen, my age, when Mama passed. She was right. Every day, I fought with myself to stem my overprotective nature.

Moments later, with an entire bag of books and assignments, we entered the Settlement House, heading straight to Mrs. Simon's office. She was sitting at her desk, pouring through papers.

I called to her. "Do you have a moment?"

Mrs. Simon stretched her neck to see around the door frame. "Is that my Hannah'la with you?" she sang. "How do you like high school? Still at the top of your class?"

"I love it." Hannah smiled. "Tillie's studying my books, too. She plans to learn everything I'm learning."

"Oh my, that's news!" Mrs. Simon said, glancing at my rounded belly.

While Hannah spoke with Mrs. Simon, I prepared tea in the kitchen. Embarrassed and annoyed to be reminded of my brief education, I hadn't planned to mention my studies. It would take a miracle for me to finish the curriculum with Hannah. Something always got in the way.

Returning to the office, I handed Hannah her tea. "Please keep my studying private. There's a lot going on right now with a baby coming and the business. I'd hate to disappoint everyone."

Mrs. Simon pressed her lips together in a thin line. "I understand, but you must keep up the work. That was the first thing you shared when we met years ago."

I set our cups on the rickety table, changing the subject. "What did those inspectors have to say?"

The creases around Mrs. Simon's mouth deepened further. "I'm afraid things are worse than we first thought. The Building Inspector is fining the owners. The airshafts were disgusting. Dr. Boro said they were knee-high with garbage and human waste. He called it 'a vile pit of disease'. But that's the least of it."

I blew on my tea, a thread of fear lacing through my veins. Listening dredged up my worst memories of living in that horrid place. I'd never forget my first whiff of the hallway when I thought I'd be sick. "What else?"

"When the Health Inspector, Rabbi, and Dr. Boro returned, they spoke for over two hours. There were at least fifty confirmed cases of disease and countless others undiagnosed. As expected, the young, undernourished, and frail have been hit the hardest." Mrs. Simon closed her eyes. "That's what always seems to happen." She inhaled sharply through her nose.

Hannah interrupted, an edge of hysteria laced through her voice. "What about Saul's family?"

Mrs. Simon hesitated, then looked into Hannah's pleading eyes. "I'm sorry, dear. Saul is very sick. Dr. Boro admitted him to the Willard Parker Hospital on East 16th Street. They're the experts."

Hannah jumped from her chair, knocking into the table, her cup rattling in the saucer. Hot tea splashed over the tabletop. "I must see him now, let's go."

Mrs. Simon reached out, grabbing onto Hannah's arm. "Sit! You will not go anywhere. What are you thinking, Hannah? Your sister's pregnant."

Hannah sunk back in her chair, stunned by the admonishment.

Mrs. Simon's voice softened as she wiped up the spill. "Dear, I know it's hard to stand by, but we must contain the spread. The apartments with sickness have been quarantined until it ends." Mrs. Simon's eyes filled with tears. "Several babies are dying."

A field of goosebumps covered my arms. "How can we help?" My head choked with memories of rocking baby Sarah while she gasped her last breath.

Mrs. Simon spoke first. "We're asking the congregation to increase contributions to the pantry, and Mrs. Katz is organizing food deliveries to quarantined homes. Rabbi plans to make announcements at services this weekend. This may be our last gathering for a while." She sighed, running her fingers through her flyaway hair, futilely stuffing the frizzy ends back into her bun. "We could use food and money. Many families won't be able to work for weeks."

Leave it to Mrs. Katz. She always found a way to make us feel useful.

Hannah turned the conversation. "What did you hear about the Jewish high school?"

Mrs. Simon answered, "It will remain open for now. Saul was the only case reported." She paused, sorting through her recollections. "The teachers have strict instructions to inform the City of any coughing or related symptoms."

We stood to leave. It felt awkward ending our conversation without embracing Mrs. Simon. To prevent the spread, everyone had curtailed hugging and kissing. I felt as if I was leaving my dear friend with an unfinished sentence.

"I need to stop at the Clinic before we go home," Hannah said, shaking me from my dark thoughts. "I have a few questions for Dr. Boro."

I hesitated, hating to disrupt the doctor after witnessing his fatigue yesterday. "Can we leave him be? Besides, the waiting room is full of illnesses. What's so important?"

Hannah huffed. "It's personal. You'll have to trust me."

Concern clawed at me. "Very well. You go ahead, and I'll prepare hot tea and a sandwich to bring to him. But go directly to his office. Cover your face completely."

* * *

Moments later, I waited in Dr. Boro's office while he and Hannah met in an exam room. I had no idea what to think. Was she sick, too?

Hannah entered the office first. Tears rimmed her eyes.

I jumped in alarm. "What's happening? I'm scared to death."

Dr. Boro followed Hannah. "Calm down. Sit," he said as he lowered himself into his desk chair. "Hannah's fine, but I need to check Eva. It seems Eva and Saul have been engaged in a little romance. I wouldn't be troubled under normal circumstances. But these days, kissing an infected person is dangerous."

I could barely move under the weight of my fear. The disease had become a runaway train. Even our new apartments and indoor plumbing couldn't protect us from the evil. I drew a deep breath, regaining my composure.

Dr. Boro stood. Pointing to the refreshments, he said, "I'll get to that sandwich in a while, but I must return to my patients now." He looked at Hannah. "If you start coughing, I want to see you immediately."

Then his eyes swept to my belly. "Two things, Tillie. I don't want to see you at the Clinic again. If you need me, send a message."

I nodded. "What's the second thing?"

"Ask Sadie to bring Eva. Today."

"Of course." I reached for my coat and straightened my hat, longing for fresh air.

Hannah didn't move. "Dr. Boro, can I borrow a book on tuberculosis? I want to learn more."

He studied her for a moment. "Of course." He leafed through the pile of Lancet medical journals on his desk and handed one to Hannah. It was titled *Professor Koch's Remedy for Tuberculosis*. "This is the most current information."

* * *

I went directly to Sadie's, Hannah at my heels. As we approached her door, I said, "You heard the doctor. You need to stay away until we know more. I'll go alone."

Hannah shot another annoyed look, then stomped to our apartment.

Knock, knock. "Hi, Sadie, it's me, Tillie."

"I'll be right there."

Seconds later, Sadie opened the door.

"Can we talk in the hall?" I asked, attempting to hide my fear.

"Sure, what's going on?" She stepped out of her apartment and closed the door.

"I just got home from the Clinic. Saul has it. Dr. Boro admitted him to Willard Parker for care. He's checking all of Saul's friends and would like to see Eva today. He examined Hannah while we were there and she seemed fine, so far." I sighed.

"Oh no," Sadie grabbed her forehead. "I'll take her right away."

A muffled cough came from the apartment. We both caught our breath.

"Do you want me to come?" I offered, terrified. "He's being extra careful, and you know it's only precautionary."

Her eyes were fixed on the door. "No, Eva and I will walk down now. You're probably right, just a precaution." She turned to the door. "I'm sorry to hear about Saul. Do you know how long he'll stay at the hospital?"

"I don't, but some apartments are getting quarantined, and Julian's school is closed."

She twisted back. "What about Rivka? We were supposed to work on the samples for Butterfield today. Can you manage on your own?"

"Of course. I'll head to the workshop this afternoon. When I finish, I'll bring the kits home, and you can check them later while we figure out how to deal with all these children stuck at home," I said, attempting to lighten her fear.

Chapter Thirty-Three

After lunch, I walked to the factory, determined to distract myself while I waited for news about Eva. No good would come from my sitting around wringing my hands. Besides, we were on a tight schedule.

My mind drifted to our customers in the western territories. This afternoon, I needed to select fabrics and assemble samples for Butterfield's approval. Unlike our country's prairie women, up north on the farms, we'd many neighbors. In the territories, women lived in isolation, forging through endless, lonely winters. The women needed something pretty to sew, holding onto the promise of spring, a fabric both sturdy and feminine. I pictured our old flower garden, the yellow and purple petunias opening their petals to welcome spring.

I was lost in these thoughts as I unlocked the door to our factory space. Before leaving the day before, I'd spread fabrics on a worktable, planning on a fresh look the morning. Now, standing over the materials and visualizing those sprays of flowers, my eyes settled on the soft yellow calico for the girl's tea dress and a dark violet for the women, like those petunias on the farm. Both were perfect for a no-nonsense everyday life, worn with a white apron draped around the front. The practical cotton prints would disguise the inevitable day-to-day splatters and stains, while the shorter ankle-length design for women and mid-calf for young girls would be both cleaner and safer than the floor-length skirts that were quickly becoming passe. Dragging one's dress on the ground and street made for filthy torn hemlines, not to mention tripping accidents.

Concentrating on the task at hand, I unbolted the violet calico. Using the pattern instructions, I measured three yards of calico for the dress and two yards of white for the apron, cutting cleanly across the unrolled bolt with pinking shears. I then cut an eight-by-eleven-inch cardboard rectangle, the kit size we'd agreed upon. Using the cardboard frame as a guide, I carefully folded the fabric, then slid it into the wrapping envelope Mr. Kraft had provided. A small paper sleeve held the pins, needles, matching buttons, thread, and grosgrain hemming ribbon. I set the pattern on top, eager to see the new outer packaging Mr. Kraft's group had promised.

After tinkering with the two samples, I packed the kits into my large satchel for the walk home. Loud footsteps clunked on the floor outside the factory door. Then a sharp banging. Alarmed, I called out, "Who is it?"

"It's Max. I must speak to you."

I pulled the door open. He stood trembling, holding his hat in his hands, his forehead dotted with beads of sweat despite the cold.

I froze, staring at his frightened face, "What's wrong?"

His voice trembled. "It's Eva. Dr. Boro thinks she's infected. Sadie took her to be tested at the hospital. I can't believe it."

I stepped backward, horrified. My mind stumbled from Eva to Hannah and how she might be next. "Maybe the tests will show she only has a cold."

"I'm praying so," he said weakly. "I'm heading home to wait with her brothers. I turned the shop over to my foreman to close later. I don't want the boys home alone."

"I'll bring dinner. I prepared beef stew yesterday. There's plenty for everyone. Maybe you'll have good news by then." I kept my voice steady, trying to sound reassuring as I watched Max scurry down the stairs.

Eva was like a second daughter to me. The girls had been fast friends from the moment Hannah came to live with us. Skittering back and forth between our apartments, their bond was as solid as sisters. And Hannah was already beside herself with concern. This news would surely devastate her.

* * *

Sadie hadn't returned from the hospital by dinnertime. I dropped off the stew and cookies with Max. About to leave, I stopped at the door and looked at his forlorn face. "Max, I don't care what time Sadie gets home. Come by and let us know."

He nodded and walked me out. "We appreciate the supper."

After returning to our apartment, I cobbled together a simple meal of leftover chicken and carrots for my family. No one complained, each of us lost in our thoughts. Finally, Abe broke the silence. "Tillie, on a brighter note, I have other news you'll want to hear."

I awoke from my silent prayers. "What is it?"

"I met with Leo Baum at his Bloomingdale's office. He asked for you and then placed his largest order yet."

"I'm so thankful that my loose lips at Lord and Taylor's years ago didn't ruin that relationship. I've learned so many lessons since those early days." As much as I enjoyed my business, I'd grown wiser, always prioritizing those closest to me.

Abe cupped his hand over mine, massaging my wrist with his thumb. "If only we had as much control over this disease."

Hannah stood, setting her silverware atop her plate to take into the kitchen. "Wake me when you hear from Sadie. I want to see Eva."

"I know you do, but we'll take our instructions from Dr. Boro."

Abe and I sat silently. With so much going on in our lives, it felt like we were on a high-wire act, battling the winds. One strong gust and all our good fortune could vanish.

I was jarred from my thoughts by a different, alarming realization. "Oh, Abe, we have only sixty days to deliver our Butterfield order. How can I keep that commitment if Sadie and Rivka can't help?" I buried my face in my hands.

* * *

The next morning, hearing nothing from Max and promising Hannah answers, I headed directly to Sadie's apartment. I gently knocked, praying for reassuring news.

Sadie, my dearest friend in the world, opened the door. I'd never seen her so exhausted, so adrift. Her face was ghost-like; her curly hair, typically tucked into a neat bun at the nape of her neck, was untethered, its curly wisps framing her face like a crown of thorns, fate mocking her. With the morning light pouring in from the windows behind, I could see the curves of her body through the thin cotton of her nightgown. Without words, she opened the door wider, turned, and walked to the dining room table, collapsing into a chair.

"Sadie," I bent beside her, cradling her in my arms, "Talk to me. What happened?"

Sadie dropped her face into her hands and leaned forward, releasing an animal-like howl of despair, sobbing, shaking. No explanation was necessary. I knew immediately that her daughter, Eva, had tuberculosis.

Chapter Thirty-Four

May 1890

F ive months later, sitting on an oak pew in the synagogue sanctuary, I could scarcely believe my family had survived the treacherous winter unscathed. One catastrophic loss followed another in our tightly-knit community. Although the tide of disease receded in March, it did little to console the families who'd lost precious loved ones. Looking right and left at my neighbors huddled together with their kin, I thanked God my little family was spared.

Behind me, to the left, an older man coughed. All heads turned. Handkerchiefs were drawn from pockets and purses. A call to arms. We'd grown accustomed to shielding ourselves from invisible germs. Germs, a word that had never been part of our vocabulary, was now sprinkled in every conversation. The man stood and hobbled out of the room. A cumulative sigh of relief followed him out the sanctuary door.

Besides those who perished, many more were hospitalized at Willard or at the Charity Hospital on Blackwell Island or left fighting to regain their health. The Mourner's Kaddish, the prayer for the dead, was imprinted in my memory, *Yitgadal v'yitkadash...* Some evenings, drifting off to sleep, the sad intonation filled the space inside my head.

Saul, Rivka's younger brother, and ten other children from Julian's school died at Willard Hospital. Many families exposed to the infected succumbed. If not with the disease, then from emotional distress. Isolation took its toll as superstition and neighbors' accusations upended our once charitable world.

With winter weather behind us today, we held Mrs. Katz's memorial service. The sanctuary windows were all opened. We mourned Mrs. Katz, an angel amongst us, for her ongoing generosity and commitment to those in need. I was transported, listening to the Rabbi's eulogy.

"Mrs. Katz found a new purpose in life after her devoted husband, Lev, passed twenty years ago. She understood pain. She understood loss. And she understood poverty. Having arrived in New York years before most of you, she and her husband scratched together a living selling pickles—the most delicious pickles in the city. They never forgot the people who helped their business succeed, and when Lev passed, and their son took over the shop, Mrs. Katz found a new purpose." He paused to allow us to consider his message. "Helping you, her community."

I thought about the evolution of my purpose—daughter, student, wife, teacher, mother, business owner, and how each shaped me into a better version of myself. What would come next?

The Rabbi continued, "Her first community-wide success was the food pantry. We will be naming it in her honor. Until she fell ill, Mrs. Katz fearlessly knocked on doors and shared provisions with those in need. But her greatest accomplishment came from the inspiration she gave to every one of us, adults, and children alike. The inspiration to give back to our community, our extended family. To trust that by giving and caring for each other, you can act as a servant of God."

"Who will help us now?" uttered an old woman in a pew behind me.

A voice answered her plea. "Others will step forward. You'll see."

I surveyed the room, spotting Mrs. Simon, another pillar in the community, and prayed for her ongoing health. Through her relentless efforts, she had raised financial support for eight adults from the tenements to leave town for a new treatment at an upstate sanitarium. Years earlier, Dr. Trudeau had founded the Little Red Cottage in Saranac Lake. Quite by accident, when convinced he would perish from tuberculosis, he decided to spend his last days in his family's hunting lodge. It was there he discovered that rest, fresh air, and nutrition could bring on a cure. We jumped at the opportunity to send congregants to him.

Eva was one of those admitted to Dr. Trudeau's sanatorium. Sadie accompanied her upstate once she was well enough to travel and stayed, declaring in her weekly letters, *I plan to bring the children back for the entire summer, so Eva has us nearby. They're building visitor cottages where we'll stay.*

I wrote back: *Such a relief. We've been so frightened for our sweet girl. I could barely hold myself together when we visited her at the hospital in February. She was so frail.*

Before Eva moved upstate, Hannah and I were permitted one brief visit. I was shocked to see how wasted her beautiful young body had become. She lay in bed with deeply sunken eyes and sallow skin, a whisper of her former self.

Now, we were encouraged by Eva's improvement and heartened by the steady flow of mail between the girls. Hannah shared a recent letter during last night's dinner.

May 1, 1890

  My dearest Hannah,

  Oh, how I miss you! I miss the city and my family, but I miss you the most, especially our talks and secrets.

  Although my progress is slow, and it's been hard to be far from all of you, I am improving. Not everyone gets better, and sometimes I'm scared. The cemetery nearby has fresh graves every week. But I try not to think about it.

  The doctor asked us to walk every dry morning, no matter how cold. So, a few of us began walking the trails around the property. I love watching the sun break through the winter clouds and feeling its warmth on my face. Mostly, it's odd to see tall fir trees everywhere. So different from the city. And wild animals leave their hiding places in the woods in the early morning hours. Can you imagine? At first, I was frightened, but I soon discovered they were more afraid of us. So far, I've seen a bear, fox, and wolf. It's like living inside a zoo.

The snow has mostly melted, but beneath the leftover ice is a lake of mud, thicker than you could imagine. There are spots where I sink to my ankles. Yesterday, I pulled my foot out, and my shoe stayed behind, sucked under forever! Mama, bless her soul, has ordered boots for me, so I won't wholly ruin or lose my shoes. I always wish you were here when funny things like that happen. We would have laughed so hard.

I think about Saul every day. You and I knew him as a quiet boy, studying and asking smart questions. But, back in Romania, he was brave. His family had a terrible life before coming to New York. On the ship, he found blankets and food. He may have snuck up to the second-class berths to find everything they needed to be warm and fed. He never said, but I suppose it's alright to steal sometimes when you're that poor.

I can still hear his laugh, like hiccups. But I especially miss his strong arms around my waist when we rode the streetcar to school. I believe he would have become someone important. Now, we'll never know.

Hannah set the letter on the table, lifting her eyes to Abe and me. "I'll bet they would have married if only...."

Abe's eyes held a knowing smile as they drifted to mine. "Love is the most meaningful part of life. I'm thankful Eva had a taste."

I sighed. "Let's pray it was her first taste." I shook off my lingering concern. "Hannah, is there more?"

"Just a little bit."

Can you speak to Auntie Tillie about visiting? You could come with Mama when she brings the family this summer. That would give me something special to look forward to.

I must end this letter now. I still get tired and will write again next week before the post. Please tell me about your family, high school, and if you like any boys.

Best friends forever,

Eva

"What do you think?" asked Hannah. "Can I go to Saranac this summer?"

"What's this about a boyfriend?" I asked.

Hannah scoffed. "There is no boyfriend! Can you answer my question?"

I folded my hands, braced for an argument. "I'm not sure what to tell you. Part of me wants to send you and keep Eva's spirits up, but another part is petrified. Let's discuss it with Dr. Boro and get his thoughts. He's always given us the right advice." Could she possibly understand the danger?

"And don't forget," I said, patting my round belly. "We have a little one arriving soon. I'm sure you wouldn't want to miss the excitement."

* * *

I hurried to the factory the following morning to work on the latest Butterfield order. Spring was in full flower in New York, with its revitalizing warmth and promise of new life. Supporting my pendulous belly with one hand, I passed flowerpots set outside stalls and storefronts. I inhaled their peaty smell, wondering what bulbs had been planted.

As I approached our factory door, I heard a chorus of women cackling. On the other side, the factory was in full swing, pulsating with the noise of industry. I marveled, delighted by the atmosphere. Rivka had organized a dozen women to tackle our largest order yet. Today, ten women from the tenements were evenly spread around five tables, measuring, cutting, and folding fabric. At the sixth table stood two women placing the notions, thread, buttons, and grosgrain ribbon into small bags, then setting those bags atop the folded fabric. A Butterfield pattern with a fabric swatch pinned to the thin paper was set on the notion bag, all stacked in a neat pile with tissue paper separating each kit, ready for delivery to Butterfield for finishing touches.

As I strolled through the room, a tiny woman caught my eye. I vaguely remembered her from my English class years earlier. Her name was Tova, a shy, mousy woman with small, sunken eyes. She had sat in the corner of the classroom on high alert, hungry, dirty, jumpy. Troubled by her appearance and assuming her family might need Mrs. Simon's extra support, one evening, I asked her to stay after class.

"I'm happy to have you in my class," I said gently in Yiddish. "How long have you been in New York?"

She began to cry. "Two months here, and my family's already sick."

"I'm so sorry. Perhaps we can help. We have a food pantry and a doctor. Can I arrange help for you?" I handed her my handkerchief.

Tova nodded. "There's no work for anyone, not even my strong, older brother."

"Perhaps we can help you there, too," I made a mental note to have Rivka stop by her apartment and discuss the factory. "May I have your address?" I asked, handing her a pen and paper.

After class, I left a note in Mrs. Simon's office concerning Tova's family and their need for services. I hoped Rivka could convince her to work for Sadie and me. It would help with income and give her extra practice with English. A week later, I was pleased to see her at one of our cutting tables. Our community was as efficient as it was poor.

Now, years later, she was still working in my factory. "I'm delighted to see you, Tova. Thank you for helping with this enormous order." I stood at Tova's workplace.

"Tank you for the work." She smiled, revealing stained, broken teeth, nodding her head up and down with enthusiasm.

Rivka walked from one table to the next, directing, correcting, and praising. Was all this responsibility too soon after Saul's passing?

I touched her arm. "You've done a marvelous job, but are you ready to take on so much?"

"It's better this way. I was losing my mind at home. Too much sadness." Her shoulders shuddered. "We have all lost people."

I changed the subject, sweeping my arm across the room. "You found wonderful help."

She knit her brows. "Everyone needs more money. I could have filled five factories."

What was I thinking? The donations from the Settlement House were only a temporary patch. This community needed to work. "Of course. I'll be right back."

I headed out the factory door to Moishe's Bakery and the kosher deli. I'd give them an extra thank you with a special lunch.

Chapter Thirty-Five

In late May, our second child, Miriam Sarah, was born. Miriam was named with an 'M' after my Oma and her middle name, Sarah, for my mother and, of course, her long-gone sister.

Unlike the first debacle, this birth was a breeze. As a matter of fact, so was the entire pregnancy. Only sixteen when Julian was born, I was bewildered by the sudden reality of adult life. This time, with far more knowledge and a circus of activity in my life, there was little time to dwell on something as ordinary as a pregnancy.

I had woken with a cramped belly but pushed through, heading to the kitchen to prepare coffee and breakfast. Just as I stirred the milk and sugar into our cups, a ripping sensation shot down my belly. Breathless, I called. "Abe, come quickly. It's started."

As he rounded the doorway, my water broke. Clear fluid gushed down my legs, soaking my new braided rug.

"Oh no, I just bought that rug. Now it's ruined!" I grabbed a towel off the counter and bent to mop up the mess.

Abe knelt beside me. "Let me get you to bed. I'll take care of this."

Hannah rushed in, still wearing her nightclothes. "What happened? Is it time?"

I struggled to my feet. "Could you get dressed and fetch Marta? And Abe, please get Julian his breakfast and walk him to school."

I tucked a clean dish towel between my thighs and hobbled back to bed, waiting for Marta. Allowing Hannah to shadow Marta was one of the wisest decisions I'd made that winter. Once she finished reading Dr. Koch's papers on tuberculosis, Hannah's curiosity about the body was unrelenting. She read her way through Dr. Boro's library until she stumbled on Dr. T. Gaillard Thomas's textbook, *A Practical Treatise on the Diseases of Women*. It was then she insisted on witnessing the miracle of birth first-hand.

Marta and Hannah remained at my side all afternoon, rubbing my back, wiping my brow through the gripping pain. Finally, it was time to push.

"Bear down. I can see the hair." Marta commanded.

I lifted my head off the pillow, shouting in her face. "I can't stand it anymore."

Hannah held her palm on my lower belly. Moments later, ignoring my plea, she shouted, "Here comes another contraction. Push!"

I couldn't resist, squeezing down with every ounce of strength.

Marta's voice was calm, reassuring. "Good job. The head's out. Next push we get the shoulders through."

A high-pitched squeal broke through. The baby was already crying and had not been fully born.

Hannah began to laugh. "Have you ever seen anything like this?"

Marta said, "Every once in a while. Baby's already complaining. Get ready for the next contraction. Deep breath, and...push!"

Miriam slid from my body onto a clean towel while Marta expertly cut the umbilical cord and Hannah wrapped the furious, screaming little body.

"Best of luck with this one," Marta laughed. "She already has strong opinions."

Hannah leaned into Miriam's reddened face. "Why so angry, dear child? Didn't anyone tell you no one stays in there forever?"

She was a cherub, almost twice the size of either twin when born, resembling her father with his dark, wavy hair.

Hannah tightened the warm, white swaddle around Miriam, rubbing the tip of her nose in the baby's cheek before handing her to me. For two months before Miriam was born, Hannah had accompanied me to my midwife visits. "I'm in love with you little girl. I love your spirit already, and you're only minutes old."

"Hannah, you're a natural," Marta complimented.

"That was so much fun! Someday, I'll be a midwife!" said Hannah.

I gazed at my newborn's face, puckered and angry at being plucked out of her blissful life in the womb. "Hang on to your grit, child. You'll need every bit in this life."

Abe and Julian, now back from school, had been waiting anxiously, bursting into the room full of vigor as soon as Marta opened the door. Abe sat beside me on the bed as we cradled Miriam. Tears rolled down his cheeks as he spoke nonstop. "I love you, Tillie. How extraordinary! Another girl, a fine blessing. You, my sweet child, will want for nothing. I promise my love and protection forever."

I watched Julian's curious face as Abe talked.

Abe twisted to Julian while he held the swaddled baby. "Come close and meet your baby sister. She may cry, but she doesn't bite."

Julian stood back; his face scrunched in confusion. "Mama, I don't understand. She was in your tummy yesterday. And there's no baby in there anymore. How'd she come out?"

I shook my weary head, hoping he would stop asking questions.

On cue, Abe sat Julian at the foot of the bed and helped him hold Miriam. "Come here, son, and hold your little sister. Stop asking so many questions, and let your mama rest. She's been working hard all day."

I wished we could freeze time. Life felt as perfect as it could possibly be without our lost Sarah. My family surrounded me in a blanket of love so pure and immense that I was overcome.

Chapter Thirty-Six

June 1890

"Good Lord, Tillie, it's beastly out there! Why a shawl?" asked Abe. "I'm *schvitzing* just looking at you!"

I rolled my eyes upward while pointing to my breasts. "They have a mind of their own these days. I have enough milk for a litter of kittens."

Laughing, Abe grabbed the satchel of new kit concepts, and we headed directly to our meeting with Butterfield. "Then, we best hurry."

The minutes crawled by as Abe, and I sat, waiting on a brightly uphol-stered settee opposite Miss Sweeney's desk in the reception area. Mr. Kraft was tied up and our meeting had been postponed.

"How's the baby?" Miss Sweeney, attempting to fill the awkward quiet, studied me from head to toe. "I can't believe you're working already. It's only been one month."

"Miriam's my delicious little muffin," crowed Abe. "Don't worry about Tillie. She's taking it slow. She has a factory full of workers helping her."

I held my tongue. They knew so little of the poor. Most women in the Lower East Side worked days after birth.

I'd no time to waste. Still a newborn, Miriam was on a three-hour nursing schedule. Although my figure had begun returning, I was breastfeeding, my body sharply attuned to Miriam's schedule. That morning, I nursed her until the moment I left home and prepared a spare bottle for Hannah to use in an emergency. But Miriam hated bottles and would impart her fury if offered one instead of my breast. I'd stuffed monthly rags in my bodice and threw on a lightweight shawl to hide the inevitable leakage.

Mr. Kraft arrived with his boss, Mr. Peters, a tall, wiry man with sparse grey hair, wearing a dashing navy suit and blue plaid cravat, no doubt setting the standard for dress at Butterfield. After Mr. Kraft's stern demeanor, I was surprised by Mr. Peter's gracious smile. He greeted us warmly, extending his hand to Abe and then to me before we all entered Mr. Kraft's office.

"I want to be the first to congratulate both of you on the birth of this fine product and, hmm, the birth of your new child." Mr. Peters laughed at his humor. He looked about. "Where's the other woman?"

Abe answered. "There's an illness in her family. She sends her regrets."

Mr. Kraft glanced at his boss, mouthing the word "women."

My face burned with anger. *He should have a sick child and see what it's like. He can't remember her name after all this time?*

Mr. Kraft handed Abe a thick sales folder. "Mr. Levine, look at the first graph. You'll be pleased to see sales have continued to grow. Pairing your fabrics and notions with our pattern and an attractive retail price was brilliant."

Abe opened the report in front of both of us. I exhaled a private sigh of relief, pleased as I scanned the page, the tension in my shoulders dissolving. *If they're selling*, I told myself, *then I don't give two hoots who does all the talking.*

Mr. Kraft opened his copy of the sales report. "We expected geographic variations, but as you see from the sales report, the kits sell equally well across the country."

I nodded at the numbers, lips pursed, pleased with my intuition. "That's what I'd predicted from the start."

Mr. Peters ignored my comment, directing his next words to Abe. "I want to seize this opportunity. Let's increase the volume and introduce new fabrics, say, another two thousand kits in six weeks? With darker, late season fabrics?"

My stomach clenched. Could I push the factory that hard? Would I need more workers?

Mr. Kraft cleared his throat. "You'll likely need capital for the next order, so we'll square up on the current payment today."

Abe added. "Gentlemen, Mrs. Levine and I are as pleased as you. But a change in the arrangement is long overdue."

The two men stared back in disbelief.

As I watched, my nipples tingled. I looked at the clock. More than two hours had passed since we left home. Every minute of waiting was met with a burning, filling sensation spreading through my breasts. "Please excuse me." I hurried to the women's lavatory to put toilet paper in my bodice.

Moments later, I returned to a heated debate.

In his calmest voice, Abe explained, "We're happy to keep the split and pricing constant but will require that you pay a fifty percent deposit on all future orders. Then we can settle quarterly after you have your sales report." I knew Abe was concerned. Once we increased scale, we'd need bank loans, and it was no secret that Abe hated borrowing. Besides, it was smart business, having Butterfield advance our working capital.

I held my breath. He hadn't discussed these changes with me beforehand. I was glued to their faces, stunned by Abe's chutzpah negotiating. His affable manner left his rivals ill-prepared for a tough negotiation. But he was right. We'd need more working capital. So why not share the risk? Butterfield had been making huge profits on our kits.

I watched Mr. Peter's face, noticing for the first time an irritated glint in his eyes. He was shrewder than I'd imagined, hiding behind his affable nature.

Mr. Kraft drummed his fingers on the table, shifting his eyes toward Mr. Peters, waiting for his boss's decision.

Finally, Mr. Peters rose. "It's a reasonable request. I'll leave you to work out the details." We all stood and shook hands. I tightened the shawl around my shoulders, crossing it at my bodice to cover the milk stains growing through my padding and thin summer dress.

Determined to end the meeting, I added, "I'll bring fall fabrics by your office later this week for approval, perhaps plaids. We'll gear up for production immediately afterward."

Mr. Kraft answered tightly. "Excellent." He handed Abe a check with a settlement invoice, averting his eyes from me. "I'll have advance payment for the new order next week when we approve the fabrics."

Leave it to Abe to solve the money challenge.

Mr. Kraft then followed us to the door. "Congratulations. I'm only sorry we didn't think of the kit idea first."

Was he kidding? But I had no time to worry about his words. My milk was seeping out, trickling down the front of my body, dampening my stomach. If I stayed any longer, it might start dripping onto the floor.

We said a quick goodbye to Miss Sweeney and hurried to the lift. Finally, out on the sidewalk, I opened my shawl and turned to Abe. The entire front of my dress was stained. "Oh, Abe, I hope I didn't leave a puddle behind. With this mess, I could have set the suffragettes back a full decade!"

He threw his arm around my shoulder, drawing me to his side. "Don't be silly. Only you could have pulled things off so well."

* * *

Another two thousand kits in only six weeks! It would be a challenge, but after the quantity we assembled a few months back during the tuberculosis crisis, I was confident we could deliver. Our growth with Butterfield had been gradual. Eight years back, we prepared a total of two thousand kits a year and now we were producing that amount every season. Even with Sadie upstate, I had things under control.

Now, thanks to Abe's sharp negotiating, we had the cash to pay for materials and wages up front without returning to the bank for another loan. And I didn't want to trouble Sadie or Max for money. They had their hands full with Eva.

That morning, I received a cheerful letter from Saranac Lake.

June 15, 1890
 Dear Tillie,
 I write with a happy heart. Eva has improved. We've come a long

way since those frightful first weeks. Dr. Trudeau still monitors her
closely, but she's moving in the right direction.

I feel guilty for not being with you, pulling my weight with Butterfield.
I'm sure you've risen to the occasion, as you always do. But I know you
understand that I must stay with Eva and put her needs above all else.
I miss the boys and Max, but thankfully, my days are complete, and I
have little extra time. When I'm not with Eva, I help the nursing staff
stock rooms, mend gowns, etc. They've invited me to eat my meals at
the Clinic in exchange for my help. I'm so thankful, as it's helped me
make friends and limit my time in the lonely, cold cabin.

The cabins are primitive, but palaces compared to the tenements.
They'll be best come summer when I don't need the fireplace for heat.
The weather here is quite harsh, and they set a cot for me outside Eva's
room when a storm is brewing.

I'm disappointed I missed the birth of your precious Miriam.
Although I was there with you in spirit through every contraction, what
I thought of most was how I'd give my right arm to start all over with
Eva. As you know from memories with your mama, our connection
with our children begins with their first cry. Treasure Miriam, love her
every moment. You are so blessed.

With deep affection,
Sadie

That Sadie! She knew how to remind me to see the bright side of life. I
closed my eyes and took a deep breath and exhaled slowly. I thought of all
the people I loved, and of Mama, and Sarah, who left me with an abandoned
heart, waiting to refill with more love. Yes, I was incredibly lucky and
determined not to forget it, no matter how busy my days became.

* * *

Abe accompanied me to Butterfield when I brought the sample kits to Mr.
Kraft for pre-production approval. I showed them to Miss Sweeney first.

"Oh, Tillie, these are marvelous! You're bringing fashion to women all over the country." Her approval was the final boost of confidence I needed before presenting my new ideas.

Seated again in Mr. Kraft's office, after the immediate business was complete, I saw my opening. "Mr. Kraft, it has been a pleasure to work with you and Butterfield on the kit concept. Now that we've established its success, I've been giving serious thought to another way to keep sales moving upward."

Mr. Kraft shifted away from me and looked toward Abe. My confidence deflated as fast as a leaky balloon. He wasn't interested in hearing new ideas from me. He was convinced Abe was the captain of the ship. I tapped Abe's shoe with mine to take over.

"As Mrs. Levine was proposing, we know from our local market that most frugal seamstresses at home reuse their patterns after purchasing the kit. To encourage women to buy more kits, we must entice them with something new and exciting. Since it's now time to prepare winter kits, why not create a fresh pattern, only attainable by purchasing the entire kit?" Turning to me, he continued, "Tillie, I know you've been working hard at this. Perhaps you can review the styles you pulled from the international magazines and your fabric selections."

"Let's see what you have, Tillie." Mr. Kraft repeated, using my first name as if I were an underling, not the owner.

After gulping down my indignity like castor oil and silently reciting my chant, *It's about the profit, not your pride*, I explained the designs, pattern modifications, and the lightweight wools I envisioned. Then, I reviewed the changes in cost and pricing. Finishing with a target date for moving the winter kits to distribution, I looked modestly at Mr. Kraft.

"Very impressive, Abe. I'll review the recommendation with Mr. Peters this week, and we can meet on Monday. Will that work for your schedules?" Mr. Kraft said, reaching into his jacket pocket. "Here's your deposit."

Both Abe and I nodded, shook hands, and left his office. Miss Sweeney shot a smile of approval, waving us out the door.

Abe laughed. "Darling, I know he got under your skin, but I applaud your self-control. Every time you hold your tongue, you make a bundle. Just keep telling yourself it's worth it."

"I know, but I loathe his condescending behavior. It's so damn insulting. Why should women need to hide in a man's shadow? I hope by the time Miriam is grown, her hard work will be recognized. I have a mind to put in more time helping the suffragettes and show these sour pickles a thing or two."

"You do that." Abe became quiet for a moment. "By the way, I've been meaning to talk to you about something he said at our last visit. Remember, Mr. Kraft said he wished they came up with the idea first?" He paused, allowing time for me to recall. "I wasn't sure if it was an offhanded compliment, but I suggest we keep our eyes peeled for anything suspicious. I'm glad things are going smoothly, but my gut is telling me not to trust them."

I remembered the remark and felt a sudden knot in the pit of my stomach. "How could they undermine us?"

"Who knows?" Abe pulled on his beard as we strolled home. We were nearing our front door when he stopped and turned to me. "Hey, I've been meaning to share an idea with you, not about work." He reached for my arm to stop me. "Do you know we've never taken any time away from here in all the years we've been married? As in, a vacation?"

I looked in his deep blue eyes, replaying his words. *A vacation?* "A splendid idea! I've read about a World's Fair in Chicago to celebrate the four hundredth anniversary of Columbus's discovery of America. What do you think about a family trip by train? I've never been farther than Papa's farm."

Abe had opened a rusty door, fulfilling his promise during our courtship to explore life together. "We'll do that, but it's two years off. I'm thinking about next weekend. With Rivka at the factory and my orders filled for the next two weeks, we can slip away for a few days with the kids after we firm up the winter order," said Abe.

"We probably could. Where should we go?"

"How about a train trip to Saranac Lake with the children before the end of summer to visit Eva and enjoy some country scenery? I know you miss Sadie."

He had said the very words I wished to hear. "Wonderful idea, we could help lift that poor child's spirits, and Hannah is beside herself to see Eva." I held Abe's hand, thinking how lucky I was. With so much misfortune in our small corner of the world, my cup runneth over.

Chapter Thirty-Seven

August 1890

T he five of us waited on the sweltering train platform: Abe, Hannah, Julian, baby Miriam, and me. The children were restless, beads of sweat on all our faces, Julian peppering Abe with questions, and Hannah removing her bonnet every few minutes to fan her face. Miriam, attuned to the mood, was crying in discomfort. Abe and I exchanged looks and sighed.

Hot summer steam rose from the concrete while the first of our three trains to Saranac Lake finally pulled in. Taking a final glance around Grand Central Station, I pondered the stark contrasts of my city. Only a few blocks south, people lived like paupers in the suffocating heat, and yet here in this part of town, there was airy, glorious architecture.

Undeterred by the temperature, Julian continued to rattle on as we settled into our second-class seats. Yesterday, he traced every mile of our route in pencil on a detailed map of New York State. "Don't forget, Papa, we switch trains in Albany and then travel west to Utica, then we switch again and ride north."

"How could I forget, son? You have our entire trip memorized, mile by mile."

Abe's and my eyes connected. Despite his young age, his knowledge of machines and their intricacies was remarkable. We were braced for a full day of Julian's commentary.

A piercing whistle reverberated through the cavernous station, and the train began to move. Despite the wheels' screeching, we stretched our arms out the train windows, waving to strangers, partaking in the momentary thrill.

"I hope it quiets down," I shouted over the din. "At this rate, we won't be able to think. Let's close the windows."

"I'm going to take Julian exploring. See you in a little while," Abe shouted back. He and Julian were out of sight in an instant.

Before long, we'd left the congestion of the city behind, entering beautiful open land. Miriam woke from time to time for a feeding, twisting her little head around curiously, looking about the cabin. But the train's movement made her sleepy-eyed and lulled her back to dreamland. Hannah was absorbed in a new suspense novel, *The Firm of Girdlestone,* by Arthur Conan Doyle. She insisted I read it when she finished, waxing endlessly about Doyle's skill as a mystery writer.

I hadn't expected any time for myself, but while Miriam slept, I opened *Great Expectations* and allowed myself the rare pleasure of dropping into a story.

A few hours later, we arrived in Albany. The second train was already on the tracks, and we hustled to board on time, Julian guiding the way, Miriam wet, crying furiously. After settling into our new seats, we were off to Utica to change trains again, and finally would arrive in Saranac Lake before dinner. Despite my excitement, I was needled by concerns about Eva. I prayed we'd find her in good condition, as Sadie had claimed.

"Abe, could you imagine traveling the entire country this way?" I said while hurriedly changing Miriam into a dry diaper. "I'd love to see the sights outside our little world in Manhattan."

"I've always wanted to see the Rocky Mountains. I hear they're a sight," he answered. "When Miriam's older, we'll plan a big trip." He gazed at her troubled little face, caught between a cry and repose.

It was close to dinner when we pulled into Saranac Lake. I gave Julian my last apple, hoping to stave off his hunger until we found a General Store with supplies. The station was minuscule, a tiny, one-room red house by the tracks. We were all stiff-legged, eager to stretch our limbs on solid land.

As our train pulled away, unblocking the vista, we were greeted with an astounding view of the mountain scenery. But scanning the scrub grass behind the platform, I saw no sign of Sadie.

"It's like a painting," said Hannah. "I'm glad Eva's in a beautiful place instead of that depressing Willard Hospital. It's no wonder people get better here."

Just as Abe and I considered renting a wagon, a man, gasping for breath, ran toward us. "Are you the Levines? Mrs. Stern asked me to take you to your cabin."

"Yes, we are," said Abe. "Where is she?"

"Got tied up at the Clinic."

Abe and I eyed each other, concerned. He swept his index finger across his mouth as if brushing crumbs from his mustache. This silent adult language was part of our lives. There was no need to upset Hannah.

The driver chatted nonstop the entire bumpy ride about the weather, the lake temperature, and the size of the latest catch, but the most impressive tale was Dr. Trudeau's story of his accidental cure. "A few years back, when the good doctor became sick, he moved here. This was where he hunted with his Pa when he was a kid. He thought he'd die here in peace, but instead, he got better. A miracle!"

"That's what I heard," I tried to pay attention while my concern for Eva rose. "It seemed the clean country air revived him."

"That's right, ma'am. The man's a good soul. He could've kept the cure to himself and lived out his life in peace. Instead, he chose to help others like me. So, he opened a Clinic and works like a dog."

Our three-room cabin sat beside Sadie's. Rob and Jake, her high school sons, were there to greet us and help Abe unload our belongings. The woodsy scent of pine trees and gentle breeze, silky against my skin, immediately evoked a sweet sense of familiarity, reminiscent of Papa's long-gone farmhouse.

Two cane rockers swayed in the light breeze on the open porch that stretched across the cabin. The interior was spartan, with an all-purpose sink, icebox, table at one end of the large room, and a fireplace with four wooden chairs arranged around an oval rust-colored, braided rug at the other. The two bedrooms contained simple cots with thin mattresses and pillows. Linens were folded at the foot of each bed.

"This is fine," I said. "We'll have a nice time here. But first, let's get food from the General Store for the icebox and fix something for dinner."

"I can do that," Abe said. "Why don't you and Hannah head to the Clinic and check in with Eva and Sadie? I'll take Julian and the baby to the mercantile and round up dinner for all of us. We must remember Dr. Boro's instructions, 'Keep the small children away from the Clinic, and Hannah must keep her distance from Eva.'"

I wouldn't forget.

Hannah and I hurried down the short path. The Clinic sat among tall pine trees on the side of the lake, its sparkling surface visible from every window. Like the cabins, an expansive porch wrapped around two sides of the grey-shingled building. Men and women sat reading, knitting, and carving wood on the slatted rockers fanning across the porch. Were they town folk?

A woman wearing a pastel, short-sleeved linen uniform with a white apron approached us. "Good evening. Can I help you?"

I remembered the tall, wing-like hats from the city hospital when Mama was hospitalized. There was none of that formality here. To my surprise, almost everyone was dressed in street clothes rather than hospital gowns, making it difficult to tell visitors from patients and removing that dreadful impression of illness.

"Do you know where we can find Eva Stern and her mother, Sadie?" Hannah asked.

The woman smiled and pointed to the staircase. "Second room on the left."

We hurried up the stairs and knocked on Eva's door.

"Come in," cried a raspy voice.

We opened the door and found Eva lying on the bed, her head supported by a stack of pillows placed atop her blanket. "I'm so happy to see you." She forced a weak smile and began to cough. "I'm sorry I'm not feeling better."

Hannah stared at her, wide-eyed with surprise. "What happened?"

Eva strained for a full breath of air. "I was caught in a flash shower last week and got soaked to the skin, then caught a nasty cold. The doctor is worried about me all over again." She reached for her handkerchief, coughing until her face turned crimson.

Hannah sat at the end of the bed and softly rubbed her friend's stocking feet. "It's okay, rest. We'll find fun things to do until your cold passes. I brought some books I can read aloud, and I'll tell you about all the kids at school."

Eva nodded. She put her handkerchief on the bed by her pillows. Fresh bloodstains from her latest bout of coughing spotted the white cotton, portending a different type of visit than I'd planned.

Eva didn't appear like a child with a cold. She looked exactly as she had at Willard Hospital before departing for Saranac, terribly thin, sunken features, dark rimmed eyes. My heart longed to see improvement, but my eyes wouldn't deceive me. Struggling to remain calm, I said, "We're so happy to be here with you. Where's your Mama?"

"She went to find the doctor before he left for the night."

"Which way is his office?"

Eva pointed to the left. "Down the hall."

I took Hannah's hand, terrified she might be next to catch it. "Come with me a moment."

I led her to the hallway, struggling to maintain my calm in a whisper. "Hannah, I don't want you close to her. Dr. Boro said, 'No hugging or kissing'. Promise me you'll sit in a chair by the door where there's a clean breeze."

"Do you think she'll be okay?" Hannah whispered back, panic lacing her voice.

"I don't know." I exhaled deeply and turned left toward Dr. Trudeau's office. Hannah would have to face Eva's fate along with the rest of us.

When I arrived at his office, I heard sniffling through the closed door. I knocked gently. "Hello, Sadie, are you in there?"

The door opened. Sadie jumped from her chair and gave me a quick hug, then led me inside. "I'm so glad you're here."

I looked around Dr. Trudeau's office. It could have been Dr. Boro's. *Do all doctors' offices look the same?* A massive wooden desk was piled high with papers. A microscope sat on the sideboard, surrounded by overstuffed bookcases crammed with worn medical books. A small oil lamp was positioned on the corner of his desk. Two worn leather guest chairs sat opposite his desk.

"Good evening, Doctor. I'm Mrs. Stern's friend, Tillie Levine, and my family just arrived."

Dr. Trudeau's pleasant face wore a compassionate smile. I ventured he was in his forties. His kind eyes shone with a depth of spirit, perhaps from bestowing hope to the dying. Standing to shake my hand, I was surprised at how thin he was. Thin with sunken eyes. *Is he dying, too?* "Hello, Mrs. Levine. I'm glad you're here, but I wish Eva was doing better."

I turned to Sadie. "I thought she was improving."

Her wide eyes were filled with apprehension. "Dr. Trudeau's worried her cold took a turn for the worse." She faltered. "Perhaps pneumonia."

My thoughts took an alarming turn as well, to a decade earlier and my little Sarah gasping her final breath. "Oh God, no."

The doctor stood. "I'd like to listen to her lungs again."

"Sadie, I'll help with the boys while you're here with Eva." I turned to the doctor. "My younger sister, Hannah, is Eva's best friend. Will she be in danger, visiting?"

"Open the windows and keep Eva quiet and resting. The more she coughs into the air, the more the likelihood of contagion. Have Hannah sit across the room. She can read to her. I don't think Eva has the strength to handle more than that."

Dr. Trudeau turned his attention back to Sadie. "Mrs. Stern, I'll have a cot set for you in the hall outside. It's unwise for you to sleep in Eva's room. I don't want you infected, too."

"But...." Sadie interrupted.

"No, buts," said the doctor. "Your other children need you too. As I said, you can sleep nearby, out of the immediate area."

Sadie's shoulders dropped.

I spoke gently. "You know the doctor's looking out for your whole family. Let's go back to Eva."

* * *

While I was at the Clinic, Abe had built an outdoor fire in a stone pit designed for cooking and heat. A large wooden table and benches for eating sat nearby. He had arranged a picnic-style dinner for our family and Sadie's boys.

"They must feed many guests," Abe said. "The store had trays of cold roast chicken, salads, sliced tomatoes, and fresh bread, more choices than I expected."

Although I vividly recalled summer evenings eating outdoors on the farm, this was all new to Julian. Fascinated by the sounds of crickets and frogs, his curiosity was piqued.

"Why don't we have crickets at home? Can we look for frogs at the lake tomorrow? What's a bullfrog? Can we bring one home?" he asked without pausing for answers.

"Julian, why don't you make a picture book of the things you've learned on this trip—the train, the animals, the insects, and picnics. What do you think about that?" asked Abe.

"Maybe on the train ride home," said Julian. "Can we go swimming in the lake tomorrow? Will you teach me to float? Are there snakes and turtles in the water? Do they bite?"

"Of course, I'll take you and Miriam to the lake tomorrow for a swim. Maybe Mama and Hannah will come, too." Abe raised one brow, studying my face.

I nodded, but Hannah was lost in her thoughts, her face full of worry. Having lost Saul months earlier, she needed no reminder of how common death from tuberculosis was. I shifted closer to her on the bench and put my arm around her shoulder. Although it felt right to travel here to support

Sadie, I now doubted the wisdom of bringing the family. After seeing the freshly covered plots in the nearby cemetery on the coach ride to the cabins, it was abundantly clear not everyone recovered.

"Hannah, she's getting the best care available. If there's a way to heal her, it will happen. Dr. Trudeau is sleeping at the Clinic tonight to keep an eye on her," I said, wishing my words could be true. "We must trust in God's plan."

Hannah nodded sadly, rose from the table, and walked up the three steps onto the porch. "I'm going to bed. I'll be heading to the Clinic early."

"Sleep's a good idea. After all the traveling, I'm beat, too." Abe glanced at me and Sadie's sons. "Let's all get some rest,"

* * *

Miriam rose early, her hungry cries splintered through the early morning stillness. I threw back my warm patchwork quilt, surprised at the early chill. If it was anything like yesterday, we'd be sweating by afternoon.

After changing Miriam's diaper, I poked my head into Hannah's room. As I expected, it was empty. I nestled under the warm covers with my baby girl to feed her. *Is this how Sadie once felt with Eva? Is this what she thinks about now as she watches her daughter struggle?* I glanced at Abe's peaceful, sleeping face and chuckled inwardly. How nice it was to be a man. Dropping my still-tired head on the pillow, I closed my eyes while Miriam suckled loudly.

While I rested, Abe propped up his body, leaning on his forearm while whispering to her. "Who are you looking at?" He repeated his words to Miriam with a laugh.

Miriam giggled with a full mouth of milk.

"Hey, you two, let me finish the feeding. It takes work to make her breakfast!" But it was too late. Miriam was lost in baby giggles, dribbling the frothy mess all over me and the bed.

Abe, amused, urged her on.

I couldn't hold back my laughter. "Come on. You know I want to get back to the Clinic. Hannah's already there. Let me finish up. When I get back, we'll pack lunch and go to the lake for a while.

"Sounds good. I'll take care of breakfast," said Abe, lifting himself out of bed. "See if you can convince Hannah to join us for a swim."

Alone on the wooded path to the Clinic, I was transported to my childhood on the farm: the tall trees, birds singing, and the piney forest fragrance. I breathed deeply, praying these memories were a good omen for Eva.

Moments later, I arrived at the Clinic and walked directly upstairs. Sadie's unmade cot sat outside Eva's door. Singing spilled from her room. My curiosity was aroused. The curtains fluttered in the breeze, filling the room with fresh mountain air. Sadie and Hannah stood in a semi-circle around Eva's bed, holding hands with a group of six other women. Eva, who looked frightfully ill, was propped upright with pillows, listening quietly. Although dark rings encircled her sunken eyes and her skin was pale as ivory, she appeared relaxed and unafraid, listening to this foreign, calming music. The soft presence of the group drew me into their soulful prayer. Sadie and Hannah hummed the tune and swayed to the music along with the ring of worshipers. Standing, listening, I wondered what type of songs they were.

Sadie's last letter came to mind.

> The women seem barely aware we are Jewish, unlike in the city south of here. The staff and patients are blind to our differences. Max has been sending deliveries of challah and sweets from a bakery in Utica to fatten up Eva. We share the treats with everyone, and now they all ask for bagels on the weekend. Can you imagine? We've introduced bagels and babka to Saranac Lake.

The song ended, and Sadie leaned over to my ear and whispered, "Christian hymns." She then turned back to the group. "That was lovely. Let Hannah and me teach you one of our prayers, too. Tillie, come join us." She reached for my hand, coaxing me into their circle.

We began to sing healing psalms with their uniquely discordant chords, and before long, the women hummed the chorus as we sang the Hebrew words.

Eva's face wore a serene glow and I felt deep gratitude that this community of different faiths could create a unique, comforting atmosphere for her. Eva glanced my way and gave me the slightest smile.

Eventually, Eva drifted to sleep, and we tiptoed from the room. "How did she do last night?" I whispered to Sadie.

"It was a difficult night. The poor child had trouble breathing, barely slept. I thought we'd lose her." Sadie's eyes glistened with tears. "She's had almost nothing to eat or drink in the last three days. How can her little body keep up the fight?" Sadie drew a jagged breath.

I wished I could offer more comfort. "The singing was beautiful."

For a moment, Sadie's face relaxed. "Sick is sick, no matter what you look like or where you come from."

"Sadie, would you like me to stay with Eva for a while? Maybe you could get some rest in your cabin."

"That's alright. I'd rather lie down on my cot while she sleeps. I'll stay close by."

"I understand." Then I turned to Hannah. "Abe and I are going to take the children to the lake for a swim and lunch. We'll come back in a few hours. Why don't you join us while Eva rests?"

Hannah clasped her hands together. "I don't want to leave her either."

I stepped close, leaning into her ear. "Don't forget what the doctor said about keeping a safe distance. I'll be back soon."

* * *

Back at the cabin, Abe had everyone ready for a swim, waiting for my return. The older boys were playing ball, occasionally giving Julian a turn. The temperature was rising, and their skin glistened with perspiration. As soon as they saw me, they ran to grab their towels and fishing poles. I hurried into the cabin to change into my bathing dress. As we hiked down the packed dirt trail leading to the beachfront, Sadie's sons, both sunburnt from fishing and swimming all summer, began naming the trees.

Julian was captivated by the different leaves and bark textures.

Rob pointed. "This is an oak tree. See the finger leaves? It's one of the strongest trees in the forest. This tree here is a maple, just as strong, with leaves like your palm. Here are elm and hickory. They cut them down to build houses and make furniture."

Years ago, I remembered Papa telling me, "The trees may look big and strong, but if the right bug gets under the bark, they will die." *Just like people. An invisible germ in the lungs and a life could come crashing down like a once sturdy tree.*

As the path veered out of the woods, the enormous lake came into view, its surface sparkling in the sunlight. I set Miriam under a shady oak tree, where she napped on a blanket. I then pulled my swim dress up to my knees and stepped into the cool blue water. Round lily pads with large white flowers floated in clusters on the surface. Dragonflies and long-legged spiders skittered from leaf to leaf, dancing above their water predators, seemingly indifferent to the dangers lurking beneath the surface. From above, birds swooped down and snapped them up in their beaks. Danger lurked everywhere.

Abe, not wasting a minute, was up to his waist in the lake, teaching Julian to float on his back.

I walked deeper, my dress floating around me, curling my toes in the lake bed's coarse sand and stone, thinking about the women who sang to Eva that morning.

During services at shul, I'd experienced the restorative role music played but knew little about the Christian traditions. That morning, I learned how similar we are, both faiths using music and worship to evoke hope and healing during the most taxing times. I found myself humming Rock of Ages as I looked off at the mountains ringing the lake. Even though Hanukkah was months away, it was my favorite song of prayer. Glancing at Abe, Julian, and Miriam, I thanked God for our little family.

Miriam woke with her typical fury, scaring the birds away from the lily pads. I stumbled out of the water to reach her. Hungry, covered in a sweaty film, her body shook with anger. I carried her to a large boulder on the lake's edge, unwrapped her clothing and removed her soiled diaper as I walked. Instead of the feeding she anticipated, I held her over the water, then lowered her enough so she could splash her little toes while I scooped water over her body, rinsing her skin. She cooed, forgetting the feeding, and looked about to her Papa and brother.

Look at me, look at me! Miriam called back.

Julian waded over to her. "Miriam, isn't the lake fun? Mama, why is she naked?"

"She doesn't have a swimdress like me. I'll dry her off in a minute."

We spent the next hour playing in the water, eating leftover chicken sandwiches, and enjoying the sweet beauty surrounding us. Around mid-afternoon, I said, "I think I'll go back and check on everyone."

Jake, sitting on a rock a few feet away, looked up from his fishing pole, "I'd like to see Eva, too. Let's bring Mama and Hannah sandwiches."

We packed our towels and leftover food, trudging back up the path to our cabins, hurriedly changing into dry clothing, and preparing a small food basket.

"I'll keep Miriam and Julian here," Abe offered.

I nodded, more than anything, I wanted my children far from the disease. I picked up my pace to catch up with the older boys, already well ahead on the path.

* * *

We went directly to Eva's room and opened the door. The silence in the hall had set me on edge. I pushed the door open. Sadie and Hannah were sitting on opposite sides of her bed, each holding one of Eva's hands. Sadie turned her tear-streaked face to her sons. "Eva hasn't woken all day. She's hot from fever and can barely breathe."

My heart fell. I struggled to fill my chest with air. "What happened?"

Sadie continued softly. "Dr. Trudeau thinks she caught pneumonia on top of the tuberculosis and may not be with us much longer." Her voice broke. "Boys, I think you should say your goodbyes."

Jake's face turned bright red, his eyes filling with tears. "Isn't there more he can do? Isn't that why we came here?"

"Mama, she was fine a few days ago," begged Rob. "How could this happen?"

"I know, I know." Sadie sniffled. "Pneumonia moves fast, and she's simply too weak from the tuberculosis to fight it."

It was all so sudden. In a blink of an eye, Eva had turned for the worse. A painful wave of sadness swept through me, thinking about our little Sarah's struggle for air. But I couldn't cry. Not yet. I must be strong for my friend, Sadie.

Hannah stood back to make room for the boys and threw her arms around me, sobbing. I leaned on the door frame while I stroked her hair, attempting to soothe her. "Oh, Hannah, I'm so sorry." I looked at Sadie's exhausted face. "Pneumonia?"

"It was brewing for days. At least that's what the doctor said." Sadie kept her eyes on Eva's face as if imprinting final memories, her tears dripping unchecked.

"I thought if I came, she'd fight harder to live," Hannah cried out. "This is so unfair. First Saul and now Eva."

It was unthinkable. Eva was dying from this loathsome disease before my eyes. There were no words of comfort I could share, so I held Hannah tightly. Digging in, I tried to think of a way to help.

"Sadie, should I send a telegram to Max?"

"No need. The nurse sent one around noon. He should be getting in later tonight," Sadie shivered, her voice breaking. "The poor man will be devastated." She gulped a sob. "Eva's his little girl."

Dr. Trudeau walked into the room; the corners of his mouth turned downward. He bent over Eva and set the stethoscope on her chest, listening for a long time, then felt her neck and wrist. Standing straighter, he turned his head to Sadie and said gently, "She's gone with the angels."

Chapter Thirty-Eight

That same morning, Max raced out of the city after receiving the telegram. Rabbi Meyers from our shul telegraphed the Rabbi he knew in Utica, who joined Max on the final leg of the train ride to Saranac Lake. But sadly, Eva passed before they arrived. The Rabbi stepped in to comfort our distraught families with prayers and worked with Abe to arrange a Jewish burial. He consecrated a plot in the Clinic's graveyard, the first Jewish burial in Saranac Lake.

Expecting Eva to rally, none of us had packed dark colors for a funeral.

Sadie refused to borrow mourning clothes from the Clinic staff. "Eva's alive in my heart. We'll bury her body here, but I'm not ready for grieving clothes!" She pounded her chest, tears flowing. "She was the joy of my life."

Max, depleted from the emotional upheaval, didn't argue. Instead, he placed his strong arm around Sadie's shoulder. "That's fine, my *bashert*."

The gravity of losing young Eva left us all unmoored. For Abe and me, it resurrected the pain of losing baby Sarah, and we grieved both children. Years earlier, our Jewish traditions had helped guide us through Sarah's death, but here in Saranac Lake, far from our enclave in the city, those rituals felt ill-placed.

Although Sadie was my closest friend, Abe and I knew to step back and give her family space. Eva had been the affectionate child, the closest to Sadie, Papa's little girl. Seemingly aware of that void, Rob and Jake hovered about their parents, holding Sadie's hand, draping an arm around Max's shoulder, stepping in to comfort and unify the family.

The staff and Clinic residents also came to Eva's graveside funeral, placing handfuls of soil on her simple pine coffin. Their words of compassion to Sadie and Max pulsed in the still air, blending like a cappella.

"Eva was a lovely young girl, such a loss."

"I'll miss her beautiful smile. She lit up every room."

"She gave the wild animals fairy tale names."

Once again, outside our insular Jewish community, we shared our sadness. Every family attending Eva's graveside funeral felt the pain of our loss, many having lost someone of their own in this unrelenting epidemic. As with Abe and me, families mourned anew, while honoring our past loved ones.

* * *

Without Eva, our travel home with Sadie's family was quiet and melancholy. I was haunted the entire train ride, unable to shake off thoughts of all the children who'd died from tuberculosis. How could man invent scientific miracles like electricity, build massive bridges but be helpless, unable to protect our most innocent from horrific diseases?

And I was worried about Hannah. At first, she refused to leave the Clinic, having decided in the heat of the moment to remain in Saranac, assisting Dr. Trudeau with his patients. Both Abe and I were steadfast in saying 'no'. Not only did we worry about her continued exposure, but I knew Papa would be frantic. As a parent, I fully understood the distress her decision would create.

"Hannah, I know you're suffering, but this is not how to deal with loss," I said after the funeral while we packed our clothing for the morning train home.

"It's not up to you. I promised Eva I'd stay and help," Hannah cried. "So many people are sick. Can't you see that?"

I struggled to keep my composure. "If you want to learn medicine, study, and become a nurse, but not this way. Papa relies on me to make the right decisions for you. What do you think he'd say?"

"You don't understand! All you care about is your stupid business," she shouted.

Equally distraught, it was all I could do to hold myself together. "You know that's not true. But what is true is that you don't always get the luxury of choosing your fate."

Hannah threw her clothing into her valise, not bothering to fold anything, withholding her words.

It didn't end there. Hannah continued grieving in her isolated cocoon, staring into space on the train and, once home, secluding herself in her bedroom. It was near impossible to draw her out, even at mealtime with the family. She flatly refused to speak to me, but even worse, refused to discuss the fall term starting in the next few weeks.

After two days, I noticed she had bitten the skin around her fingernails, and three of her fingertips were bleeding. Remembering years earlier when she picked at her eyelashes and brows, my concern heightened. "Oh, Hannah, let me bandage your fingers."

She drew them under her skirt. "No. I'll stop. Go away."

I asked for Abe's help when he returned home that evening. "Please try to get through to her."

He went directly to her room and sat on the bed. After rubbing her back, he said, "Hannah, I know how you feel. You know I've lost people I loved, too. It takes time and patience."

"No, it won't get better. I imagine running up to Eva's apartment to pick out first day of school outfits. Then I realize," she sniffled, bereft, "she's not home. That she'll never be home again."

Abe held Hannah and rocked her in his arms like a small child.

* * *

After a third day, I sought Dr. Boro for advice. Unfortunately, when I arrived at his Clinic, he had a full waiting room. His receptionist assured me he'd stop by my apartment during his evening visits.

True to form, he arrived after dinner, walking into the apartment slowly, looking more weathered than unusual. The epidemic was taking its toll on him. I decided to waste no time.

I pointed to Hannah's room. "She's been in there for three days and has barely touched any food. She's unable to shake her grief from Eva's passing."

Dr. Boro's eyes were hooded, solemn, exhausted. "Please come in with me. Are there chairs by the bed?"

"Yes. Can I bring in a tray of tea and sandwiches for you and possibly Hannah?"

"That would be good." Dr. Boro started toward her room. "I haven't eaten much today either."

I quickly prepared a cold supper in the kitchen, listening to their muffled voices seeping through the space under the door, glad they had begun without me. What if Dr. Boro couldn't shake her out of the sadness?

I knocked and entered, setting the tray on the second chair, and sat at the foot of the bed.

Hannah was propped up on the bed appearing engaged. She reached for a sandwich. A wave of relief rushed through me.

Dr. Boro also helped himself to a sandwich, "Food is restorative. It helps provide the fuel for living," he locked eyes with Hannah, "and for healing."

Hannah chewed slowly, watching his face.

Dr. Boro spoke in careful measures, allowing each thought, like moist raindrops on dry soil, to soak in fully. "This dreadful disease has taken many of our dearest family and friends; it's affected us all. Hannah, it's clear you are in great pain, having lost Saul and now Eva, who was like a sister to you. I'm sure you feel overpowered.

He looked from me to Hannah. "Do I have that right?"

She nodded.

He cupped his hand on her shoulder. "It's called grieving, and it's as normal as joy. But to work through it, you must be kind to yourself and stay close to those who love you. I can't promise your sadness will fully pass, but I can promise the pain in your heart will lessen."

Hannah and I both nodded. My eyes filled. I'd never met another living soul with Dr. Boro's ability to reach into the core of a person with such compassion.

He turned his head back to me. "I'd like Hannah to follow a schedule.

First thing in the morning, she will make a good breakfast and take a long walk with her baby niece in the carriage. With all the ruckus, she's barely gotten to know Miriam. Then, until school begins, I'd like to see Hannah help the teachers arrange their classrooms at the Settlement House School. They can use an extra set of hands. Tillie, you can talk to Mrs. Simon about the details."

Again, I nodded, wondering if Hannah would comply.

"Finally, could you help her find a companion for the morning trolley to school? She's dreading the ride without Eva. Perhaps you can ask Eva's brothers to accompany her."

My eyes drifted to Hannah's. "Sweetheart, Abe or I can go with you."

She shook her head. "I'd rather go with a classmate."

I understood. She was still blaming me. I knew it was part of her grieving, but it hurt nonetheless.

"Hannah told me wonderful things about the tuberculosis Clinic in Saranac. While I agree it was best to bring her home, I believe her interest in medicine is genuine." Dr. Boro said.

Hannah interrupted in a burst of anger. "Tillie wouldn't let me stay. She insists on treating me like a child!"

Dr. Boro turned to Hannah. "You are part child and part adult. Don't blame Tillie for doing her job. I would have done the same thing."

Hannah huffed.

Dr. Boro continued, "As I was saying, we discussed the books she borrowed, and I'm impressed with her knowledge. If she works on healing herself first, and if you agree, she can help me at the Clinic a few hours a week once school is underway."

I felt a pang of fear and blurted. "Is it safe? I'd die if she caught it."

Dr. Boro's tone was even. "Nothing in life is entirely safe, but I'll teach Hannah skills to reduce her risk and limit exposure to contagious patients." He paused before adding, "You need to discuss this with Abe and your father. Then, let me know."

Dr. Boro turned to Hannah and gently placed his hand on hers. "But before you come to work with me, you need to heal. Eva wouldn't want you hiding in your room. So put one foot in front of the other and walk off some of your sorrow."

"I will, Doctor Boro," Hannah said, her voice steadier than I'd heard in days. "I promise."

A week passed. Hannah followed Dr. Boro's instructions to the letter. She gradually began to eat more and took Miriam for a daily walk in her carriage. I was pleased to see her excitement when she joined her old teachers in the afternoon, helping set up their books, art supplies, and musical instruments. One evening, she walked to Sadie's apartment, and an hour later returned smiling.

"Rob and Jake were so sweet. They invited me to ride the streetcar with them both ways when school starts. Jake said they always thought of me as their other little sister."

"You're helping each other. Losing Eva was a terrible blow for them as well," I said sadly.

Chapter Thirty-Nine

The following day, I walked to the factory, feeling relieved but empty of emotion. Hannah, still hurting, was hanging onto school, a resolute force to pull her forward. I kept reminding myself that grieving wouldn't pass at my convenience. It would stay with us for a while. Still, there was much catching up to do at the factory and with Rivka.

As I entered the room, she embraced me in her strong arms. "I wish I knew the right words."

I was drained and shook my head. I couldn't talk about Eva or the disease anymore.

We nodded. Words felt pointless.

My eyes scanned the room. Rivka was finalizing the late summer order for Butterfield. *Industry, that's what moves us forward.* Stepping back, I examined the piles of finished packages organized in stacks on each table. "These look beautiful. Tell me, how did things go these last weeks? Any problems?"

"Not at all. Everyone's happy to have work." Rivka raised her brow as if there was no way I could understand their circumstances. "But once the kits are delivered, many of us need a few days off. Some are moving to Brooklyn and need time to settle in before their children start school. You know how it is."

With the proliferation of new apartment buildings in Brooklyn and a steady income saved through the epidemic, my workers and their surviving family were packing up their sparse tenement homes, much like Abe and had done years ago. They all worked hard for this step upward and needed to leave their sad memories in the tenements.

I remembered our move quite clearly. But I was put off by Rivka's tone, suggesting that I was living in an entitled world entirely different from hers. I knew my sensitivities were heightened, but instead of reminding her of my losses, I chose to swallow my words and move forward. "Yes, of course. That's a grand idea. Let's get the kits inspected and pack them in the cardboard cartons I ordered."

Rivka met my words with a head nod. "I'll make sure the delivery is made and clean up the workshop so it's ready for next season. Then we'll lock up tight."

I hoped their break proved to be more uplifting than mine had been. "Mr. Kraft and Mr. Peters approved the winter concept. They will have their new dress patterns ready any day. The timing is perfect for the next round of orders."

"I'll drop off the key later in the week." She paused, a full smile covering her face. "What is it you say here in America? Welcome to the land of opportunity?"

For the first time in our history, the workshop closed. Most of the workers were excited as they collected their pay, including a bonus of five paid days off, and hurried to their homes to finish packing and moving.

Later that evening, at my dining room table, Sadie and I poured over the ledgers.

"Are you sure you're up to work matters? This can wait, Sadie."

Sadie sat erect, determined. "No, sitting around is torture. At least before, there was hope. Let me start getting involved again. You know what they say about idle hands."

We'd made a staggering amount of money from the kits. But we were still way over budget on our expenses. "Sadie, can you check with Max about the fabric price? I'm wondering if he increased his prices while you were up in Saranac."

Sadie bent her head to the side, appearing puzzled. "I'll ask him later. But I can't imagine he would do something like that without discussing it with us first."

"I'll check with Rivka tomorrow." I was expecting her at my home in the mid-morning to drop off her key. I had a special bonus set aside to thank her for the time I was in Saranac.

* * *

The next morning, right on schedule, I heard a knock at my door. I had made a pot of tea and wanted to review the ledger with Rivka.

I opened the door. It was Tova, the quiet little woman in the factory. "Good morning. This is a surprise."

She averted her eyes. "Rivka asked me to drop off the key. She's in Brooklyn this morning cleaning her new place."

"Of course. I understand." I should have figured she wouldn't have spare time for tea. I took the key. We'd work through the fabric issue next week when she returned.

As I tidied the kitchen, I thought I'd send a gift to Rivka for her new home, then realized I didn't have her new address. I ran out of my apartment, down the stairs and through the front door, hoping to reach Tova on the sidewalk. But in her drab clothing she had vanished into the crowd.

* * *

The next few days were painfully quiet. I spent them sorting out the upcoming Butterfield order, collecting the notions and other supplies, and distributing them on worktables. Thursday, I stopped at Max's factory to place the fabric order, having selected the designs with Sadie the evening we reviewed our books. His factory was buzzing with activity. I signaled to him from across the room and walked into his cluttered office to wait. The sight was dizzying: piles of paper scattered over every inch of his desk, filmy cups of unfinished coffee, and bolts of fabric leaning against every inch of free wall space. The light streaming in through the smeared window lit particles of dust floating in the air. I could scarcely breathe.

Finally, Max broke free and joined me. He sat, all business, reviewing the upcoming order I handed to him. "This looks fine, but would you mind paying for the woolens in cash tomorrow? I need to pay suppliers this week, and they prefer I pay ahead."

"Of course. While we're on the topic, I've been meaning to ask you something."

Max's brows rose.

"Did Sadie mention that we found a discrepancy when we reviewed the books last weekend? Did you raise your prices? It seems our fabric costs are over budget."

He cocked his head. "Yes, she asked me, and I told her that I haven't changed anything."

I screwed my face. "I don't understand the overage."

Max looked off into the factory, his eyes captured in thought. "Did Rivka tell you about the defects she found? She's been here a few times ordering extra bolts. I told her I'd refund for the defects when she brought the damaged fabric back to me. That way, I can handle it directly with my supplier. I'm still waiting for the defective bolts."

This was the first I'd heard of damaged fabric. "No, but I'll check on it. I'll get them to you next week when she returns. In the meantime, I'll do my best to get payment to you tomorrow." I tucked the thought away, relieved to have an explanation, but wondering why Rivka hadn't mentioned it.

I knew Friday would be busy. It was Hannah's second day back at school, and I worried she'd need me. In addition, I had planned a visit with Mrs. Simon at the Settlement House in the afternoon. I would squeeze in the bank run and pay Max after tea. It would be tight, but Max always delivered for us, and I couldn't disappoint him, "Will late afternoon work?"

"Of course. Just remember, the factory closes at four for Sabbath. If you can't make it, stop by first thing Sunday. I'll be here."

It would be close. Typically, I did the banking in the morning, stopped at Max's, and put the money in his safe, but Friday was jammed. To make matters worse, Miriam's nursemaid would only be available after lunch.

* * *

The following day, I hurried from the Settlement House to the bank, arriving right before the guard latched and bolted the door at three-thirty. Immediately after, I ran to Max's factory with a bulging envelope of cash in my purse, but by the time I arrived, his door was locked. Frustrated, sweating, my feet throbbing from dashing about in my new fall shoes, I decided to head over to my workshop around the corner. I'd lock the cash in my desk and bring it to Max on Sunday morning.

It felt odd to open my factory door and face an empty room. Peaceful, but I was accustomed to the buzzing of workers chattering in Yiddish and Russian, fabric bolts bouncing around the worktables while they were unrolled and measured, pinking shears snipping through the calico. The room was immaculate. Tables gleamed, tools were properly stored in canisters in the center of the tables, chairs squared off. Not a stray thread left behind. The dozen wooden worktables held the materials for next season, in perfect rows like valiant soldiers awaiting their next command. The last time I remembered that feeling was when we opened this new location years back, and Sadie and I had just finished arranging the room.

The evening sun was setting, sending ribbons of light through the tall windows lining the street. Sadie and I had come so far. Granted, we had our share of heartache, but neither of us had allowed our losses to beat us down. I prayed that after suffering Eva's death, Sadie would reengage.

I crossed the room to my desk in the corner, unlocked the drawer, and placed the cash envelope beside the ledgers, all twelve hundred and fifty dollars; enough money to purchase two thousand kits worth of fabric from Max or four years of one employee's wages.

Everything was in order as I relocked the drawer and placed the desk key in my bag.

As I turned to the door, I heard a soft rustling, a scratching noise across the room. *Damn, I better check.* I looked at my watch and walked to the center of the room. My eyes circled the entire workshop, floor to ceiling, as I turned my body about in a full circle. I didn't see anyone or anything out of order. *For God's sake. Our mouse problem is back.* I made a mental note to buy more traps.

Short on time, I hurried home, thinking about the beautiful woolens in the winter order, remembering our dull scissors. They needed to go to the silversmith for sharpening next week. I could see it in my mind, twenty busy women, scarves covering their hair, bent over the tables, cutting, meticulously folding and ironing fabric. Then, filling small wax bags with notions and assembling them into tidy packages to be stacked and delivered to Butterfield. I could barely wait.

* * *

Sunday morning, I returned to the workshop for Max's payment and to set mouse traps. Several Jewish factory owners in my building were already busy working. Their doors and windows were propped open, beckoning a cool breeze inside. Although still early, the interior heat was already oppressive.

Opening the door, I imagined seeing a pack of mice racing for cover. At first glance, nothing appeared amiss, but as I turned left toward my desk, I screamed. "Oh, my God!" My desk was in shambles. Running closer, I saw that the drawers were ripped to shreds, turned upside down on the floor. The lock was gone. Wood chips were strewn everywhere. My heart pounded. *No, please, no!* As I looked frantically about the room, I saw the ledger intact on the floor.

I fell to my knees, crawling under the desk, searching. I couldn't find the envelope! A small fortune, gone. I grabbed my hair and screamed. "No, no, no!"

Within seconds, neighboring tenants ran into my shop. "What happened? Are you alright?" they called out, one by one.

"I've been robbed!" I screamed at the men like a mad woman. "Someone broke in and took my money."

Mr. Eidelman, a factory owner on my floor, crouched low beside me, the fringes of his tallit shawl sweeping the floor. Reaching into his trousers, he drew a handkerchief and handed it to me. "Are you hurt?"

I shook my head, wiping my dripping nose and eyes, hysterical. "It happened before I got here."

He rose. "I'll get the police," then disappeared around the door.

Mr. Diamond from the factory below helped me into a chair while new faces poked their heads through the door, all curious as cats.

I scanned the group and pleaded, "Someone, get a messenger and find Abe!"

Mr. Diamond leaned into my face. "Where is he?"

An hour earlier, over coffee, Abe had rattled off his sales stops for the morning, all Jewish customers who worked on Sunday. I prayed the messenger could track him down.

"I need my husband," I sobbed.

Mr. Eidelman returned, holding a whiskey bottle in one hand and a delicately painted floral China teacup in the other. He filled the teacup halfway and said in his thick Russian accent, "The boys went for police. While we wait, dink dis. I guarantee you'll feel betta. Not too much, or it'll put hair on da chest."

I looked at him, shocked, then laughed hysterically. Was I losing my mind? I took a deep breath and tried to collect myself.

I'd never tasted whiskey before. I swallowed and gasped for air as the burn traveled down the back of my throat. The piercing liquid penetrated my head, drying my runny nose.

He nodded. "Take another."

I did, and without his urging, a third...

Within minutes, the muscles in my face relaxed, and my shoulders dropped. "This works. Are you sure about the hair?" I smiled thinly at Mr. Eidelman, embarrassed by my outburst.

"You'll see. It'll be okay. People get robbed. It happens more than you dink. Maybe coppers can catch dem."

Within the hour, two policemen entered my factory. They were young and handsome, opposite in appearance. The first was fair, red hair, watery blue eyes, and a field of freckles across his face. The other had chestnut hair, deep blue eyes, and a pointy nose. Both were young, likely rookies stuck with Sunday duty.

Mr. Eidelman signaled with his hand. "Over here. Dis lady, Mrs. Levine, is the boss and was robbed."

"A lady boss? Where's the man?" asked the red-haired officer in his brogue, scanning the workshop, his eyes searching.

The other officer was incredulous. "You mean you own the place?"

My relief was short-lived. I'd hit my breaking point, sick of insults from men. Slapping my hands on the table, I rose, standing erect. Then, leaning into their faces, locking eyes with theirs, I spoke in a steady voice laced with a fury that surprised even me. "Yes, officers. Tillie Levine is my name, and my partner is Sadie Stern. We own the factory and have been robbed. Are you two little boys experienced enough to find the thief?"

The air about us stilled.

"Sorry, lady, meant no harm," said the dark-haired officer, looking at his shoes. "I'm Officer Murphy."

The other cleared his throat. "Yes, ma'am. I'm Officer Kelly. Let's go over everything you saw."

Their mothers were likely the last women who'd scolded them in such a harsh manner.

Rapidly recounting the last twelve hours, I insisted, "We must act immediately. Don't give them time to get away. It was money for our next shipment of fabrics. People's jobs are at stake."

"We'll go to the tenements and find this Regan," said Officer Kelly.

I corrected him before they could leave the office. "No, I said her name's Rivka. She may have already moved."

"Then, we'll get her address from the neighbors." Descending the stairs, Officer Murphy muttered to his partner, "Whoever heard of a name like Rivka? I'll never get used to these daft names."

I looked at Mr. Eidelman and rolled my eyes. "Do you think they're capable? They'll never find a Regan in the tenements. The Irish left those buildings for Five Points years ago."

Moments later, Abe raced into the workshop. He embraced me tightly in his long arms. "Are you alright?"

I mumbled into his sleeve, "I'm better now that you're here. They stole my cash. It was so much money, enough for all the winter fabric." Tears resurfaced. "Mr. Eidelman brought over whiskey. It helped."

"Not too much of that stuff." Abe took the teacup from my hand. "I saw the police leave. Where're they going?"

"To find Rivka, but I think she moved, and I don't have her new address. Could you get Sadie?"

"Will you be okay without me? No more whiskey, though. We need you thinking straight." He twisted to Mr. Eidelman and eyed the half-filled bottle on the table. "Thanks for helping settle her down."

Mr. Eidelman winked and returned to his shop, bottle in hand.

Within the hour, Sadie arrived, the police at her heels. While waiting, I replayed the last few days in my mind. I couldn't imagine any of my workers pulling such a stunt.

Officer Kelly said in disgust. "The lady's gone. There're new tenants now, and no one on her floor knew where she'd gone.

Officer Murphy chimed in. "Doesn't anyone speak English? It was like squeezing blood from a stone."

Officer Kelly shrugged his shoulders, hands spread open. "It's as if she vanished into thin air. Didn't she have friends?"

I thought hard. Was it possible Rivka was the thief? No, it couldn't be. She'd been loyal since the beginning. But, her aloofness had always set me at a distance.

"Who else had a key?" Abe stormed. "This is outrageous!"

I blurted, "No one. Tova dropped it off last week."

"Who's Tova? Where does she live?" barked Officer Murphy.

Sadie looked hard at me. "I never liked that woman. Never looked me straight in the eye." Then, turning to Officer Kelly, she said, "I'll take you there, and if she's not home, we'll check Grand Central."

"There's no time to waste." I grabbed Officer Murphy's arm. "Sadie, you go to her apartment, and I'll go to the train station."

"I'm coming with you," said Abe. "We'll get to the bottom of this."

* * *

Two hours later, we reconvened at the police headquarters. Sadie, Abe, and I sat on one side of a metal table in a concrete block interrogation room. Tova sat alone, opposite us, her face ashen.

Within minutes after arriving at the train station with Officer Murphy, I spotted Tova hiding, clinging to her valise like a mouse with cheese. She was wearing a russet overcoat, far too warm for the sweltering heat, cowering in the shadow of a tobacco shop. I shouted, pointing to her. "There she is!"

Officer Murphy and the station police pursued Tova, grabbing her arms before she could run across the tracks.

I held the valise, following the officers while they dragged her into the police wagon. We all climbed aboard and rode to the station for questioning while Abe retrieved Sadie and Officer Kelly.

"I did nutting," cried Tova, her chin quivering.

I opened her valise, exhaling a sigh of relief. It contained one change of clothing, a towel, a hairbrush, and my envelope. I dumped the envelope on the metal table, but only half of the stolen money was there. I glared at Tova, my face hard. "Where's the rest?"

"Dat's all I have." Her crying swelled as if it could soften my fury.

Sadie's voice rose over the clamor. "Where's the rest, Tova? You must know."

At that point, a senior officer stepped into the room. Despite the heat, he was dressed in full regalia, a three-quarter woolen double-breasted coat, thick belt, bully club, and domed hat. He bent into Tova's face, shouting, "Answer the woman!"

Tova jumped, shuddering in fear.

He repeated, this time even louder. "I said, answer her!"

Tova broke, spilling her story in broken English. As it turned out, her family, crowded into the tenements like so many others, had been overcome by consumption. Her parents and brother had died, and no one would come near Tova. She was tainted; the neighbors were all frightened she carried the disease. A disease that left her alone in this foreign world. Unable to pay the rent, she was cast out onto the streets. After a week of sleeping in alleys and washing in our factory lavatory, she spotted Rivka selling our calico to a street vendor. When Tova confronted her and threatened to report Rivka's theft to me, Rivka let Tova sleep in the factory.

They arranged for Tova to leave at the end of the last shift along with the workers and sneak back later. Although this arrangement had worked for a few weeks, Tova knew it couldn't last.

Still, in her early twenties, she was convinced no man would ever marry her if they knew of the family's terrible health misfortune. So, she planned to run away and start a new life.

"But how did you know about the cash in the desk? The factory was empty when I left it there." I probed.

Tova sniffled. "I was hiding in a little closet and could hear you open and close the drawers."

The mice! How stupid of me.

Sadie pursued, "But how did you get the key?"

Tova cocked her head in disbelief, speaking to us like we were brainless. "We made a spare."

"That's what we get for trusting our employees." Sadie scoffed. "Where's Rivka?"

Tova shrugged her shoulders. "She told no one, not even me. Took her half and ran."

Abe muttered, "Damn, she could be anywhere, even on a boat back to Russia for all we know."

I sat stunned by this avalanche of wrongdoing. "But why? We treated you so well, like family. Don't you know we were once poor, too?"

Tova snorted. "We were never family! You got rich off our sweat. Rivka wanted a bigger piece. You were fools to trust her."

* * *

We left Tova at the police station to face her arrest. Sadie and I walked silently to Max's factory, digesting the day's events. Abe headed home.

My heart was still racing when we arrived at the factory. All I could manage was a few words, handing the partial payment to Max. Then, after

Sadie filled him in on the robbery, I promised, "We'll get you the rest this week. I'll get a loan from the bank."

He shook his head. "Consider it a loan." You and Abe are our dearest friends. Keep your shipment on schedule. We'll sort it out."

The afternoon light faded as Sadie and I left his factory. The beginning of autumn's evening chill laced through the air. Goosebumps ran down my bare lower arms. I used to believe in the goodness of mankind. Had I been wrong? Or was it a world of extremes? Max and Sadie's deep generosity versus trusted employees who stole?

I turned to Sadie. "Max didn't have to do that. Let's go back to my place, have something to drink, and figure out how to dig out of this."

* * *

I opened the parlor windows, summoning the cool evening air into the room. Sadie settled at my table while I prepared tea. I mused, "I can't believe I was so trusting."

Sadie watched me pour. I could see she was deep in thought. "You ran the factory alone for months while I nursed Eva in Saranac. Consider Max's loan my share of the profit during that time. You don't need to repay a nickel."

"No, Sadie. That's not right." I knew I couldn't allow her to bear the brunt. "If Rivka had confided in either of us, we would have helped her. It was my duty to know something was amiss."

Sadie shook her head. "You can't know everything. It takes both of us to manage this business. It's a big job and keeps getting bigger." She sighed, "Besides, I imagine Rivka went crazy after losing Saul. That's how I feel, crazy. Nothing matters the same way now."

I pulled Sadie into a hug. "It's still so soon. Give it time." I held her until she relaxed and said, "I can't believe Tova was living there all along. Stupid me, I thought she was a mouse."

For the first time in months, Sadie laughed. "Let it go. It's over. We both know there are much worse things in life."

CHAPTER THIRTY-NINE

But I couldn't let it go so fast. "She wasn't a mouse. Tova was a rat!"

IV

Part Four

"I think the degree of a nation's civilization may be measured by the degree of enlightenment of its women."
—Helen Keller

Chapter Forty

September 1890

The Jewish New Year, Rosh Hashanah, was in early autumn this year. Papa and Rebecca, at my request, had invited Sadie's family to join us at his farm in Sullivan County. I hoped a change in their routine might soften the harshness of celebrating this first holiday without their dear Eva.

Papa waited for us at the train station in a new red wagon pulled by his spry young horses. Infinity and Zero, our childhood horses, had long departed this world. Papa had foresight when he named them. Our family had come a long way since he and Mama arrived in New York. My oldest brother, Nate, had joined Papa's business, growing it into the largest poultry farm in the area. Joseph was an architect downtown, having completed his degree from Columbia University, and I had my dress kit business. We all held high hopes for Hannah now that she was recovering from the loss of Eva and back to her intense studying.

In only one month, the season had changed. Although it was a warm, bright fall day, the trees were no longer green. As we bumped along, we saw brilliant red and umber leaves hanging precariously on the branches, clinging to the final days of warmth and nourishment before turning brown, dropping to the soil below.

Sadie leaned into my ear. "I haven't had an opportunity to tell you that Jake met a girl at Saranac Lake. But her family lives in Chicago. They've been writing to each other the last few months. He's talking about moving out there after he graduates this year."

I wrestled with a mixture of joy and concern. "Isn't it a bit soon?" How would Sadie feel, losing two children in one year?

She cocked her head to the side, exhaling deeply. "I don't know. In a few years, maybe Max will sell his factory, and we'll follow Jake. I don't want to be far from our grandchildren. And it could be a fresh start."

It was a new year with new ideas and plans in the making. Was it time for Abe and me to reassess our lives, too?

* * *

Rebecca greeted us with a hug, then pulled me alone into the dining room. Over the years, we had patched up our differences, both committed to restoring a united family, writing to each other regularly. That was how I learned of Rebecca's dressmaking business in her farm community.

Weeks earlier, I had shown Rebecca's designs to Mr. Baum at Bloomingdale's, and shortly after, he invited her to visit the city for an interview.

Rebecca clasped her hands, her eyes buzzing with excitement. "I haven't been this excited in years! I don't know how to thank you." Her face radiated joy. "Imagine, Bloomingdale's! And that Mr. Baum is such a clever little man. I never stopped laughing."

"Did you bring your apple honey cake?"

"I did, just as you suggested. You'd think the man hadn't eaten in years, and he's as round as they come." Rebecca tittered. "He kept calling me his new, secret weapon. That he was going to make a killing. Get it?"

Her excitement infected me. "Oh, that's Mr. Baum alright. Full of puns. I'm thrilled for you, and it's about time you got the recognition you deserve. Which design did he buy?" I asked as I thought back to my meeting in his design studio a few weeks ago.

I had joined Abe for a routine sales call, and as always, Mr. Baum was exuberant. "Tillie, I hear you're a big *macher* downtown with those dress kits. And, of all things, to partner with Butterfield. Pure genius," he said, biting into a bialy piled high with fixings, smearing cream cheese on the curl of his moustache.

I handed him a cloth napkin.

"That's what happens when you bring good Jewish food my way." He pumped his brows. "I lose control. Delicious!" He took another bite, speaking while he chewed. "I'm surprised they did business with you plucky Jewish women—even though all their customers are women. Fashion's a crazy world. Butterfield still thinks men should decide what everyone wears."

I scoffed. "They're not interested in doing serious business with Sadie and me. We bring Abe, with his smooth New York accent, as a front to pacify them. They think he runs the company." I shrugged. "I've convinced myself not to dwell on it too much, even though it sometimes drives me mad. In business, the money you make is the only thing that matters."

Mr. Baum chuckled. "You're a wise girl, and you'll sleep better at night if you're rich than if you're right." He paused, wiping his mouth with his napkin. "Bloomingdale's should have come up with this kit idea first. The brothers have been so wrapped up catering to the new money that they forget the poor make up two-thirds of the city."

I wished all men thought like Mr. Baum. It would make my life far more pleasant. "Speaking of talented women, I'm hoping you'd take a look at my stepmother's work. She's quite a seamstress and designs all her garments."

I pulled Rebecca's meticulous designs from my oversized satchel and laid them across the front edge of the worktable. Then, I unfolded a tissue paper packet containing a dress and spread it along the rear edge. "I think she has a gift."

Mr. Baum studied each drawing with full concentration. Then he walked to the back edge of the table, lifting the garment, examining the dress. First, the exterior, moving his skilled hands inch by inch over the fabric, scrutinizing the pleats, seams, bound buttonholes, and darts. Finally, he turned the dress inside out and studied the hidden seams and lining.

I held my breath as if it were my own work.

"A gift is an understatement." His voice was thoughtful, serious, a tone I hadn't heard from him before. "Can you get her into the city to meet me? Self-taught, I presume?"

I let out my breath. "Of course."

Back in the dining room, Rebecca continued to gush. "In the end, Mr. Baum selected a winter three-piece ensemble with a bell-shaped ankle skirt, a matching narrow jacket, and a white, thinly pleated blouse. He'll accessorize with a velvet hat and a small pull-string purse. He couldn't decide which of Max's spectacular fabric samples to choose, so he picked them both!"

I smiled. "Leave it to Sadie to send the best."

Rebecca waved me off. "I'm not done, there's more! He selected a deep purple and navy brocade for the skirt and jacket. His milliner plans to construct a small hat in purple velvet with a navy and red plume. A clean, sophisticated design. Today's woman is too busy for all the frippery. The other combination is green with blue accents."

I caught Rebecca's excitement. "I love the look of brocade and velvet. That'll be exquisite." The trip to the city was a far cry from her monotonous life on this remote chicken farm.

Hannah, leaning on the door, had been listening. "Do the jacket and blouse have puffed sleeves? I love that style."

"Of course! That's what everyone wants, but Mr. Baum and I laughed about it. We think the mutton leg sleeve, as they call it in the business, like the bustle, won't be here too long. And, the best part, he wants me to work on a casual spring line. He said women are buying special clothes for recreation. Can you imagine? Pants for bicycles! I need to learn more about it. I'm excited to try something new."

Rebecca had come alive in a manner I'd never seen before. Did we all possess hidden talents, repressed by our life circumstances, only waiting for the right opportunity to strike?

She paused. "You know, I think he really likes working with women. He's different than most men."

Papa crept into the room, placing his arm around Rebecca's waist. "What's this about trying something new? Getting tired of the 'ole rooster?"

"Oh, you sweet man. How could I ever get tired of you?" Rebecca reached up to kiss Papa's cheek. "And the best part is I can work from home and still keep an eye out for Abby and your Papa."

I was relieved to see Papa looking spry. My brother Nate had warned me that Papa was slowing down and might need to visit a doctor. He wrote, *Papa runs out of air and he's sleeping every afternoon.* I thought I'd ask Rebecca to bring him to the city and see Dr. Boro before the winter when he was certain to find more excuses to delay.

* * *

Our families filled two large wood tables we'd pushed together. The holiday meal began with challah. Papa invited Max to say the *Hamotzi,* a special prayer intoned before breaking bread.

"Time for the Rosh Hashanah questions!" Papa shouted in his sing-song voice above the commotion. "I have candy for those with good answers."

Sadie looked confused.

I nudged her. "One of our crazy Isaacson traditions. Don't be too surprised; we've invented many."

Sadie's face turned inward. She whispered, "I suppose we all did."

Abe asked, "Julian, do you know why the challah is baked in a round loaf on Rosh Hashanah?"

"That's easy, Papa. It symbolizes the year and how it turns in a circle of seasons that never ends."

Papa pitched a candy across the table to Julian. "That's true, but we also wish at Rosh Hashanah that our good fortune and blessings in life also continue without an end."

After the *Hamotzi,* I served a tray of sliced apples with honey for dipping.

"Abby, why do we dip apples in honey?" Rebecca asked.

Abby smiled. "The honey is to wish everyone sweetness in the year ahead."

Julian interrupted. "Can I say something, Mama?"

I nodded, sighing loudly.

"Did you know that on most fruit trees, the leaves grow first and then

301

protect the fruit? But apples grow before their leaves, with no protection, like the Jews. Right, Opa? We don't have the same protection as others." He smiled at his Opa. "Do I get another candy?"

I stared at my son, wishing the world were a kinder place. All children should grow up feeling protected.

"Very true, Julian." Papa tossed him another candy. "I hope you never, ever experience what your Oma, God rest her soul, and I lived through in Germany before we came to America. Nothing here in New York is as ugly as it was in Europe when they chased Jews with guns and swords."

"Papa, *de kinder.*" I pointed to Miriam. "Let's remember, this is a happy holiday."

After clearing the apple plates, Rebecca and I brought platters of tender brisket, gravy, sweet noodle pudding, and honey-glazed carrots to the table. It was followed by a dessert tray teeming with apple honey cake, dried fruits, and cinnamon cookies.

After everyone was sated, the children peeled away from the table to play, the men headed outdoors for a walk to inspect the farm, and the women cleared the table. We lined up in the kitchen to help Rebecca wash, dry, and store the dishes.

Once we finished, I strolled out to the front porch and found Papa cheering for the youngsters as they played ball.

He glanced my way with a satisfied smile. "Come sit."

I dragged a rocking chair close to his, and before I could voice my concern about his health, he launched into a memory, recounting his voyage to America forty years earlier. I marveled at his new-found skill as a raconteur. Leaning back in his white wooden rocking chair, he drew a full breath of air, sailing back in time. Mama had always shared a rosy picture of their adventure, but Papa's retelling was an entirely different matter.

"The sailors were a bunch of drunks, pounding at the women's cabins at night when they felt randy. We men took turns hiding in the galley to guard the women and children so they could rest." He paused, collecting his scattered memories. "There was nowhere safe for the young ones to play. The deck floors were disgusting from slop buckets tipping that if we weren't careful, we'd slip and fall into the stinking mess. By the end, when we saw New York in the distance, I thanked God we'd made it safely. You know, that was before Ellis Island and the great Mother Liberty greeted folks."

It was difficult to visualize the harbor without the grand statue.

He stopped to reflect, "I knew then nothing in life, that is until your mama got sick, could ever be as terrible as that trip."

I screwed my face. "Papa, that's the first time I've heard the story that way. Mama always made it sound like a romantic adventure."

He scoffed. "Just like your mama to see the bright light in everything. She passed that gift to you, Tillie." He paused, inhaling a nostalgic breath. "Don't ever lose it."

I decided to discuss his health later in a letter. Why spoil this special moment? I'd spent hours of my life remembering his messages of love and wisdom, especially when difficult times struck. I hadn't expected a new one this afternoon.

* * *

After a lavish breakfast of leftovers, the following day, Nate brought us back to the station. We boarded the train south, swinging our worn valises into the overhead racks and setting our picnic baskets, filled with leftovers and apples from Papa's new orchard, on the floor beside our feet.

Having waited for the trip home to speak with Sadie, hesitant to discuss business during the holiday, I was ready to plan the upcoming season. "Would you mind sitting with me? We can firm up matters for the Butterfield meeting next week while we travel."

Sadie touched my forearm. "Before anything, I want to thank you for inviting my family. We had a wonderful time. The boys' smiles gave me hope. It made the holiday much easier to bear, instead of another sad day, reminding us of our loss."

The train screeched as it pulled away from the station. Within moments, it was chugging along at a steady clip on the ride back to Grand Central.

Satisfied that I was beginning the New Year helping my best friend, a *mitzvah*, I laid out my thoughts. "Sadie, have you been following the newspaper stories about the banks?"

She answered quizzically, "A little, but I don't fully understand. We don't borrow much or hold stocks. Do you think we'll be affected? Max isn't too concerned."

"I'm not sure I fully understand all that happened, but last winter, two large railroad companies went under. That set off a reaction in the stock market and the farmers who depend on the railroads to transport their harvests to market. Right now, I'm trying to think ahead."

Sadie thought aloud. "Why do you think it would affect the kits? Will women forgo new dresses?"

I considered her question. "They may hold off on store-made garments. In the past, during tough times, women made their clothing." I paused for a moment, searching deeper. "And now many have sewing machines. What if it triggers the opposite, an increase in kit orders?"

Sadie's brows shot up. "That's fascinating. Do you think New York banks will be impacted?"

"I don't know, but we should stay alert. If the banks are hit, we won't be able to borrow anything."

Sadie crossed her arms. "I'm grateful we haven't needed to depend on the banks. Max has never trusted them."

I nodded. "We should probably keep sales volume steady and work off our cash flow. I'm curious to see what we hear at Butterfield."

Chapter Forty-One

October 1890

Miss Sweeney greeted us with enthusiasm, taking in our new fall dresses as we entered the Butterfield office. "It's so nice to see you! Mr. Kraft will be with you shortly. Your outfits are fetching."

I handed her a basket of fresh apples. "Something healthy for a change." I laughed. "These are from my Papa's farm up north. The children picked them yesterday."

She dipped her nose into the basket, inhaling the sweet perfume. Just as she lifted her head, Mr. Kraft and Mr. Peters exited the elevator.

A broad smile broke across Mr. Peters's face as he reached for Abe's hand. "Good morning, Tea with Rose! I'd like to join your meeting this morning, and it's not only to sample the delicious pastries you bring."

"Fresh picked apples today." Miss Sweeney glowed as she held up the basket.

Mr. Kraft, indifferent to the food, gestured to his office door. "Please come in." He'd grown his mustache longer and was using a copious amount of wax to curl the ends upward. While it was the new fashion these days, it made him appear sneaky.

We settled into our customary seats at the conference table.

Mr. Kraft handed out the prior months' sales report. "As you see, demand continues to increase. Abe, your idea to switch designs was brilliant. It refreshed interest in the product. Not only did the adult kits sell well, but we also sold all the children's."

I nudged Sadie's shoe with mine. *That was my damn idea! But as usual, Mr. Kraft wouldn't give me the credit.*

"You know what that means?" asked Mr. Peters.

I jumped in. "Before we discuss upcoming orders, I'd like to hear your view on the banks and if they could impact the business."

"Such a timely question, dear." Mr. Peters darted his piercing eyes my way.

Something odd in his expression set me on edge. Was he acting more patronizing than usual? *He must think I'm an outright idiot who can't read headlines!*

"We predict our pattern business will be one of a few that grows. Our Board thinks many families will have less to spend, so they'll be growing their own vegetables, so to speak. The men will take out their hammers to repair their homes, and women will dust off their sewing machines to make the family's clothing." Mr. Peters laughed, clearly enjoying his country's ill fortune.

Mr. Kraft added, "Last year, we worried off-the-rack clothing would depress sales, but the opposite is happening. Now that Tea with Rose has an established name, it's time to build volume. We'd like to introduce another three new dress patterns and increase the order to ten thousand units for each design."

I gulped. "You're suggesting we increase the women's kit production to thirty thousand? What about the children's kits?"

"For now, we'd like to double them." Mr. Kraft replied. "We expect some women will refashion their old garments for their daughters. Like they used to."

"Let's see. In total, you're asking for an additional thirty-two thousand units. By when?" Abe asked.

"We'll need half by November 30th to ship for the Christmas shopping season and the remainder by year-end," Mr. Kraft answered. "Our new patterns are completed and ready. We've begun producing them."

Sadie and I locked eyes. There was no way we could possibly manufacture that kind of volume in our current factory. I gave Abe a swift kick under the table.

"That's an astounding opportunity. Tillie and Sadie, what are your thoughts?" Abe asked.

"It is thrilling, but we haven't the capacity," answered Sadie carefully.

They must have planned this all along. After all, they have new patterns ready to go! I was furious. It took every ounce of self-control to contain me in my chair. "That's a tall order to guarantee. Our factory is working at full speed to meet the current orders. An increase of this size requires a larger space, tripling our workforce, and that's only after we firm up volumes with our suppliers." I couldn't suppress the hostile edge in my voice. "We would need to secure greater volumes of fabric and notions in addition to your patterns. That would require bank loans.

Sadie fiddled with a curl that had freed itself from her bun. "As you know, this isn't the best time to ask for a loan."

"What happens if we can't deliver?" Abe asked.

Mr. Peters cleared his throat. "We've considered that possibility, Mr. Levine. Would you be inclined to entertain an offer from Butterfield to buy Tea with Rose, name rights and all?"

Sadie gasped loudly. Her loose corkscrews bobbing about.

I felt faint; the room started spinning. Gripping the seat of my chair, I took a deep breath, regaining myself, then looked at Abe's face, wondering how he'd respond. Never in a million years had we expected this morning's discussion to turn this way.

Abe laughed and shook his head in disbelief. "Gentlemen, I must admit, I wasn't prepared for this. How about we meet later in the week once we talk it over with our bank and attorney? You've given us much to consider."

Mr. Peters handed Abe an envelope. "That's fine, but we'll need a decision by the week's end. Look over our offer in the meantime."

As I rose to leave, I watched Mr. Kraft twisting the end of his mustache. Was he hiding a sinister smile behind that waxy curl?

Moments later, out on the sidewalk, Sadie cried, "Those snakes! They want to steal our company. I'll bet their offer is terrible."

"We won't let them!" I snapped. "Abe, open the envelope. I want to see what they offered."

Abe ripped open the envelope and stepped closer to me, giving both of us a full view.

Sadie said impatiently, "Are you going to tell me, too?"

I gazed at the ground, sighing deeply. "Forget it. You're right, Sadie. It's another insult. They want to steal it from us."

Abe pocketed the letter before I could grab it from his hands and rip it to shreds.

Sadie stood up straight. "Well then, we'll stop at the bank and set up a credit line, work around the clock, and hire more workers. Then we can stay in our current space until we see if the kits sell."

I was silent, discouraged, not the least bit hopeful, given the gloomy national news, that we could obtain a credit line.

Sadie took my hand. "Come on, Tillie. It's not like you to give up."

Stunned, we walked the block to the bank in silence. I was bewildered, struggling to conjure a way to answer Butterfield's challenge without losing Tea with Rose. Opening the heavy bank door, we were greeted by long lines of stern-faced customers standing restlessly, facing the brass-barred teller windows. A young man in line was rubbing the back of his neck raw, muttering to himself.

Sadie whispered to Abe. "What's going on here? Why the lines?"

"If this is anything like twenty years ago when my parents lost their business, people are pulling their money out. It's probably not a good day to ask for a loan."

"Do you think the bank will fail?" I panicked. "Abe, do we have money here?"

Abe looked at the crowd. "No, don't worry. Ours is safe, under lock and key at home. Remember, I bought a good safe after the robbery?" He looked at his pocket watch. "But I've got a meeting of my own to get to in an hour. Why don't you set up an appointment for tomorrow? I can join you then, and hopefully, things will have settled down."

CHAPTER FORTY-ONE

"What if they close the bank?" Sadie asked.

"We'll have to take our chances. Just try to get an appointment." Abe looked at his pocket watch. We'll talk later at home." He kissed me on the cheek and hurried out.

Sadie and I walked past the lines to a receptionist, requesting an appointment with the loan manager. Every eye on the line followed us with suspician. But, instead of an appointment, we were led directly to a table in a conference room.

We sat down, unprepared for a meeting. I wished Abe hadn't left. Nothing was happening as planned. Sadie and I eyed each other, both apprehensive. She was twisting her hair again, unspooling her bun. I wondered if my face reflected her anxious expression.

I leaned over the table, whispering. "Stop playing with your curls. You'll look like Medusa if you keep it up. We need to look polished and prepared, even if we aren't."

Sadie nodded, inhaled through her nose, tucking her wiry curls back into her chignon, and folded her hands on the table.

Moments later, two men entered the room, each wearing a monocle held firmly in place by a frowning crease on their noses. Although their faces were cast in similar expressions, one man was quite tall and the other a full head shorter.

The first man, the older and taller of the two, pointed at his partner and bowed his head ever so slightly. "Good morning, ladies. My name is Mr. Pinter, and this is Mr. McCracken. How can we help you today?" Both men ran their eyes up and down our garments.

I answered, "We came to arrange an appointment for tomorrow together with our husbands. We hadn't expected to meet with you now."

"It's rather busy, but we can spare a moment." Mr. McCracken smiled thinly.

I was confused. With those long lines in the lobby, why were they bothering to meet with us? But I took a breath and launched into an explanation of our business and the amount needed for expansion.

"You foolish woman," Mr. Pinter scoffed, once again taking in our expensive and fashionable clothing. We thought you were planning to withdraw your money."

Mr. McCracken threw his hands to the ceiling. "Didn't you see the lines in the lobby? Are you two daft?"

"Ladies, there's no way in burning hell any banker in his right mind would loan money to a couple of women, especially now, during a market crash," Mr. Pinter admonished, pushing back his chair. "You're wasting our time."

"Good day, ladies." The men huffed as they stormed out, leaving Sadie and me sitting in a stunned silence.

We gathered our belongings and hurried through the bank lobby to the sidewalk.

Sadie exclaimed. "Could you believe their rudeness? And I thought Butterfield was bad,"

I was ready to explode with frustration. "I've had enough of these brutes! There must be something we can do."

* * *

Abe, Sadie, and I sat in the parlor that evening, sharing our outrage. I made a pot of tea and set leftover apple honey cake on the table.

Sadie began. "Imagine how much money we'd make if only we could find a way to increase production."

I sensed there was more to the story. "But what if they're wrong? If we find a lender, borrow to the hilt, and the kits don't sell, then what? If the demand is temporary and a year from now women return to off the rack, we'll have to shrink the factory and let people go. We've never done that before."

Abe shook his head, raising his voice. "This was a set up. He said the patterns were ready. They've planned this for months."

"I don't have the stomach to fire our workers." Sadie paused. "And if they're wrong, it could bankrupt us."

I wondered aloud, "What if we demand Butterfield gives us more money up front."

"I doubt they would; they'll make the upfront money a loan," Abe took his time, his thoughts forming as he spoke. "They'll insist on making Tea with Rose the collateral. You'll walk deeper into their trap."

I exhaled loudly. "What bastards. I would have thought after all these years they'd be better partners."

Abe continued, not listening to a word I said. "Tea with Rose is only a few years old. How attached are you? Think about it. Sadie's talking about moving to Chicago in a few years. You could sell it for a good price and invest in something else, like the apartments being built everywhere around us."

I looked toward the children's bedrooms, "Miriam is still young, and if we ramped up as much as they want, I'd never see her."

Sadie considered Abe's earlier remark. "Abe, do you really think they planned this take-over?"

Abe nodded his head slowly. "My guess is they've had their eye on your business ever since it took off. Butterfield's big and rich. They could bide their time and wait for the right moment to strike."

My stomach churned. I felt small and exposed. "We've worked so hard. I can't believe how evil they are."

Abe sighed. "I see it happening with little factories all the time. Many are too small and local to compete and are forced to sell out to bigger factories that can handle national-sized orders and bear greater financial risk." He sat back in his chair. "I'll probably end up selling my button business too."

My eyes shot to his. "That's news. How long have you been thinking about selling out?"

Abe shrugged. "On and off for a while. There's little need for a middleman selling buttons."

"So, you think they're simply being smart businessmen?" Sadie asked.

Abe smirked, tilting his head. "Partly. Loyal relationships are hard to find in the business world. That doesn't excuse them for ambushing you. But you can outsmart them right back."

I looked hard at my husband, still digesting his announcement.

We sat thinking, sipping our tea, nibbling on the cake. I thought about

311

how its sweetness symbolized the start of the Jewish New Year. Suddenly, I pictured Mr. Baum stuffing his face with Rebecca's cake.

"Oh, I know! I've got it." I jumped up with delight. "What about talking to Mr. Baum at Bloomingdale's? They have the workspace, their own designers to make patterns, distribution, and everything else needed to make it work!" I was buzzing with excitement. "You know he always loved the kit idea. Remember when he said he was sorry they hadn't thought of it first?"

The corners of Abe's mouth turned up. "Yes, he did, and it could be good for the Bloomingdale brothers, help them ride out this bad patch. After all, they're going to lose customers for a while."

Sadie chimed in. "Don't forget, there's nothing in our contract that says we can't do business with others."

Abe leaned back in his chair. "Don't count on Bloomingdale's buying you out right away. But they may be willing to test the water." He chuckled, "The men at Butterfield underestimated you two."

I sighed, "We must tell Mr. Baum the whole truth that Butterfield tried to buy the company for a pittance of what it's worth. I want a completely above-board negotiation."

Sadie nodded, "I agree, even if we don't get the top price."

Once Sadie and I decided to sell, we moved fast. The winter season was practically upon us, and we only had a few weeks to spare. The workers in our factory needed a new shipment to work on, or we'd have to let them go.

Chapter Forty-Two

"You're beginning to feel like family!" Mr. Baum's voice belted out across the busy workshop when Abe, Sadie, and I walked into his design shop at the end of the week.

I laughed. "Is that good or bad?"

Sadie whispered to me. "Is he always this friendly? Quite a change from Butterfield."

"And who is this lovely woman?" Mr. Baum asked, studying Sadie with his broad, toothy smile.

"I thought you'd like to meet my partner and closest friend, Sadie Stern," I said, pleased with his gracious reaction.

Mr. Baum reached for Sadie's hand and gave it a hearty shake. "Any friend of Tillie's is a friend of mine."

Sadie's face looked starstruck, her eyes wide.

Mr. Baum turned back to me. "Tillie, it's a hectic day. Can we get started?"

"Absolutely, I brought lunch." I set my picnic basket on his conference table.

"See, only the best parts of family, good food but no nonsense." Mr. Baum laughed as he rubbed his hands together. "Let's eat."

Sadie giggled. "Tillie and Abe, you've been hiding your best customer. How could you?"

We sat around the work table in his office. While we ate, I described the situation we were facing with Butterfield. "It's time for us to sell. But before we do, Sadie and I'd like to see if we can interest you and Bloomingdale's."

"Bloomingdale's to buy Tea with Rose?" Mr. Baum's eyebrows darted up to his hairless dome.

At this point, Abe interjected, "Yes, or work together with us. Consider putting your name on the kit during this terrible market. It's a perfect strategy for a department store like yours." Then, he shifted his eyes to Sadie and me. "And these ladies prefer to work or sell to honest people rather than stay in a business relationship they can't trust."

"An interesting proposition. I'd think you were kidding if I didn't know you so well." Mr. Baum said. "You brought Rebecca to me out of the blue, and she's brilliant. I'll remind the brothers of that when we talk. Who knows? Maybe this idea could work."

For the first time in days, I allowed myself to feel hope. I took a deep breath and felt my tight shoulders relax.

"Here's the thing, Mr. Baum," I said. "We must move fast. We haven't committed to a winter line with Butterfield and must substitute a partner. Otherwise, we'll be forced to sell to them or close our doors. And we have a factory full of loyal, hard workers ready to start our next season's order."

"First, would you stop calling me Mr. Baum already? Leo is the only name I answer to."

A good sign.

"I commend your sense of duty to your workers, and of course, if the brothers Bloomingdale's want to bite, they may prefer to put their toe in first and see how twelve months of a partnership works before buying."

Sadie crossed her arms. "I like the idea of Bloomingdale's stepping into Butterfield's place for a year and testing it out. That gives us more time to decide, too."

Leo wiped his mouth with his napkin, setting it down firmly on the table. "Good. Knowing the boys as I do, I don't think they'd buy any other way, especially in a down market."

Sadie and I looked at each other and nodded in unison. Until Leo mentioned the possibility of a trial, we hadn't considered remaining the owners. So, I was relieved to hear Sadie's endorsement.

"We can do that. We only need a Bloomingdale's pattern, new labeling, and an agreement. Then, we can replicate our process with Butterfield,"

I said, digging into my satchel for sample kits and the most recent sales volumes to leave with Leo.

"Do you think you can have patterns printed in time?" Abe asked.

"Are you kidding? Of course, I can." Leo rubbed his chin. "Aha! I'll put Rebecca on the design. She'll know what a novice seamstress would enjoy."

I took silent pleasure in working with a man with nothing to prove.

I handed Leo the kits and folder. "Is there anything else you'll need for your pitch to the owners?"

"Yes," he said with an amused tone. "You, Sadie, and Abe wouldn't hurt." Leo stretched his arms open. "Do you think I can pitch this idea as well as you?"

Sadie gasped. "But we've never met them. What are they like? Would it be smarter to have Abe do the pitch? We've found most men prefer conducting business with men."

Mr. Baum stood, his hands placed firmly on his hips. "No, do it the same way you just did with me. They'll want to know who they're dealing with. They're more serious than me, so no joking around. But they're good people."

He headed to the door. "Don't move. I'll ask for a meeting date before you leave."

A moment later, he hurried back to the office, his jowl jiggling while he ran. "Now! They're both here, the father and son. They want to hear what you have to say. Bring the sales report and sample kit."

Sadie and I jumped out of our seats. I was shaken at the prospect of meeting the 'brothers,' the giants who grew this store from their Upper East Side clothing bizarre years ago. "But, Leo, we haven't practiced." This was happening far too fast for me.

A loud guffaw escaped his full grin. "You just did, with me. You'll be fine." He reached for my arm. "Come, let's not waste their time."

Sadie and I hurried behind Abe and Mr. Baum to the elevator. We entered silently, waiting for the attendant to take us to the top floor. Upon leaving the elevator, I caught Abe's eyes.

He nodded his head with a soft smile. "Show time, ladies."

Although I wanted to absorb his lightness, Abe's humor panicked me further. "Abe, can you warm them up and give us a moment to collect our thoughts?"

He nodded as we walked briskly into a beautiful conference room containing a large mahogany table, upholstered armchairs in enchanting jewel tones, and soft, botanical wall coverings. A stunning crystal chandelier cast a warm glow through the room.

As we found our seats, two gentlemen entered: one quite old with white hair, spectacles, and a heavy mustache; the other, a younger version, also wore spectacles, a full mustache, and a tightly trimmed beard. Both were dressed in crisp autumn suits.

Mr. Baum darted to them, extending his hand. "Thank you for allowing this interruption in your busy day." He introduced each of us, explaining Abe's history with Bloomingdale's and the recruitment of Rebecca, all in under three minutes.

We had never encountered anyone quite like these two men. I was winded at the pace of the meeting, my head spinning like a top as I struggled to organize my thoughts.

Lyman Bloomingdale, the son, spoke abruptly. "Let's see what you have. Lay it out on the table."

While Sadie followed his instructions, setting the kits and finished dresses across the surface, I started without Abe. "We've come to interest you in a unique opportunity that will help Bloomingdale's weather the bad market. We had been working together for the last several years with Butterfield, but frankly...."

Sadie interrupted, "They tried to rob us blind!"

The air stilled as her heated words reverberated off the walls. My palms grew damp. *How could she blurt out such a thing?*

The older man, the father, one of the original founders, suddenly laughed. "They did, did they? This is a story I want to hear. I've always disliked that crowd."

The next hour flew by, starting with a report on our continually growing past sales. Our graphs and regional reports passed back and forth between the men as they pointed out tidbits of information to each other. They seemed starved for a hopeful idea. Finally, Sadie demonstrated the content of the kit packets. Abe explained how this lower-priced product could help the store reach a new stratum of customers, bringing money in from a fresh geographic population who could soften the market blow for them just as it would have for Butterfield.

Within an hour, we had ourselves a new partner. As Leo predicted, they insisted on a year of partnership before discussing the purchase of Tea with Rose. Our timing could not have been better. Every business in New York City was frantically searching for ways to buffer the bank failures, and our kit was no longer an experiment. It had proven success.

The three of us danced out of the building onto the busy sidewalk, excited beyond words. Finally, we were out of the morass.

Chapter Forty-Three

With the Bloomingdale's deal finalized, Sadie and I set an appointment with Butterfield. It was the first time we'd come so close to failure, navigating the high-wire challenge of financial success. Butterfield thought they had us cornered, but we were hopping mad and could barely wait to put those charlatans in their place. Better yet, we did not need Abe for this meeting.

Poor Miss Sweeney. She looked confounded when we walked in without Abe or pastries. I tried to greet her with a warm smile, but the knots in my stomach must have shown on my face.

"Um, is everything alright, ladies?" Miss Sweeney's eyebrows knotted together; a concerned frown crossed her face.

"Yes. Can we wait in Mr. Kraft's office?" Sadie asked.

"Of course," Miss Sweeney answered in a whisper.

When Mr. Kraft sauntered in moments later, Sadie and I were sitting at the conference table, ready to pounce. He fiddled with his waxed mustache, holding a file. Mr. Peters followed him, wearing a haughty expression. We knew he thought we'd come to cave to his offer.

We stared at the men in frosty silence, having decided to let them speak first. Then, finally, Mr. Peters' eyes darted to the door. "Where's Mr. Levine?"

Sadie replied, "Gentleman, we brought Mr. Levine to earlier meetings for your benefit since you prefer speaking to a man. For the record, Mrs. Levine and I own one hundred percent of Tea with Rose and have made every decision from the very start."

Mr. Kraft looked astounded. "But what about the contracts?"

"All signed by Tea with Rose. Have another look," I said, keeping my voice low and measured although my heart was pounding.

Sadie jumped in. "Check with your attorneys if you need to. Everything was properly executed. But that's not our purpose today."

Mr. Peters cleared his throat. "Perhaps we should get down to business."

"We should. Because, as of today, we're concluding our business with you." Sadie looked Mr. Kraft straight in the eye.

Mr. Peters' nostrils flared as he spoke through his teeth. "What do you mean? Aren't we going to work through the sales contract? I understood that was the purpose of today's meeting."

I reminded myself to stay calm. After all, we had the upper hand.

"Gentlemen, let me be clear," I explained. "Our partnership with Butterfield has been fruitful for both of us over the years. But it was built on false assumptions. In all fairness, these existed on both ends. Your attitude toward women forced us to pretend Abe was the owner, so we did. But the worst part was that you lulled us into trusting your word, thinking you were genuine partners, you know, through thick and thin."

Sadie snarled, "Then, you attempted a takeover to force us to sell at a God-awful price."

Mr. Peters cleared his throat and lowered his voice. "We didn't intend our offer to come across that way. We only want to seize a rare opportunity. We expected a negotiation. That's all part of the process."

"Well, sirs, you were evidently happy to take us down that road without warning," I said. I wouldn't let him fool us again into thinking he was being realistic. "Giving us no advance idea about your plans and no reasonable alternatives. Before sharing anything with us, your patterns were in production, placing us in an impossible corner." I sat straighter and forged on. "You would have made a fortune working with us as partners. But you were greedy and chose not to."

I gave my words a moment to sink in. "So, we did what any smart businesswomen would do. We shopped around until we found an alternative."

"Who?" Mr. Peters blasted at us.

I ignored his outburst. "An excellent choice. As you know, in this dreadful market, everyone is biting at the bit."

"Don't forget, our name is trademarked," Sadie added.

Before they could respond, I rose from my chair. "We'd like to thank you for your years with us. I believe we've finished our business today."

Mr. Kraft's head was rocking back and forth so fast I thought it would detach from his body. "You can't do that! Besides, who'd ever partner with a couple of foolish women?" He sniffed in a long breath before adding, "And for the record, it's unseemly for a nursing mother to wet herself at work. You should have been at home caring for your baby, not leaking milk in a conference room!" he barked, projecting spittle across the table.

Sadie and I turned toward the door as Mr. Peters half-whispered to Mr. Kraft, "They're just a bunch of shifty Jews."

How dare he speak that way! A visceral anger snaked through me. But I held my head high, turned back to face Mr. Peters, and said through clenched teeth. "For a bunch of shifty Jews, we're the ones who respected the partnership. You pulled this devious move, trying to trick us into folding So, consider this a courtesy call. Our attorney will contact you for our remaining sales commissions. Not a penny less. Good day, sirs."

* * *

The next six weeks were spent furiously replicating our typical shipment volume. Rebecca added a dress pattern with a lovely sash, enabling it to go from daytime with an apron to church on Sunday. Mr. Baum selected the fabric and notions. By keeping the volumes steady, we completed the shipment on time, delivering it to Bloomingdale's for packaging and distribution. Bloomingdale's used their creative talent to create gorgeous labels, placing our tea rose name front and center, disguising the fact that the Butterfield name was no longer there.

They had a knack for enticing the buyer. The prior year, they had employed a marketing wizard, Mr. Dugan, who called upon a brand-new Midwestern-based catalog business, Sears and Roebuck, who had established a national sales base through their watch and jewelry business. Sears and Roebuck recently had expanded their catalog to include everyday household goods and clothing and wanted our product. Our timing could not have been better!

I looked around the room. After weeks of furiously preparing kits, the workshop was a disaster. Scraps of fabric were strewn across every table and chair, dust-balls laced with colorful thread, and stray buttons collected in every nook and corner.

"Can you believe we finished the order on time?" I marveled, looking at the clutter, toasting our success with a drop of plum schnapps.

"We have the best factory in the city," Sadie burped, then covered her mouth with her fingertips. "We should have a party to celebrate." She lifted her dainty teacup in the air for another toast. "Maybe we'll invite Mr. Eidelman next door over with his whiskey. I'll wager it tastes better than this stuff."

Chapter Forty-Four

December 1890

Winter's darkness wrapped its arms around the sky before we sat for dinner. I prepared a fragrant roasted hen rubbed with melted butter, onions, and dried herbs. The skin was perfectly salted, browned, and cracking crisp. I bought yams at the local market and baked them with the hen in the oven. Bloomingdale's' order had shipped, and I could finally relax and enjoy a meal with my family.

"I've got great news!" Hannah crowed as she sat down beside Miriam's highchair.

"Let's hear it," Abe replied.

"I just received my marks from the fall semester, and they were perfect in every subject. I can't wait until college. As a matter of fact, I plan to concentrate on biology." Hannah beamed.

"Hannah, I couldn't be prouder." I smiled. "Still thinking about nursing?"

She scrunched her face, drawing back. 'I'm going to be a doctor, like Dr. Boro."

I stared at her with the most profound admiration. Never in my wildest dreams would I have imagined college for myself, then medical school. All I had wanted years ago was to finish high school. "Well then, that is what you will do. How far we've all come." I was pleased my hard work helped open doors for Hannah's dreams. Although it took years for me to set my course, I was satisfied with my life and all I had created, starting with a supportive, loving family. Mama was right years ago when she told me that the most important, enduring part of life is your family.

Hannah's voice interrupted my musing.

"I'm more certain than ever. I'm as smart as any boy in high school. I know I can do it." Hannah puffed her chest. "And I may attend another delivery this weekend. Marta will need me if Mrs. Aaron goes into labor. That will be my sixteenth."

I thought back to my father's comment years ago when he argued with Rebecca about my high school dream, *she's smarter than all the boys.* I was pleased that I'd done well with Hannah.

Julian looked at Hannah with a quizzical expression. "I still don't understand how...."

Abe cut off his question. "Julian, how was school today? Didn't you have an arithmetic test?"

Hannah smiled knowingly.

We finished dinner listening to Julian rattle on about how he solves multiplication problems in his head. Finally, Hannah and Julian cleared the table and headed to their rooms to tackle schoolwork. Miriam trailed behind Hannah.

Could my life be any more perfect? I entered the kitchen, tied my apron, preparing to wash the dishes.

Abe stepped behind me as I scrubbed the plates with a soapy rag. "Can I give you a hand and dry? He ran his finger down my spine.

I answered with a naughty laugh. "Sure, Abe, I'd love a hand. What else is on your mind?"

"Tillie, I saw our accountant today and can't believe how well we've survived this awful market. Most people in our business have struggled with all the bank failures, mostly from over-borrowing as my parents had. So even though my button business has contracted, connecting Tea with Rose with Bloomingdale's was a brilliant move."

"That's wonderful, Abe! We dodged a disaster." I knew that so many of our business contacts had lost their livelihoods. Success and failure were a game of chance. "Do you think Bloomingdale's will be interested in buying the company in a year?"

"Yes, if sales continue as they've been. But you and Sadie may change your minds. Think it over carefully."

"I feel blessed, especially while others have struggled. The money is wonderful, but my family matters to me most. Just like Mama told me it would, so many years ago."

Abe leaned down and kissed my cheek. "The day I first saw you, standing in your father's farmhouse parlor, was the luckiest day of my life. I fell in love the moment I looked into your eyes. You've always been beautiful, but how could I have known you were so intelligent and determined, too?" He hugged me around my waist, resting his head on my shoulder. "Except for little Sarah, life has been perfect."

I thought back to those turbulent early years and how my love for Abe had grown. "I wanted you from the start. Bringing a gift for Rebecca and not me was a clever trick. I was intrigued by a man who would know to do that."

"I have another trick up my sleeve," Abe chuckled, pressing his body further into my back, pushing my heavy hair away, kissing my neck. "How about we get these dishes done and celebrate."

I needed no convincing to spend precious time alone with Abe. "I'll be in right after I put Miriam to bed. Could you check on Julian and let him know we're turning in early?"

Moments later, door locked, we were undressed and kissing each other deeply under the warm quilt. "You have such a beautiful body," Abe whispered as he stroked my breasts, gently grasping my nipples and sending thrilling waves of excitement down my body.

"Mm, you too," I said as I nibbled on his ear lobes, pulling on his curly chest hair.

Suddenly, Abe stopped kissing me, fingering my left breast more deliberately.

"What's the matter?" I cried. "What are you doing? You're hurting me!"

"Tillie, I feel something. Here, give me your hand." He placed my fingers on the underside of my breast. "What is that?"

My amorous mood vanished as I examined my breast. There was a hard lump the size of a pea under the skin. I felt the other breast, soft, with nothing unusual. A flood of fear coursed through me as I thought of the morning fifteen years ago at the farmhouse, Mama holding the teapot, crying. *Oh, please, God, not me!*

I jumped out of bed, turned on the light, and stepped in front of the bureau mirror. My breasts looked normal in the reflection. I touched each one, prodding the skin and nipples. Both were soft under my fingertips except for the bump in the underside of my right breast.

I lowered myself back into bed and lifted the covers to my neck, trembling.

"Did you feel anything else?" Abe asked, raising himself on one elbow, his voice trembling.

"No, just that one spot." I began to weep. "This is what happened to Mama. I'm not ready to die! The children are so young. They need me." I turned my face into the pillow to muffle my sobs. "I'm terrified."

Abe drew me into his arms. "We'll have Dr. Boro see you first thing in the morning. Maybe it's nothing. He'll tell us."

Generally, hearing Dr. Boro's name brought instant reassurance, but not now. Not with the thoughts of Mama's death pulled fresh from my memory. "I don't know why I hadn't noticed. That's what happened to Mama. First, they cut her up, and then she died from an awful infection. It was dreadful." My body trembled. *Oh, Mama, now I know how you felt.*

"Tillie, I'd never let that happen to you, to us." Abe held me in his arms until my sobbing subsided. "I refuse to lose my wife and best friend."

I looked at his loving face. His eyes glistened with tears.

I tried to fight the angry edge in my voice. "I wish it were up to you. But Papa had no control, and you don't either."

Abe drew a loud breath through his nose. "That was years ago. We will fight this!"

I sighed, knowing that my life was in the hands of fate.

Abe wiped his tears away, gripping me tighter as if he could protect me from this fierce army lurking inside me. "Let me get some brandy. It'll calm us down, so we get a little rest."

I knew we were powerless; sleep would be elusive for both of us.

Hours later, I lay in bed listening to Abe's uneven breathing, both of us tossing and turning, wishing this horrifying discovery was a night terror, longing to return to that moment, hours earlier, when I felt my life was perfect.

* * *

Dr. Boro waited in his office with Abe as I dressed after my exam. Although I could easily slip into my clothing without a second thought, I now focused on every move, clinging to each familiar step as I tried to restrain my emotions. First, I hooked my corset and adjusted my breasts. Would this be the last time I touched them? *No, don't think that way!* Then I fastened the tiny pearl buttons on my blouse, noting that the top button had become loose and needed mending. *Why did I care?* I finally slid the skirt over my head, clasping the hook fastener at the waist.

Marta poked her head in the door and looked at me. "Are you almost ready?"

"I am," I whispered hoarsely.

She took my hand as we entered the office. Dropping slowly into the chair, I absorbed Dr. Boro's somber expression, a harbinger of words to come. His concerned eyes, eyes that typically sparkled, told me everything I needed to know. His news would be bad. His countless, fearful conversations with past patients echoed in the office like ghosts. How many times had women gripped the same armchair I was now squeezing, bracing for words that would pierce more deeply than any sword?

I drew in a deep breath.

"I've always been honest with you, so I'll speak directly," Dr. Boro said softly, looking at Abe's face and then mine. "I'm concerned. The lump is dense. On its own, that could suggest cancer. Your mother and grandmother had breast cancer, and although we don't understand the family connection, we know one must exist. I've seen it run in patients' families like yours many times. For some reason, it places you at a higher risk."

He paused for the devastating news to settle. Abe reached for my hand, and Marta held my shoulder.

"I'd like you to see Dr. Arnold at Mount Sinai this afternoon. He's one of the best surgeons in the city. I've referred women to him, and his patients do well."

My chest tightened. "Dr. Arnold? Did you know he took care of my mother fifteen years ago?" I couldn't hold my tears back any longer. "He and Dr. Montgomery mutilated her; then she died from infection. She never returned home to say goodbye to my brothers and sister."

Marta handed me a handkerchief.

"Surgery has improved since your dear mother died," the doctor said. "If we're lucky and nip this early, you have every chance of recovery. Let's see what he says."

I closed my eyes and squeezed Abe's hand.

Abe squirmed in his chair and cleared his throat. "Dr. Boro, isn't there someone else besides Dr. Arnold? There must be others."

Dr. Boro shook his head. "No, he's the best in the city, and I trust him."

"Alright, we'll clear the afternoon and take a ride to the hospital," Abe said gently, turning to me. "If it turns out he recommends surgery, we'll come home first and talk to the children. We'll get through this together."

I looked into Abe's bloodshot eyes, a web of tiny veins. Was he awake all night like me? Through the veil of exhaustion and shock, I could see inside his compassionate heart and knew he would stay close, making me feel safe.

"If you need an operation, I will ride up and check in on you at the hospital." Dr. Boro said. "I know a few people up there."

"I'll come, too," said Marta. "You won't be alone."

I nodded and dried my eyes as a fresh concern woke my senses. "What about Hannah and my sweet baby, Miriam? Will they get it, too?"

Dr. Boro reached for my hand. "Right now, there's no way to know. You don't need to worry about that today. Today, we'll take care of you."

Chapter Forty-Five

A be and I rode in a coach uptown to Mount Sinai. The temperature had risen, and people filled the sidewalk, enjoying the day, talking and laughing. I wished I could seize their happiness as I usually would. But right now, it felt like false joy. In no time, winter's ogre would arrive, complete with its epidemics. This flash of warmth was no more than a tease.

The early morning snow had turned to slush. Sidewalk sweepers cleared the watery mess, pushing it into the streets, converting it into an ankle-deep smelly concoction of melted snow, garbage, and manure, befitting my dour mood.

Although the hospital building hadn't changed over the years, the neighborhood was now unrecognizable. The low, shabby wooden storefronts I remembered were replaced with sturdy brick and stone apartment edifices, much grander than the hospital. A hospital worker stood by the door and directed us to the Women's Clinic. The room smelled fresh, the windows cracked a hair, beckoning in clean air. Hues of blue and violet were used to decorate the walls and furniture, creating a sense of calm. In one corner, a colorful children's play area was decorated with a Mother Goose motif and filled with toys and books. The entire space, including the windows, was sparkling clean.

We signed in with the receptionist and I handedher Dr. Boro's office notes. Abe and I chose two seats in the bright light, far from the others.

"It may smell fresher than Bellevue years ago, but it's still a nightmare," I said. "When I was with Mama, I never realized how terrified she was. And to make matters worse, a rude woman criticized her dusty clothing, soiled from the ride down. I was in my own world then, preoccupied with missing school, with no clue what she faced until days later when she was dying. I'm ashamed of myself."

"Darling, it's different here. Besides, you were too young to understand back then. No one expected her to do poorly."

I nodded, remorse filling my heart, realizing there was no way to change the past.

He kissed my cheek, stroking my hair. "Try to trust in our future. You're one of the most optimistic people I know. Dr. Boro would never have sent us here if he didn't believe it was for the best."

The minutes ticked by as we held hands, lost in our thoughts. Finally, the receptionist called my name. "Mrs. Levine, please come to the desk."

We rose and hurried to her. Just then, the door leading to the exam rooms opened. I couldn't believe my eyes. Her hair was grey, her back slightly bent, and her face a web of lines, but I could never have forgotten her soft, understanding grey eyes.

"Nurse Sophie? Is that you?" I whispered. "You're not at Bellevue anymore?"

The nurse nodded, studying my face. "It is. How do I know you?"

"I was there years ago with my mother, Sarah Isaacson. She had a breast operation." Then, lowering my voice, I swallowed hard. "She died from infection."

"My goodness, that was more than a decade ago. I remember your mother and poor father." Nurse Sophie's expression brightened. Then, her eyes shifted to Abe. "And who is this?"

Abe reached out his hand, "I'm Tillie's husband, Abe. I'd like to stay with my wife if you don't mind."

"I'm afraid you can't come back quite yet, but I'll get you when the doctor is ready to discuss his findings." She reached around my shoulder and hugged me. "Don't worry about your wife. We're old friends."

"It's okay, Abe. I'll be alright." I patted his arm, remembering how attentive Nurse Sophie had been with Mama and her kindness to Papa and me.

329

Nurse Sophie spoke softly as we walked to the exam room. "You have a very handsome husband. So, tell me, any children?"

I held back a surge of tears. "Yes, a nine-year-old son, Julian, and a daughter, Miriam, who's one. Too young to lose their Mama."

"Stay calm, dear; I'm right here with you. And we'll get you home to those sweet children in no time."

I was reliving a bad dream—undressed, gowned, and waiting for the doctor, just like Mama. But this time, it was me, sitting on the unforgiving exam table, displaced, a field of goosebumps sprouting on my uncovered arms. I missed the familiar textures of my own clothing.

A soft knock. The door opened as Dr. Arnold and a younger, red-haired man entered. I stared at Dr. Arnold. He looked older and more distinguished, carrying himself with an air of confidence, his back erect, sporting a beard and spectacles.

"Good afternoon, Mrs. Levine. I'm Dr. Arnold, and this gentleman is my surgeon-in-training, Dr. Kahn."

"We've met before. You and Dr. Montgomery operated on my mother years ago at Bellevue." My voice shook. "She died."

The room fell silent. Both doctors looked at me, both at a loss for words.

Dr. Arnold spoke. "I'm sorry about your mother, Mrs. Levine. We can talk about that in a moment. But I need to examine you, and then we'll discuss a plan. Please lie back. Is anyone here with you?"

His remark was too automatic. Did he care my mother died at his mentor's hands? I felt crushed. "My husband, Abe, is waiting outside." I lay back as instructed.

Dr. Arnold opened my gown and slowly palpated each breast, measuring the lump with his fingers. "Looks about a centimeter. May Dr. Kahn examine you?"

I looked at Dr. Kahn. He was so young. He gazed at me with compassion; his eyes relaxed, head slightly cocked to the side, appearing like someone who understood sickness.

"I'll be gentle," he reassured me.

I nodded my permission.

His fingers lacked his mentor's experience, but they quickly found my lump, pushing it under the skin like a pebble mixed into loamy soil. "I feel a small, isolated lump," he said.

Small, should I be relieved? What did his words mean?

Dr. Arnold said calmly, "Nurse Sophie, could you please get Mr. Levine from the waiting area and have him join us? Mrs. Levine, you may dress. We'll return in a few minutes,"

He didn't seem alarmed. So maybe it was nothing to worry about after all.

* * *

Moments later, dressed, I sat on the table while everyone stood around me. Five adults crammed into a tiny exam room. Abe stood beside me, his comforting hand resting on my lower back.

Dr. Arnold began. "Doctor Boro was wise to send you, Mrs. Levine. Unfortunately, there is a growth that must be removed."

The tension of the last twenty-four hours made me unravel. I took deep breaths to restore my calm, but a ragged sob broke through.

Nurse Sophie, standing behind me, leaned into my ear. "Breathe slowly. We're all here to help you. Let the doctor finish."

I gulped back my tears, desperate for a way out. "What happens if I don't have surgery? You said it was small."

"You're right. It is small, probably early stage. We hope it hasn't done much damage. But, if we delay, I'm afraid the tumor will grow, spread, and eventually take your life. Unfortunately, that's how breast cancer behaves," Dr. Arnold said.

I stared at him and then at Dr. Kahn, whose eyes never left my face. Despair filled me, rising to my chest, forcing me to curl forward as in prayer.

Nurse Sophie rubbed my back. "There's every reason to be hopeful, Mrs. Levine. As the doctor said, it is small."

Dr. Arnold interjected. "But time is crucial. I would like to schedule surgery later this week.

"Does that mean I can go home first?" I asked with a rush of relief.

Dr. Arnold nodded, appearing eager to move on. "Of course, you can. Dr. Kahn, please check the operating theater for availability, and I'll review the process with the Levine's."

One last question gnawed at me. "Doctor, what about infection? That's what my mama died from days after surgery. I'm afraid that will happen to me." I strove for calm. "Everything looks shiny and white, but is the hospital truly clean?"

Dr. Arnold's face registered surprise. "I've never been asked that question before." He clasped his hands in front of his chest. "We understand the role of germs better now and have modified our techniques accordingly. We use carbolic acid in the operating theater before dressing the wound. Ten years ago, we used it for bandage changes and found our patients were more prone to infection. Now we apply it at the end of surgery. As a result, your chance of recovery is far greater. It's very unlikely misfortune will happen again." He leaned toward me and gave my shoulder one pat.

I felt my body drop, the tension releasing, satisfied with his explanation.

Dr. Arnold then shifted his eyes to Abe. "But I must also advise you that the operation involves removing a considerable amount of tissue, including the entire breast and part of the chest musculature. It's a significant disfigurement, even after she heals. She won't be the same woman as before."

Abe knitted his brows and exhaled through his nose. I could feel his anger rising. But, instead of unleashing, he draped his arm around my shoulder and pulled me into his side. Then, locking eyes with Dr. Arnold's, he said, "Doctor, you worry about your job and make sure she leaves here alive. I'll handle the rest. She'll always be every bit the woman I'll ever want or need."

* * *

An overwhelming force seized my body, pulling me down into a viscous, gripping sleep. Through my heavy eyelids, I felt heat and brightness. I forced my eyes open a crack and saw sunlight streaming into the room. It took too much effort to open them fully. My mouth was parched as if I was crawling through a desert. No words would come. Voices drifted in and out. I couldn't tell who was talking or what was said.

Finally, "Wake up, sweetheart, wake up." A deep, familiar voice. I strained to remember. *Whose voice was it?*

I forced my eyelids upward again and saw vague shapes.

"Water. Mouth. Dry," I whispered. "Where am I?"

"You're at the hospital,"

"Abe?" I slurred.

Abe spoke softly in my ear. "Darling, you're fine. It's over."

Seconds later, I forgot what he said. Again, I fought the stranglehold of sleep.

Another man's voice. "Open your eyes, my precious. It's Papa."

I wrenched my eyes wider, focusing on the faces suspended over mine, Abe and Papa. I was still alive. I tried to smile.

Papa's tears dropped gently on my cheeks as he kissed my forehead. "Thank you, dear God, for sparing my precious daughter."

"Everything's fine. The surgery went well." Abe rubbed my hand lightly and then kissed my palm. "I love you so much."

Hannah gazed at me from the foot of the bed; her lips turned upward in a slight smile. She winked at me with reassurance.

But the moment vanished as I felt a grip of deep pain grow at my right chest. "It hurts. I can't breathe." I panicked as my chest refused to expand while I filled my mouth with air.

"I'm getting Nurse Sophie," Hannah hurried away.

"I'm going to be sick." I began to cry, but tears intensified the pain. I choked them back. I began to shake uncontrollably. *I'm going to die.*

Seconds later, Nurse Sophie was by my side. "I'm here and giving you something for the pain."

A needle pricked my arm. I uttered, "Sick."

She placed a pan under my chin, understanding my shorthand in a blink. "Go ahead, dear. I'm holding the pan. That sick feeling is from the chloroform. It will pass." Nurse Sophie sat by my side, holding my good shoulder still. "I'm not going anywhere."

I lay my head back steadier. The pain slowly dissolved, releasing its excruciating clench. "Water, please. My mouth—so dry."

"Only a little. Spit it out in the pan. No swallowing until your stomach steadies." Nurse Sophie poured a small amount into a cup.

Relieved, I opened my eyes and breathed again deeper this time. For the moment, the thick fatigue lost its hold, and my memory sharpened. I looked at Papa, Abe, and Hannah surrounding my bed. "I'm so glad you're here."

"We've been at the hospital with you the whole time. We love you." Hannah rubbed my foot from where she stood at the base of the bed. "I know it hurts, but the surgery was successful. The tumor was smaller than they thought. You're going to be fine."

Nurse Sophie spoke softly, scanning the anxious faces of my family. "You should let her rest,"

Everyone gathered to leave but Abe, who leaned in my ear. "Darling, Sadie has the children, and I'm not leaving the hospital. I'll take a walk and let you close your eyes. I'll be here when you wake next."

I relaxed, knowing Abe, my bedrock, would stay nearby.

Alone with Nurse Sophie, I watched her reposition my thin blanket and take my temperature and pulse. I felt her gentle breath over my face, odorless, rhythmic, and soothing as she glanced at me occasionally with a reassuring smile. "Everything looks fine. You've gotten through the surgery like the brave soldier you are. It's time to close your eyes and relax. Rest, healing, and time are what you need most. I'll have more pain medicine for you when you wake next."

I began to drift. The shock of knowledge broke through. "Wait! My breast. Is it really gone?" I cried out, knowing in the core of my being that it was no more. But still, I needed her to tell me out loud to make it real.

Nurse Sophie positioned herself on the wooden chair, reaching for my hand. "Yes, dear. The doctors removed all the diseased tissue. Of course, you'll look different when you finish healing, but you'll be a healthy woman."

I nodded sadly; a lone tear traveled down my cheek. *How could life be so cruel?*

Nurse Sophie studied my face. "I believe your mama, Sarah, God rest her soul, was at your side, protecting you. You'll be back home with your sweet family in no time." She patted my hand.

I closed my heavy eyelids, imagining Mama, her long chestnut hair and loving face. *Oh, Mama, are you with me? I made it. I'm alive.* I silently repeated my intonation: *I made it; I'm alive,* as I felt the cumulative power of my family's love and reentered the dense forest of sleep.

Chapter Forty-Six

February 1891 - Two months later

I tilted my head toward the sun, its bands of light shooting through breaks in the winter clouds. My eyes shut, I drank its momentary warmth. I didn't mind that winter had arrived with its frigid temperatures. Eight weeks indoors convalescing had taken me over my limit. First, trapped in an antiseptic bubble of over-attentive nurses for a month at the hospital. Air saturated with the toxic sweet smell of carbolic acid was overwhelming. My doctors advised me to spend the second month in a convalescence home, but I insisted on returning home with Abe to our children. Abe then hired a nurse to help me during the day, but we didn't need her for long because Hannah never left my side. Although their demonstration of love and commitment had its charm, I was desperate to break free.

Sadie held my right hand as we circled the city block again. "Haven't you had enough? I'm freezing." She tightened the scarf around her neck.

I exhaled slowly, thankful for the fresh, crisp air and the absence of pain on my left side. "I suppose. Can we talk over tea? We have decisions to make."

Sadie guided me up the apartment steps into the foyer, then pressed the elevator button. "We'll go to my place. A different view for you."

Settled into Sadie's parlor, sipping piping hot tea, she began. "Now I can appreciate how burdened you were when I wasn't available during Eva's illness. Running the factory is far too much for one person."

I felt awful leaving Sadie to handle the Bloomingdale's account. As expected, the first order sold out in weeks, and they insisted on a second, larger order with more designs. It was non-stop. A year ago, I would have viewed our popularity with excitement, but now it felt burdensome. I was ready to let go.

I adjusted my weakened arm with my right hand, setting it across my lap. "I don't know if I'll ever get proper use of my left side. My fingers constantly tingle, and my muscles are still weak. Not good for factory work." I cleared my throat and paused. "Maybe we should consider selling Tea with Rose."

Sadie smiled. "You're reading my mind like you always have." She shifted in her chair. "Max and I have been poking around, seeing what other factories are up to. Lots of small businesses are selling to larger ones. It so happens that this is the perfect time to sell. Our kits are so unique and successful that the demand will never be higher, and the factory runs like a charm with our trained workers. We can get a top price. Who knows how long it will last?"

I nodded, "I believe you're right about that."

Sadie bent her head to the side, searching my eyes. "But I worry about you. What will you do instead?"

I sat back, rubbing my left hand to relieve the tingling. "Abe and I have been discussing our options, too. He's been following the construction of new buildings. Apartments are going up every month all over the city and Brooklyn. He's dying to get involved and ready to sell off his button inventory." I paused, "What about you and Max?"

Sadie brushed away a tear, etching a trail down her cheek. "The one good thing I can say about being busy was I didn't have time to brood about Eva. My memories used to keep me up at night, but now I'm too exhausted to think about anything. Max and I have decided to follow the boys to Chicago and start fresh. It's a question of timing. He will need to sell, and so will we."

My fragile emotions bubbled to the surface. "What will I do without you? How will we remain close? I can't imagine."

She took my right hand in hers. We sat without another word.

* * *

An hour later, I entered my apartment and was greeted by the mouth-watering scent of apples and sugar baking. "Yum, what are you making?" I wiggled out of my coat and hat, placing them on the pegs.

Julian called back. "Hannah's teaching me how to make an apple pie."

Miriam was sitting on the parlor floor by the radiator, deep in concentration, deftly brushing the hair of her baby doll. She didn't look up when she spoke. "Mama, me make pie, too?"

I knelt beside her, surprised by the number of words she had strung together. "Such a lovely doll. I will teach you too, Miriam, when you're a little older and can reach the counter."

I strolled to the kitchen door. "What a nice family scene."

Hannah turned to face me, her wavy hair falling free from its bow. "How was your walk with Sadie? Feel better? Any improvement in your arm?"

"I'm happy like a tigress let out of her cage. The arm is stubborn, though, refuses to cooperate."

Hannah set the rinsed preparation bowls and knives on the counter to dry. "The surgeon said it would heal in time. I borrowed a book from Dr. Boro and was reading about brachial nerve damage." She shook the soapy water from her hands. "Sometimes it takes months. Let's do some strengthening exercises after dinner."

I awkwardly lifted a towel and bowl, attempting to help. "You should be using your free time to study. I'm ready to do more."

Hannah took the bowl from my hands, her brows drawn. "How could you suggest such a thing? You were younger than me when you took me in. Since that time, you have treated me like a rare jewel—every single day of my life. My schooling can wait."

I drew her close, nuzzling my face in her hair, inhaling its sweetness. "Abe will hire someone to help with the chores and cooking. You, young lady, will live your dream and become a doctor. Not only for yourself—for both of us." I said, "And for Mama."

A Note from the Author

Fact – Fiction – Family Folklore

As a work of fiction, great effort was made to build the setting of this story with correct historical detail – early farming in Harlem, Jewish migration to Sullivan and Ulster Counties, the Lower East Side, and the evolution of the garment industry. Epidemics were frequent throughout this period, with the highest incidence in lower Manhattan, where population density, poor housing and nutrition, and overpopulation were rampant. Bloomingdale's and Lord and Taylors were among the first department stores in the city, and Butterwick was the first national dress pattern company.

That said, the non-family characters and plot are all fiction. Since I was a child, buttons fascinated me, and I have jars of unusual buttons in my office. My collection started during my middle school years, when I began sewing clothing on the porch of our summer lake home. For that reason, making Abe a button salesman was a natural and sentimental fit. It also was a fresh approach to illustrating the fascinating transformation of the garment industry – from tenement factories and product salesmen to mass production of off-the-rack clothing – all in just a few decades. The Butterick company name was intentionally altered to differentiate its misdeeds in the story from the actual company's esteemed reputation, but the Delineator was their fashion periodical. As a quasi-seamstress, having used many gorgeous Butterick patterns throughout my life, that story twist came from left field. I place the blame entirely on my characters, railroading my careful plotting. Such is fiction. The Bloomingdale's family is authentic, but their storyline is pure fiction.

Family folklore is fascinating. Many of us listened to tales about our ancestors from the time we were small children. But how much of it is true? The following is what I discovered in my genealogical research: Mathilda's family emigrated through a passenger port in Hamburg in 1866, arriving at Castle Garden intake center in New York City late spring of that year. Mathilda was a one-year-old at the time. I found her later in a 1900 census record, living with Abraham and their son, Julian, in a row house north of Central Park. Abraham was twelve years her senior. Tillie was sixteen when she wed. Abraham noted on the census form that his profession was 'wooles,' Tillie's was homemaker. I found no marriage or death records for either Abraham or Tillie. As for folklore, the farm in Harlem was always included in their very brief story, as well as Tillie dying from a woman's disease. Therein lies my connection to her BRCA1 genetic defect.

The following bibliography helped craft the setting of the story and contains many of the lesser-known, spellbinding facts:

- *Our Crowd*, Stephen Birmingham
- *The Excellent Doctor Blackwell*, Julia Bond
- *The Pocket, A Hidden History of Women's Lives*, Barbara Burman and Ariane Fennetaux
- *The Bowery*, the Strange History of New York's Oldest Street, Stephen Pau DeVillo
- *Suffrage, Women's Long Battle for the Vote*, Ellen Carol Dubois
- *Victorian and Edwardian Fashion, A Photographic Survey*, Alison Gernsheim
- *Damnation Island, Poor, Sick, Mad and Criminal in 19th Century New York*, Stacy Horn
- *My Notorious Life* (fiction), Kate Manning
- *From Midwives to Medicine, The Birth of American Gynecology*, Deborah Kuhn McGregor
- *The Doctors Blackwell*, Janice P. Nimura
- *Bellevue, Three Centuries of Medicine and Mayhem at America's Most Storied Hospital*, David Oshinskyospital, DHosHosp
- *When Abortion was a Crime, Women, Medicine, and Law in the United*

States, 1867-1973, Leslie J. Reagan

- *The Gospel of Germs, Men, Women, and the Microbe in American Life,* Nancy Tomes
- *The Women's Suffrage Movement,* Sally Roesch Wagner

Acknowledgements

Taking the formidable plunge into novel writing would never have happened without instruction, feedback, and encouragement.

An early, untitled draft of *Threadbare* sat on my credenza for over a year while I completed and published *In the Hands of Women*. I was fortunate that my characters and plot struck contemporary chords: women's rights, immigration, disease, fortitude, and finding mature love. Readers asked for more, so I dusted off *Threadbare* and revised it for publication.

My love for research comes from my parents, who were both avid readers and enjoyed pulling historical trivia out of their hats at the dinner table and with friends. Our set of *World Book Encyclopedia* was heavily worn. I realized how fascinating the past becomes when we zoom in on a micro level and explore the ways people's lives were affected by the times in which they lived. What a fabulous way to learn history!

In that vein, my thanks go to the numerous historical museum staff in NYC and locally in Morris County, NJ. With their help, I found obscure maps of neighborhoods, rare books, and magazines of that day. Without fail, they were cheerful and supportive.

As a fledgling writer, I immersed myself in classes, personal coaching, independent critique groups, and friends willing to read and provide feedback. Specifically, Harriette Sackler, formally of Level Best Books; Michelle Cameron at The Writer's Circle in New Jersey; my writing partners: Ananya Holland and Marleen May; and my book club and personal friends: Patti Bleicher, Peggy Barnett, Carla Errico, Laurie Kalb Kaswiner, Lisa Ozer, Ilene Rosenbaum, Sandy Sachs, and Debbie Spicehandler. Thanks to my editor, Verena Rose, for her excellent feedback and Shawn Reilly Simmons for the stunning cover art.

My profound thanks to my husband, David, for his unflagging encouragement and to the medical workers: physicians, physician assistants, and nurses in my family and professional life who helped fact-check and imagine the experience of injury and illness before contemporary medicine—the vaccines, treatments, and medications we now take for granted. My specific appreciation goes to my son Ben Taylor, MD Surgery, and Steven Papish, MD Oncology. And an endless thank you to my trusty, tireless trio of exceptional daughters: Laura Johnson, PA, Laura Taylor, RN, and Caroline Hodge, PA, who generously shared hours reading, commenting, and exploring plot options.

The last expression of gratitude is the trickiest to express. I had every reason to relinquish hope in May 2009 when I received an incurable cancer diagnosis. But with the rapid advances in treatment over the past decade, a team of superbly talented physicians, the loving support of my husband, family, and friends, and finally, an unshakable belief in the power of hope, I was able to fulfill my life-long dream of writing.

About the Author

A cancer diagnosis, a genetic defect, and a lifelong fascination with the history of medicine led Jane Rubin to put pen to paper. After an ovarian cancer diagnosis in 2009, Jane, then a healthcare executive, poured her energy into raising research dollars through the Ovarian Cancer Research Alliance (OCRA) and learning more about her familial roots. Her research led her to her great-grandmother, Mathilda (Tillie), who arrived in New York City in 1866, at the age of sixteen, married a man twelve years her senior, and later died of 'a woman's disease.' Then the trail ran cold. With limited facts, Jane was determined to give Mathilda a fictional life of her own, imagining her rags to riches life, fight with terminal disease, and the circumstances surrounding her death. Threadbare is a tribute to her.

Ms. Rubin's research of the history of New York City, its ultra-conservative reproductive laws, and the state of medicine during that era has culminated in a suspenseful, fast-paced, historical fiction series. Her engaging characters confront the shifting role of midwives, the dangers of pregnancy, the infamous Blackwell's Workhouse, and the perilous road to financial success. *In the Hands of Women* (Level Best Books) is Ms. Rubin's debut novel. Her previous publications include her essay memoir, *Almost a Princess, My Life as a Two Time Cancer Survivor*, and numerous essays in trade journals.

Ms. Rubin, a graduate of University of Michigan (MS) and Washington University (MBA), retired from a 30-year career as a health care executive to begin writing full-time. She lives with her husband, David, an attorney, in Northern New Jersey. Between them, they have five adult children and seven grandchildren.

SOCIAL MEDIA HANDLES:
FB: Jane Loeb Rubin
Instagram: @janeloebrubin
LinkedIn: Jane Loeb Taylor Rubin
Goodreads: Jane Loeb Rubin

AUTHOR WEBSITE:
https://JaneLoebRubin.com

Also by Jane Loeb Rubin

In the Hands of Women (2023 Level Best Books)

Almost a Princess, My Life as a Two-Time Cancer Survivor (2010 IUniverse)

Printed in the USA
CPSIA information can be obtained
at www.ICGtesting.com
CBHW030827021124
16831CB00001B/1

9 781685 125813